"You're not spending the night," Riley told him.

Straker's gray eyes leveled on her. "Sure I am. Why else the backpack?"

Why else indeed. She should have connected the dots sooner. "Then what?"

He shrugged. "The morning will bring what the morning will bring."

"To hell with you, Straker. You have a plan and you know it. What is it? Do you think Emile had something to do with the dead body? Do you think he's going to contact me? Has *already* contacted me?" She thrust her hands on her hips, in full outrage now. "Are you going to follow me around just in case I'm up to something nefarious?"

"Nefarious?" He grinned. "I've been in law enforcement for ten years, and I don't think I've ever used that word."

She all but sputtered. "You listen to me. I do not need and will not tolerate a reclusive, lunatic FBI agent with post-traumatic stress disorder in my hip pocket."

His eyes were narrowed; his body was rigid. She wasn't nervous, but she was on high alert. He said, "Two things."

"Okay."

"One, I don't have PTSD. I'd have PTSD if the guy'd shot his hostages. He didn't. He shot me. So, no PTSD."

She nodded. "No PTSD."

"Two, you need a drink."

CARLA NEGGERS

ON FIRE

MIRA®

ISBN 1-55166-541-7

ON FIRE

Visit us at www.mirabooks.com

Printed in U.S.A.

To my nieces and nephews: Blythe, Sarah Mae,
Tommy, Rose, Chris, Timothy, David,
Sarah Elizabeth, Emily, Dan, McKinzie, Scarlett
and Marena...and to Kate and Zachary...
you're a great bunch!

Prologue

Riley St. Joe sloshed through three inches of frigid seawater. The *Encounter* pitched and rolled under her, its old metal hull moaning and creaking as it took on more water. *Trapped like rats on a sinking ship,* she thought. Her stab at humor caught her by surprise— but it helped keep her on her feet as she made her way to her grandfather. They were in the diving compartment deep in the bowels of the ship, a raging engine fire and catastrophic flooding cutting them off from the rest of the crew.

After three decades at sea, the *Encounter*—the old minesweeper Emile Labreque and Bennett Granger had had refitted as an oceanographic vessel—was going down in the North Atlantic. There was nothing Riley could do about it. More to the point, there was nothing her grandfather, the stubborn, brilliant, visionary oceanographer Emile Labreque, could do about it.

She grabbed his thin arm. He was seventy-five, wiry and fit, and he had to know what was happening.

He knew his ship better than anyone. He stared at the watertight door that had shut fast against the fire and flooding, sealing them in the bowels of the ship. "Emile, we have to take the submersible," she shouted. "We don't have any choice."

"I'm not going anywhere. The pumps will handle the flooding. The crew will put the fire out."

"The pumps won't do anything, and if the crew's smart, they're getting into the life rafts now. Emile, the *Encounter*'s sinking. If we stay here, we'll go down with it."

He tore his arm from her grip. His dark eyes were wild, his lined, leathery face and white hair all part of the legend that was Emile Labreque. He took a deep breath. "You go. Take the submersible. Get out."

"Not without you."

"I need to see to the crew."

"You can't. Even if you could get the doors open, the fire's too intense. And if you didn't fry to a crisp, you'd drown. Sam will have to see to the crew." Sam Cassain was the ship's captain, but Emile would consider the *Encounter* and her crew his own responsibility. Riley struggled to stay on her feet. *Rats. We're trapped like rats.* She fought off panic. "Emile— damn it, you know I'm right."

He knew. He knew better than she that the *Encounter* was lost. An engine explosion, a spreading fire, a hull breach—they had only minutes. "The submersible's only built for one," he said.

"It'll handle two. Sam would have sent out an SOS

by now. The Coast Guard's probably already on their way. They'll pick us up before we run out of air."

"We'll have three, maybe four hours at most."

"It'll be enough."

Emile placed a palm on the watertight door, shut his eyes a moment. The *Encounter* was as famous as he was, the base for his oceanographic research, the documentaries he'd taped, the books he'd written. Now, its day was done.

He turned to her. "We're out of time. Let's go."

Five hours later, Riley numbly accepted a blanket from a Coast Guard crewman and wrapped it around herself. The crewman was saying something, but she couldn't make out his words. She'd stopped shaking. Her eyelids were heavy, her heart rate steady. But her hands were clammy and very white, and she simply couldn't make out what he was trying to tell her.

I must be in shock.

Her throat burned and ached from tension and fatigue, from gasping for air as oxygen slowly ran out in the tiny, cramped submersible she and Emile had shared for almost four endless hours.

"My grandfather." She didn't know if her words came out. "How is he?"

The crewman frowned as if she'd made no sense.

"Emile—my grandfather."

"We're going to get you some help, okay?" The crewman touched her arm through the blanket. "Just hold on."

"I'm not hurt." She felt as if she were shouting,

but couldn't hear her own words. "The crew—are they all right? They made it to the lifeboats?"

"Miss St. Joe—"

Something in his face, his tone, sent a stab of dread straight through her. *Oh God.* "How many? How many died?"

The eyes of the nearby crew turned toward her, and she realized she must have shouted this time. The crewman winced. He was Coast Guard all the way. Every death at sea pained him. He said nothing, and Riley knew. There had been deaths aboard the *Encounter.* Not everyone had made it off alive.

A man yelled, and she looked up and saw three crewmen holding back Sam Cassain. He was tall and tawny haired, a thickly built man, a firebrand, a good captain with a propensity for mouthing off. He would speak first, think later.

Riley saw her crewman grimace, as if he wanted to protect her from Sam's words. Too late. She could make them out clearly.

"Five died," Sam yelled. "*Five.* And it's your goddamned grandfather's fault. The great Emile Labreque. He's responsible. He knows it."

"Who?" Riley clenched the blanket tightly around her, her fingers rigid, her stomach lurching. "Who died? Sam, for God's sake—"

He couldn't have heard her, but he shouted, "Bennett Granger's dead. He fried in the fire. He never had a chance to make it to the lifeboats. Think Emile should be the one to tell your sister, your brother-in-law?"

Riley couldn't speak. Bile rose in her throat. Bennett Granger was the chief benefactor and cofounder of the Boston Center for Oceanographic Research. He and her grandfather had been friends for fifty years. His grandson had married Emile's granddaughter, Riley's sister. *God. Who would tell Matthew and Sig?*

"Get him out of here," her crewman shouted.

"You mark my words, Riley St. Joe," Sam said, his voice deadly. "I warned Emile. I told him the *Encounter* was an old girl and we needed to take more precautions. He wouldn't listen. His mission always came first. Now five people are dead. That's on his shoulders, not mine."

Riley struggled to get to her feet. The crewman held her by the elbow, keeping her from going after Sam—or from passing out. "Don't," he said softly. "There'll be an investigation. This will all sort itself out in due time."

"But Emile—my grandfather—"

"He's in the infirmary. He'll be okay."

Every part of her, mind and body, was spent. She couldn't even lick her parched lips. "The fire was an accident. It wasn't Emile's fault. It wasn't anybody's fault."

The crewman made no response, but his eyes told her everything. He agreed with Sam Cassain. He believed Emile Labreque was responsible for the explosion and the fire that sank the *Encounter* and killed five people.

Riley clutched the folds of her blanket. *Bennett.*

Oh, God. She wished she could start the day over and save the *Encounter,* save Bennett, save the crew. But the old ship was gone, and five people were dead, and Emile...her grandfather, she thought, was doomed.

One

Riley ignored the slight tremble in her hands and jammed the two ends of her high-performance paddle together. She zipped up her life vest. There was no reason to be nervous. She'd kayaked the coves and inlets of Schoodic Peninsula since she was six years old. Today's conditions were near perfect: a bright, clear, still September morning, halfway between low tide and high tide.

She squinted at her grandfather, who'd come down from his cottage to the short stretch of gravelly beach to see her off. "Come with me," she said.

He shook his head. "You go on. You need to get back out on the water."

"I've been out on the water. Caroline Granger had us onto her yacht for a cocktail party Friday night."

"Cocktails." Emile snorted. "That's not getting out on the water."

She knew what he meant. She hadn't been on a boat, a ship, even a kayak, since the *Encounter* disaster a year ago. On the Granger yacht off Mount

Desert Island Friday night, she couldn't make herself go below. She'd never been claustrophobic, not until the watertight doors had shut her and Emile into the diving compartment, not until the two of them had endured the hot, cramped, terrifying hours in the experimental submersible.

This had to end, she told herself. She was a scientist, director of marine and aquatic animal recovery and rehabilitation at the Boston Center for Oceanographic Research. She couldn't get spooked about the water.

"I shouldn't kayak without a partner."

Emile shrugged. "You'll stay close to shore. Just watch out for fog rolling in later."

"You're sure you won't come with me?" she asked him.

"I can kayak anytime I want."

One of the perks of his exile, he seemed to be saying. After the disaster of the *Encounter*, Emile Labreque had shocked the world by retiring to the Maine fishing village where his family had settled generations earlier. It had been his home base for years; he owned a small cottage, where Riley and her sister had spent summers growing up. He looked after a small, private nature preserve on a part-time basis. The last hurrah of a legend.

He eyed Riley as she dragged her shocking pink, sit-on-top ocean kayak to the water's edge. He wore his trademark black Henley and khakis, and at seventy-six, he was as alert and intense as ever. She'd inherited his lean, wiry physique, his dark hair and eyes, his sharp features—and, some said, his single-mindedness.

"You're planning to stop on the island?"

She nodded. "I packed a lunch. If the fog doesn't roll in, I'd like to have a little picnic on the rocks, like the old days."

He gazed out at the water. The bay sparkled in the morning sun. Labreque Island was farther up the point, almost at the mouth of the bay—a tiny, wind-swept landscape of rock, evergreens and sand that had been in Emile's family since the turn of the century.

"I should warn you. John Straker's staying at the cottage."

"Straker? Why? What's he doing back here?"

"He took a couple of bullets awhile back. He came home to recuperate. I let him use the cottage on the island."

Riley digested this news as if it were a hair ball. John Straker wasn't one of her favorite people. He'd left the peninsula years ago to join the FBI. A lot of people in his home village couldn't believe the FBI had accepted him. She'd only seen him a few times since. "Who shot him, criminals or his friends?"

"A fugitive who took a couple of teenagers hostage. It had something to do with domestic terrorism."

"Right up Straker's alley. Anyone else hurt?"

Emile shook his head. "You know, John's not much company on a good day."

"This is true. I'll just have to keep to the other side

of the island. He won't even know I'm there. I didn't realize the cottage on the island was still inhabitable.''

''He's fixed it up a bit. Not much.''

''How long's he been out there?''

''Since April.''

She shuddered, then grinned at her grandfather. ''Well, tough. I'm not afraid of John Straker. Will you be here when I get back?''

''I doubt it.''

She hesitated, debating. ''I'm stopping in Camden on my way back to Boston. Is there anything you want me to tell Mom and Sig?''

''No.''

Riley nodded without comment. Perhaps, she thought, too much had been said already. Her mother and sister—Emile's only daughter and older granddaughter—blamed him for the *Encounter,* for Bennett Granger's death, for the deaths of four crew members and friends, for Riley's near death. For Emile's near death and the shattering of a lifetime's reputation.

Of course, everyone blamed Emile for the *Encounter.* Except Riley. Sam Cassain's assessment of what had happened—his conviction that Emile had cut too many safety corners—wasn't enough for her. She needed hard evidence before she could damn her grandfather to the pits of hell. But she was in a distinct minority.

Emile wished her well and started back along the path up to his rustic cottage. Corea, Prospect Harbor, Winter Harbor, Schoodic Point. These were the places of her childhood, tucked onto a jagged, granite-bound peninsula, one of dozens that shaped and extended Maine's scenic coastline. Riley knew all its inlets, bays and coves. It was here she'd discovered her own love for the ocean, one that had nothing to do with being a Labreque or a St. Joe but only with being herself.

It was here, too, that she'd drawn blood in her one and only act of out-and-out violence, when she'd hurled a rock at John Straker. He was sixteen, she was twelve, and he'd deserved it. His own mother had said so as she'd handed him a dish towel for the blood and hauled him down to the doctor's office. He'd required six stitches to sew up the slit Riley had left above his right eye. She wondered if he'd had to explain the scar to the FBI. Amazing they'd let him in. Bonked on the head by a twelve-year-old. It couldn't bode well.

Now he'd been shot. Domestic terrorism. She grimaced. Well, she had no intention of letting a cranky, shot-up FBI agent ruin her picnic on her favorite island.

She slid her kayak into the incoming tide. Given the warm weather, she'd opted against a wet suit and wore her Tevas without socks. Maine water was never warm, but she'd be fine. Her shirt and drawstring pants were of a quick-drying fabric, and she'd filled two dry packs with all the essentials. One held her picnic lunch. The other held everything she might need if she got stranded for any reason: waterproof matches, rope, emergency thermal blanket that folded up into a tiny square, rations she'd eat only in an emergency, aluminum foil, portable first aid kit, flashlight, compass, charts, whistle, marine band radio, extra water and her jackknife. And duct tape. She'd zipped an extra compass, matches and a water bottle into her life vest, in case she got separated from her kayak.

All in all, she deemed herself ready for anything, even a recuperating John Straker.

She laid her paddle across her kayak and walked into the ankle-deep water, which wasn't as cold as she'd expected. Maybe sixty-five degrees. Downright balmy for this stretch of Maine. She dropped into her seat, did her mental checklist and set off into deeper water, her strokes even and sure, all uneasiness gone. This was what she needed. A solo kayak trip in the clean, brisk Maine air, along the familiar rockbound coast with its evergreens, birches, wild blueberry bushes and summer cottages. The water was smooth, glasslike, the air so still she could hear the dipping of her paddle, the cry of gulls, the putter of distant lobster boats.

Yes, she thought. Emile was right. She needed to get back out on the water.

Two hours later, she was tired, hungry and exhilarated. A fog bank had formed on the eastern horizon, but she thought she'd be finished with her picnic and safely back at Emile's before it arrived. The swells and the wind had picked up on the ocean side of Labreque Island, but she worked with them, not against them, as she paddled parallel to shore, looking for a landing spot. The island was a mere five acres of sand, rock, pine, spruce and a few intrepid beeches and birches, all of which took a pounding from the North Atlantic winds, surf and storms. The ocean side had imposing rock ledges, and the water tended to be choppier—but Emile's ancient cottage, and thus John Straker, was on the bay side.

The waves pushed her toward shore. Despite the island's rugged appearance, its ecosystem was fragile, Riley knew. She wanted to find a spot that would provide a smooth landing for her and an unintrusive one for the island. Just an inch of lost soil could take hundreds of years to replace. A sandy beach was her first choice; next best was a sloping rock ledge.

She found a spot that would do. It wasn't great— little more than an indentation amid the steep rock cliffs and ledges and deep water swirling around huge granite boulders. The swells had picked up. If she capsized and bonked her head on a rock, she'd be seal food. This, she thought, was why one didn't kayak alone. She concentrated, maintaining her center of gravity. A tilt to the left or the right could turn her over, even in a stable ocean kayak. She maneuvered her vessel perpendicular to the shore and, with strong strokes, propelled it straight toward the rocks.

Rocks scraped the bottom of her kayak, and she jumped out, yelping at the sting of the much colder water. Moving fast, she dragged the craft up onto the rocks, not stopping until she was well above the tide line. She sat on a rounded boulder, warmed by the midday sun, to catch her breath. Despite the worrisome fog bank hovering on the horizon, the view was stunning, well worth the small risk of running into Special Agent Straker.

It was hard to think of him as an FBI agent. The John Straker she'd known had been intent on becoming a lobsterman or a jailbird. She'd never believed he'd leave Washington County. His parents still lived in the same house where his mother had grown up, a ramshackle place in the village. His father was a lobsterman. His grandfather had worked in the local sardine canneries.

At the thought of him lurking just a few acres through rock, trees and brush she began to set up her picnic: an early Mac, wild-blueberry muffins, cheddar cheese, two brownies and sparkling cider. Using her jackknife, she carved the apple into wedges and the cheese into thin slices, then layered the two.

Perfection, she thought, tasting the cheese and apple, smelling the sea and the pine needles and the barest hint of fall in the air. Seagulls cried in the distance, and trees and brush rustled in the breeze. Everything else fell away: the stress and trauma of the past year; the questions about herself, her family, her work, what she wanted, what she believed; the breakneck pace of her life in Boston. She was here, alone on an isolated island she'd first visited as a baby.

She was on her first brownie when she realized the fog bank had moved. She jumped to her feet. "No! I need more time!"

But the fog had begun its inexorable sweep inland, eating up ocean with its impenetrable depths of gray and white. Riley knew she couldn't get back to Emile's before it reached the bay. She paced on the rocks, cursing her own arrogance as she felt the temperature drop and the dampness seep into her bones. The mist and swirling fog quickly blanketed the water, then the rocks, then the island itself. Her world shrank, and she swore again, because she should have known better and skipped her island picnic.

"No use swearing," a voice said behind her. "Fog'll do what it'll do."

Riley swallowed a curse and came to an abrupt halt on her boulder. Straker. He materialized out of milky fog and white pines, exactly as she remembered him. Two bullets and his years as a special agent of the Federal Bureau of Investigation hadn't changed him. He was still thickly built, tawny haired, gray eyed and annoying.

"You're the oceanographer," he said. "You should have known the fog'd get here before you could sneak off."

"I'm not clairvoyant."

"I knew."

Of course he'd know. He was the Maine native who knew everything. As if timing a fog bank were part of his genetic makeup. "Have you been spying on me?"

His eyes, as gray as the fog, settled on her. He didn't answer. His heavyweight charcoal sweater emphasized the strength and breadth of his powerful shoulders. He didn't look as if he'd been shot twice. He didn't, Riley thought, look as if he'd done anything with his life except fish the coast of downeast Maine. He looked strong, fit, at ease with his island environment—and not happy about having her in it. But wisely or unwisely, she'd never been afraid of John Straker.

"Well, Straker, if possible you're even worse than I remember."

"Fog could be here for hours. Days. It's going to get cold."

It was already cold. "I tried not to disturb you."

"I spotted you through my binoculars. You're hard to miss. You looked like you were paddling a pink detergent bottle."

"It's a bright color so boats will see it. Forest green and dark blue wouldn't stand out against the background of water and trees."

He narrowed his eyes, the only change in his expression. "No kidding."

He was making fun of her. No matter how much time she'd spent in Maine, how many degrees she had or what her experience—no matter how long he himself had stayed away—he was the local and she was the outsider. It was an old argument. He still had the scar on his right temple from one installment he'd lost.

"I thought Emile would warn you off. I'm not much company these days."

"Emile did warn me, and you've never been much company, Straker. Where were you shot?"

"Up near the Canadian border."

The man did try one's nerves. He always had, from

as far back as she could remember. When she was six and he ten, he'd enjoyed jerking her chain. He jerked everyone's chain.

"Obviously your smart mouth's still intact," she stated.

"Everything's intact that's supposed to be intact." He squinted out at the fog and mist; there was no wind now, no birds crying near or far. "You could be here until morning. Have fun."

Naturally, he had no intention of inviting her back to the cottage to wait out the fog—and Riley would freeze to death before she asked. "I love the fog," she told him.

He vanished into the trees.

She thrust her hands onto her hips and yelled, "And don't you dare spy on me!"

He was gone. He wasn't coming back. He'd let her sit out here and freeze. When she'd been eleven and gotten into trouble in high winds after taking one of Emile's kayaks into the bay without permission, Straker had plucked her from the water in his father's lobster boat. He'd been unmerciful in telling her what an idiot she was and had promised that next time he'd let her drown.

And she'd cried. It had been awful. She'd been cold, wet and scared, and there was fifteen-year-old John Straker threatening to pitch her overboard if she didn't stop crying. "You made your bed," he'd told her. "Lie in it."

"Bastard," she muttered now. She'd never intimidated John Straker. That was for sure.

She scooted off her boulder and unstrapped her dry pack. *Damn.* She was supposed to be back in Boston tonight, at work in the morning. She'd come to Maine last Wednesday for a round of fund-raising dinners, meetings and informal lectures at the Granger summer home on Mount Desert Island. Caroline Granger, Bennett's second wife and now his widow, had decided to end her year of mourning and invited the directors and staff of the Boston Center for Oceanographic Studies north, perhaps to indicate she was ready to take her husband's place as the center's benefactor.

No one had mentioned Emile Labreque, living in exile a stone's throw to the north. Riley hadn't even told her father, Richard St. Joe, a whale biologist with the center, that she was extending her stay a few days to visit her grandfather.

With a groan of frustration, she dug out her emergency thermal blanket. It looked and felt like pliable aluminum foil. She unfolded it section by section, telling herself it'd be worse if she'd been unprepared. There was no shame in having to use her emergency supplies.

Still, she felt self-conscious and humiliated. She blamed Straker. He enjoyed seeing her in this predicament.

She climbed up onto a different boulder and threw the blanket over her shoulders. It was effective, but unromantic. A fire was a last resort. Fires on islands could be deadly, and even a small campfire could scar a rock forever. She'd have to find a sandy spot.

She clutched her crinkly blanket around her, her windbreaker already limp and cold from the dampness, and followed a narrow path along the top of the rock ledge. It was just past high tide, and below her only the water's edge was visible through the shroud of fog. Her path veered down among the rocks. She took it, relieved to have a safe outlet for her restless energy.

Fog was normal, she reminded herself. It wasn't like an engine explosion and a raging fire aboard a ship. This wasn't the *Encounter*. This was a great morning on the water with an aggravating ending— but not a traumatic one, not a dangerous one.

The path came to an end at the base of a huge, rounded boulder that Riley remembered from hikes on the island in years past. In happier days, she thought. Her parents, her sister, and later Matthew Granger would pack a couple of coolers and head out to Labreque Island for the day. Emile and Bennett had seldom joined them. There was always work, always the center. Now Bennett was dead, Emile was living in exile, his daughter wasn't speaking to him and his granddaughter's marriage to Matthew Granger was in turmoil.

Her sister's husband had made a brief appearance on Mount Desert Island, long enough to demonstrate he hadn't put the tragedy of the *Encounter* and his father's death behind him. Matt shared Sam Cassain's belief that Emile should be in jail on charges of negligent homicide.

Riley shoved back the unwelcome rush of images

and plunged ahead, leaping from rock to rock, heedless of the fog, her flapping blanket, the memories she was trying to escape.

She walked to the edge of a flat, barnacle-covered boulder below the tide line. At its base, water swirled in cracks and crevices with the receding tide, exposing more barnacle-covered rocks, shallow tide pools, slippery seaweed. Her Tevas provided a firm grip on the rocks, although her toes were red and cold.

Should have packed socks, she thought. Straker had probably noticed her bare feet and smugly predicted frozen toes. She pictured him sitting by the cottage woodstove, warm as toast as he waited for the fog to lift and his unwelcome visitor to be on her way.

She leaped over a yard-wide, five-foot-deep crevice and climbed up a huge expanse of rock, all the way out to its edge. At high tide, the smaller rocks, sand and tide pools that surrounded its base now would be covered with water, creating a mini-island. She stood twenty feet above the receding tide. Ahead there was nothing but fog. It was like standing on the edge of the world.

Straker could have given her five damned minutes to warm her toes by the woodstove and have a cup of hot coffee. He could have lent her socks.

"Never mind Straker," she muttered into the wall of fog.

Something caught her eye, drawing her gaze to the left. She peered down at water, rocks, seaweed and barnacles. Probably it was nothing. Fog could be deceiving.

Not this time.

Riley felt her blanket drop, heard herself gasp. *Oh God.*

Amid the rocks, seaweed and barnacles, facedown and motionless in the shallow water, was a man's body.

Straker heard Riley yelling bloody murder and figured he had no choice. He had to see what was up. He walked out onto his rickety porch, where a pale, white sun was trying to burn through the fog. With any luck, the stranded Miss St. Joe could be on her way in less than an hour. She had always been... inconvenient.

He heard her thrashing through the brush alongside the cottage, heedless of the maze of paths that connected all points of the small island.

"Straker—Straker, my God, there's a dead body on the rocks!"

He made a face. A dead body. Uh-huh.

He went back inside. His two rooms were toasty warm. He had a nice beef stew bubbling on the stove. The fog, the cold, the shifting winds were all reminders that summer was coming to an end. He couldn't stay out here through the winter. A decision had to be made. What next in his life?

"Straker!"

Riley didn't like sharing her island with him. She wasn't above conjuring up a dead body just to get back at him for leaving her out in the cold fog. He'd known her since she was a precocious six-year-old who liked to recite the Latin names of every plant and creature she pulled out of a tide pool.

She pounded up the stairs onto the porch. She didn't bother knocking, just threw open the door. "Didn't you hear me?"

He stirred his stew. The steam, the rich smells were a welcome contrast to the cold, wet presence of Riley St. Joe. She was small and wiry like Emile, with his shock of short dark hair, his dark eyes, his drive and intensity. She had her mother's quirky laugh, her father's straight nose. She was difficult, competitive and a know-it-all. And she seemed to have no idea how much he'd changed since he'd left Schoodic Peninsula.

It was a great stew. Big chunks of carrots and red potatoes, celery, onions, sweet potatoes, a splash of burgundy. Not much meat. Since getting shot, he'd tried to be careful with his diet. His FBI shrink had urged him not to isolate himself, but his FBI shrink hadn't grown up on the coast of Maine. Two hours out of the hospital, John had headed home. When Emile caught him camped out on Labreque Island, he'd offered him use of the cottage. There was no telephone, no mail, not much of a dock and the only power source an old kerosene generator and wood. Straker had accepted.

As a consequence, Emile's younger granddaughter was in his doorway. He glanced at her from his position at the stove. She was pale, shaking, eyes wide.

"I heard you," he said.

"Bastard—why didn't you come? You know more about...*oh, damn.*"

She turned even paler. Straker put down his slotted spoon. Hell. Maybe she *had* seen a dead body. "Finish your sentence. This is good. I want to hear what it is you think I know more about than you do."

"Dead bodies."

It was almost a mumble. He said, "The fog can fool you."

"Damn it, Straker, you don't need to tell me about fog. I saw his—his—his hair and his hand—" Her eyes rolled back in her head. "I think I'm going to throw up."

He sighed. Damned if he needed *that.* "Bathroom's in there."

"I know where the damned—"

She interrupted herself with a curse and lurched across the linoleum floor to the short hall that led straight to the bathroom. It was in an ell tacked onto the cottage. In the old days, there'd just been an outhouse. Straker had locked her into it once when she was eight or nine and especially on his nerves. Emile hadn't been too pleased with him. Riley, the little snot, had screamed and carried on far more than was necessary. Straker had it in the back of his mind that was what she was doing now. Exaggerating, going for the drama.

He followed her, although not with great speed or enthusiasm. Still, if she choked on her tongue or something it was a long trek to an emergency room.

Between moaning and swearing at him, she got rid

of the contents of her stomach. She managed fine. Straker, leaning in the doorway, found himself noticing the shape of her behind as she bent over the tank. He grimaced. He'd been out on his deserted island longer than he'd thought.

Leaving that realization for later pondering, he went out to the kitchen and checked the kettle he kept on the woodstove. The water was bubbling. He got down a restaurant-style mug Emile had probably lifted from a local diner a million years ago, dangled a tea bag in it and poured in the hot water.

Riley staggered back into the main room. She was trembling visibly and had a wet washcloth pressed to her forehead. Her color had improved, if only from the blood rushing to her head from pitching her cookies.

"It was the brownie," she said, dropping onto an ancient wooden folding chair at the table.

Straker shoved the mug in front of her. The table was in front of a big picture window overlooking the bay, still enveloped in fog. "I thought it was the dead body."

"I wouldn't have thrown up if I hadn't eaten the brownie."

But she didn't smile. There was no spark in her dark, almond-shaped eyes.

"I don't have a phone," he said. "We can use the radio on my boat to notify the police. I'll go have a look, make sure you weren't seeing things."

"I'll go with you." She tried a sip of the tea, the

tea bag still dangling. "I don't want to stay here alone."

"If the guy's dead, he's not going to come crawling in here."

That rallied her. She pushed her chair back so forcefully it almost tipped over. She was still trembling, but she squared her shoulders. "Just let's go."

She took a couple more quick sips of tea, wiped at her face once more with the wet washcloth and pushed past him to the door. She looked a little wobbly, but Straker kept his mouth shut. Riley wasn't one to like having her weaknesses pointed out to her. He wondered if this was her first dead human. Her job put her in contact with stranded whales and dolphins.

Then he remembered last year's tragedy. Five dead, a narrow escape with her own life. She hadn't retreated to a deserted island to lick her wounds. Physically unharmed, she'd returned to her work at the Boston Center for Oceanographic Studies. Straker doubted she'd acknowledge any mental scars from her ordeal.

He followed her along a wet, winding path. She pushed hard, although her head had to be pounding and her energy drained from being sick. The fog continued to hang in, thick, damp and cold, reducing visibility to just a few feet despite the sun's attempts to burn through.

Straker felt the familiar tightness in his chest and incipient sense of panic that had nothing to do with following Riley St. Joe to a corpse. Fog had come to

make him feel claustrophobic, as if his soul had
spilled out of him and claimed the rest of the world.

Maybe he should have picked a cabin in the Ari-
zona desert.

"There." Riley stood on a rock ledge and pointed
toward the water, which Straker could smell but not
see. But he knew this stretch of coastline, knew the
rocks, the tide pools, the currents. She turned to him.
Her skin, hair, eyes had all taken on the milky gray-
ness of the fog. "He's caught on the rocks. The tide
must have brought him in. He might go out again with
high tide, but I don't think so. I can show you—"

"I'll find him."

Straker charged down the rocks. He'd grown up on
this coast, was comfortable jumping from rock to rock
in any weather. And his physical wounds were long
healed. He was in better shape now than he'd been
in the past two or three years. But he wasn't ready to
go back to work. He trusted his instincts, his training,
his experience. It wasn't that. He just didn't have
much use for people. In the past six months, he'd
grown accustomed to life alone.

Now a body had washed onto his deserted island.
Maybe it was an omen. If he didn't go back to work,
work would come to him.

Of course, Riley had said nothing about murder. It
was probably some poor bastard who'd taken a header
off his boat.

The tide had moved out, and he made his way over
barnacles and slick seaweed. He came to the water,
just a few inches deep now. A giant hunk of granite

loomed to his right. Riley would have been up there, he reasoned, looking down at the water.

Gravelly sand shifted under him. He stepped up onto a flat brown boulder, still wet from the receding tide. Not far ahead, waves slapped gently against rocks and sand.

He sensed the body before he saw it. His muscles tensed as he called upon the discipline and professionalism his work had instilled in him. He'd seen dead bodies before. He knew what to do.

This one was still, bloated, soaked. He'd put on jeans and a red polo shirt for his final day. He was about five feet off, facedown, as if he'd tripped and fallen running in from the water.

The gulls had been at him.

Straker turned away.

Riley materialized a few yards behind him. "You found him?"

"Go to my boat. Radio the police. I'll wait here."

"Why? If he's dead—"

He looked at her. She was ghostlike, smaller than he remembered. "I'll fight off the gulls."

Two

Lou Dorrman tied up his boat and tossed Riley's pink kayak onto Emile's dock. She thanked him, hoping he'd make short work of dropping her off, then head back to the island. But he climbed out onto the dock after her. He was the local sheriff, a paunchy, gray-haired, no-nonsense cop who'd said for years that John Straker would come to a bad end. Someone was bound to shoot him, run him over or beat him senseless. That a body had turned up on the island where he was recuperating was no surprise to Lou Dorrman.

That Riley was there, too, obviously troubled him. He glowered at her. "What're you doing hanging around John Straker?"

Her teeth chattered. The fog had burned off, leaving behind a warm, sunny afternoon, but she couldn't stop shivering. It was nerves and dehydration—and the lingering, horrible image of the man she'd found on the rocks. Straker had made her put on an overshirt after the police had arrived. She'd had to roll up the sleeves about six times to get them to her wrists. The heavyweight chamois smelled of sawdust and salt water.

"I was having a picnic," she said.

Dorrman nodded without understanding. "Hell of a picnic."

"Do you have any clues about the body—who it was—"

"Not yet. There was no identification on him. The medical examiner will do an autopsy. We should know more soon."

Riley thought she saw something in his eyes. "What is it, Sheriff?"

"Nothing. We have to do this one step at a time." He shifted, eyeing her with a measure of sympathy. "You going to be okay? I imagine Emile's out and about somewhere. I'll have to round him up before too long, seeing how that's his island."

Last summer, it was Bennett Granger and four members of the *Encounter* crew. This summer...a dead body on Labreque Island. Riley pushed back the nightmare, the familiar sense of unease. "I'll be fine on my own, thanks." She still couldn't stop shivering. "Sheriff, you don't think Straker had anything to do with this, do you? I know he was shot six months ago—Emile said it had to do with domestic terrorism."

"Domestic terrorism. Hell, that's FBI talk. Let's just take this one step at a time, okay? You'll be around awhile?"

"I'm supposed to head back to Boston tonight. I

have to be at work tomorrow. I was planning to visit my mother and sister in Camden on the way. I gave your deputy numbers where you can reach me."

"All right. Go ahead. I'll let you know if CID has any other ideas." CID was the Criminal Investigation Division of the Maine State Police; Straker had already explained they'd handle the investigation. Dorrman cuffed her on the shoulder. "Rough day, kid. Put it behind you."

While he sped back across the bay, Riley half carried, half dragged her kayak up to Emile's cottage, its dark-stained wood blending into the surrounding spruce-fir forest. This was his home now, not just his periodic getaway. It hadn't changed in years. She welcomed the familiarity of the smells and sounds, even the exposed pine roots in the path as she returned the kayak to the attached shed.

Her legs almost gave out on her, as if she were climbing Mount Katahdin instead of a few porch steps. She collapsed onto an old Adirondack chair. The wind had shifted. There wasn't even a hint of fog in the clear September air. It was cool up on the porch, out of the sun, which only made her shivering worse.

Emile's door was shut tight. She doubted he'd have heard the news yet. She felt acid crawl up her throat at the unbidden images of bloated flesh, pesky gulls swooping down on the hapless body.

She sprang up out of the chair. "I should have skipped that stupid picnic."

Then Straker could have found the body on his

own. Or the sea could have had it back. She struggled with the same disconcerting feeling of helplessness she'd experienced at her first whale and dolphin strandings when she was a teenager volunteering on a rescue and recovery team. Their mission was to end the suffering of animals beyond help, get the healthy ones out to sea before they died on the beaches and treat the injured, taking them back to the center for rehabilitation and, whenever possible, their eventual return to the wild. Now it was her team—but she would never get used to the death and suffering.

The man on the beach had been long past suffering.

She decided to leave Emile a note. Sympathy, commiseration, allaying her fears, venting—such niceties wouldn't occur to him. He would expect her to continue on to Camden and Boston. He wasn't heartless; he was simply oblivious. The urge to share her woes with him arose more from the shock of the moment than any rational reasoning on her part. She'd arrived too late to do the man on the rocks any good, and now her experience felt unfinished, as if she should do more, know more.

Would Straker dismiss the dead man and resume his isolated island life without a second thought?

She found Emile's spare key on the windowsill and let herself in. Even less rational than wanting to cry on Emile's shoulder was trying to get into John Straker's mind. Time to get her things and be on her way.

But when she set off, she ended up on the side street above the village harbor, where Straker's parents lived in a serviceable house that was at once home, shop and project. It had been in a constant state of flux for as long as Riley could remember, with gardens going in and coming out and discarded house innards piling up in the yard as various rooms underwent renovation. The glassed-in front porch served as a catchall for yard sale findings Straker's mother planned to fix up. She was clever at fixing things up, even if she tended to underestimate the time she would require. Summer people and locals alike employed her talents in furniture restoration and upholstery—they just knew not to expect quick results.

John Straker, Sr., was a lobsterman, his pots piled up outside the garage. It was a hard, good life, and if he regretted not having his son around to share it, he would never let an outsider like Riley St. Joe know about it.

She went around back, and Linda Straker called her into her cluttered kitchen, where she was elbow deep in one of her craft projects. She had an unlit cigarette tucked between her lips. She was a strong, stubborn, imaginative woman with hair that frequently changed color—today it was brunette—and a few extra pounds on her hips.

Her son had inherited her gray eyes. They settled on Riley. "You're here about that dead body?"

"You heard."

"Not much happens around here I don't hear about. Where's Emile?"

"I don't know. On the nature preserve, I expect. I'm on my way back to Boston." Riley dropped into a chair; she felt awkward, as if she were twelve again and Mrs. Straker would offer her a glass of Kool-Aid. "Actually, I'm not sure why I stopped by."

"Because you're afraid that body's got something to do with my son and it's going to come back and bite you in the behind." She took a breath, made a pretend drag on her cigarette. Her eyes were serious, experienced. "It could, you know."

"Why do you say that?"

"Because that's the way it's been with John since he saw the light of day thirty-four years ago. He's an FBI agent now, Riley. He's seen and done things since you nailed him with that rock when you were twelve. If I were you, I wouldn't mess with him."

Riley fiddled with a length of twine. "Too late."

"You couldn't have just pretended you didn't see that body and gone on your way?" She gave a long sigh. "No, I suppose not, and if you had, John would have known it and come after you. No way out of this one, Riley. If you're going to go toe-to-toe with him again, don't rely on luck. That's my advice. Take good aim, and if you do hit him, run like hell."

In spite of her tension, Riley managed a laugh. "I have no intention of seeing your son again, never mind throwing rocks or anything else at him."

The back door banged open, and Straker glared in at the two women. If Riley had still had any doubts he wasn't eighteen anymore, they would have been dispelled. He radiated hard-edged energy, the kind of raw intensity she'd expect from a man who'd gotten himself shot twice.

"Speak of the devil," Linda Straker said, unperturbed.

He kicked the door shut behind him. "St. Joe—damn it, what the hell are you doing here?"

Riley groaned. "I'm talking to your mother. I'm allowed. Aren't you supposed to be holed up on the island?"

"He comes into town every now and then for supplies," his mother answered for him.

He turned to her. "I thought you quit smoking."

"I did. It's not lit."

"Then what are these for?" He picked up a package of matches that Riley hadn't even noticed and tucked them in his jeans pocket. "You'll be puffing away the minute I leave."

She dropped her cigarette into a brass ashtray shaped like a lobster. "There. Nazi. I deserve a cigarette after hearing you found a dead body."

"I didn't. Riley did."

"You could have taught school like your sister," his mother said, "or taken up lobstering like your father. You could have opened up a law practice in town. But no, you have to join the FBI and get shot, bring dead bodies to town."

"That body has nothing to do with me."

"Then it has something to do with Emile Labreque. Either way, you'll get involved. You've always had a soft spot for Emile. He believed in you when no one else did. Even I had my doubts."

"Mrs. Straker," Riley said carefully, "just because

the body was found on Labreque Island doesn't mean
Emile—"

Straker didn't let her finish. He fingered a paper
doily. "What're you making?"

His mother bit off a sigh. "Your Christmas present.
Keep your mitts off."

"I stopped by to reassure you. I knew you'd hear
what happened." He shot Riley another nasty look,
as if she'd been the one who squealed. "It's nothing
to worry about, probably just some poor bastard who
fell off his boat."

"No one's been reported missing. You'd think—"

"Don't think, Ma. Just let the police handle this
one. And I'm fine, in case you were wondering."

She glowered at him. "The hell you're fine.
You've been sitting out on that island for six months.
Half the town thinks you're a raving lunatic."

His jaw set hard. "I've said my piece."

He about-faced and walked out. Just like that.
Linda Straker snatched up a huge pair of scissors.
"That terrorist didn't do half the job on him I could
do right now."

Riley judiciously said nothing.

"I'll tell you the truth, Riley. We all breathed a
sigh of relief when he went out to Labreque Island to
recuperate instead of up into the spare bedroom. I'd
just as soon tend a wounded tiger as him."

Riley knew the minute she agreed with her, Linda
Straker would turn on her. "Will you excuse me, Mrs.
Straker?"

"Go on," she said. "Go after him. You're looking

good, Riley—I meant to say that right off. I wasn't sure what to expect after your grandfather's ship went down.''

"That wasn't his fault, you know."

"You never know with ships," she said, and Riley, suddenly feeling the walls closing in around her, shot outside.

She caught up with Straker in the driveway. "Where are you going?"

He whipped around. Every muscle in his body seemed tense, rigid, as if he was ready to burst out of his skin. "Back."

"Back where?"

"The island."

"I've got your shirt. It's in my car." She eyed him, becoming aware of a strange sense of uneasiness. His mother was right—he wasn't the same kid she'd bloodied all those years ago. But she wasn't intimidated. "You look as if you want to lock me in an outhouse."

His eyes sparked, and his mouth drew into a sardonic smile. "That's not it."

Riley nearly choked. Bullet wounds, a six-month self-imposed exile. Women probably hadn't been on his short list of things to do. Well, she'd walked into that one. "Are the police finished?"

"No."

"Did you offer to help?"

"No."

"You know, Straker, if I had a rock..." Riley didn't go on. She'd pushed her luck enough with him.

"What else are you doing in town, besides reassuring your mother?"

His eyes turned to slits. "Are you being sarcastic?"

"I'm not afraid of you, Straker."

"That always was your problem."

He turned and started down the narrow street. Riley sighed. "What about your shirt?" she called after him.

"Keep it."

"Do you need a ride?"

"No."

"How did you get here?"

He glanced back at her. "I live on an island. I took a boat."

"I hate you, Straker," she called. "I've always hated you."

"Good."

She got in her car and drove in the opposite direction. She was agitated and restless and faintly sick to her stomach, and she didn't trust herself not to run Straker over. She headed out to the nature preserve, but Emile wasn't around. Neither was his car or his boat. She stopped back at his cottage. Same thing.

She gripped the wheel. "Well. Push has come to shove."

It was time to head to Camden and face her mother and sister. The first time she'd spent any time with her grandfather since the *Encounter,* and she'd found a dead body. No way would this go over well.

Two hours later, Riley rang the doorbell to her mother's little, mid-nineteenth-century gray clapboard on a pretty street above Camden Harbor. When the black-painted front door opened, she surprised herself by bursting into tears.

"Emile," Mara St. Joe said, tight-lipped. "*Damn* him."

"It's not him—he didn't do anything." Riley gulped in air, feeling like a ten-year-old. She brushed her cheeks with her fingertips. Thank God she hadn't fallen apart in front of Straker. "I found a dead body."

"I know. I heard on the radio. It's Emile's fault. He never should have let you kayak alone."

She whisked Riley into the front parlor. This was her parents' first house—her mother's first house. Two years ago, Mara St. Joe had declared she'd had her fill of living aboard research vessels and in whatever rented apartment was nearest their work. She'd grown up like that, she'd raised two children like that and she'd had enough. She chucked her puffin and guillemot research and set off to picturesque, upscale Camden, with its windjammers and yachts and grand old houses built by legendary sea captains and shipbuilders. She became a successful freelance nature writer and bought a house. For a while, Riley wondered if her parents would call it quits, but if they'd ever considered it, they hadn't told her. Her father was free to come and go as he pleased, which seemed to suit them both. Her parents had, and had always had, an unconventional marriage.

"Sit," she said. "Catch your breath."

"Mom, I'm fine. It was just pent-up tension."

"It was just your *grandfather*."

She half shoved Riley onto a wing chair. The parlor was decorated in antiques and antique reproductions in rich woods and soothing colors. Her mother, Riley thought, was not a patient woman. She was taller than Riley—taller even than Emile—with dark hair streaked white and eyes that could flare with sudden bursts of anger. People said her mother, Emile's one and only wife, who'd died when Mara was two, had possessed a similar temper. At fifty-five, Mara knew all too well the particular kind of pain her father could inflict. It wasn't his work that drove her crazy, she'd said—it was his single-mindedness. She didn't care if it was in a good cause, it was workaholism by any other name, and it left her out. It left everyone out.

"Would you like a cup of tea?" she asked, obviously restraining herself.

Riley shook her head. "I'm okay now. I should have called and told you. I didn't mean for you to hear the news on the radio."

"I had it on while I was working. Oh, Riley." She brushed back her hair with one hand and paced; she had on jeans and a plaid flannel tunic, her writing clothes. "Emile should have known better. And John Straker of all people..." She groaned in disbelief. "My God!"

"He let me throw up in his toilet."

Her mother spun around at her. "He's a lunatic! Living out on that island alone the past six months.

What *could* Emile have been thinking when he let you go out there?''

"He didn't let me. I just went. Mom, for heaven's sake, I'm not twelve.''

"I still blame Emile.''

Riley sank into the chair, spent. She smiled wanly at her mother. Her reaction was exactly what she'd expected, perhaps even needed. "I'm so glad to see you, Mom. Is Sig home?''

"She's out walking. She'll be back any minute. Come, I'll make tea. You'll feel better in no time.'' Mara exhaled. "*Damn* Emile.''

She was having twins.

Sig St. Joe slipped into the enclosed back porch of her mother's house, which she'd fashioned into her first real studio in years. She had a worktable, 140-pound cold-pressed paper, tubes of watercolors, a dozen brushes, water jars, boards—everything she needed except inspiration.

She flopped onto a studio bed she'd covered in old quilts and pillows, just like her girlhood bed in the loft at Emile's cottage. She'd spotted Riley's car. She couldn't face either her sister or her mother right now.

Twins.

She was just over four months pregnant and had told no one, including her goddamned, miserable, self-absorbed husband.

Sig sighed. That was another quarter for her mason jar. She was on a campaign to stop swearing. At the rate she was going, she'd be broke by the end of the week, or she'd have to dip into her Granger money. God forbid. She'd rather wash her mouth out with soap.

She could feel the babies move. Just a flutter. Probably they were already jockeying for position. She wasn't prepared to have one baby, never mind two. But maybe in the long run it would be easier, because she had no intention of getting pregnant again. After Matthew Granger, she was through with men.

One day she'd have to explain to her babies what a flaming asshole their father was.

Flaming *jerk,* she amended, mentally putting another quarter in the jar.

He was rich, he was handsome and he was convinced her grandfather should be in jail for negligent homicide. "Emile's criminally responsible for my father's death. Admit it."

Sig didn't want to admit anything. She wanted Matt to work through his anger and grief and accept that they just didn't know what had happened aboard the *Encounter.* No one did. The boat was at the bottom of the North Atlantic. The official investigation was inconclusive.

No, she thought, *don't go there.* Thinking about the *Encounter* and her father-in-law's tragic death—the tragic deaths of the four crew members—spun her around in circles. There was nothing she could do. There was nothing Matt could do, only he couldn't accept that, at least not yet and maybe not ever.

She just wanted to bury herself in a heap of quilts and stay out here all night, pretend she was ten again, sleeping out at Emile's with her sister. She'd felt so safe at ten. Whatever her family's oddities, she'd never felt anything but safe with them. Now here she was, thirty-four, pregnant, estranged from her rich husband, a failure as an artist and about to be a failure as a mother.

Sig glanced over at her worktable, where another of her abandoned paintings was still taped to her large board. The porch didn't go with the rest of the house. It had been added in one of the various renovations over the past century or so, and her mother wanted to get rid of it. She wanted a dooryard garden. Well, it made a lousy studio. The light was bad, and there was no heat. Sig knew she couldn't work out here much longer. It was time. She had to figure out her life.

What would she do with twins?

They'd be *Granger* twins. She shuddered. It wasn't as bad as bearing the Prince of Wales, but it was damned close. Maybe she just wouldn't tell Matt about his babies. Spare him the torture of explaining to the rest of Beacon Hill that not only had he married Emile Labreque's granddaughter, he was now providing the murderous madman with *great-grandchildren.*

The door from the kitchen opened, and Riley said in an unusually small voice, "Sig? Mom thought she heard you."

"I'm here wallowing in self-pity. Come on out. Mom send tea?"

"And raisin toast."

"Good. I'm starving." Eating for *three.* She eyed

her younger sister, who looked so damned tiny and smart—and something else. "Jesus, what happened to you?"

"It's a long story. I'm okay."

Riley set a tray on an old gateleg table their mother had found at a yard sale and painted creamy white. Sig had messed it up with watercolor spills. Splatters of cobalt and lemon, dots of purple, one big splash of crimson. She loved spills.

"You don't look okay," Sig said.

Riley ignored her comment and sat on the other end of the studio bed. Sig was tall and leggy, like the St. Joes. When they were kids, Emile had called his granddaughters Big Dog and Little Dog until Mara told him to stop it, he'd give them a complex. Emile didn't understand things like complexes.

Sig blinked back sudden tears. She hadn't seen her grandfather in a year. Not since the *Encounter*. "You've been to see Emile, haven't you?"

Riley poured tea and placed a triangle of toast on the side of each saucer. Mara had gotten out the good china. Definitely something was up. Sig shifted uncomfortably, her voluminous dress drawing across her swelling abdomen. She realized her mistake, but too late.

Riley gasped, nearly dropping the teapot. "Sig— you're pregnant!"

Sig managed a wry smile. "The trained scientist speaks."

"When—how—" Riley blushed furiously, bringing much needed color to her cheeks; for a woman consumed with the doings of sea beasts of all kinds, Sig was amazed at how downright prudish her sister could be. "I mean, how far along are you?"

"A little over four months. I can feel them move."

"*Them?*"

"I found out on Friday I'm having twins. I've been trying to absorb it ever since." Saying it out loud didn't make her feel any more in control of her situation. "I haven't told a soul."

"Mom—"

"She doesn't even know I'm pregnant, never mind having twins. Neither does Matt. I haven't seen him in…well, ages."

Riley handed her tea and toast. "Looks as if you saw him within the last five months or so. He's on Mount Desert Island. I ran into him. He made a brief appearance at one of Caroline's dinners. He managed not to mention his vendetta against Emile." Riley picked up her tea again. "He was staying on his boat. I would think he's still there."

"It doesn't matter. He's so eaten up with anger and grief over what happened to his father…." Sig waved a hand, dismissing Matthew, all the upheavals of the past year. "I just don't care anymore."

The color had drained back out of Riley's face. Sig silently chastised herself. There was no point in bringing up past horrors when obviously some new one had her sister in its grip. Bennett Granger was dead. He was one of the finest men Sig had ever known, and he and Emile had been friends and partners for fifty years. That his death had led to more tragedy and pain only compounded her sorrow.

"Where's Mom?" she asked.

"She's slipped off to the market. She insisted I stay for dinner. She's cooking lobster." But Riley didn't seize the opportunity to proceed with her own problems. "She knows, Sig. You know she does. She's just waiting for you to say something. You can talk to her—"

"She never wanted me to marry a Granger."

"That's because she was afraid you'd end up living in his shadow and indulging his whims. When she realized Matt's a regular guy, she came around."

"He's not a regular guy. He's a goddamned blue-blood with too much money and not enough common sense."

"You sound as if you hate him."

"I wish I did. My life would be so much easier." Sig quickly sipped her tea and bit into the raisin toast; her mother had slathered on the butter. "I said 'god-damn,' didn't I? That's another quarter for the mason jar."

"You've quit swearing again?"

"I was doing pretty well until I found out I'm having twins." She inhaled, unable to concentrate on anyone's problems but her own. "I want these babies, Riley. I want to be a good mother."

"You will be. You just won't be conventional. You haven't started smoking again, have you?"

"Not a chance. And how're your vices?"

Her sister grinned, and some of the usual spark came back into her dark eyes. "I have no vices."

"Ha. You're like Emile and Dad. The seven seas are your vice."

"My passion," Riley amended.

"Same difference. Now, are you going to tell me why you look like absolute shit?" When Riley didn't answer, Sig winced. "I've really fallen off the wagon this time. I've been swearing like a sailor."

But Riley had shut her eyes, and she squeezed back tears.

"Riley..."

"I found a dead body and almost threw up on John Straker."

"Holy shit," Sig said. "No wonder Mom's making you lobster."

Three

❧⟳⟳⟳⟳❧

Straker didn't settle quickly back into his routines. He heated his stew and took a steaming bowl of it onto his porch. It was early for lunch, but he didn't care. The police had packed up late yesterday and left, at least for now. The island was quiet again, the waves, wind, gulls and familiar putter of lobster boats the only sounds. The return to solitude didn't have the impact he'd expected. A few days ago, the quiet had soothed his soul. Now, twenty-four hours after Riley St. Joe and a dead body had violated his tranquility, it was getting on his nerves.

He spotted Lou Dorrman's boat making its way across the bay toward the island and went down to the rickety dock. The sheriff tied up, jumped out and greeted him with a curt nod. It was as if Straker's old life had reached into his new life to remind him there was no escape. "What's up, Sheriff?"

"We just got word from the medical examiner. He won't have final results for a while, but his preliminary exam suggests our John Doe took a blow to the head.''

Straker went still. ''Accident?''

''CID's treating it as a suspicious death. We need to know what role the head injury played in his death, did he take the hit before he was in the water, after—maybe when he washed in on the rocks.''

''I don't know how he could have washed ashore, with the tide and the currents out here. Doesn't make sense.''

Dorrman frowned. He'd gone to school with Straker's father, had once dated Straker's mother. ''You have any visitors out here the past few days? Besides Riley.''

''Christ, Lou, if I offed someone, I wouldn't dump his body on the rocks for Riley St. Joe to find.''

''Answer the question.''

''No. No visitors. And if our John Doe had spent any time on the island, I'd have known about it.''

''He wouldn't have anything to do with one of your FBI cases?''

''If he did,'' Straker said pointedly, ''I wouldn't be sitting on my porch eating a bowl of stew.''

Dorrman didn't back down. ''I wish you'd picked somewhere else to sit around for six months. You're a burr on my butt, Straker. See to it we can find you if we have more questions.''

Straker eyed him, took in the red face, the unusual level of aggravation, even for Lou Dorrman. ''What else?''

''What do you mean, what else?''

"Something else is eating at you."

The sheriff huffed and gazed out at the water a moment. "I can't find Emile."

"Hell."

"I checked his cottage, I checked the preserve. His boat's gone, his car's gone." Dorrman shifted his back to Straker. "I don't like it. A dead body turns up on Labreque Island one day, Emile disappears the next."

"Did you check inside his cottage?"

"I can't do that without a warrant."

Straker could. "Give me a lift?"

Twenty minutes later, they put in at Emile's dock. Straker didn't wait for Dorrman. He headed up to the old man's cottage, mounted the steps and tried the door. Locked. He held the doorknob, leaned his shoulder against the door and, putting his weight into it, pushed hard.

The door came on the second push. Piece of cake.

"Christ," Dorrman said from the bottom of the stairs, "I don't believe you."

"I'm his friend. This is what he'd expect. I'll be out in two minutes."

Emile's cottage was more cheap old man than world-famous oceanographer. He'd left most of his old life behind. The only remnants were copies of his books and documentaries on a shelf in the main room and a few pictures of his family aboard the *Encounter*. He'd taken out the trash, left a mug in the dish drainer, unplugged the coffeepot. Straker checked the downstairs bedroom. A tidy sailor to the last, Emile had made his bed, too.

Straker took the steep, ladderlike stairs up to the loft and came across a red bra, size 34B, under a creaky twin bed. It provided no clues as to Emile and his whereabouts. It did, however, provide fresh insight into Riley. She'd never been neat, but Straker wouldn't have expected her to favor red underwear.

Best to keep his mind on the task at hand.

He joined Dorrman back outside. "He cleared out."

"Kind of makes you wonder, doesn't it?"

"Not my job to wonder. I'm going to take a drive down to Boston." A sudden wind gusted off the bay; he was thinking up his plan as he went along, knowing already he'd regret it. He should go back to Labreque Island and reheat his stew. "I'll let you know if I run into him."

"You do that. Keep in touch."

"You want to bug my car, make sure I don't take off to Alaska?"

Dorrman sucked in a breath, controlling his irritation. "If it were up to me, Straker, you'd be hauling in lobsters with your old man. You're not fit to be an officer of the law. Never have been."

"Does that mean if I'd been killed instead of wounded six months ago you wouldn't have marched in my funeral parade?"

Dorrman's mouth stretched into a thin, mean grin. "There'd have been a fucking brawl over who got to lead that parade."

Straker took no offense. Louis Dorrman didn't like him. A lot of people didn't like him. But Straker had friends, and he had people he trusted—and he did his job. He'd never been the most popular guy around. It didn't worry him. What worried him were the dead body Riley St. Joe had found on his island and where Emile had taken himself off to.

The sheriff grudgingly gave him a ride back to the island and waited while Straker packed up, grabbed his car keys and rinsed out his stew bowl. He didn't need to come back to find the place overrun with ants.

He climbed back into Dorrman's boat. "My car's at my folks' place."

"I know," the sheriff said, as if to remind Straker he knew everything that went on in his town. He was the one who'd stayed, who hadn't gone off and joined the FBI. Dorrman gunned the engine and sped across the bay.

Riley picked up eggplant parmesan from her favorite Porter Square deli on her way home from work, where, mercifully, no one had heard about what had happened yesterday on Schoodic Peninsula. She kept the news to herself. When she'd left Mount Desert Island, she'd said only that she was taking a long weekend. She hadn't mentioned going to visit Emile.

With any luck, there'd be a message from the police on her answering machine telling her the man she'd found had been identified, he'd died in a tragic accident, end of story.

She had a one-bedroom apartment on the third floor

of a triple decker just off Porter Square in Cambridge. There was no message from the police on her machine. There was one from her mother, asking her if she was all right. Nothing from Richard St. Joe. Her father was in Bath, checking on the *Encounter II*, the state-of-the-art, ecologically friendly research vessel the center was having built. He would be back tomorrow.

She heated her eggplant parmesan in the microwave and whisked a bit of balsamic vinegar and olive oil together for her salad. It felt good to reacquaint herself with her routines. After dinner, she'd put in a load of laundry and clean out her fridge.

Her telephone rang, and she grabbed the portable out from under a newspaper on her kitchen table.

"What would you do if I told you I was on the curb outside your apartment?"

Straker. Her stomach knotted. "You have a sick sense of humor, Straker. You're not on my curb. You live on a deserted island. You hate people. You wouldn't traipse all the way to Boston just to aggravate me."

"You wouldn't invite me in?"

She tightened her grip on the phone. He sounded close. She remembered he didn't have a phone on the island. She took her portable into the front room, knelt on her futon couch, leaned over and pulled back the blinds so she could peer down at the street.

It was dark, but she could make out a beat-up, rusting gray Subaru station wagon with Maine plates.

"Damn it, Straker, you *are* on my curb!"

"So, do I get to come in?"

She hit the off button and tossed her phone onto the couch. What did he think he was doing? Six months alone on an island—and now Boston? He'd kill someone. Someone would kill him. He was not fit for the civilized world.

It was the body. Something must have happened.

She was hyperventilating. She clamped her mouth shut and held her breath, forcing herself to count to five. If she didn't let Straker in, what would he do?

If she did let him in, what would he do?

She unlocked her door and took the two flights of stairs two and even three steps at a time. She picked up so much momentum, she almost went head-over-teakettle down the front stoop. After throwing up, all she needed was to split her head open at Straker's feet.

He had his window rolled down.

Riley caught her breath. "I can't believe you drove all the way down from Maine."

He popped the last of a Big Mac into his mouth. "Now that you mention it, neither can I."

"What do you want?"

He reached for a backpack on the floor in front of the passenger seat, rolled up his window, locked his door and climbed out. He looked just as powerful and strong and unflappable on her Porter Square sidewalk as on Labreque Island. The city didn't make him any more or less than what he was—a man she would be wise to avoid. His own mother had said so.

"Our body came with a nasty blow to the head," he said. "CID's treating it as a suspicious death."

"You mean—what—" Her stomach rolled over. "Are you suggesting he was *murdered?*"

"That's my bet."

He hoisted his backpack over one shoulder and started for her front stoop as if he'd just told her a dog had peed on her rug. Riley stayed on the sidewalk next to his car. She couldn't move. Her knees wobbled. He wasn't just John Straker, obnoxious teenager from her past. He was an FBI agent. He'd been shot twice by some dangerous nut on the FBI's Most Wanted list. He'd spent the last six months as a recluse.

Straker turned back to her. He shook his head. "You aren't going to throw up, are you?"

That unmoored her. She brushed past him and walked up the steps with as much nonchalance as she could fake. She prided herself on her ability to look reality square in the eye. Right now, the reality was that Straker was here, and she had to deal with him. She headed upstairs, assuming he would follow. He did.

"I figured you for a condo on the water," he said from behind her.

"Too expensive."

"Well, I guess you're comfortable among Cambridge eggheads."

She glanced back at him, cool. "Don't inflict your stereotypes on me, Straker."

He shrugged. "Tell me your apartment won't have egghead written all over it."

"Just shut up."

She could feel his grin as she pushed open her door. He'd always known how to jerk her chain. He walked in past her, took in her living room with her stuff stacked and spread out everywhere and gave her a smug wink. "I rest my case."

"I haven't had a chance to clean—"

"You have enough books and magazines and crap in here to start your own think tank." He walked over to her computer table, cluttered with printouts and Post-it Notes. The wall behind it was covered with nautical charts. He ran a finger over the flamingo Beanie Baby she kept on her monitor. "Egghead with a touch of kook."

Riley gritted her teeth. "Straker, I swear I don't know how people stand you."

"They don't." He abandoned her computer and came closer to her. It was as if he'd brought an electric current into her apartment; the air sizzled. "You're looking a little green at the gills. Want me to fetch you a drink?"

"No. I want you to tell me why you're here."

He lifted a stack of *Audubon* magazines off her futon couch, set them on the floor next to a stack of *Smithsonian* magazines and sat down. "Emile took off."

"What do you mean, he took off?"

"I mean he took out the trash, made his bed, locked up and vamoosed. No car, no boat. He probably hid one—my bet's on the car. Emile's a sailor at heart. He'd go by water if he had a choice.''

Riley ignored a sudden chill and uneasiness. ''You're thinking like an FBI agent instead of someone who knows Emile. He does this sort of thing. He'll go off for days at a time without telling anyone.''

''Does he always hide his car?''

''You don't know he hid it. He could have just used it to haul supplies to his boat, then didn't want to take the trouble of driving it back up to the cottage, so left it.''

Straker shook his head. ''I don't think so.'' He leaned back and stretched out his thick legs. Riley didn't remember him being so earthy. He seemed to exude sexuality. It had to be deliberate. A way of throwing her off balance in case she was hiding something from him. He glanced around. ''No cat?''

''What?''

''I figured you'd have a cat.''

She groaned. ''This is outrageous. I think you should leave.''

''I'd have to sleep in my car. I don't have enough dough on me for a hotel.''

''Don't you have a credit card?''

''Nope. I got rid of all my plastic after I got shot.''

He was perfectly calm, controlled and irritatingly at ease. Riley sputtered, ''You can't think…''

She fought the overwhelming sense she was losing her mind. The man she'd found may have been murdered, Emile had slipped off and John Straker, who'd been living on a deserted island for the past six months, was in her apartment. She hadn't had a man in her apartment in months, not since after the *Encounter,* when the oceanographer she'd been casually dating said for her to take a few weeks to pull her head together, he'd be in touch. He hadn't been in touch, and her life had gone on. She had her work. Romance would take care of itself.

She winced. It was dangerous to think about romance with John Straker standing inches from her. "You're not spending the night," she told him.

His gray eyes leveled on her. "Sure I am. Why else the backpack?"

Why else indeed. She should have connected the dots sooner, like out on the street. "Then what?"

He shrugged. "The morning will bring what the morning will bring."

"To hell with you, Straker. You have a plan and you know it. What is it? Do you think Emile had something to do with that dead body? Do you think he's going to contact me? Has *already* contacted me?" She thrust her hands onto her hips, in full outrage now. "Are you going to follow me around just in case I'm up to something nefarious?"

"Nefarious?" He grinned. "I've been in law enforcement for ten years, and I don't think I've ever used that word."

She all but sputtered again. "You listen to me. I do not need and will not tolerate a reclusive, lunatic FBI agent with post-traumatic stress disorder in my hip pocket."

He got to his feet, crumpled up his Big Mac wrapper and walked through the dining room into the kitchen. Riley followed him. She wondered if she'd said something wrong. If she'd said a lot wrong. She reminded herself that everything she'd said was true and thus it might have been wiser on her part not to say it out loud. What if he snapped?

He glanced back at her. "Trash can?"

"Under the sink."

He pulled open the cupboard and tossed in the crumpled wrapper. He turned back to her. His eyes were narrowed; his body was rigid. She wasn't nervous, but she was on high alert. He said, "Two things."

"Okay."

"One, I don't have PTSD. I'd have PTSD if the guy'd shot his hostages. He didn't. He shot me. So, no PTSD."

She nodded. "No PTSD."

"Two, you need a drink."

"I don't need a drink. I don't need anything—"

He sighed. "Now I remember why we threw rocks at each other when we were kids. Do you have whiskey or is wine it?"

"Wine's it."

He plucked a half-full bottle of chardonnay from her refrigerator. He didn't bother tracking down her wineglasses, just filled two juice glasses. He handed her one. "Toast?"

She was past arguing. "Sure."

He clinked his glass against hers. "To the first thing Riley St. Joe needs."

"I don't know the first thing I need."

He winked. "That's why we're toasting it."

"Huh?"

"One night on your futon. Tomorrow I'll figure out whether I need to jump into your hip pocket or not."

"I won't let you."

"Sweetheart, I'm a pro. You won't even know I'm there."

Straker had never slept on a futon. As sofa beds went, it wasn't bad, and he had to admit it was better than that thing in his cottage Emile called a mattress. It was the clutter and the city noises that got him. And perhaps the presence of Riley St. Joe under the same roof. At least she didn't have a cat. If he'd had to put up with a cat, too, he might not have endured.

She was up at the crack of dawn, putting coffee on, humming to herself, digging through piles for odd items she tossed into her leather tote bag. Straker had a pretty good idea she'd forgotten she'd let him sleep on her futon.

Suddenly she gasped and went still. She had her back to him. He figured she was trying to make herself disappear. She had on oversize, black-watch-plaid flannel boxers and a T-shirt with a guy snowboarding down a mountainside on the back. She had slender, shapely legs. The boxers were too big for him to make out the shape of her bottom. Forget the T-shirt; he could fit in it. He could also get it off her in one fell swoop. She was small, sexy and not as easy to figure out as he remembered. From what he could see, she didn't have much of a life. He guessed she'd gone underground since the *Encounter* disaster. Instead of a deserted island, she'd picked think-tank clutter.

He sat up and rubbed his overnight stubble. "You wear boxers to bed, huh? Not me. I sleep in the buff."

She didn't turn around. "I'll put more coffee on," she mumbled, and quickly retreated to the kitchen.

He pulled on his pants and shirt and for once didn't bother checking the scars on his lower right side and thigh. His wounds had healed. He could climb tall mountains if he wanted to.

He went to join Riley in the kitchen, but she'd already dashed off, presumably to her bedroom for more clothes. He poured himself a cup of coffee, made a spot at the table and sat down to mull over his options. Yesterday his mission had seemed clear. Find Emile. Start with Riley. *Boom*. Here he was.

This morning, things were muddier. Riley had a job and didn't want him around. Emile could be anywhere. Neither necessarily had any connection to the body found on Labreque Island.

The telephone rang. Who'd be calling at seven in the morning? He waited a half beat after the final ring before picking up the portable.

Riley was talking. "Sig—slow down. What's wrong?"

"Mom just talked to the police." Sig spoke rapidly, obviously not getting enough air. "Riley, they've identified the man you found. Oh, *Jesus*."

Straker stiffened. This wasn't good news. He could hear Riley gulp in a breath. "Tell me."

"It's Sam Cassain," Sig said, sobbing.

Riley was silent. Then, in a strangled whisper, "Oh, my God."

Straker frowned. "Who the hell's Sam Cassain?"

Sig almost screamed. "Riley? Who's that? Who's there?"

"Straker, get off my damned phone!"

He didn't move. "Who's Sam Cassain?"

"John Straker?" Sig said, more calmly now. "Riley, what's he doing in your apartment? Are you *crazy?*"

This wasn't getting him anywhere. Straker hung up and went into the bedroom. Riley was sitting on the edge of her unmade bed in her work clothes, no shoes. Her eyes were huge. Her skin was pale. She stared up at him. "I'll call you later, Sig," she told her sister, and hung up.

"Who's Sam Cassain?" Straker repeated.

She placed a shaky hand on her forehead. "He—he was the captain of the *Encounter.*"

The pieces fell together. "He's the one who laid the blame for the explosion and fire at Emile's feet."

She nodded dully.

"He turns up dead on Labreque Island, and Emile disappears. Police'll be calling you next." He thought a moment, ignoring her increasing paleness. "Strike that. They'll come see you in person. You didn't recognize him?"

"No. I didn't get that close a look, and the gulls…"

He remembered. "Emile must have figured it out."

"How could he? He never saw the body."

"Instincts," Straker said.

She slid to her feet. Her room was as cluttered as the rest of her apartment, but with feminine touches—a pair of earrings on the nightstand, a botanical print of beach plums above the bed, little jars of creams and perfumes on the bureau. She stood in front of him, smart, professional and quite pretty. And annoyed. "I don't want you listening in on my phone conversations."

"Would you have told me about Cassain if I hadn't?"

"Probably."

"Probably" wasn't good enough, but she was too unsteady and shaken for him to press the point. He made her drink a cup of coffee and eat a piece of toast, and when she protested about him driving her to work, he ignored her and coaxed her into his car. The rush-hour traffic into Boston reminded him why he'd retreated to an uninhabited island to recuperate. Lots of stimuli out here on the city streets. Cars, lights, horns, traffic helicopters, blaring radios, construction.

Riley sat beside him, hugging her overstuffed leather tote on her lap so hard her knuckles turned white.

"Remember to breathe," he said.

"I am breathing."

"Not from here." He poked her breastbone. "From here." He poked her low on her diaphragm. He could feel smooth, cool skin under her creamy blouse. More stimuli. "Slow, deep breaths. How well did you know Sam Cassain?"

"He was the *Encounter*'s captain for seven years. He was tough, no-nonsense and not one to suffer fools gladly."

"Who hired him?"

"Emile did. His last captain had died of cancer. He was a scientist, too, and when he died, Emile wanted someone new who'd tend the ship and leave the science to him. The *Encounter* was old." She swallowed, her gaze locked straight ahead, as if she couldn't turn her head. "The center had already commissioned a new research ship. It's costing a fortune, but it'll have all the latest ecological and technological advances. We're calling it the *Encounter II*."

"Who's in charge of it now that Emile's out of the picture?"

"My father."

Straker took Storrow Drive along the Charles River, then cut over to the waterfront. More construction. No room for the five million other cars on the road. The center was located in a renovated nineteenth-century warehouse on its own wharf. A huge, whimsical stone fountain out front featured various marine mammals.

"You can just drop me off on the curb," Riley said.

He hated the idea of dumping her and retreating.

Cassain's body had been found in Maine, and Emile had exiled himself to Maine. But the two men's relationship had begun here, in Boston.

"I think you should hire me to feed the penguins or something," he told her.

She blanched. "No."

"Why not?"

"I'm not in a position to hire you, and I don't want you underfoot." Now that he'd seen her in her boxers, underfoot probably sounded less threatening to her than in her hip pocket. "And you wouldn't fit in."

"I'd fit in. I grew up on the ocean. I probably have more practical knowledge about the ocean than most people who work here."

She managed to peel one hand off her tote and place it on the door handle. "For God's sake, Straker, you haven't been around people in *six months*. Even on a good day you're not volunteer material. Please. Just let me go to work and put this all into perspective."

While she talked, he formed a plan. She didn't need to know it. It would just upset her, and she was upset enough. He said, "Okay. See you around."

Her brows drew together. She'd put on a little bit of makeup, but not enough to hide how pale she was. Her lips were plum. They were also well shaped. He had a feeling she didn't have a man in her life. She made a face, obviously having no idea what he was thinking. "I don't know if I like the idea of you running around out here by yourself."

He grinned. "I'm a big boy."

"I'm not worried about you. I'm worried about *me*."

"Think I'd do something to embarrass you?"

She didn't answer. "You aren't on this thing officially, are you?"

"Nope. Sleeping on a futon in your apartment isn't part of my job description."

"What if I promise to call you if I hear from Emile?"

"Okay."

"Do you have a cell phone in this car?"

He gave her the number.

"Thank you." He assumed she meant for not pressing his case about the penguins, which was a misreading of the situation on her part. "This'll work out. I know it will. Emile's probably just checking out puffin nests."

Straker gave her an hour to get settled. He parked in her spot in the garage, bought a cup of coffee from a sidewalk vendor and sat by the stone fountain. The coffee was hot and strong, and he sipped it slowly as he avoided pigeons and tried not to let his thoughts run full speed ahead of him. One thought came to him crystal clear, impossible to ignore.

Riley St. Joe was trouble. She always had been. He had the scar on his forehead to prove it.

Four

Riley holed up in her small, cluttered office and worked all morning. After her long weekend, she had plenty to do. She tried not to think about Emile or Straker. Emile worried her. Straker simply annoyed her. He always had. He took pleasure in it. The shock of having him roll off her couch that morning had nearly done her in. The dark stubble on his jaw, the unbuttoned shirt. He was earthy, masculine and relentless.

Forewarned, she told herself, is forearmed. She needed to remember that nothing ever penetrated John Straker's hard shell enough to reach his soul, not two bullets, not a dead body on the rocks.

It was Sam Cassain's body she'd found.

She shut her eyes, the faint beginnings of a headache pressing against her temples. Sam was dead, Emile was missing—and Straker? She didn't know what Straker was up to. It might have made more sense to keep him where she could see him, but she had nowhere to tuck an FBI agent.

Her father poked his head into her office. "Busy?"

She smiled. "Just pretending."

If anyone fit the stereotype of the hyperfocused scientist, Riley thought, it was Richard St. Joe. He was tall and thin like Sig, but with none of her sense of style. He was oblivious to his typically ragged appearance. Today he had on jeans, a navy thermal shirt and water sandals with thick socks. His scruffy beard was grayer than she remembered. He hadn't been aboard the *Encounter* when it caught fire and sank last year. Instead he'd been aboard a university research ship, conducting a seminar on right whales, when the first distress calls came in. He'd had to wait hours before he learned that his daughter and father-in-law had survived.

"Your mother called—she told me about Sam." He looked as if he'd been fighting off panic, irritation, trying to figure out how to confront an adult daughter and colleague. "Why didn't you tell me you were going to see Emile?"

"I didn't think of it."

"You didn't have to sneak off. I know he's your grandfather. It's not as if I'd forbid you to see him."

"But you can caution me against it," she said, knowing that was exactly what he'd have done.

Richard pushed his bony hands through his salt-and-pepper hair as if he'd like to pull out every strand. "Only because I think he's become insanely reckless and selfish. Sam—you can't think there's no connection between his death and Emile. There *must* be." He almost trembled with exasperation. "My God!"

"I'm trying not to jump to any conclusions."

"I'm not talking about conclusions, I'm talking about *logic*." But he checked his raging emotions and softened, giving her a quick hug. "Thank God you're all right. Let's hope the worst is over for you. At this point I don't give a damn anymore about Emile, but you…" He tousled her hair as if she were seven. "I care about you, kid. I'm sorry you had to go through what you did."

"At least I didn't know it was Sam. If I had…" She shuddered, leaving it at that.

"I know. Let's hope the police make quick work of this. Riley, you know I have no desire to see anything more happen to Emile—"

"It's okay, Dad. I understand. He shouldn't have taken off the way he did."

"Yeah. Keep me posted, will you?"

She promised she would. Her father, her mother, Sig. Emile. In their own way, they were a family, and they cared about each other. As tough as her parents were on Emile, Riley knew it pained them to see what they believed had become of him. And it frustrated them that she disagreed with their assessment. She was the only one who still refused to believe Emile Labreque had become a dangerous disgrace to his work, his reputation and himself.

Not two minutes after her father left, her extension rang.

"Don't you have your own secretary?"

Straker. "Where are you?"

"I'm on break."

"From what?"

"I'm learning how to feed sharks."

"What?"

"I signed up for the volunteer-training program for people with PTSD. Abigail Granger happened to be in the volunteer office when I stopped by. I understand this program was her idea. Get them to connect with nature, toss a few fish to the sharks and they feel better about what they've been through. She walked me through the paperwork."

"You're shameless. There's a hot poker in hell with your name on it, I swear. That program is for people with a serious psychological disorder."

"I went to an island for six months. I connected with nature. I feel better."

Riley gripped the receiver so hard her hand hurt. "You went to an island for six months because you can't get along with anyone."

"I've made friends with a couple of Vietnam vets this morning. Now, they've got real demons to fight. I didn't want to lie to them, so I told them the score. They liked it when I told them you had a Beanie Baby sitting on your computer. You have quite the tiger-lady reputation."

"You're the most obnoxious man on the planet. You conned Abigail."

"Nope. I told her I'm shadowing you because I don't trust you to mind your own business and I needed a cover story, and she showed me to the sharks."

"You did not."

He laughed.

"I hate you, Straker."

"You hold that thought. You staying in for lunch?"

"I'm not telling you."

"Okay, I'll find out on my own—"

"Yes! Yes, I'm staying in for lunch." She hated him, hated him, hated him. But his laugh still resonated, low and deep. He was a very dangerous man. "You?"

"Abigail's bringing us clam chowder."

He hung up, and Riley had to pry her fingers off the receiver.

She raced down to the volunteer office, where, indeed, Abigail Granger had ordered clam chowder lunches for her volunteers.

"Would you like some?" she asked. "We always order extra."

Riley smiled stiffly. "No, thanks. I was just checking out a rumor."

Straker was there. He hadn't lied. Abigail wasn't the sort who'd see through him. She was thirty-nine, fair-haired and fine boned, with striking blue eyes and a well-honed sense of style and grace. She never griped about anyone or anything, although she was divorced and the mother of two teenage boys away at school.

Like Bennett Granger, her deceased father, she wasn't a scientist, but her dedication to the Boston Center for Oceanographic Studies was total. She'd taken his place on the board of directors. If she wanted to fall for John Straker's phony sob story, she could.

"I heard about your terrible ordeal this weekend," Abigail said. "I'm so sorry. How are you doing?"

From her tone Riley guessed she hadn't heard that the body had been identified as Sam Cassain. Abigail had never said what she believed happened to the *Encounter*. Matthew Granger—her brother and Riley's brother-in-law—was the one who knew. Emile was responsible, period, never mind that he'd been like a second father to Bennett's two children, showing them how to tie knots and sing to the periwinkles. His downfall had left a void in their lives, too, even if Abigail repressed it and Matt raged against it.

Riley decided she didn't really want to tell Abigail it was Sam's body she'd found. "I'm okay."

Abigail frowned. Her expensive navy suit, although simple, looked out of place amid the stripped-down furnishings of the volunteer office. The center had a policy of putting its funds into research, public displays and facilities that benefited its marine and aquatic population—not into plush furnishings for staff and volunteers. "I understand you were visiting Emile."

"I spent Monday night at his place on Schoodic."

"Riley? Are you all right?"

She attempted a shaky smile. "It's just been a tough few days." There was no way around it. She had to tell her. "Abigail, I heard this morning—the body I found. It was Sam Cassain."

Abigail clutched a stack of papers with her long,

thin, manicured fingers. "That's *awful*. Does Henry know?"

Henry Armistead was the center's executive director, handpicked by Bennett Granger. He'd won the board's gratitude for his impeccable handling of the public relations nightmare the *Encounter* tragedy had presented. Sam's death would give the gossip and the center's critics fresh life—reason enough for Riley to have gone straight to him first thing that morning.

"I don't know," Riley admitted. "I haven't told him."

"I think you should," Abigail said with certainty. "I imagine the police will want to talk to him about Sam. And reporters…" She took a breath, regaining her poise. She would think of the center first. She always did. "We need to put a strategy in place for handling the inevitable questions. Oh, Riley, this is horrendous. You know Sam was in Maine over the weekend, don't you?"

Her head spun. "He was?"

"Yes, I thought you saw him. He stopped at the house on Friday before the cocktail party. He said he just wanted to see how we were doing." She faltered, suddenly awkward. "Oh, dear. What if we were the last people to see him alive? How on earth did he end up on Labreque Island, of all places? It *must* have been an accident."

Riley half wished she'd taken her grandfather's cue and cleared out for a few days. Then people could have jumped to the wrong conclusions about her, too. "I have no idea, and I'm trying not to get ahead of myself with questions I can't answer. I should have talked to Henry sooner. I'll go see him now.'' She hesitated, debating. ''Will you be talking to Matt? Sig knows about Sam, but I doubt she—''

''I'll get in touch with him,'' Abigail said, briskly polite. Whatever her opinion of her brother's marital problems, she would never say.

Riley ducked out without bringing up the topic of oddballs who might have shown up that morning for the PTSD volunteer program. She went out to the exhibits. No sign of Straker. The low lighting gave the sense of being underwater as tourists, school groups and businesspeople on their lunch hour intermingled, checking out exhibits that ran from small aquariums to the huge, multistory saltwater tank.

The PTSD volunteers, she knew, stayed in the bowels of the center, away from any hint of crowds. But she didn't see Straker there, either. Maybe his clam chowder had arrived. Riley had no desire to disturb the rest of the group's lunch. With a huff of exasperation, she stormed outside to collect her wits before she ventured up to see Henry.

A stiff breeze gusted off Boston Harbor, bringing with it the feel of autumn. She wanted to be out on the water now, in her kayak, paddling with the wind. Just imagining it helped calm her.

Straker materialized at her side, his impact like a hot gust. ''Nice fountain. Dolphins, whales, otters, seals. I like the walrus, myself. A fountain with a sense of humor, which is more than I can say about most of the people who work here. You're an intense group.''

"What did I do to deserve you on my case?"

His gaze cooled. "You found a dead body on my island."

"I thought you were having lunch with your PTSD friends."

"It was yuppie clam chowder. Now, a good haddock chowder with a pat of butter and a sprinkle of black pepper—that would have had me." He laid on his downeast accent, but Riley could see the tightness in his jaw, the hint of tension in his eyes. They were good eyes. Alert, expressive, as cool and impenetrable a gray as a Maine fog. She shook off the image, wondering what had got hold of her. He went on, "I expect I owe Abigail Granger an apology."

"For what?"

"I was pretty much a jerk to her. I lied, and I put her on the spot."

"You've never apologized before for being a jerk."

He scowled. "You're smart, Riley. But you're not sweet." He started off without a word.

"You aren't really going to apologize to Abigail, are you?"

"I might." He glanced back at her, a spark of humor lighting his face. "You know, she's a hell of a lot nicer than you are."

"Sam Cassain stopped in to see the Grangers on Friday," Riley blurted.

He stopped. She could see his FBI-trained mind

clicking into gear. This wasn't the mind she knew. She knew the mind that wanted to drown her. She had to remember this wasn't the boy she'd known on Schoodic Peninsula.

"On Mount Desert?" he asked.

He said it, *dessert,* the way the locals did, as in the French *Mont Desert,* or barren mountain, for its hills of pink granite. She nodded. "Abigail told me."

"Where did Cassain live? What's he been doing the past year?"

"Last I heard he was working on the docks in Portland, but he still had his place down here—out in Arlington, I think. He hadn't settled into a new job, so far as I know."

Straker continued on his way without comment. Riley sighed. The man could drive her to the brink if she let him. She turned back to the fountain. More people had drifted over for a bit of fresh air during their lunch hour. Suddenly the idea of going back to work, trying to concentrate, didn't appeal to her. She was restless, frustrated, still absorbing the potential ramifications of Sam Cassain turning up dead on Labreque Island. She wanted to find Emile—and she wanted to know what Straker was up to next.

"Riley? I thought that was you."

Hell, she thought. Henry Armistead. He'd got to her before she could get to him. From his grim expression, she guessed he'd heard the news. Bennett had lured him east from California three years before to serve as the center's executive director. He was fifty-one, handsome and polished, and Riley, oblivi-

ous to such things herself, had heard rumors of a bud-
ding relationship between him and Abigail Granger.

"I was just coming to see you," she said lamely.

"A little late, I'd say. Maine State Police investigators are on their way. They want to talk to Abigail,
Caroline Granger, your father and me about Sam's
death. They said they might want to ask you a few
more questions, too."

She nodded. "I understand."

"I wish I'd known about this before the police
called."

"You're right. I'm sorry. I've been preoccupied."
She stopped, picturing the body lying facedown in
low tide. "I didn't recognize him. It never occurred
to me..."

"It must have been a terrible moment for you,"
Henry said softly. "Riley, Sam's body turning up on
an island your grandfather owns..." He inhaled. He
was gray haired, formal in his dark gray suit. His
dress and manner, his sensibilities, fit with the Grangers more than they did the Labreques and St. Joes. "I
can only imagine what the police must be thinking."

"We shouldn't jump to any conclusions just because there was bad blood between Emile and Sam.
For all we know, Sam could have been on his way to
tell Emile he'd changed his mind about the *Encounter*
and wanted to mend fences. There's just no telling."

"I know Emile's your grandfather, but..." He
sighed. "Well, never mind. It's obvious you have a
blind spot where he's concerned, which is understand-

able. I just hope Emile hears the news that the police want to talk to him, and comes in.''

''I'm sure he will. This isn't the first time he's taken off without telling anyone. Since he's retired, he doesn't have to answer to any of us.''

Henry tilted his head back slightly and gave her a long look, the kind that reminded her who was boss and who wasn't. ''That's true. He doesn't. But you, Riley—I want to make sure your priorities and obligations are clear.''

''Of course they are.''

He looked dubious. ''Your sister is estranged from Matthew Granger. Sam Cassain placed responsibility for the deaths of five people, including Bennett Granger, on your grandfather's shoulders. Now he's dead and Emile's disappeared.''

''I was there, Henry.'' She kept her voice low, under control. ''I know what happened.''

''Perhaps you should take the afternoon off,'' he continued more gently. ''We can see where things stand in the morning. With any luck, this will all have sorted itself out by then.''

Riley stood rock-still, not certain where this was leading. ''Henry, I have work to do. Is this a suggestion or a request?''

''You've been walking the razor's edge for a year. I know it's difficult for you to accept Emile's culpability with regard to the *Encounter*. It's difficult for all of us. I'm being very straightforward with you, Riley. You're not neutral. If you were, you wouldn't have been on Labreque Island in the first place.''

"I took a vacation day and kayaked over for a picnic. It's not as if—"

He held up a hand, stopping her. "I know, I know. I'm not criticizing you. You're in a difficult position. I ask you to keep in mind how important the Grangers are to this institution. Bennett's death and the *Encounter* controversy were tough blows to absorb. I'm not sure what else that family can stand before they turn their attentions elsewhere."

And their money, Riley thought bitterly.

It was as if Henry read her mind. "It's not just their financial support we can't afford to lose. It's their enthusiasm, their passion for the center's work."

"Abigail's, you mean. Caroline doesn't seem that interested in oceanography, and Matt—"

"Take the afternoon off," Henry interrupted sharply. "And take tomorrow off if you need to."

She nodded. Her throat was tight, dry, her voice strangled. If Henry knew about Straker and his shark-feeding, he'd probably fire her. He'd only worked at the center for three years. He didn't understand the connections between her family and the Grangers, that losing Bennett Granger was tantamount to losing a second grandfather.

"What about the dinner tonight?" she asked.

He winced, obviously having forgotten Abigail's bimonthly dinner for the center's staff. "You'll have to attend, I suppose. It would be awkward and obvious if you didn't. Abigail understands your torn loyalties. We all know you were nearly killed on the *Encounter* yourself."

"So was Emile."

"Emile doesn't place the same value on human life that the rest of us do. That's the problem. That's what led to the *Encounter* disaster. We all see it, Riley, even if you can't." Henry straightened, squaring his shoulders as if he knew he'd gone too far. "Well, I've been as brutally honest as I can be. Forgive me. I'll see you this evening."

He started out across the plaza, and Riley shook her arms and hands to loosen up the tensed muscles. *Was* she that blind to Emile's faults? Her mother, her father, her sister, her boss—everyone believed his passion and dedication to his work had turned pathological. She was his last defender.

What did Straker think?

"You don't care what Straker thinks," she reminded herself out loud.

She went back to her office, packed up her leather tote and made it out to the parking garage before she remembered she'd come in his car. Well, fine. She'd take the *T* home.

Then she spotted the rusting back end and Maine license plate of Straker's Subaru in her reserved space. Of all the nerve.

"What're you doing, quitting early?"

His voice came out of nowhere, echoing amid the concrete. She was so startled she jumped, and suddenly he was behind her, like a mugger who'd been lurking in the shadows. He caught an arm around her middle, steadying her. "Whoa, don't fall over." He grinned, his eyes sparkling with self-satisfaction. "I didn't know I'd have that effect on you. Riley St. Joe, gone weak at the knees.''

"You snuck up on me."

"I was already here. Gossip in the shark tank had you sent home for the day. I turned my pail of fish over to one of my new buddies and came on up.'' His arm lingered on her middle; she could feel his thick fingers on her side. "I figured it'd slip your mind I'd done the driving.''

"Straker, you can let go of me now.''

His arm didn't move. She tried not to nestle into it, sink into him and let him absorb all her frustrations and fears. "You won't faint and fall over?''

"No.''

"Throw up?''

He was enjoying himself. His arm was warm across her back, strong, unexpectedly reassuring. She sucked in a breath. "No.''

"You know,'' he said close to her ear, his fingers digging just a little deeper into her side, "I think you're the first human I've touched since I got out of the hospital. I've wrestled with a few lobsters and picked through the tide pools, but you're the first woman—''

"Are you comparing me to lobsters and blue mussels?''

He grinned and patted her on the hip. "Nope. Not a chance. I kind of thought you'd have thorns. However, it turns out you don't.'' He laughed. "Oops, better let go. I can feel your blood starting to boil. Don't want to burn myself.''

"Straker…"

He dug into his pocket for his car keys. "Relax. I meant boiling because you're pissed, not boiling because you want me to do a little more than put my arm around you, although who knows."

"*I* know."

"Uh-huh." He went around and opened the driver's door first. "You get sent home for talking out of turn?"

"Henry Armistead doesn't think I'm neutral where Emile's concerned. He thinks I'm on Emile's side."

"Aren't you? I am."

"You're an FBI agent. You can't take sides."

"I'm not here because I'm an FBI agent. I'm here because I'm Emile's friend."

"And if I get in your way?" she asked.

"You were born in my way."

He climbed in and reached over to unlock her door. She debated getting in. She could still take the *T*. But if she did, Straker would just beat her home. It would accomplish nothing, except perhaps confirm for him that she was out of her mind and out of control, willing, as the saying went, to cut off her nose to spite her face.

Also, he'd assume he'd got to her with his ridiculous comments about boiling blood and that pat on her hip. Which he had, only because she'd had a hell of a day. Otherwise she'd be impervious.

She settled into the passenger seat, her eyes pinned straight ahead. She could still feel the weight and warmth of his arm. Not a good indication of her mental state. She struggled to concentrate on his reason for being in Boston in the first place. Emile. "So you don't think Emile had anything to do with Sam's death?"

"I have no idea."

"But if you're on his side—"

"That doesn't mean I have an opinion about what he's done or hasn't done. He's my friend."

"I guess you have your 'priorities and obligations' sorted out."

He glanced at her, a darkness coming into his eyes and penetrating right through her. "I do."

Sig painted until she was bleary-eyed and her hand was so cramped she couldn't open her fingers. She stared at the watercolor paper taped to her big board. Splashes of gold, pumpkin, fiery red, muted burgundy on a full-body wash of autumnal blue. Beautiful. Inspiring. And one or two brushstrokes away from being mud.

She collapsed onto the studio bed, the strain of standing pulling at her lower back. Her eyes burned. Her breathing was rapid and shallow. She tired more quickly. All those hormones.

She didn't want to think. She *wouldn't* think. She would drag herself back to her feet and paint some more. Turn the damned thing into a raging mess. She didn't care.

The kitchen door cracked open, and her mother said, "Sig, I have work to do. I can't keep him entertained forever. He's not leaving until he talks to you.''

''I know, I know. I'm sorry.'' She flopped back against the cushions and groaned. ''Okay. Send him out.''

Mara started to speak, abandoned the effort and withdrew inside, where, somewhere, she had Matthew Granger waiting about as patiently as an angry, caged tiger. *My husband,* Sig thought with a pang. *The son of a bitch thinks he's the only one who has problems.*

She wrapped a plaid shawl over her shoulders and pulled a thick chenille throw up over her bulging stomach. It was cool enough out on her porch that Matt shouldn't be suspicious, and he was suspicious by nature. She had no intention of bringing up her pregnancy, telling him she was having twins, when he'd popped in unannounced and uninvited, his only reason for being in Camden obvious. Sam Cassain was dead, and Emile was missing. Otherwise Matt wouldn't have taken one step in her direction.

The bastard, she thought. The single-minded, self-righteous, self-absorbed *bastard.*

That's two quarters for your mason jar, she reminded herself.

''Sig.''

That voice. She shut her eyes. It still could turn her to liquid. It had since she was fourteen, although it was years before she'd realized it wasn't just his voice that drew her to him.

She looked up as he walked onto the porch. Well, he hadn't changed. He was handsome as hell and so goddamned rich he couldn't hide it even when he wore jeans and a sweatshirt. He was fair-haired, blue-eyed, tall, lean and angular. This was the man she'd married. The man she'd loved. The man whose babies she carried.

She summoned all her bravado and ability to lie through her teeth. "Hello, Matt. Excuse me for not getting up, but I've been on my feet since dawn. Mom made you tea?"

"An entire pot, yes."

Good. If all else failed, he'd have to hit the bathroom. "What brings you to Camden?"

She hated how awkward she sounded, how formal. She'd always been able to talk to Matt, even when they were kids and he and his father and sister would sail up to Emile's from the big Granger house on Mount Desert Island.

He crossed his arms on his chest. "You know what."

She stifled a surge of irritation. Smug bastard. If she weren't so obviously pregnant, she'd jump up and uncross those arms, make him stop treating her like a recalcitrant nine-year-old. "Just tell me, Matt. Don't tell me what I know and don't know."

She could see the flash of anger, the tightening of the muscles in his arms. They knew exactly what buttons to push with each other, good, bad and indifferent. As if he were counting to ten to keep from exploding, he walked over to her board and eyed her painting. She wished she'd covered it, but the paint was still wet. He'd taken art history classes as an undergraduate at Harvard. He'd been to most of the world's great museums. A damned art snob.

He glanced back at her. "It's nice to see you painting again."

Another gush of annoyance. She was in just the mood to take exception to everything he said. But if she let him get to her, she risked forgetting she was hiding twins. She'd end up throwing off her blanket and having at him, and he'd know. She had no idea how he'd react, and she didn't want to find out. Not today. Not on his terms.

"I've been up to Emile's," he said. "I've talked to the police. Sig, if you have any idea where he's gone—"

"I don't." She hadn't seen her grandfather in months. She shared her mother's concern he'd gone right off the deep end—but she refused to give Matt the satisfaction of driving the wedge between her and Emile even deeper. "If I did, I wouldn't tell you. I'd tell the police. This is their problem, not yours. They're not going to go off half-cocked and stick their nose where it doesn't belong."

He spun around on his heels, eyes narrowed, thin, regal mouth clamped shut. He took a calming breath. Grangers didn't lose control. "I didn't come here to argue with you."

"Sam Cassain's death isn't your concern. Or mine. Let the police do their job."

"We were on Mount Desert Island last week. Caroline, Abigail, her kids, myself." He moved closer, his gaze probing, as if he could see right through her blanket to the two babies growing inside her. "Armistead and your father were there, too. And your sister."

"I know. So what? It's got nothing to do with me."

"Sam Cassain showed up."

"What?" She almost popped to her feet, but caught herself in time. "Why? What did he want? Did you see him? Riley didn't say a word—"

"She didn't see him. My point is that the police understandably want to know how he ended up dead on Labreque Island." Matt was silent a moment, all his churning emotions back in check, under tight Granger wrap. "He had the good sense to resign after the *Encounter*. It would have been easier on everyone if your father and sister had followed his lead, too."

"And quit their jobs? That's absurd. They didn't do anything wrong. For God's sake, Riley nearly *died.*"

"They were in the middle of a controversy. They still are. Honor would dictate—"

"Don't you dare talk to me about honor." Sig tightened her grip on her shawl and throw. Her fingers were cold and stiff, the rest of her burning. Her head spun. "It's not as if you've ever given a damn about the center."

His eyes flashed. He smiled nastily. "I know what I've given a damn about and what I haven't."

She knew what he was saying. After three years of marriage, four years of loving him so hard at times she thought she'd die, she knew how to read between Matt Granger's lines. He blamed her for leaving their house in Boston. He wanted to come and go as he pleased, talk to her when the mood struck, pace in silence when it didn't. He wanted it all his way because his father was dead and her grandfather was responsible.

"You're not going to guilt-trip me, Matt. I didn't walk out on you. You walked out on me. Maybe not physically, but emotionally you left long before I did."

"I asked you to understand that I needed time to sort things out. Goddamn it, Sig, if my father had been responsible for Emile's death, what the hell do you think you'd do? What you'd think *I'd* do?"

Her stomach rolled over. She could feel every drop of blood draining from her head. *Shit.* She was going to pass out. The stress, the hours on her feet, the roiling hormones. Him.

"Sig? What's wrong?"

She pushed her head down off the edge of the couch, careful not to expose her belly to his gaze. "I'm okay."

He made a move toward her.

She held up a hand. "Matthew, I'm okay."

He went all rigid and composed blueblood. His half-closed eyes slanted down at her. "You should learn to pace yourself."

If she weren't about to pass out, she'd have thrown something at him. Pace herself. The goddamned *nerve*. Instead she raised her head, which still spun, and croaked, "Anything else?"

A mistake.

She could see the lightbulb of suspicion click on. He took a step back and studied her, clinical, objective, sealing his fate. She wouldn't tell him a thing. She'd be *damned* if she told him.

"All right," he said. "What's going on here?"

"What do you think's going on? My grandfather's missing, my sister found Sam Cassain dead and *you* have the audacity to come here and accost me just for having Labreque blood in my veins."

"I've hardly accosted you, Sig."

"Go back to Boston. Go sort out your goddamned 'issues.'" She sank back against the pillows, drawing her throw up to her chin. She could feel a flutter of movement. Her babies. *Their* babies. "I don't have anything to tell you."

He knotted his clenched hands into fists, inhaled and about-faced without another word.

When she heard his expensive car screech down the street, Sig burst into tears and sobbed into a pillow so her mother wouldn't hear. It was so obvious, so painful. Her husband thought her grandfather—her own flesh and blood—was not just capable of criminal negligence, but of murder.

She squeezed her eyes shut, as if it would help block out the tumble of thoughts and the harshness of the reality she was facing. She was pregnant, she was alone and her family was in deep, deep trouble.

After she couldn't cry anymore, she stumbled over to her painting. Her lower back still ached; her head still swam. Her nose was stopped up. She brushed at her tears and tried to focus on the image before her.

Something was trying to emerge. Something *right*. It wasn't just blobs of color.

Bullshit.

Matt hadn't commented on its quality because it stank.

It was mud. Pure mud.

She grabbed her mop brush, dipped it in water and soaked the entire paper until all the colors had bled together and what she had was just how she felt. An ugly mess, a mishmash that didn't know what it was or wanted to be.

Five

Straker took a hot shower to rid himself of the smell of dead fish and the lingering sense he should have kissed Riley in the parking garage. He'd exercised powerful restraint. He wondered if she had any idea how close he'd come to cranking up the tension between them another notch or two.

As it was, he couldn't imagine wanting a woman any more than he did her. Circumstances, however, made him cautious. After months and months of celibacy, he couldn't be sure he wasn't simply reacting to her proximity, the intensity of the situation itself. He had never before in his life thought about kissing Riley St. Joe.

Kissing her, hell. He wanted to take her to bed.

He swore under his breath. What was wrong with him?

"You're a goddamn madman," he muttered to himself.

He washed quickly with an almond-scented soap. Like so much of Riley, her bathroom was a surprise, soft and pretty, with nary a regular bar of soap in sight. He'd had to pick through a basket of little soaps and gels with scents like rosewater, lavender, goat's milk and strawberry. The shower curtain, the array of sponges, the pink razor, the shampoos and fragrant soaps and gels all served as tangible reminders that he was a man in a woman's shower.

He'd never been much on relationships. It wasn't just the job. It was him. Sex with a woman was one thing. The give-and-take of a long-term relationship was another. He'd never been much good at give-and-take.

He dried off with a fluffy towel, pulled on his clothes and banked down his physical frustration before he returned to the front room. Riley was different from most of the women he knew, it was true. She had no illusions about him—she'd know what she was getting into if she got into bed with him.

No, he thought. She wouldn't. She thought she was still playing games with the teenager he'd been.

He found her sitting on the floor, lacing up a pair of battered running shoes. "I'm going for a run," she said without looking up.

If a shower was his way of restoring his equilibrium, maybe a run was hers. "Where?"

"On the river. I won't be long. I need to burn off some restless energy."

Likewise, he thought, but running wouldn't do it for him. He made no comment.

She glanced up at him, took a quick breath as if she could guess what he was thinking, and returned to her task. She finished with one shoe, started on the next. "I didn't expect that body to be Sam Cassain."

Straker sat on the edge of the futon. "You want some company?"

Her dark eyes met his. "No."

He grinned. "Think I'd be distracted by the sight of you in running shorts?"

"That wouldn't slow me down. That would slow you down. You're the one who's been sitting out on a deserted island the past six months. Not me."

"You're saying you wouldn't be distracted by the sight of me in running shorts?"

"You don't even own a pair of running shorts."

He was tweaking her and she knew it. "How do you know?"

"I know."

"I own shorts. I just don't have any of those high-tech, flimsy things." He leaned back, enjoying himself. "They don't look as if they'd hold in everything they were supposed to hold in."

She jumped up. She had good muscle definition in her slim legs; probably elsewhere, too. "I don't like where this conversation is going. You're complicating things."

"There's no man in your life, Riley. I'm not complicating anything."

"You've *always* complicated things, Straker. That's why you ended up in the FBI." She shot him a look. "And how do you know I don't have a man in my life?"

"A woman's bathroom tells all."

"Bastard," she muttered, and headed for the door.

"Did you stretch?"

"I'm fine."

No stretches. She wasn't going to plop down in front of him and do toe touches. He liked that. It meant she knew she was getting under his skin and wasn't too sure what to do about it. A run on the river was a start.

After she left, he put on a pot of coffee and settled in at her cluttered kitchen table. Beyond the occasional urge to pelt each other with rocks, there'd never been anything physical between him and Riley, nothing even remotely sexual. If he could beam himself back in time and tell his sixteen-year-old self that eighteen years from now he'd want Riley St. Joe so bad it hurt, he'd probably fling himself off Schoodic Point.

Of course, Riley wasn't twelve anymore.

He poured a cup of coffee and debated whether this new development—or this new twist in a very old development—would get in the way of finding Emile. Nah. Would it get in the way of getting his head sorted out after two bullets and six months alone on an island? Not if he didn't turn stupid.

"Well, ace, stupid is as stupid does."

Riley was the first woman he'd touched—virtually the first woman he'd had *any* contact with—since his self-imposed isolation. Of course he'd think about her in her red bra, covered in rosewater soapsuds in her shower, doing toe touches in her little shorts. It was natural. Like ducks and imprinting or something.

He raked both hands through his hair in frustration. Why the devil did it have to be Riley St. Joe who'd paddled out to his island? She was all wrong. She'd never be anything but all wrong. She liked doing things like donning big rubber boots and wading into ice-cold water to help stranded whales. She lived in Cambridge. She had a lot of science degrees. She was maybe a notch above Emile when it came to social skills. Her family was weird.

And he, John Straker, wounded FBI agent, someone she'd known and disliked pretty much all her life, was the last man on the planet she'd want fantasizing about going to bed with her.

He swallowed the last of his coffee and shot to his feet. No, she wouldn't—and that was half the problem. She was out there trying to run off the same fantasies he was having.

He wanted to find out how Sam Cassain's body had ended up on Labreque Island. He wanted to find out where Emile had taken himself off to. If shadowing Riley would help him get answers, Straker needed to maintain a high degree of self-control.

She burst in after her run, and he knew he was doomed. Even with sweat glistening on her arms and legs and dampening the ends of her hair, he found her sexy. He wanted to take her into the shower, peel off her running clothes slowly and completely, and go from there.

"I've got a dinner tonight," she said. "I need to get dressed. Can you check the local news and see if they've picked up the story about Sam yet? I'd like to know what I'm in for."

"Sure."

She frowned. "Are you okay? Maybe you should go for a run. It energized me."

That wasn't what he needed to hear. Something about his expression must have told her so because she took a step backward, gulped and quickly retreated into her bedroom.

Another night on the futon just wasn't going to work. He'd rather strap on an IV and jump back in his hospital bed than torture himself trying to spend another night under the same roof with her. Swearing softly, he flipped on the tiny television in the front room.

One of the local stations had the story: "Mystery and tragedy once again swirl around world-famous oceanographer Emile Labreque." The report didn't have all the details. It said the death of the former captain of the ill-fated *Encounter* was under investigation and police were as yet unable to locate Emile, who had a habit of vanishing for days at a time without notice.

The report didn't mention who had found Cassain, and it called the island where his body was discovered "uninhabited."

The news shifted to a traffic report. Straker shut off the television and considered the ramifications of reporters on Riley's doorstep. It was bound to happen. Right now they'd just want a quote from her as the granddaughter of the famous, tragic Emile Labreque. When they found out she was the one who'd spotted Cassain's body on the rocks, they'd swarm.

Toss a recuperating FBI agent into the mix, Straker thought, and there'd be no peace. He wanted to maintain some level of maneuverability and anonymity. Riley was already cramping his style. Reporters would do him in.

The doorbell rang. Reporters already? He looked out the window and saw two cops on the doorstep of Riley's building. Maine CID. Hell, he'd rather have reporters. He debated hiding in a closet, but his car was parked two down from theirs. Beat-up Subaru, Maine plates. He couldn't pretend he'd gone back to his island.

Riley emerged from her bedroom in a simple black dinner dress that was perfect for her trim little body. She hadn't put on her stockings or shoes, and she had a towel wound around her wet hair. The intimacy and normalcy of the moment struck him, reminded him of the barren life he led, not just since Labreque Island, but before. For a long time work and the occasional affair had been enough. He'd thought after his months alone on a five-acre island he'd go back to that life. Now he wasn't so sure.

Of course, he reminded himself, it wasn't exactly normal to have two state cops at the door.

She adjusted a small earring. "Someone's here?"

"It looks like a couple of Maine State Police detectives."

Her earring flew out of her hand. "Can you let them in? I'll slip on some shoes and comb my hair."

She squatted down, running a palm over the floor in search of her earring. Straker could feel her nervousness. No one liked having the police at their door. "I suppose they want to talk to me about Sam." She scooped up the earring, a tiny bit of gold, and got to her feet. Her towel had come loose. He watched her swallow. "And Emile. Damn. Straker, I don't know anything."

"Tell them that."

"You think it'll be that easy?"

"No."

The doorbell rang again.

She nodded at him. "Go ahead."

He trotted down the stairs and opened up for the two detectives. "John Straker," the older of the pair said, shaking his head. Teddy Palladino. Straker knew him to say hello. He was a stringy, smart detective on the verge of retirement. "You go to an island to recuperate and a stiff lands practically on your doorstep?"

"Lucky me."

"Yeah. Well, I'm not surprised Sheriff Dorrman thought it might be someone out to kill you." He grinned at his own sick humor, then frowned, beady eyes narrowed. "What're you doing here?"

"I was just watching TV."

The detective snorted. "Dorrman warned me about you, Straker. I take it you're not here in any official capacity?"

"No."

"You a friend of the family or just Emile?"

"I've known Riley St. Joe all my life."

Palladino let the sideways answer go. "She in?"

"She's powdering her nose just for you." Straker motioned up the dark, narrow staircase. "After you, gentlemen."

Riley was waiting on the futon couch. She'd finger-styled her damp hair, slipped into stockings and low-heeled shoes and rosied her cheeks and lips with a bit of makeup. She looked poised, if a little pale. Straker saw the detectives take in the clutter, the nautical charts, the flamingo Beanie Baby. They didn't know what to make of her, either. If he had his island, Straker thought, she had her kooky egghead apartment. A narrow escape from death, a grandfather's reputation shattered, five people dead. The *Encounter* disaster had left her with her own demons to fight. This was a good place to keep them at bay.

Palladino introduced himself and his partner, Chris Donelson. "We'd like to ask you a few questions, Miss St. Joe."

"Sure."

He turned to Straker. "You mind taking a walk for a half hour?"

"I'll go put my feet up in the bedroom."

"What, you don't trust us?"

"Nah. I just could use forty winks."

He was wide-awake. He had no intention of sleeping, but if he left the building, he wasn't sure that, in her current frame of mind, Riley would let him back in. She'd never admit it, but she was close to snapping. Sam Cassain dead on Labreque Island, Emile gone and now two Maine CID detectives in her living room—it was enough.

On his way back to her bedroom, he heard Palladino say, "You know the body you found on Sunday has been identified?"

"Yes, it was Sam Cassain." She said it as if she were in science class. "He was captain of the *Encounter* until it sank last year."

"And you didn't recognize him?"

"No."

Straker shut the bedroom door behind him. He'd let Palladino and Donelson do their job. Riley would hold up, and she had nothing to hide. She had no more idea of what was going on than any of them did.

The bedroom was softly lit, the colors warm and soothing. Straker took in things he'd missed that morning when he'd barged in after Sig's call. She had a fluffy down comforter and lace-trimmed sheets, the bedstand piled with a mix of popular novels, magazines and work-related documents and texts.

He noticed a watercolor on the wall, recognized the surf and rocks of Schoodic Point. It was signed in the lower right corner by Sig St. Joe. Straker stared at the painting. It captured both the resilience and fragility of the Maine coast, as well as its beauty—everything he missed most during his years away at college, law school, Quantico, his various assignments with the FBI, first in the Boston field office, more recently with a counter-terrorism unit based in Washington. Where to next—he didn't know.

Looking at Sig's painting, he could understand, if not articulate, why her little sister worked so hard rescuing and rehabilitating marine animals—why the world's oceans so consumed her family. It was different from the forces that had driven Strakers to sea for generations, although his lobsterman father always seemed to understand Emile's passion and dedication to oceanographic research and conservation.

Straker pulled his gaze away. He hadn't chosen a life on the water. He couldn't predict what would happen to the North Atlantic in fifty years—but he could predict what questions the detectives were asking Riley St. Joe. They would ask her what she knew about the animosity between her grandfather and Sam Cassain, details about their working relationship over the years, her take on the *Encounter* tragedy. They'd ask her how she'd come to be on Labreque Island to find Sam's body. Why she was visiting Emile, why she hadn't told anyone, why she was kayaking alone, how she'd come to be caught in the fog. They might get to Emile's relationship with the center he'd founded, the Granger family, his own family. But they might wait on that, too.

They'd ask her if she had any idea where her grandfather was. Straker was convinced she didn't, not because she wasn't above hiding that information from him. If it suited her, she'd lie to him—but she didn't know because otherwise she wouldn't be here, dressed for dinner. She'd be out pestering Emile. She'd never let him just sneak off on her. That wasn't her style. She thought she had the right to know everything. It was the same natural curiosity that had led her to learn the Latin names of seaweed and mussels and all the other little creatures in a Maine tide pool.

Straker sat on the edge of her bed. Dangerous territory. He felt a little as if he were trespassing. He concentrated on the questions at hand. He was operating under the assumption that Emile had taken off on his own because he'd guessed the identity of the body Riley had stumbled on. But what if he'd run into trouble? What if he'd been hurt, kidnapped, killed?

Straker jumped up from the bed. Time to quit dithering. He needed to get out of here. He needed to go after Emile without Riley breathing down his neck. Or him breathing down hers.

Palladino pushed open the bedroom door. "Walk out with us?"

My turn, Straker thought. He started toward the door. "Let's go."

Riley talked herself out of skipping Abigail's dinner. She needed her routines. She needed her friends and colleagues. She also needed to get away from Straker, she thought, but that wasn't working out too well. He had all but stuffed her into his car to give her a ride to Beacon Hill.

"I could have taken the subway or driven my own car," she repeated for at least the fourth time as he drove up Mount Vernon, Beacon Hill's widest and most well-known street. "It's not as if I need a body-guard."

"I'm being nice."

"No, you're not. You're just a control freak. That's why you joined the FBI."

He glanced at her as if she'd turned purple. "You don't know what you're talking about."

"Well," she said, "I don't need you to give me a ride home. I'll take the subway or get a ride from someone at the dinner."

"Take a cab. Don't take the subway."

"Straker, it's not as if someone's going to hit me over the head and dump my body on the rocks. We don't know Sam was murdered."

"I know," he said.

She scowled. "You're in fine form tonight. A control freak and a know-it-all. That's Louisburg Square." She pointed to an intersection up ahead. "Drop me off on the corner. I'll walk to Abigail's."

"Don't want to be seen with me?"

"Absolutely not. What are you going to do?"

He pulled over to the curb. His rusting Subaru with its Maine plates didn't exactly fit in with the expensive cars and stately town houses. "Go back to your apartment and rummage through your underwear drawer."

"You are such a jerk."

He grinned, the evening light darkening his gray eyes. "I'll go back and watch TV."

"Liar. You're going to snoop around here. If you cause me any trouble, Straker, I'll have your head. I swear I will. These are my friends and colleagues. This is my *job*."

"Looks like a Beacon Hill dinner party to me."

"I'm serious. I'm already on thin ice. You wouldn't be easy to explain if I hadn't just found Sam dead."

Straker leaned back in his seat. He didn't look too worried. "Sure you can handle a brick sidewalk and cobblestones in those little shoes of yours?"

She jumped out of the car without bothering to answer. Instead of heading up Mount Vernon, he lingered. Riley felt his gaze on her as she negotiated the brick sidewalk to Louisburg Square, famous for its cobblestone streets and graceful nineteenth-century homes on a small, enclosed private park. After her husband's death last year, Caroline insisted on moving to a condo on the water, and Abigail had reluctantly moved back into her childhood home. Matthew and Sig had a town house on Chestnut Street, two blocks over. At least for now. Riley didn't want to speculate what would happen if her sister's marriage ended in divorce.

Most of the guests had already arrived, gathering in the parlor of the elegant bowfront house. Good, Riley thought. That reduced the chances anyone had seen her arrive with Straker. She did *not* want to have to explain him.

Caroline Granger was the first to greet her. "Riley, I'm so glad you decided to come tonight. It's the very best thing you could do for yourself."

Her warm words helped Riley to relax. She'd come

to admire Caroline's grace and fine manners, her acute sense of duty. Just sixty, an attractive woman with silvery-blond hair, her life had been in limbo since Bennett's sudden, horrible death aboard the *Encounter*. They'd been married only seven years. This was Caroline's second experience with widowhood. Her first husband, a corporate executive, had died of a heart attack when she was in her early forties. She had no children, and she'd taken great pains not to overstep with Bennett's two adult children. She was the sort of wife who made her husband's interests her own, and even now, she was doing what she could to support the center and provide a smooth transition to the next generation of Grangers.

"I heard about Captain Cassain," she said. "I can't imagine what it must have been like for you."

"It was pretty awful."

"Yes, so I gathered from what the police told me. They interviewed me earlier this afternoon. They asked about Sam's visit to Maine. He stopped by the cocktail party—did you see him?"

Riley shook her head. "No. I spent most of the cocktail party trying not to hyperventilate, so I was glad just to be back on *terra firma*. I'll get over it, but that was my first time on a boat since..." She didn't finish.

"I understand," Caroline said quickly. "Well, Sam didn't stay long. He was in a good mood. But..." She smiled. "Enough said about that. How's Emile? I heard he's gone off on one of his jaunts. His timing's awkward, but I told the police this was vintage Emile.

I miss him. I know that's heresy in some quarters, but it's true.''

"It was good to see him." Riley swept a glass of champagne from a nearby table. She knew she should abstain from alcohol under the circumstances, but the champagne went down easily. "I think he likes his new life."

"So long as he's close to the ocean, he'll do fine." Her eyes misted, and Riley wondered how many glasses of champagne she'd had. "Ben loved your grandfather. They accepted each other's weaknesses along with their strengths. Even if Emile did make a mistake, Ben wouldn't have wanted to see him..." She stopped herself, manufactured another society smile. "It's a tragedy. I'm sure everyone can agree on that much. Now, tell me, how is Sig?"

"Painting again," Riley said, and they chatted for another minute before Caroline melted into the throng of other guests.

Her champagne finished, Riley slipped out to the courtyard, one of Beacon Hill's many "secret" gardens. She paused at a classical stone fountain. The gurgling water and sweet scent of end-of-the-summer flowers calmed her, made her feel less exposed and vulnerable. She blamed Straker. Seeing him with the two Maine detectives had forced her to admit he wasn't the obnoxious, raging teenager she'd pelted with a rock at twelve—nor was he a salt-of-the-earth Maine lobsterman like his father. He was *an FBI agent*. Confident, disciplined, self-possessed.

"Hey, kid."

She smiled at her father. He'd put on his one dinner suit, but no matter what he wore, Richard always managed to look rumpled—and dinner parties just made him awkward. "Are you hiding, too?" she asked.

"Not yet. I saw you and came on out. Everything okay?"

"I was thinking about how I could go for a dozen whales stranding themselves on a Cape Cod beach right about now. Isn't that awful?"

"It would take your mind off things."

"I shouldn't have come. Everyone knows about Sam. Everyone thinks Emile had something to do with his death. They won't say so, but it's obvious."

"Is that what you think?"

She sighed. "I'm trying not to think."

"I was thinking about Sig." He glanced around the perfect little courtyard garden, shaking his head. "Do you believe she's happy as a Granger?"

"She's not a Granger. She's a Labreque-St. Joe. She just married a Granger. It's a fine distinction, but one that's important to her, I think." Riley caught herself. "Or was my glass of champagne one glass too many and I'm not making any sense?"

"No, you're making a great deal of sense. You know, I always thought Sig and Matt loved each other, and the rest—his money, her obliviousness to it—wouldn't matter."

Riley grinned at him. "Is this my pragmatic father talking?"

He smiled. "I'm a romantic at heart. Why else

would I spend a lifetime working to save a doomed species of whale?'' He faced the fountain, his eyes half-closed, almost sad. ''You can ask someone to give up some things, but not their identity, not their soul.''

''Do you think that's what Matt's done with Sig?''

''I don't know. I worry about them—but there's nothing I can do.'' He pulled at his beard, seemed to shake off some dark thought. Then he smiled, embarrassed. ''You see why I avoid dinner parties? I'm lousy at small talk. Two glasses of champagne and I turn into a blowhard.''

Riley wondered if he knew Sig was pregnant, but it wasn't her secret to tell. ''Sig'll be okay. She's tough.''

''You're both tough. Emile and your mother wouldn't have had it any other way. Me, I'd like to have spoiled you rotten.'' He gave Riley's arm a gentle squeeze. ''This will all work out. Sam's death, Emile. I know it will.''

Dinner was announced. It was served buffet style, a comfortable mix of Beacon Hill elegance and practical informality. Even after decades of attending Granger parties, Riley thought with affection, her father still looked as if he expected a live lobster to crawl out of his pockets at any moment. He was much more confident and at ease studying whales.

She managed to avoid anything controversial or seriously awkward through the main course, and was just starting to eye the dessert table when Matthew Granger barged into the elegant dining room.

Abigail gasped. "Matthew! What's wrong?"

Fatigue clawed at his handsome features, and his blue eyes searched among the guests gathered in the sparkling dining room. He wasn't dressed for dinner. His clothes were casual, expensive, wrinkled. He quaked with outrage, the out-of-control, obsessed antithesis of the well-bred, contented man Riley remembered waiting for his bride at the altar.

His angry gaze fixed on her. "Why the hell is John Straker hanging around outside?"

Suddenly the maple cheesecake didn't look so good. *Damn* Straker. What kind of FBI agent was he that he couldn't snoop without being seen? Riley noticed Henry Armistead's eyes narrowing on her with instant concern and suspicion, and she heard Abigail's sharp intake of breath, saw her father sink back in his chair in total confusion.

Caroline Granger frowned, a sliver of blueberry tart on her china plate. "Matthew, who on earth is John Straker?"

Henry answered, his gaze, like Matt's, not leaving Riley. "He's the FBI agent who was with Riley when she found Sam on Labreque Island. It's not yet public knowledge."

"Oh. Oh, my." Caroline required about two seconds to realize this was a nasty scene in the making. She reached a hand toward her dead husband's son. "Perhaps you and Riley can discuss this in the parlor."

Matt didn't move. His eyes continued to bore into Riley. "Where are you two hiding Emile?"

Half the guests listened with open interest. The rest just sat or stood in quiet shock, either pretending not to listen or wishing they were somewhere else. Riley could have stabbed Matt with her dessert fork. If Sig had been there, her sister would have cheerfully done the honors.

Riley's displeasure with both her brother-in-law and Straker kept her steady on her feet. "I don't know where Emile is, and John Straker isn't my responsibility. Or yours." She ignored the knife twist in her stomach. "That's all I'm saying to you, Matt, while you're in this mood. If you'll excuse me, I'm going home. It's been a long day. Abigail, thank you—"

"Don't expect me to feel sorry for you," Matt interjected, his jaw clenched, his expression unrelentingly harsh.

Abigail, horrified, got to her feet. "Matthew!"

He ignored her, stayed on Riley's case. "You covered up for Emile last year with the *Encounter*. If you hadn't, maybe he'd be in prison right now and Sam Cassain would be alive."

Richard St. Joe shot to his feet, no longer paralyzed with confusion. "All right, Matt. That's enough."

Matt spun on his heels and stalked out of the dining room. Abigail gave her guests a panicked, embarrassed look and went after him. Riley started to shake. Her father swore under his breath and followed Abigail and his son-in-law. "Goddamn it, Matt," he growled, "pick on someone your own size."

Caroline took charge of the social situation. She smiled ruefully. "Matthew's been under a terrible strain. We all have. My apologies, everyone. Abigail has a lovely dessert table—I've already sampled the blueberry tart. Let's end the evening on a high note, shall we?''

The guests dutifully took her cue, resuming conversations and starting for the dessert table. Riley waited for her chance to go out and find Straker, if he hadn't already made good his escape.

Henry Armistead came to her side and grasped her elbow. ''Let's get you out of here.'' His tone was gentle, but he was firmly taking charge. ''You have some explaining to do.''

Six

Straker eased into the shifting shadows of Louisburg Square and considered his options now that the jig was up. Matthew Granger had made him. Presumably he was inside flaring his nostrils at Riley. When he finished with her, she'd beeline for the door and come for Straker's head.

Sneaking around Beacon Hill had been a tactical error. He'd known it when he'd parked his car on Louisburg Square after wandering the narrow streets. However, he hadn't liked the idea of leaving Riley up here alone, never mind that she was among friends, colleagues, even family. Sam Cassain had been murdered. Straker would bet his FBI badge on it.

He had two options, neither of them good. He could run or he could stand and fight.

He wondered how long he had before Riley stormed out.

He'd considered intercepting Granger, but it wouldn't have done any good. It wasn't as if Granger had it wrong. Straker knew Riley hadn't told anyone she had an FBI agent on her case—why would she? At least Granger wouldn't shoot up the place or beat someone senseless. He'd just get cold and nasty, which Riley could handle.

Then she'd hunt Straker down.

He supposed he could make for Maine while he still had his balls attached, or maybe go back to her apartment, let himself in, turn on the tube and pretend her brother-in-law had made a mistake.

The hell with it. Damned if he'd run. He wasn't afraid of Riley St. Joe.

He went still, eased back into the shadows as a familiar figure walked down Pinckney Street at the end of the square.

Emile.

The white hair, the wiry physique, the hurried gait. It couldn't be anyone else.

The old man must have sensed Straker's presence because he stopped abruptly, as if he'd forgotten something. He turned around and bolted back up Pinckney.

Straker swore under his breath and lit out after him. The months of running on Labreque Island, with its rocky coastline and network of paths, had strengthened him, but he'd lost his feel for pavement, cobblestones, brick sidewalks, city air. Pinckney was a steep, narrow street suited to horse-drawn carriages, its brick town houses flush with the sidewalk. With virtually no front yards, shrubs, fences or trees, there was nowhere for a sneaky old man to hide.

Old-style black lanterns and glittering windows provided some light, but not enough. Straker hoped he hadn't screwed up and wasn't chasing some rich old codger who was calling 911 on his cell phone.

Pinckney crested and flattened out, and Straker moved into the middle of the quiet one-lane street and picked up his pace. Damn it, Emile was in his seventies. He couldn't outrun a trained FBI agent.

No. He couldn't.

Straker slowed his pace. If he were seventy-six and had a man forty years younger chasing him, he'd duck into a doorway or alley and hope for the best. He wouldn't try to outrun him.

"Come on, Emile." Straker spoke loudly, without shouting. "Don't make me check every damned cubbyhole on this street."

He waited, pacing. He didn't know how much longer he had before Riley hunted him down.

Three or four town houses back down Pinckney, the old man stepped out from an elegant doorway. Straker had run right past him. Emile walked up the street. Straker walked down, and they met just above Louisburg Square.

The artificial night light made Emile look older, thinner, less capable than he did on windswept Labreque Island. He was out of breath.

"I didn't mean to wind you," Straker said.

"I was winded before you spotted me. Damned hills."

"You need to turn yourself in to the police,"

Straker said with no further preamble. "Tell them what you know. You can't solve this on your own."

Emile ignored him. He coughed and spat.

"Running makes you look bad. It diverts the police from going after Sam Cassain's real killer."

The dark eyes, without their usual spark, focused on him. "You followed Riley here?"

"Let's just say I wasn't on Abigail Granger's guest list."

Emile shook his head, seemed to stare off into the dark. "Abigail—she's stepped right into her father's shoes, hasn't she? She was always devoted to the center, after him to pay more attention to volunteers and membership, public relations. Fund-raising."

Straker inhaled. "Emile…"

The old man shrugged, visibly melancholy. "Well, the center's not my concern any longer."

"Emile, I know one of the detectives on the case. I can help you get through this."

Emile wasn't listening. "I know Riley, John. She's not going to mind her own business if she thinks I know anything about Sam's death. She'll hound me, she'll hound you if she thinks you know where I am. Get her out of here. Take her back to the island with you."

"She's not going to listen to me any more than you will." Straker reined in his impatience, tried to be objective, coldly calculating. A pity Detectives Palladino and Donelson weren't here. Straker would turn Emile over to them without a qualm. "Emile— what the hell's going on?"

The old man leveled his dark gaze on Straker. "I'm leaving. You can stop me. You have the strength, the will. I can't outrun you. I only ask that you think first, then let me do what I must do."

Drama. The Labreques had a knack for it. "Which is what?"

"I didn't kill Sam. I don't know who did it."

And that was all Emile planned to say. He turned and walked down Pinckney, toward Charles Street, daring Straker to follow him. Straker seized up with frustration and no small measure of irritation. Duty, instinct and common sense told him to drag Emile to the police. If anything happened to him—if the old man did something stupid—Straker would look back to this moment for the rest of his life, knowing he'd made the wrong choice.

If Sam Cassain had been murdered and Emile knew anything about it—or if the killer even *thought* he knew anything about it—Emile was in over his damned, stubborn, know-it-all head.

On the other hand, if Straker didn't let his old friend do what he felt he had to do, he would have to live with that, too. When he was seventy-six, he wouldn't want someone half his age making his choices for him.

He tightened his hands into fists. "Hell."

Emile reached Charles Street. Straker had to make up his mind.

But he knew he already had, and he cursed himself as Emile turned right, toward Storrow Drive, the

Charles River and all points north, south, east and west.

He was gone.

The Red Sox were playing at home, Straker thought. He could take in a game, forget Sam Cassain, Emile Labreque and Riley St. Joe. After the game, he could pack his toothbrush and head to his island, make a nice pot of soup, watch the sunrise.

He walked back to Louisburg Square. The Granger dinner had broken up. He stood next to his car, expecting Riley to burst out onto the cobblestone street in her little black dress.

Instead Abigail Granger joined him. She was elegant, poised, the lamplight catching her high cheekbones and making her skin seem pale and bluish. He'd never apologized to her for lying his way into her volunteer program and taking advantage of her generosity.

"Riley left." Her cool eyes stayed on him. "You don't have PTSD, do you, Mr. Straker? Or am I supposed to call you Special Agent Straker?"

"John will do, although most people just stick to Straker. Actually, I do have PTSD. Or I did. Technically. I don't happen to put myself in the same category as the Vietnam vets I met today." He felt a rare twinge of regret. "I'm sorry I misled you."

"You didn't *mislead* me, Mr. Straker, you *lied* to me."

"Fair enough. Where's your brother?"

"He left, too. He's not..." Pain flared in those cool

eyes. "I should have canceled tonight's dinner. I thought it would help...."

"Maybe it did, only you can't see it right now."

"Matt was rude to Riley. He made a terrible scene. She must have been humiliated, but it's impossible to tell with her. She holds her emotions in check, and she's loyal to her family. Matt *is* family to her." She brushed a trembling hand through her hair, fought back tears. "He and Riley have had the worst of it this past year."

"You lost a father, too."

"But I'm not married to Emile's granddaughter. My brother is." Her eyes cleared, and they turned cold as they fastened on Straker. "I would hate to see Riley used, Mr. Straker. By you or anyone else."

"I guess my shark-feeding days are over, huh?"

Her eyes widened in surprise, and she made a delicate hiss of total frustration. "I won't even dignify that with an answer," she said without raising her voice, then sailed back in her expensive, historic house.

Straker gave Riley another thirty seconds. Then he knew for sure. She wasn't coming after him. Which meant only one thing. The pain in the ass had given him the slip—she must have seen him and Emile talking and gone after her crazy grandfather.

"Damn."

He shot into his car. He didn't have a Beacon Hill resident's sticker like Abigail Granger did, but he hadn't gotten a parking ticket, either. It was his one bit of luck that evening.

* * *

Riley's feet hurt, and she couldn't get a good long stride going. Her little black shoes and little black dress weren't designed for following a crazy old man through city streets.

She'd lost Emile at the Alewife Station. It was the last stop on the subway's Red Line. She'd hoped he'd get off at her Porter Square stop and go to her apartment. But he hadn't, and with a grim certainty, she knew he'd boarded a bus and headed to Arlington Heights, where Sam Cassain had a house. Riley couldn't remember the name of the street. It was on one of the hills near the Lexington border and the route of Paul Revere's ride. She'd walked up from the bus stop. The night air had turned cool. She wished she had a sweater. Going after Emile had been impulsive.

Numb with fatigue and frustration, Riley was past caring if Emile knew she'd spotted him, if Straker had gone FBI on her and was following them both.

Her talk with Henry hadn't gone well. He was furious with her for not telling him Straker was in town, staying at her apartment. He didn't buy her excuse that she hadn't wanted to involve the center. The center *was* involved. The police had questioned him that very afternoon.

By the time she got outside and saw Emile sneaking down Pinckney Street and Straker pointedly *not* going after him, it was more than she could take. She'd slipped over to Mount Vernon, cut down to

Charles and took off after her grandfather. Let Straker
hunt her down. Let him worry. She didn't care.

Now here she was, not lost exactly, but uncertain
of where to go next in the maze of streets. Sam's
house, she recalled, was a small 1920s single-family
Cape Cod with a one-car garage underneath suitable
for a Model T. She thought the house was red. Maybe
dark brown.

Riley paused at a corner, tidy middle-class houses
all around her. She wanted to scream. Emile must be
headed this way. But why?

She heard sirens several blocks away on Massachusetts Avenue, the main thoroughfare that ran from
downtown Boston through the western suburbs. A
few yards ahead of her, a man was walking a black
lab. The dog was agitated, yanking on his leash. The
man tightened up on it and quietly ordered the dog to
heel.

A yell came from someone out of view. Two teenage girls ran up from a side street. They were breathless, gulping for air. "Fire!" One of the girls grabbed
the man and pointed up the street. "There's a house
on fire! You should see the flames!"

"Oh, no." Riley took a deep breath. She could
smell smoke now.

The black lab barked, jumped at the girls. The sirens were louder, closer, the fire trucks' horns blaring.

The second girl cried out. "Look—look, you can
see the flames! My house is across the street. What
if it catches fire?"

"The fire engines are on their way," the man with

the dog reassured her. "They'll get the fire out before it spreads."

Riley stood motionless on the sidewalk, her feet aching, her mind reeling. Up on her right, perhaps a block away, the dark sky glowed orange. A line of emergency vehicles roared past her.

She shivered. Sharp pains shot through her chest. "Emile," she whispered, and broke into a run.

She couldn't make good time in her evening shoes. She was tempted to kick them off and run in her stocking feet, but knew that would only draw attention to herself. She followed the path of the emergency vehicles, toward the fire's glow. The two girls ran past her, more excited than panicked.

Riley's head throbbed. When she turned the corner and saw a nondescript red Cape engulfed in flames, her stomach lurched.

Residents of the neighborhood had come out onto their lawns and walked into the street, as if they thought they should stop themselves but couldn't. Someone said, "It's that sea captain's place. The one who was found dead in Maine."

The police set up a line to keep onlookers back. Firefighters swarmed over the burning house, working madly to contain the fire and keep it from spreading to other houses on the quiet residential street.

Riley melted into the edges of the gathering crowd. She stood on her tiptoes, searched faces, backs, physiques, hair for any sign of Emile. Her teeth chattered. She was cold now, scared.

Sam hadn't left his iron on, she thought. He was

dead, undoubtedly murdered, and someone had set fire to his house.

Emile. How could Straker have let him go? Were they in cahoots?

Her gaze fell on a figure on the far side of the crush of onlookers. Not Emile. Matt. There he was, hands shoved in his pockets as he stared at the burning house.

Had he followed Emile? Or had Emile followed him?

"What in God's name is going on?" she whispered, forcing down her frustration. The police would know this was Sam Cassain's house. Riley didn't need to call attention to herself—or to her brother-in-law.

She squeezed between an older couple, pushed past a young family, a throng of teenagers, two ten-year-olds on bicycles. She slipped under elbows and stepped over feet and used her small stature to her best advantage, but she lost sight of Matt. People were packed tightly, eyes fixed on their dead neighbor's burning house. They didn't know she had to get to Matt, talk to him, find out what he knew, why he was there.

She finally broke from the crowd, but Matt was gone. She ran up the street, away from the fire. Was he on foot? Did he have a car? Had the police recognized him?

A car rattled behind her. She spun around.

A beat-up Subaru with Maine plates. Another inch and it would have run her over. Straker had the passenger window rolled down, and eyed her darkly from behind the wheel. "Get in, St. Joe."

"You—"

"Now."

She wanted to get off her feet. She wanted to get away from the police, the firefighters, the burning house. But she resisted. "You let Emile go. What were you, out of your mind?"

"Goddamn it. Get in here or I'll come out there and drag you in."

She was so cold. "What if he's inside?"

"The firefighters will handle it. There's nothing you can do."

She didn't move. She couldn't speak. Emile. Matt. What were they doing here? What was Straker doing here?

"In, Riley. Now." When she still didn't move, he unclamped his seat belt. "The hell with it. I'm coming after you."

"No, don't."

She pulled open the door and slid in beside him. Her stocking snagged on a torn section of the passenger seat. She sank back, numb.

"Dead bodies and fires. You're a menace, St. Joe."

"Go to hell."

"No 'thank you, Straker, for rescuing me'? It's just like that time when I pulled you out of the bay in your kayak. What were you, nine? A damned ingrate. At least you cried." He eased down a side street, not going too fast. "I always figured you hated me because you cried in front of me."

"I hated you because you gloated."

He glanced over at her. "Do you want to cry now?"

"No." She settled into her seat, fighting tears. "I want to find Emile."

Straker stayed under the speed limit until he reached Massachusetts Avenue. Then he accelerated, tight jawed, eyes on the road, arms tensed as he negotiated traffic, stoplights, pedestrians. It was a straight shot to Porter Square.

When he turned onto her street, he glanced sideways. Riley saw no humor in his eyes. No softness. If anything, he was even madder than when he'd picked her up. He didn't say a word. Neither did she.

He parked in front of her house and pulled on the emergency brake with such ferocity it nearly broke off. He stared straight ahead and swore under his breath. Viciously.

"Hey," Riley said, "I'm the one who should be mad. You skulked around after I'd asked you not to. You ended up siccing Matt Granger on me. Then I go outside and see you watching Emile slip off into the night. Did you two cook up something? Did you plan to meet him on Beacon Hill? Did you know he'd head for Sam's place?"

Straker didn't answer. He didn't even look as if he were listening.

"Well, obviously you did. No other reason for you to be there."

He slammed his palms on the steering wheel. "Damn it, Riley."

"What? I'm just speaking my mind."

"Your mind can get you into a lot of trouble."

She started to answer but some primitive instinct told her he was a man pushed beyond all limits. Before she could slip quietly out of the car and give him a chance to cool off, he dropped an arm over her and hauled her to him. He didn't give her a chance to take in a breath. His mouth found hers. It wasn't a tender or tentative kiss, but had all the hunger, passion and need of a man too long on a deserted island, too abruptly catapulted back into the world of people, death, police and fires. He was in no mood to hold back, but took from her what he wanted, even as she could feel him fighting for self-control.

She knew she should push him away. Help him regain his senses. Instead she kissed him back, soaked up the feel of him, let him bring her back to life. He was warm, strong, kissing her with such unrelenting intensity she couldn't breathe, couldn't think. If he'd waited until they were in her apartment, they'd be on the floor by now, clothes ripped off. Nothing would have stopped him.

Or her, she admitted as his palm cupped her breast through the thin fabric of her dinner dress. He placed her hand on him, as if to make crystal clear what would come next. He was thick, hard. She imagined the feel of him inside her. *Yes.* She wanted him tonight, *now.*

If they didn't stop immediately, they wouldn't. In another half second there would be no going back.

She pressed her palm against him, gave a silent moan as desire burned through her.

He pulled back so suddenly she lost her balance. Her hand flew back to her lap almost of its own accord.

His breathing was fast and ragged. His eyes had turned a dark charcoal. He ran the back of his hand over his mouth. "For three or four minutes I didn't know if you were trapped in that fire or not." He bit out each furious word, then paused, his narrowed gaze settling on her. "I didn't know which way I wanted it."

"Well." She checked her own breathing; at least she wasn't shivering and numb anymore. She licked her lips. Now she knew what her friends meant when they said they'd been kissed senseless. That had never happened with her and her various oceanographers. Not like this. She cleared her throat, tried to regain her equilibrium. "That's not a very nice thing to say to a woman you've just ravaged."

His mouth twitched, almost in spite of himself. "Ravaged? Forget it, St. Joe. You've got too many clothes left on to make that claim."

"You're an outrage, Straker. I must have inhaled toxic fumes or something to have wanted—to have just..." Her body still reeled with wanting him. "Never mind."

He grinned. "Sure. It's pretty obvious what you wanted, anyway."

Sex, she thought. Hot, torrid sex. That's what she

wanted. And that's what she'd have gotten. And nothing more.

Or less, she thought with a fresh surge of desire. She silently cursed her treacherous mind. What was wrong with her? It wasn't as if *she'd* spent the last six months on a deserted island and John Straker was the first man she'd seen.

But he was the first she'd kissed in...well, forever. The occasional celibate date was about all she'd managed in the past year. It was as if she'd shut down after the *Encounter*.

Such thinking would get her nowhere. She had to take control of herself. What did she want?

She reached for the door handle. Never mind want. What made sense? "You're still sleeping on the futon."

"As you wish." His tone was wry, sexy, as if he knew what was going on inside her.

"Or feel free to go back to Maine." She gave him a cool, sideways glance. "I can manage just fine without you."

"If not for me, you'd be sitting under a hot lamp, answering questions from a couple of irate cops."

"That's ridiculous."

"No, it's not. If I were a cop and saw Riley St. Joe in front of Sam Cassain's burning house, I'd pounce."

"You did pounce," she muttered, and slipped quickly onto the sidewalk.

Straker was right behind her. He slammed his door a bit harder than seemed warranted. She glanced at him. The sexual energy was still sparking between them like a dangerous downed wire. If she didn't do something to dissipate it, she couldn't possibly let him back into her apartment. She'd have to be mad.

"Matt Granger was there," she said. "At Sam's."

He grimaced. "Hell."

"He could have been following Emile, too. Or me."

"Or the damned Pied Piper. Who knows?"

She unlocked the door to her building. The apartment on the first floor was occupied by three medical students, the second floor by a young couple with jobs in Boston's financial district. Riley wondered if they'd seen her in the car with Straker.

She pushed open the door, glanced back at him as he followed her in. "Did Emile tell you he was headed to Sam's place in Arlington? Is that how you ended up there?"

"Emile didn't tell me a damned thing, Riley. I let him go on his way because I was going to have to use bodily force to stop him. And because he asked me to." Straker sighed, obviously trying to make sense of his own behavior. "He's a persuasive old cuss."

"It's his one-track mind. He just exhausts you."

They started up the stairs. Riley finally kicked off her shoes and walked in her stocking feet.

"To answer your question," Straker said from close behind her, "I heard about the fire on the radio. I drove out to Arlington and looked for the action."

"Did you expect to find me there?"

"No. I knew I'd find you."

Her message machine was full and her telephone rang thirty seconds after they entered her apartment. Reporters. Riley had no intention of talking to any of them. Straker turned on the television to a regional all-news channel that was covering the fire. It was under control, and early reports from eyewitnesses suggested it might have been caused by an explosion. Investigators suspected arson. No one had been inside the house.

"The *Encounter* fire was caused by an engine explosion," Riley said for no reason. Her mind was skipping around, trying to make connections where none necessarily existed. "It was an old ship. A refitted minesweeper from the fifties. I just figured it was one of those things. But Sam blamed Emile."

"Riley, we're not going to make sense of this tonight."

"It's so…" She threw up her hands, let them fall to her sides as she felt her frustration build. At least for a few minutes, with Straker in the car, she'd been unable to think. "It's unbelievable Emile was heading for Sam's place right as it went up in flames."

"But you didn't see him there," Straker said.

"I wonder if he was set up, if someone tipped him off…." She stopped, her stomach twisting. "What about Matt? Why was he there? Damn. If you hadn't come along, I might have caught up with him."

"And done what?"

"I don't know. Made him tell me what's going on. He must know something. What if Sam said something to him on Mount Desert last week?'' She paced, another call coming in; she ignored it. ''I suppose I should tell Sig.''

Straker flipped off the television. ''And what would that accomplish?''

''Matt's her husband—''

''So?''

Riley didn't answer. Straker headed into her kitchen, his calm a distinct contrast to her growing agitation. So many questions, fears, countless stabs of doubt. What if she made the wrong decision? What if she did the wrong thing? She stood in the kitchen doorway and watched as he filled a kettle with water. ''What are you doing?''

''Making you tea. If you don't settle down, you're going to blow a gasket.''

''I'm not going to blow a gasket.''

Not just agitated, she thought. Contrary, too. Argumentative. Straker ignored her and rummaged through an assortment of teas she had in a basket on her counter. It was an older kitchen, charming, serviceable. He seemed as at ease there as he did anywhere. He chose a chamomile tea bag and dangled it in a mug.

The phone rang. She snatched up the portable and hurled it across the room.

Straker eyed her knowingly. ''See?''

She could hear her message machine taking the call in the next room. Her mother's voice came on. ''Riley? Are you there? Your father just phoned. He told me about the fire at Sam's. He's worried about you. I am, too. Call me—''

Riley grabbed the portable off the floor where she'd hurled it. "Hi, it's me. Mom, I'm fine. There's no need to worry."

Straker arched a brow at her.

Her mother gasped in relief, half sobbing. "Riley! Oh, thank God. I was afraid you were caught in the fire. After the *Encounter...*" She couldn't go on. "Are you *sure* you're okay?"

"Yes." She made an instant decision not to give her mother all the details about her evening. Emile, Matt, her presence at the fire. Kissing Straker in his beat-up Subaru. "Thanks for checking up on me."

"I hate the thought of you being there alone."

In her mother's view, having Straker camped out on her futon might be worse than being alone. He poured boiling water into her mug. Naturally he was listening. He was on alert at all times, never mind when a suspicious death and a suspicious fire were at hand. It was his nature. His training.

"Riley?"

"Sorry. I'm a little distracted. The past few days haven't been easy, that's all."

"You can always stay with your father." He had a studio apartment in the North End of Boston, getting up to Camden when he could. "You know that, don't you?"

"Of course."

"And me—you're welcome here."

"Thanks."

Her mother sucked in a breath, and Riley could predict what was coming next. "Your father told me about Matt's behavior tonight. It's inexcusable. *Was* John Straker outside?"

"As a matter of fact, yes, he was."

"But that was none of your doing," her mother said.

"No." It was the truth, as far as it went.

"Good. I know he's an FBI agent, but I can't..." She paused. "I have my doubts about him, that's all. I can't help it. He's been living out on that island for months and months, and he's in tight with Emile."

And he was making her chamomile tea. "Right. I'll be careful." But Riley felt an immediate tug of regret at deceiving her worried mother—and she'd learned the hard way over the years that bad news was best delivered early and completely. She had to get this over with. "Mom, John Straker's staying here."

"In your apartment? With you? *Riley.*"

"It's okay. I can handle him." She ignored another arched brow. "Mom, Emile will be okay, too."

"I don't give a damn about Emile. I'm past caring about him."

But this was a lie, or denial. He was her father, and Riley was convinced that for all her frustrations and fears, Mara still loved him. It wasn't a point they could argue. "You haven't told Sig about Matt showing up at dinner and being such an ass, have you?"

"No, I don't see the need. You just be careful, Riley St. Joe. I came close enough to losing you last year. I won't go through that again.'' Her tone softened, lost some of its vehemence. "If you need me, I'm here.''

Riley thanked her, and after they hung up, she sank onto a chair at the kitchen table. Straker shoved a mug of fragrant, calming chamomile tea in front of her. "Your mother wasn't comforted by my presence?''

"I'm not, why should she be?''

She crossed her ankles. One foot kept jiggling. Her hands had started to shake again. She could see the tea jumping around in her mug as she tried to take a sip. Straker had given it to her straight, no honey, no milk, no sugar. He sat on another chair, watching her with those cool gray eyes. He wasn't shaking. The only indication he'd been through any kind of ordeal was a slight frown.

"I suppose tonight was nothing to you,'' she said.

He shrugged. "You weren't in the fire. Emile wasn't in the fire. I managed not to kill anyone despite all provocation. I'd say I got off light. You, on the other hand, had Matt Granger go berserk on you, then made the mistake of following Emile instead of minding your own business.''

"So I got what I deserved?''

"I think you did.''

She used both hands to grip her mug. He was the most obnoxious man on the planet. Yet not even an hour ago, she'd all but had sex with him in his car. It was the fire, of course. Sirens, flames, the crush of people, adrenaline. On an ordinary Thursday night, she wouldn't have let him touch her, much less touch her where and how he had.

He smiled. "Wishing we hadn't stopped when we did?"

"What?" She shook off her thoughts as his words sunk in. "What are you doing, reading my mind now? You really do have a lot of gall, Straker."

"You were looking distracted."

"Because of the fire," she said.

He smiled in that confident, disbelieving, know-it-all way. "Ah."

"Just because you've been sitting on a deserted island for the past six months doesn't mean *I* have. I'm not as hot to trot as you are."

"You were thirty minutes ago."

"That's projection."

He settled into his chair and laughed, cocky, genuinely amused. "You still can't believe you kissed me back, can you?"

"It is rather hard to swallow. But I understand, and I forgive you. We'd just had a shock, and you haven't—well, I'm the first woman you've come in contact with in quite a while. It's only natural, if you think about it, that you'd end up throwing yourself on me."

"Jesus. You're amazing." He sat forward, holding up two fingers. "Two things. One, you enjoyed what we did down in my car as much as I did. I know you did. You know you did."

She squirmed and said nothing. Her tea, at least, was soothing.

"Two, this six-months-on-a-deserted-island bit will get you only so far. You're using it as an excuse for 'succumbing' to my demands or some damned thing. I'm not an animal. I can control myself."

"That was self-control down in your car?"

He grinned. It was almost like a caress and set her skin tingling. "That was supreme self-control."

She took a breath. Sometimes she should know when to leave well enough alone.

"My point is," he continued, "you bear responsibility for your own actions. If you kiss me back, it's because you want to, not because I demand it."

"I see. Well." She cleared her throat, sipped her tea, decided he didn't know the first thing about what she wanted. She was aware of his eyes on her, aware of his...self-control. If she so much as breathed the idea, he'd take her to bed. "Six months on Labreque Island hasn't reverted you back to caveman status. Okay. That's good."

His eyes flashed, sexy, knowing. "That's not what I said. I said I could control myself. I didn't say my months of isolation haven't had an effect."

"You mean you do feel—"

He cut her off. "'Caveman status' covers it."

This wasn't going well at all. She felt exposed, as if he could see right through her dress, and she wondered if "caveman" conjured the same images in his mind as it did in hers. With a shaky hand, she tucked a few stray hairs behind her ear. "Now that we have that straight—"

He laughed. "We don't have anything straight, but go ahead."

"We have to find out more about the fire at Sam's. How it happened, if it was arson, why Matt was there—and Emile. Where he was."

Straker shook his head. "*We* don't have to do anything."

"That's true. You can go back to Maine."

"You try a body's patience, St. Joe."

His voice was low, serious, not as irritated as she could have expected. She drank more tea, closing her eyes briefly as she tried to let the chamomile calm and soothe her. "You've done enough. Tonight... fetching me at the fire. Thank you."

"I wish I had a tape recorder. Riley St. Joe thanking me."

She leveled her gaze at him. "Are you always this aggravating?"

"You've known me since you were a tot. You tell me."

"You were beyond aggravating at sixteen."

"That's when you gave me the scar above my eye. You were pretty much a pain in the ass yourself. Nose in a book, and when it wasn't, you had to go around telling people how many individual hairs there were on a sea otter."

"A hundred thousand. I also hiked and kayaked."

"You were and still are a show-off."

"At least I wasn't mean, and I didn't go around trying to humiliate twelve-year-old girls."

"You were impossible to humiliate. You had too

high an opinion of yourself.'' He got to his feet, enjoying himself. ''If I'd noticed even the smallest chink in your armor, I'd have left you alone. Instead you opened up my skull for me.''

She smiled, remembering her shock at the blood, his barely controlled rage. He hadn't thrown a rock back at her. ''It's a good thing I didn't live in Maine year-round. We'd have killed each other.''

''Nah. We'd just have ended up in bed together a lot sooner.''

''*Straker!*''

''Not when you were twelve. I'd have waited a few years.''

''That's it. I'm locking my door tonight.''

She jumped up, set her mug in the sink, tried to push back a mix of images that had nothing, nothing, to do with the reality of the man standing in her kitchen. He'd stirred her up, and she needed to settle down and recognize that she and John Straker had always been a volatile combination.

''Front door or bedroom door?'' he asked, languid, deliberately sexy.

''Both. I swear, Straker, if I could do it, I'd handcuff you to your futon.''

It was a mistake. His grin was slow and easy, and he slouched against the doorjamb, one knee bent, his eyes half-closed. ''I think I have a set of cuffs down in the car if you want to give it a try.''

''No wonder my mother worries.''

''She's a smart woman, Mara St. Joe.'' He sauntered back into the living room, where he sat on the futon couch and stretched out his legs, relaxed. His mind was still working, however, she knew. "Take a nice hot shower and go to bed, Riley. Anyone calls or pounds on your door, I'll get rid of them."

"The police…"

"They didn't see you at Sam's," he said, "but they'll probably want to talk to you."

She nodded, the enormity of what had happened tonight sinking in. "This makes it more likely he was murdered, doesn't it?"

"His death might just have been inconvenient for someone who didn't want the police pawing through his stuff. We don't know, and because we don't know, we need to keep an open mind."

"Is that what you do as an FBI agent?"

"Nope. I get out my six-shooter and shoot everyone in sight."

In spite of herself, she laughed. "You're impossible."

"Hot shower. Bed."

"You?"

"Cold shower. Lumpy futon. But after you, of course."

Seven

❧⟨∞⟩❧

Straker ordered a breakfast roll-up thing at one of the food stalls at Quincy Market, a short walk from the Boston Center for Oceanographic Research, where he'd dropped Riley off for the day and parked in her spot in the garage. It was ten o'clock on a lousy Friday morning. He'd woken up with a score of reasons why he should be back on the island and damned few why he should stay in Boston. The prospect of sleeping with Riley counted as a reason to clear out. So did the prospect of not sleeping with her.

He had a choice of eight different kinds of coffee. He stuck with Colombian, black, no sugar, and took it and the roll-up into the rotunda, where he stood at a wooden counter that serviced the throngs eating on the run, but still had the feeling of a trough. The place was empty. The drizzle and low clouds made everything seem close and claustrophobic. At least Boston Harbor was practically across the street. If worse came to worst, he could rent a boat and clear out.

Worse *had* come to worst. He'd let Emile Labreque

go on his merry way, and he couldn't get Riley St. Joe out of his mind.

He bit into his roll-up. Scrambled eggs, ham, cheese, peppers, onions. It wasn't breakfast on his porch looking out at the sunrise, but it wasn't bad.

He knew he was exaggerating. Worst-case scenario wasn't kissing Riley. Worst-case scenario was if he'd taken her to bed last night. They'd come close. Too damned close for sanity's sake.

She hadn't repeated her previous morning's mistake. She'd come out of her bedroom dressed for work, right down to panty hose and shoes, and had announced primly, "A good adrenaline rush can make one do the silliest things, can't it?"

He'd resisted comment. If thinking of the sexual currents between them as silly kept her on the straight and narrow, who was he to disabuse her?

He finished his roll-up and took his coffee to a pay phone. He put a collect call through to a Maine state detective who owed him big-time. "I'm not one to call in a favor," he said, "but I need to know what you guys have on Sam Cassain."

"It's not my case, Straker."

"I know. Get me what you can. I'll wait." He read off the number at his pay phone.

Ten minutes later, he had his information. His friend was straightforward, detailed and professional. The medical examiner had determined that Sam Cassain had drowned after a blow to the back of the head had probably knocked him unconscious. It looked deliberate, but there were a lot of ways a man could get knocked cold working a boat.

In the days before his death, Cassain had stopped at the Granger house on Mount Desert Island. He'd seen Abigail, Caroline, Matthew, Richard St. Joe, Henry Armistead and other members of the center's staff and its Maine supporters.

"Oh," his friend said, "and we talked to Mara St. Joe. En route to Mount Desert, Cassain stopped in Camden and saw her."

This was a surprise. "Why?"

"Don't know."

"What about Emile?"

"He's not an official suspect, but he's their best bet. Doesn't look good, him taking off like that. Palladino thinks Riley St. Joe's holding back and has at least a fair idea of where grandfather could be. You, too."

No point mentioning they'd seen him last night. "What about the fire at Cassain's house down here?"

"Arson. Looks like a time-delayed device, crude. Massachusetts police are cooperating with us. Well, that's it. That's all I've got. We're square, Straker. Next time you call, it better be because you've got something for me."

Straker tossed his empty coffee cup in a trash can and headed back to the Boston Center for Oceanographic Research. Sam Cassain had been to see Mara St. Joe. Ten to one Riley didn't know, which meant Mara hadn't told her. Interesting.

He let this latest piece of information simmer while

he concentrated on his surroundings. He passed a trio of men in expensive suits, two women in expensive suits, an old woman walking a cocker spaniel and a bunch of beefy guys in hard hats. The hard hats were working the interminable Big Dig, a massive project that had already added the Ted Williams Tunnel under the harbor and now was sinking the Central Artery.

The noise of traffic and construction coupled with the dank weather and his frustrated inactivity magnified Straker's overall squirreliness. For two cents he'd clear out. He didn't have to go back to the island. He could go anywhere. He could go back to his damned job, where there were rules, procedures and no slim, dark-eyed oceanographers.

But he walked past the center's marine mammal fountain and up to the main entrance, where he got the steel eye from the security guards and was told he wasn't welcome back. Abigail Granger must have put out the word. The guards wouldn't even let him pay up and visit the exhibits like a normal tourist. No trust. No sense of humor. A bit of an overreaction on Ms. Granger's part, but there wasn't much Straker could do about it.

This wasn't going to work. He stood in front of the fountain and contemplated his situation. Shadowing Riley would drive him over the brink. He needed to get moving on his own Big Dig, find out who'd killed Sam Cassain, what it had to do with Emile and Matt Granger and maybe even Mara St. Joe. He needed to get this mess unraveled, sorted out and tied up with a ribbon before someone did something stupid. Like Emile. Like Riley. He remembered the feel of her breast, the taste of her mouth. Like *him*.

Abigail joined him at the fountain and smiled coolly. Dressed in a sleek navy raincoat, she had an umbrella and briefcase tucked under her arm, and her hair was pulled back, ready for a gale-force wind. "What are you going to do when it starts to rain?" she asked.

"Buy an umbrella."

Her quick laugh didn't reach her eyes. "You enjoy being irreverent, don't you?"

"No."

"Well, I've got it figured out now. Sometimes I can be incredibly dense. You're making sure Riley doesn't get into trouble because of Sam's death. Did Emile put you up to it? She was almost killed last year. We've all become rather protective of everyone who survived the *Encounter*."

"I'm not looking out for Riley. She can look out for herself."

"I see." Abigail seemed nervous, out of her element, but she maintained her poise. "I suppose you heard about the fire at Sam's house last night. This is all…" She faltered. "It feels as if everything's spinning out of control."

"Maybe it is."

She shot him a look. "You're no comfort."

"I've been told that a lot. Your brother blames Emile for your father's death. Do you?"

"I try not to think about it." Her voice was quiet

and sincere, all coolness gone. "No one can fault Emile for his dedication to his work. Without him, this center never would have come to fruition. My father had money and a passion for oceanography, but not Emile's vision or expertise—or sheer energy. He and my father had so many, many good days. That's what I prefer to remember."

"You're dedicated to the center," Straker said.

She smiled, her eyes warming. "Yes. Henry and I share the same vision. My father and Emile were very old school. They didn't oppose our ideas—they were simply indifferent. With so much competition for people's time and money, Henry and I are convinced we need to increase the center's visibility, give it more life, more spice. We *must* do more to reach out to the public. My father was satisfied with a stodgy quarterly newsletter. That's not enough these days."

"Sounds as if you two have a lot of plans for the future."

"That's been the one bright note in this otherwise dreadful year."

"What about Sam Cassain?"

Her eyes narrowed; the coolness returned. "Sam's death has nothing to do with the center or my family." She frowned, looking past Straker. "Here comes Henry. He's not very happy with you."

Henry Armistead edged in between them, touching Abigail's arm. "Sorry to keep you waiting, but I was delayed."

"Oh, it's no trouble, Henry." She smiled awkwardly. "Do you know John Straker?"

Armistead's manner changed. "I certainly know of him." He gave Straker a frosty, pursed-lip once-over. "I asked security not to allow you onto the premises. Unfortunately, there's nothing I can do about our public spaces."

The fine drizzle had turned to a light rain that collected on his gray hair. Like Abigail, he had an overcoat, a briefcase and an umbrella, which he didn't unfurl.

Straker had on a sweatshirt, jeans and running shoes. He didn't care about a little rain. "So I'm persona non grata because I fed a few sharks under false pretenses?"

"There was last night in Louisburg Square as well," Henry said. "I'll be straightforward with you. I was in favor of calling the police. I'd already heard about your intrusion earlier in the day here at the center." He tilted his head back slightly. "I simply will not tolerate having someone on my staff stalked."

Straker frowned. *Stalked?*

"I understand you're with the bureau. You were shot earlier in the year while apprehending a federal fugitive."

The bureau. He liked that. "I'm on leave."

"You're an expert on domestic terrorism, correct?"

"Nah. I just catch regular old bad guys."

"That's not what I hear. Well, I expect the stress of your work coupled with your long recovery and

self-imposed isolation have taken their toll. It's on
that basis that I'm giving you another chance."

"Another chance for what?"

The older man squared his shoulders and took in a
breath. He was supercilious and commanding, but
Straker could see Henry Armistead wasn't sure he
wanted to be telling a nutty FBI agent to buzz off.
"Riley doesn't want you here."

"Riley?"

"If you're keeping watch on her, for any reason,
it's without her consent. That makes you a stalker, or,
to put it more kindly, a potential stalker."

"She told you I was stalking her," Straker said.

"That was the implication, yes."

He should have left Riley St. Joe out on her kayak
in the middle of the North Atlantic all those years
ago.

Spots of color formed high on Abigail's cheeks.
She hadn't popped her umbrella, and the drizzle,
heavier now, was matting down her fair hair.
"Henry," she said.

"I'm almost finished." Armistead straightened,
whipped open his umbrella and held it over her. He
turned back to Straker. "We've been enduring a media assault all morning thanks to the arson fire at Captain Cassain's house last night. Kids, I suspect. They
probably heard he'd died and decided his house was
fair game. In any case, I have no desire to compound
my problems by taking this matter with you any further. I can count on your cooperation?"

Straker got the picture. If he showed his face at the

center again, it was off to the clink with him as a wounded FBI agent who'd lost his grip.

"No problem," he said without expression. His fight wasn't with Armistead. It was with Riley.

Armistead politely, but coldly, excused himself, took Abigail by the arm and escorted her across the plaza. She didn't say a word. Straker found a pay phone in the garage, dialed the center's switchboard and had them put him through to Riley's office.

"That kiss last night must have frustrated you more than I realized."

"What?"

"You're trying to buy time, St. Joe. It won't work, not with me. You're not weaseling out of this one. You told Armistead I'm stalking you. Now he's barred me from the premises."

"Stalking? I have no idea what you're talking about."

She wasn't going to come clean. Straker clenched the phone. He was losing objectivity. Control. All he wanted to do was march up to her office, grab her and finish what they'd started last night. *That* was where this stalking nonsense had come from. She knew what the score was between him and her, and she'd panicked.

He had to act, and he had to act now. Too much was at stake. He needed his mind back. He needed to be able to sit and calmly, objectively, put the pieces together.

"All right," he said. "Have it your way. If you

end up with your ass in a sling, it's your own damned fault. I'm out of here.''

''Wait—where are you going?''

He hung up. Screw it. He didn't answer to Riley St. Joe.

He got his car out of the garage, paid full price for parking because he didn't have her with him to get the discount, and negotiated the narrow, busy streets to get on I-93 North. He wasn't leaving much at Riley's place. His toothbrush and razor, a couple of changes of clothes. Nothing he couldn't replace.

Camden was about four hours north. He'd stop in for a word with Mara St. Joe and Sig St. Joe-Granger, and after that, he'd see.

Riley stuffed what work she could into her leather tote. She was just grabbing files and reports, dumping them blindly into her bag as she fought back her sense of frustration and humiliation. How could she have been such a coward?

She had let Henry Armistead maneuver her into implying that Straker was stalking her. Now Straker was furious with her, Henry still had his doubts, and she was supposed to lie low for a few days, even at the risk of letting her work pile up.

First thing that morning, Henry had popped into her office, paced in front of her desk. There wasn't much room, but he'd been agitated, troubled by the terrible position he—or more important, the center—was in. ''It's not your fault you found Sam's body,'' he'd told her. ''But with the media attention and the police scrutiny, I think we'd all be better off if you kept a low profile for a few days. Relax this weekend. Take Monday off. Then let's see where we are.''

"Henry, I'm already backed up—"

"We can't have John Straker skulking around. I know you can't help it that he was on the island when you found Captain Cassain. Nevertheless…'' He sighed. "You know what I'm saying.''

"You're saying I inflicted him on the center.''

"He's unpredictable, a loose cannon if you will. If you take a few days off and let the authorities figure out what's going on, perhaps he'll go back to Maine. That would be best for all of us.''

Riley could understand his frustration and anxiety. The job of executive director of an oceanographic research institution, while never easy, wasn't supposed to include things like suspicious deaths, fires and FBI agents lurking on the premises.

"I don't have any control over what Straker does,'' she'd said. "And I don't think what I do or don't do should be dependent on him.''

Henry rubbed the back of his neck as if he were in pain. "Riley…I can't risk another incident like last night. Give this some time.''

"You mean you can't risk alienating the Grangers.''

He lost patience. "Of *course* I can't risk it!''

"I'm not responsible for what John Straker does,'' she said.

"No, you're not. Riley, I wouldn't want anyone to question your priorities and obligations. I understand your devotion to Emile, your loyalty to him in the face of what everyone else so clearly believes happened last year.''

The past few days had given any critics she had more ammunition. She liked Henry. He was good for the center. And it was the center he cared about, not Labreques, St. Joes, or even, ultimately, Grangers.

He'd gone on quietly, ''If Mr. Straker is acting against your will, then, in my judgment, he can be accused of stalking you.''

She'd seen her opening and had seized it.

She dropped onto her chair now, her tote on her lap. She didn't know what had come over her. Sure, she'd gotten herself off the hook with Henry. But she should have anticipated what would happen—what *did* happen. Straker's description was circulated to security, and he was barred from the premises.

And he'd found out about it.

It was the kiss.

It wasn't the kiss. That was absurd. She'd been kissed before.

But not by John Straker.

She was so far in over her head she didn't know if she'd ever come up for air. The man she'd kissed last night, the man she'd thwarted at every turn, was an FBI special agent. He wasn't a marine scientist. He wasn't even the teenager who'd tormented her as a kid.

She'd checked the Internet for various accounts of the incident that had nearly killed him six months ago. He and his team had tracked down three men wanted in connection with a string of armored car robberies. The thieves had killed four guards, seriously injured three. They were using the money to fund their own private, paranoid domestic army, with plans to target an array of state and federal government buildings and private institutions.

Straker and his team had managed to arrest two of the men without incident. The third took two teenagers hostage, shooting Straker in the leg and abdomen. The terrorist made the mistake of believing Straker was dead instead of just damned close to it.

None of the accounts went into great detail about John Straker. All portrayed him as skilled, well-trained, professional and courageous. That he was also obnoxious and sexy and couldn't get along with anyone didn't enter the picture.

Way, way over her head she was.

Now she'd turned a respected FBI agent into a would-be stalker.

"He's going to shoot me dead," she said out loud, then noticed Abigail in her doorway.

She smiled a bit formally. "Henry told me you were taking some time off—I'm glad I caught you before you left. I don't know if Caroline's told you, but I'm joining her in Maine this weekend. Sam's death has dredged up all the pain and controversy we'd hoped we'd put behind us." She shuddered, not going further. "I'm sure you understand."

"Of course. My father left an hour ago. He claims he needs to run up to Bath and check on the progress of the *Encounter II*."

"He'll be so much happier when he can spend more time at sea."

Riley nodded. "It's going to be a beautiful ship."

"He invited you to go with him, didn't he?"

"Pleaded would be more accurate. If I'd known Henry was going to kick me out of here, I might have accepted Dad's offer. Have a good trip. Give my regards to Caroline. We've all had a pretty awful few days."

Abigail lingered in the doorway. She bit her lower lip awkwardly. "I was wondering—do you think it'd be okay if I stopped in Camden to see Sig? It's been ages."

"If you're asking me if she'd see you, I don't honestly know." There was still the matter of Sig's pregnancy. If Abigail noticed and Sig didn't mention it, her sister-in-law wouldn't say a word. "She won't be ugly about it or anything. She'd just say she's painting and can't be disturbed."

"I don't want to get involved in her and Matt's problems. I just—well, I don't know what I'm thinking at this point." She smiled, the strain of the past few days evident in her delicate features. "Caroline invited Henry, too. We're driving up together."

Riley wasn't surprised, but she didn't know what to say. "Oh."

Abigail blushed. "Maybe if we're not here for the media to pester, it'll help diffuse the crisis atmosphere."

"What about your brother?" Riley asked. "Is he going to Maine with you?"

"I haven't seen Matt since last night. I'm sure this

has all been a nightmare for him. Caroline and I are worried about him. Henry is, too. That's why I want to see Sig. If she can do something, suggest something we can do..."

"You don't think he had anything to do with Sam—"

"No!" She shrank back in horror, deeply offended. "How could you possibly say such a thing?"

Riley debated telling Abigail about seeing Matt at the fire last night, but quickly rejected the idea. She'd have to explain her *own* presence there. She said quietly, "I don't mean to imply he had a hand in Sam's death. Forget it. I don't know what I meant."

"It's all right. We're all on edge." Abigail regained her poise, even managed a soft smile. "Have a good weekend. I hope when we see each other next this will all have resolved itself."

"I hope so, too."

After Abigail left, Riley turned out the lights and headed for the subway. Straker and his car, she knew, would be long gone from her spot in the parking garage.

The rain had stopped, but gray clouds continued to hang over the city. The subway ride and walk back to her apartment did nothing to calm her. She climbed up her front steps, rummaging for her keys, and almost screamed when she heard a movement behind her.

She whipped around, keys in hand.

"Whoa," Matthew Granger said. "You could poke an eye out with those things."

"That was the whole idea."

He looked haggard and drawn, as if he hadn't slept in days. "You can hit me for last night if you want. Just leave my eyes alone, okay?"

It was an apology, and Riley accepted it. "You're not worth hitting, Granger. I'm not even going to ask what possessed you, because I know. We're all under a lot of stress right now."

Sheepishness, however, wasn't her brother-in-law's long suit. Although clearly exhausted, he stood tall, patrician, his emotions under rigid control. "I know you mean well, Riley, but—"

"Don't let's start, okay?"

"I saw Emile on Beacon Hill last night. So did you. So did John Straker."

He paused, his piercing eyes narrowing. Riley resisted the urge to explain, to defend Emile, to distance herself from Straker. Matt hadn't gone to the trouble of intercepting her just to apologize. He had an agenda, and she needed to let him get to it.

"Funny." He came up another step, still two down from her. "Not an hour after Emile turned up on Beacon Hill, Sam's house caught fire."

So he hadn't seen Emile in Arlington. Riley shrugged. "Funny you were at Sam's yourself."

She hadn't caught him by surprise. He remained coolly under control, last night's rage dissipated. This was the Matthew Granger who could charm and infuriate at will. "So that *was* you. I thought so. You must have followed Emile."

He was trying to trap her into confirming his suspicions. Riley didn't bite. "Emile? Did you see him at Sam's?"

Matt exhaled slowly, not rising to her provocation. "I didn't come here to go round and round with you. Riley, something very nasty and dangerous is going on. If Emile's at the bottom of it or not, it doesn't change the facts. Sam Cassain is dead—murdered— and his place was torched." He paused, letting her digest his words. His gaze was serious, fraternal, just this side of patronizing. "You need to pull back."

"So do you," she said automatically.

He hissed through his teeth. This was her day to try everyone's patience. "I know you care about Emile. I know you believe in him. But whatever his role in this business is, you know damned well he wouldn't want you meddling."

"And what are you doing if not meddling?"

"I'm not here about me. I'm here about you."

"Well, thank you very much. Why bother? What difference does it make to you what I do?"

"If I didn't make the effort and something happened to you..." He averted his gaze, and she could see the dark circles under his eyes, the stubble of beard on his jaw, the difficulty he was having maintaining his unyielding stance. "It's tough enough between Sig and me right now as it is."

"You don't need a dead or beat-up sister-in-law mucking up the works."

His eyes flashed. "Bluntly put, no, I don't."

She swallowed. "You should go see Sig."

"I saw her yesterday." His eyes gleamed with affection, even humor, but sadness and frustration quickly crept in. "Why do you think I was in such a rotten mood last night?"

He couldn't know Sig was pregnant. He'd seen her, and he still hadn't figured it out. Riley groaned inwardly. He was even more thickheaded than she'd imagined. Wouldn't a husband somehow divine these things?

As if she knew anything about husbands. Or even men. The one man she'd kissed in recent months she'd just sent packing as a stalker.

"Honestly, Matt," she said, shaking her head with a sudden smile. "Sig can have you. If you were my husband, I'd have poisoned you by now."

He laughed, but somehow ended up looking even more haggard. "I can't wait to meet the poor bastard who falls for you, Riley. It'll be a hell of a show." He trotted down the steps; when he reached the sidewalk, he glanced back at her, deadly serious. "I just gave you good advice. Follow it."

Fifteen minutes later, she had her backpack crammed with essentials—underwear, flannel boxers, toothbrush, makeup, water sandals, hiking socks, hiking clothes, regular clothes. The phone rang twice while she was packing. Reporters. With any luck, she'd get out before they or the police could land on her doorstep.

Straker had gone back to Maine. He must have. Where else would he go? Caroline Granger was en route, Abigail, Henry, her own father. Her sister and mother were already there. Riley had no idea where Matt would end up.

So. It made sense. *She* would go to Maine, too.

Eight

─❦─

Sig lay on the studio bed with her feet up and the hem of her voluminous dress pulled to her knees. She wasn't wearing socks. She stared at her legs and wondered if she'd get varicose veins. She'd been on her feet again all day, painting, sketching, playing, but at least she'd gone for a long walk, too, not letting the off-and-on rain deter her. Now she just wished someone would bring her tea and toast. If she could, she'd stay on her mother's porch forever. She had no desire to go out into the cold, cruel world. Let someone else slay the dragons.

It was the fight or flight principle at work, she knew. She would choose flight every time. Riley, of course, would choose fight.

Someone knocked on the back door, and Sig yawned. No doubt it would be the same person who'd been ringing the front doorbell, which she hadn't bothered to answer; her mother was out. It wasn't Matt. Matt wouldn't have bothered knocking. Maybe it was a dragon after all, she thought.

She roused herself enough to see John Straker's deadly, sexy face in the doorway. "A dragon indeed," she said to herself, then called, "Door's open."

He came in, and the years since she'd seen him fell away. He was the same John Straker she'd known since childhood, never mind the FBI and six months on Labreque Island recovering from bullet wounds. He was fit, agile, alert and just impatient and irritated enough for her to know Riley was under his skin. *Good for you, Sis,* she thought. Straker was the perfect kind of man for her sister—in her face, impossible to intimidate, *there.* Riley would never tolerate the kind of unconventional relationship their parents had.

"I tried the front door," he said. "You didn't hear the doorbell?"

"No, I did. I just didn't bother with it, and Mom's off to the post office."

His gaze dropped to her abdomen, and he said with typical Straker frankness, "You're pregnant?"

"Oh—shit, it's that obvious?"

"Nah. I'm a trained FBI agent."

She smiled. "It *is* that obvious. Mom hasn't said a word."

"Then she's minding her own business, which isn't a dominant gene in this family. Husband doesn't know?"

She sighed and shook her head. Matt had stood right where Straker was standing, and he hadn't no-

ticed. Of course, she'd had a blanket pulled up to her
nose.

"Well, good luck. Shouldn't you avoid paint
fumes?"

"They're watercolors, and I have good ventilation
out here." She dropped her feet to the floor and stood
up, feeling a mild strain in her lower back. "You've
always been one to cut to the chase, haven't you?"

He grinned. "I thought this was small talk."

"For you, maybe."

He walked over to her worktable and eyed the
painting on her board. It was inspired by her mother's
yellow mums, spatter layers of yellow and white. Her
best work of the summer. "You planning to sell any
of your stuff?"

"I don't know. I haven't given it much thought."

"Are you any good?"

She smiled. "I like that particular painting. I guess
it's a start."

He turned to her, his gray eyes taking in her sweep
of dress, her bulging stomach, her wild hair hanging
down her back. "What're you doing up here in
Maine, Sig?"

"Hiding."

"From what?"

She blinked rapidly, trying to keep back the tears.
Damned hormones. "Myself, mostly." She breathed
through her nose and refused to cry. "What about
you?"

"That's simple. I'm looking for Emile." Straker
took a couple of steps toward her. He radiated

strength, virility, toughness. Sig wouldn't be surprised if her sister hadn't even noticed. "I think he's out to track down whoever killed Sam Cassain."

Sig could feel the weight of the past few days, the seriousness. A man was dead. *Sam* was dead. "I think so, too."

"But you," Straker said. "You're just hiding."

"I understand you were on Beacon Hill last night. I heard my husband behaved like a perfect jackass. You saw what it's like. I don't fit in. There's no place for me there."

"So? Make your place."

"Matt thinks Emile should be in jail." She wondered why she was telling this man anything, much less her deepest thoughts and feelings. "He's obsessed with proving that my grandfather's negligence and arrogance led to the *Encounter* tragedy. He won't let go. His father died a terrible death, and Matt wants vengeance. Justice, he'd say."

"What about you?"

Her shoulders slumped. "I just want the whole thing to go away."

"It won't, not until the police have Cassain's death settled. Emile thinks it's murder. Otherwise he wouldn't have taken off."

"What do you think?"

"It's murder. I'd look to the *Encounter* disaster for clues."

She was definitely dealing with cut-to-the-chase John Straker. It was a quality that had made him few friends, even in high school. The friends he had, Sig knew, would die for him. "Riley didn't come with you, did she?"

"I let her fry in her own fat awhile. She's a damned pain in the ass."

"She's not in any danger—"

"Only from me. I might strangle her."

Sig smiled, saw the scar her sister had put in his forehead. "You two."

But he didn't smile back. "I need to find Emile, Sig. He was in Boston last night. He must have a base—a friend's house, an old campsite, a pile of rocks somewhere. Do you have any ideas?"

"No, I wish I did. I haven't had much to do with him the past year. To be honest, I'm not so sure Matt's not right about him. Emile..." She threw up her hands. "You know what he's like."

"When you and Riley were kids," Straker persisted, "you must have had places the three of you talked about, visited. If you think of anything, even if it's unlikely, let me know."

"Where will I find you?"

"Hell if I know. I'll check back with you from time to time." He moved to the kitchen door, listened. "I think I hear your mother coming in. I need to talk to her. You staying out here?"

Sig nodded. "Forever if I could."

He hesitated at the door. "Your husband might be a jackass, but unless you think he'd hurt you or the baby, you should tell him he's going to be a father."

"I don't recall asking for your opinion," she said, more as a point of information than out of anger.

"Don't worry—it's free."

"And it's babies. I'm having twins."

He grinned and gave her a wink. "Hell. Maybe you shouldn't tell him. Or if you want to give him a heart attack, lay the news on him without any warning."

"You're terrible!"

"So I've been told. By the way," he added, pulling open the door, "I figure I had about a two-hour head start on your sister. She'll be here before nightfall."

"She knows you were headed here?"

"No."

"Then how—"

"Trust me. She hasn't changed since she was six years old. She'll be here."

Mara gave him about three minutes before she insisted on serving him tea and a fresh, gooey coconut macaroon in the front parlor. She wore drawstring pants and a plaid flannel overshirt, and every instinct Straker had said she was holding on to the last shreds of her sanity and self-control. Her family was in crisis. Her father, her two daughters. It couldn't be easy. She was tense, preoccupied and couldn't stand still.

"I have a few calls I need to make," she said. "Would you excuse me? I won't be long. Then we..." She swallowed, unusually nervous. "Then we'll talk more."

"Sure."

The time out would give him a chance to consider how much was left unsaid among the Labreques and St. Joes. He set his cup and saucer on the gleaming butler's table. Mara had gotten out the good china. He felt like a nineteenth-century ship captain home for a spell with the womenfolk.

She claimed Sam Cassain had stopped by late last week merely to say hello, not to drive the wedge between her and her father deeper; not for old times' sake; not, apparently, because he knew he was about to be killed.

Straker didn't disbelieve her. He thought there was more.

The front door banged open, and Riley burst in. She'd changed from her work clothes to jeans and a high-tech hiking top that delineated the shape of her breasts probably more than she'd want him noticing. Or not. She scowled. "I should have known I'd find you here."

"You did know. That's why you came."

That didn't sit well. She stormed around the living room. The long drive and long days had taken their toll. This was bluster. Fatigue. Even buried anguish. She flew at him, her jaw set hard. "Where's my mother?"

"Back in her office. She had some calls to make. Sig's gone for a walk." He sat back on Mara's handsome couch, which wasn't particularly comfortable. "It's been a rough few days for them, too."

She gave a tight nod. "I know. They won't admit it, but they're worried about Emile. They don't want to see him in over his head."

"That goes for you, too."

She sank into a wing chair and kicked her feet out

in front of her. He could see some of the frustration and anxiety wash out of her now that she was in a safe place, with people she cared about and who cared about her, even if he was among them. "I'm sorry," she said abruptly, without looking at him.

Straker made no comment.

"I shouldn't have gone along with Henry's suggestion that you could be a stalker. It was...stupid." She rubbed her forehead, not because she had a headache, Straker reasoned, but because she hated admitting she was wrong. "He's upset with me for finding Sam's body, for bringing you onto the scene last night and enraging Matt. He offered me a chance to throw you to the wolves, and I did."

"You were trying to save your own neck?"

She nodded, obviously not proud of herself.

Straker picked up his teacup. "I thought it was because I'd kissed you and you were scared of what came next."

"I wasn't scared then," she said. "And I'm not scared now, because nothing comes next."

She slid off her chair and poured herself a cup of tea from Mara's china tea service, then sat back down. She still hadn't met his eye. "Then you had cold feet," he said.

"You only get cold feet when you stop yourself from doing something you deep down want to do or know you need to do." Now her eyes lifted, zeroed in on him. "So that leaves cold feet out."

No, that left cold feet in. But Straker decided not to push her. She'd had a lot of time to think things over on her solitary drive up to Camden. "Armistead tell you to get out of town?"

"To lie low is more like it." She sipped her tea, which was only lukewarm. "I want to find Emile before he runs afoul of the wrong people."

Afoul? Maybe it was the antiques and the nineteenth-century atmosphere, Straker thought. "What makes you think you won't run 'afoul' of the same people?"

She set her teacup in its saucer. "I know how to shoot."

"Jesus Christ," Straker breathed. "All this mess needs is Riley St. Joe armed to the teeth. Did you slip a gun into your backpack?"

"No, I don't even own one. You're the FBI agent. You must have all kinds of guns."

"Riley. Forget it."

She refused to give up. "I can always use tranquilizer darts."

"Sit back," he said softly. "Tell me about your work."

"I don't want to tell you about my work. I want to find Emile."

"What does the director of recovery and rehabilitation for the Boston Center for Oceanographic Research do?"

She sighed. Her dark eyes fixed on him. "I know what you're doing."

"If I were a dolphin," he said, "would I want Riley St. Joe to rescue me?"

It worked. She gave another sigh and started. She

explained the basic philosophy of the center's recovery and rehab program, the constant search for funds, the training and mobilization of volunteers when there was a mass stranding, the ongoing research. Straker tried to pay attention to her words, but it was her manner that captivated him—her passion, her common sense, her dedication. This was work she loved. Work she could never give up. He'd once felt the same way about his own work, but not in a long time.

Mara St. Joe joined them in the parlor. A pair of reading glasses hung from her neck, and she fingered them nervously as she greeted Riley. "John said you'd be along. Did you have much traffic?"

Riley shook her head, a tiny spark in her eyes all that suggested she didn't like the idea of him predicting her movements. "I'm sorry I didn't call ahead."

"There's no need. You're always welcome here." Mara dropped her glasses, but didn't seem to know what to do with her hands. She seemed unusually ill at ease, even for someone whose daughter had recently found a dead man. "Riley, we need to talk. I have something I—something you deserve to know."

Graceful exits weren't one of his strengths, but Straker got to his feet. "I could use some air. I'll take a walk around the block."

Mara seemed relieved. Riley just seemed confused, as if she couldn't imagine what her mother might tell her that she didn't already know. Straker had a policy of avoiding mother-daughter conversations whenever possible. It was bad enough when his own mother got him by the ear and sat him down. Hadn't done that in years, not for lack of provocation.

He ran into Sig halfway down the front walk. The clouds were moving out over the water, the sky clearing. "I see Riley's arrived," she said. "She boot you out?"

"I took my cue."

Her face clouded, and she nodded with understanding. She was breathing hard from her walk, her cheeks red from exertion and the stiff breeze, but she wasn't winded. "Then she's telling her. Damn. I think I'll sneak around back. You want to join me?"

"That depends."

"Then you don't know," she said.

He remained silent.

"I thought you came up here because you knew."

"To be honest," he said, "I haven't thought much about you St. Joe women until Riley came screaming into my cottage about a dead body and threw up."

Sig's eyes narrowed on him. She'd combed her hair and braided it, put on comfortable shoes. At the right angle, she didn't look pregnant in her flowing dress. She was artistic, creative, intense in ways different and less obvious from her scientist sister, mother, father, grandfather. And Straker could see her debating what to tell him, wondering if she'd said too much already.

"You have no reason to trust me," he said.

"It's not that. I just don't know if it's my place—"

"Sig, a man is dead, murdered. Your grandfather is missing. Even if what you have isn't directly related, if you think it might help me figure out what's going on, stop it from escalating, then you should tell me. If not, feel free to keep it to yourself.''

She licked her lips, bit down hard.

"Is it about Sam Cassain?" Straker asked. "He stopped here last week."

Tears glistened in her eyes, spilled almost immediately onto her cheeks. She flicked them away with her fingertips, as if furious. "I can't stand it—I cry at the drop of a hat." She made a valiant attempt at a smile, gave up before it had formed. "My mother and Sam had an affair."

"Damn."

"I know. It happened just before she bought her house here. It didn't last. Sam was never Mom's type, and vice versa. I guess my parents almost split up—the affair was their wake-up call to make changes, which they did."

"What happened when he stopped by last week? What did he say? How long was he here?"

She shook her head, eyes lowered. "I don't know what he said. I stayed in my studio. He left after about twenty minutes."

"And Riley doesn't know," Straker said.

"I'm sure Mom's telling her now."

"Who else knew?"

"Everyone," Sig said bluntly. "My father, Emile, the Grangers. It was a fling, a wake-up call for all of us, herself included, that something was wrong. She moved up here, and things have worked out since.

She didn't want Riley to know about Sam—I guess none of us did.''

"Why?" But Straker could guess.

"It's hard for any of us to live up to her expectations," she said. "It's not that she's hard on us, it's that she believes in us so much. I suppose we just want to pretend we're as good as she thinks we are."

Straker couldn't see it, maybe because Riley didn't think much of him to begin with. "Emile?"

"Emile is her idol. He would want to disappoint her least of all."

Riley sank into a hot bath sprinkled with a few drops of essential oil of rosemary. It was supposed to revive her. Good. She needed reviving. She had things to do before nightfall, and she couldn't let her confusion and anger, her total frustration, get the better of her.

Straker and her mother were down in the kitchen. She could hear Straker's terse laugh, her mother's strong, confident voice. They were getting along fine considering she'd warned Riley not fifteen minutes ago to watch out for him, that he wasn't normal. Her mother and Sig wouldn't expect him to be charming. Well, no one would.

Her conversation with her mother had been awkward, painful and brief. Riley shut her eyes and breathed out over the steaming water, tried to absorb the unexpected news, tried not to picture the bloated body on the rocks of Labreque Island. Sam Cassain. Her mother. *Good God.*

She wasn't as put out about being the last to know as she might have anticipated. She was often oblivious to personal undercurrents. Rivalries, jealousies, mad crushes, personality conflicts, the occasional illicit affair. It wasn't that she wasn't interested—more often than not she just didn't notice. Through example and edict, Emile had taught her to stay focused on her work.

Yet even he'd known about her mother's affair with the captain of the *Encounter*.

With deliberate effort, Riley concentrated on her breathing. Eventually her mind drifted. Her body relaxed. After a while, she became aware the water had cooled. A knock came at the door. "Riley?" Straker's voice, like a bucket of boiling water in her tub. Her skin felt as if it were on fire. "You didn't go down the drain, did you?"

"No, I was just getting out."

She moved, the water stirring, and she went still as she pictured him out there in the hall, listening. Imagining her in the tub.

"Straker? You still there?"

"I haven't moved a muscle."

His voice was deep and low, like liquid heat down her spine. She kept very still. "Could you go down and heat up a can of soup or something? I'm starving."

"I can do soup," he said, and she thought she detected a trace of knowing humor in his tone.

She waited until she heard his footsteps on the stairs. Her skin was prune-wrinkled and pink, but she shivered when she stepped out of the tub. She rubbed herself down with one of her mother's big, soft towels. Like the rest of the house, the bathroom was tasteful, understated and comfortable. It bore little resemblance to the series of functional apartments and houses her parents had rented when she and Sig were growing up.

Riley could remember when her mother had shared Emile's excitement and vision for their work, for the center. His growing fame and the pressures of his single-mindedness—her husband's single-mindedness, her own—had put a subtle, ever-present strain on everyone.

Relationships weren't easy even when you had everything in common, Riley thought, sprinkling herself with powder. She and Straker didn't have anything in common, and whatever was going on between them, it could hardly be called a relationship. Just because she couldn't stop thinking about him in the most basic, physical ways didn't mean a thing. He was a rough, competent, utterly masculine man, and what she was feeling was…simple biology.

So why was she sorry she'd sicced Armistead on him? Why did she want to hear him laugh?

Don't even think it, she warned herself, and quickly pulled on her clothes.

Her mother had a bowl of steaming, homemade bean soup on the kitchen table. "John's back talking to Sig," she said. "He doesn't seem as…unbalanced as I expected."

"He believes in Emile."

Her mother looked pained. "So do I, Riley."

"I didn't mean it that way." She sat in front of the soup, wished she could stop her mother from being so defensive. "Straker considers himself Emile's friend, but that doesn't mean he thinks Emile couldn't have—" She stopped abruptly. *Couldn't have killed your ex-lover.* "It doesn't make any difference to him if Emile's done something or not."

"John's always had his own way of looking at things." Her mother attempted a small smile, twisted her hands together as she paced in her homey kitchen. "I'm sorry. I'm not trying to put you on the spot. I'm not proud of myself. For Sam, for not telling you when I found out it was his body you'd found."

"You don't owe me an apology or an explanation." Riley tried the soup, but she'd lost her appetite.

Mara leaned against the counter and shut her eyes, her regret, her pain, evident. Her father was missing; Sam Cassain was dead. "I hadn't seen Sam in ages, not even after the *Encounter* went down. I didn't want to see him."

"Why did he stop by?"

She shrugged. "I don't know, just to say hello, he said. He seemed content, almost smug. I think..." She chose her next words carefully. "I think our affair was a coup for him. I was a scientist, Emile Labreque's daughter, Richard St. Joe's wife—your mother. I saw that last week, and frankly, I didn't like it. I didn't like him. I didn't like myself."

Riley wanted to crawl under the table. This sort of introspective, heart-to-heart talk with her mother made her squirm. She tried more of her soup, but her stomach rebelled.

"Sam Cassain was a selfish, greedy man," her mother continued. "His needs always came first, and he wasn't afraid to ask for what he wanted. I guess I needed that in my life at one time."

"Mom, I'm not judging you—"

"No." Her smile reached her eyes. "Of course you're not. It's long, long over. I love your father. We worked things out. That's all that matters."

Riley nodded. "I guess I'm as thick-headed as Emile. I never suspected a thing. You sure you're all right?"

"I'm fine."

"I plan to head up to Schoodic, stay at Emile's—"

Her mother winced. "I wished you wouldn't."

"I'll be okay. I can't just sit back, I have to do something. If I can find Emile—"

"You think it'll make a difference?" Mara asked.

Riley ignored the trace of bitterness in her mother's voice. "I'll be careful," she said. "I'll go on back and say goodbye to Sig, see what Straker's up to."

"You know where I am if you need me."

When Riley ducked onto the back porch, she found her sister standing next to a packed overnight bag. Straker was nowhere in sight.

"Straker left," Sig said. "He told me to tell you he needs room to maneuver and you should go find some whales and dolphins to save."

Riley groaned. "I hate him. I've hated him since I was six years old."

"You're so full of it. You know, he's better looking than I remembered. And sexy. My God, don't tell me you haven't noticed. I know it's not just my raging hormones. Well." She slipped a shawl over her shoulders, further concealing her pregnancy. "I've decided to help you look for Emile."

"What? Sig, you're pregnant. You can't."

"I'm not helpless. And Emile's my grandfather, too."

Riley frowned at her sister and searched her face for clues to her real motives. Sig loved Emile. There was no question of that. But that wasn't why she'd packed up. Sig had always had a laissez-faire attitude toward their grandfather. She wasn't one to meddle in his decisions and actions, whether he was filming a documentary on whales or having his reputation ripped to shreds by tragedy and reckless accusations. Her policy, from as long as Riley could remember, was to stay out of it.

"It's Matt," Riley said. "Isn't it?"

Sig made a face. "No wonder Straker snuck off on you. He told me you're a pain in the ass, and you *are*."

"Sig, you don't think Matt had anything to do with Sam's death, do you?"

But her sister went pale, mumbled, "I don't know," and hoisted her bag onto her shoulder. She leveled her dark eyes on Riley. "For my sake, and the sake of my babies, I have to find out. He's in this thing up to his eyeballs, Riley. I just don't know how or why or where it's all going to end."

"Oh, Sig," Riley said. "Does Mom know you're going?"

"I packed while you were in the tub. She's opposed, but she knows she can't stop me. That's why she's not seeing us off. I'm thirty-four years old. I know what I have to do." She set her jaw. "If I don't go with you, Riley, I go alone. It's that simple. Your choice."

"Like that's any choice. All right, but here's the deal. The *second* I think you're pushing it, I'm hauling you back here or straight to a hospital. I won't have you endanger your health on my watch."

Sig sniffed. "I'm not on your watch. I'm on my own watch. And I have been for some time." She attempted an encouraging smile. "I know what I'm doing."

"Good, because I sure as hell don't."

"That's another quarter for my mason jar." She yawned, not exactly looking up to traipsing after her seventy-six-year-old grandfather. "I'm thinking of exempting hells and damns. What do you think?"

Riley laughed. "I think Straker'd be happy he didn't stick around. This whole family's nuts."

Nine

~~~⚬⚬⚬~~~

They stopped for lobster rolls and wild-blueberry pie and made it to Emile's before Riley had to stop a third time for Sig, who constantly sipped water, to go to the bathroom. "You're going to be impossible in your third trimester," Riley told her.

"I hope so. I hate suffering in silence."

The air was cool and still, the tide out, the last of the dark clouds pushing east and exposing a starlit sky. Riley breathed in, feeling herself relax. She could smell the ocean, spruce, pine, and for an instant, she was carefree and six again.

"We should build a bonfire and toast marshmallows," Sig said beside her, obviously sharing her mood. "Maybe Emile would smell them, wherever he is, and come to his senses."

"Do you think he's out here somewhere?"

"I don't know. I gave up a long time ago trying to figure out how he thinks."

Riley unlocked the door to their grandfather's cabin, and they carried their gear inside. The place seemed empty, almost uninhabited. She turned on lights and built a fire in the woodstove while Sig, looking more exhausted than she'd ever admit, flopped onto the couch. "You still believe he can do no wrong, don't you?"

"You mean Emile."

"Of *course* I mean Emile."

Riley opened the dampers on the stove, struck a match and set her kindling ablaze. She watched the flames, remembered the orange glow of Sam's house last night, the crush of firefighters and police and on-lookers, and Matt Granger there at the edges of the crowd. Her brother-in-law. Sig's husband. Riley hadn't told her sister about seeing him at Sam's, about her encounter with him earlier that afternoon. It was obvious Sig wasn't here because of Emile. She was here because of Matt.

"I was nearly killed last year." A skinny piece of kindling caught fire, blackened and smoked as the flames ate it up. Riley kept her back to her sister. If she didn't, she was afraid Sig would guess she was hiding something. "Those hours in the submersible with Emile will haunt me to my dying days. We were hot, couldn't breathe. We were so sure we were going to die."

"Even Emile?"

"I think he already knew Bennett was dead—I think he thought we'd all be lost. Everyone aboard the *Encounter*. He never said. He's so stoic. His only concern was me, what had happened to the crew. He didn't care about the ship, his mission, his research."

She sighed. "We were cut off from Sam and the crew. We wanted to believe they got into the life boats, but the fire and flooding were so horrific, we just didn't know."

"Sam always struck me as self-serving, but you have to admit he never benefited from accusing Emile. His own career went down the tubes this past year."

But Riley was back in the submersible, hot, gasping for air. "I didn't panic." Sig seemed to know what she was talking about. "Maybe it was shock, I don't know. Emile never said a word about how he thought the ship caught fire."

"Well, that doesn't surprise me," Sig said. "If you're about to suffocate or drop to the bottom of the ocean, what difference does it make who did what?"

"I suppose. Still, when the Coast Guard picked us up and Sam started flinging accusations, Emile never defended himself. I don't know if he blamed himself out of a sense of honor because the *Encounter* was his ship, or if he really believed he'd cut safety corners—or if he just didn't want to credit Sam's accusations with a response."

Riley shut her eyes. She thought she'd had all this worked out. That she'd done all her post-trauma work and she would never again feel this crawling sense of panic. Her narrow escape in the submersible, she realized, would be with her forever.

"Riley? Look, if this is too hard for you to talk about—"

"It's not. I'm fine." She took a breath, held it, let

it out slowly; she couldn't lose control when Sig had so much more at stake. Twins, a faltering marriage. "The question is, do I believe Sam's version of what happened to the *Encounter?* Do I believe Emile's arrogance and obsession with his work caused it to go down? The engine should have shut off. If the automatic safety features weren't working properly, if there'd been a crewman posted…" She turned, faced her sister. "I don't want to blame Emile, but the truth is, I don't know what happened to the *Encounter.*"

Sig frowned, stretched out on the couch, her shoes off. "It blew up, caught fire and sank for a reason. Five people died, Riley, including my father-in-law."

"Don't you think I know that? I was *there.*" She grabbed a small oak log, shoved it on the burning kindling, nearly smothering the flames. "It was an old ship, Sig. Unless we go out and dredge it up, we'll probably never know for sure what happened."

Sig was silent.

The fire was throwing off heat now, and Riley turned to her sister, could feel the warmth on her back. "I'm sorry. I don't mean to upset you—"

"I'm pregnant, I'm not sick. And I'm not fragile. Don't tiptoe around me, okay? If Sam…" Sig thought a moment, fidgeting, pulling at the fringe on her shawl. "If he was murdered, we have to assume someone would have a motive to kill him. What if he had proof the *Encounter* was sabotaged—or of criminal negligence, something?"

"What, and he brought it to Emile and Emile killed him?"

"I don't know. Maybe, maybe not. Maybe it was phony proof and Emile cracked, or maybe Sam came after him for revenge and Emile killed him in self-defense. Maybe Emile didn't have one damned thing to do with killing him. How the hell would I know?" She paused, eyes narrowed. "And how would you know?"

Riley kept her cool. "I've worked side by side with Emile since I turned thirteen. He didn't kill Sam. Sig, come on. You know he didn't."

"All right. Let's do it your way. For the sake of argument, let's eliminate Emile as a suspect. Let's say someone else killed Sam. Let's say Sam had evidence of neglect or sabotage—proof something went very wrong aboard the *Encounter* and it wasn't just one of those things, something beyond anyone's control."

"He just pinned it on the wrong person?"

"Right. What would he do with that kind of proof?"

Riley didn't hesitate. "He'd try to make a profit."

"He wouldn't go to the police?"

"No. When Sam railed to the Coast Guard and then the rest of the world about Emile, it wasn't for the sake of justice. It was for revenge, and to keep anyone from blaming him for what happened. I'm not saying he was evil or even particularly bad, he just looked out for himself."

"Until someone hit him on the head and let him drown."

Riley shuddered.

Sig pulled her shawl more tightly around her shoulders. "This is scary."

"Yep. I think I'll turn on another light."

She stopped halfway across the living room. "Did you hear that?"

"Hear what?"

Then, from outside, came a muttered curse in a voice that was distinctly male but unidentifiable, followed by heavy footsteps on the front porch.

"Grab the poker," Sig said, even as Riley reached for Emile's ancient blackened iron poker by the woodstove.

The door opened. Riley had her poker poised, ready for battle.

Straker walked in and shook his head. "I don't believe you two. The two of you put together don't have the sense of one hermit crab."

"Scare us to death, why don't you?" Riley didn't lower her poker. He filled the room with his presence, his broad shoulders and glower and total self-possession. "Why didn't you knock?"

"Because I was hoping someone had stolen your car and left you in a ditch somewhere." He bit off another curse, his gray eyes narrowed, unyielding. "Why the hell aren't you still in Camden?"

"We're trying to find Emile."

"I'm sure that's just what we all need—a pregnant woman and a know-it-all oceanographer out here in the wilderness searching for a man who doesn't want you to find him."

Riley lowered her poker a fraction of an inch, just

because it was heavy and she was tired. She doubted
he was too worried about her taking it to him, but she
wanted him to know she wasn't intimidated. "I wish
I'd never gone to your cottage to throw up."

"You didn't come there to throw up, you came
there for my help and good advice—which right now
is to go back to Camden."

"Obviously I was in shock or just out of my
mind." The poker went down another few inches, in
spite of her desire to do something productive with
it. This man drove her wild. She didn't know what it
was about him. "You belong on a deserted island,
Straker."

Sig wiggled her toes and leaned back against
Emile's ancient throw pillows. "You two fight it out.
I'm beat."

Her words didn't break the tension. Straker was
clearly in no mood to back down. He thought he had
the upper hand. Riley knew she was being obstinate,
but his presence had thrown her off balance, made
her hyperalert, aware—of him, herself. She noticed
the shape of his shoulders, the way his sweater fit over
his chest, the thick muscles in his thighs, the set of
his jaw and the cool, foglike gray of his eyes.

She couldn't control her attraction to him, couldn't
bank it down even when he was standing there yelling
at her, disgusted and cranky because she wasn't
marching to his tune.

He took three long steps across the room and
snatched the poker from her hand. "As if this would
do any good."

"It would if I used it," she grumbled.

She noticed the tensed muscles in his arms and shoulders as he smacked the poker back by the woodstove. The fire was going nicely now. It filled the room with the smell of burning oak, made the cottage homey, welcoming, less cold and empty. Yet she could feel the sprawling blackness beyond the flames and the glow of Emile's old lamps, out across the dark bay and the dark acres of the nature preserve. Straker wouldn't feel it. This was civilization compared to what he was used to.

He turned to her, no sign he was softening. "I take it you two plan to spend the night here."

"Good work, Straker. I guess they taught you deductive reasoning at Quantico."

She regretted her sarcasm almost immediately. What was the matter with her? But they must have taught him self-restraint, too, because he didn't react. "And tomorrow?"

"We don't know yet." She grabbed a birch log out of the wood box. "Don't you worry about us. Feel free to take all the room you need to maneuver. We don't want to cramp your style."

"You cramped my style when you paddled your kayak to the island for your damned picnic." He sighed, glancing around the old cottage. "I planned to stay on the island, but I could camp out here—"

"No!"

Sig sat up on one elbow, her eyebrows raised. "Why not? You know, Riley, if Sam really was murdered—well, I wouldn't mind having an FBI agent sleeping on the couch."

Riley shook her head, adamant. "I've had Straker under my feet for two nights. *I* need room to maneuver." She turned back to him, sensed he'd dipped into his last reserves of patience. He needed the island. She needed him on it. For once they were in sync. "Go on. We'll be fine. All your stuff's on the island or in my apartment. You don't even have a toothbrush."

"I don't like the idea of you two out here alone."

"We *like* it out here alone."

"Riley—"

"It's okay, Straker. Really. We'll be fine." She managed a sincere smile. "Thanks for checking on us."

He sighed. "All right. But if you need me—"

"We'll send up flares."

He clenched his teeth without a word, whipped around and marched back outside. The floor of the old cabin shook when he pounded down the front steps. Riley ran to the door and peeked outside, made sure he wasn't pitching a tent out on the rocks. She heard his boat, saw its lights, then watched it speed out across the starlit bay.

"Holy shit." Sig peeled off an afghan from the stack at the end of the couch and pulled it up over her. "You do get under that man's skin."

"He's up to something."

"Of course he's up to something. He's a frigging FBI agent."

"I hate him," Riley said, but her heart wasn't in it.

Sig grinned. "Ha! He's under your skin, too." She planted her feet firmly on the floor and stood, rubbing her lower back. "I always thought you'd end up with some expert in clams or porpoises or something, and here it is an FBI agent." She chuckled to herself. "John Straker no less. A son of the Stone Coast."

"I'm glad you're having a good laugh at my expense."

"It's not at your expense. If I weren't here, God knows what you two would be doing right now."

"Sig!"

"See?" She was smug. "You were thinking the same thing. I'll bet he was, too."

"Would it do any good for me to tell you you're way off track?"

"It would not."

Riley let her sister enjoy her victory. Arguing would only further convince her she was right. They left a light on downstairs—"for the bogeyman and the bathroom," Sig said—and collapsed under heaps of quilts in the twin beds in the loft.

But neither fell asleep quickly. Riley stared at the sloped, wood-paneled ceiling and listened to the ocean and the wind, imagined Straker alone on his tiny island and tried not to think about how much she wished she'd asked him to stay. He had her confused, aching with longings she didn't understand or care to explore.

She could hear Sig's bed creak as her sister turned

onto her side. Riley bit back tears. She wasn't being fair to Sig, either. She was holding back on her about Matt last night at Sam's, about this afternoon outside her apartment. It wasn't right. Sig deserved to know. Riley knew she was being protective—*over*protective, maybe—because of her sister's pregnancy. *I'm not sick.* But how much could Sig take?

Riley rolled over, facing her sister's bed in the darkness. "Sig, are you sure you should be here? I can take you back to Camden in the morning. It's not just that you're pregnant. You lost your father-in-law, your marriage is under tremendous strain and now you've got Sam's death and Emile." *And Matt*, Riley thought. *Who knows about him?*

"I'm fine. Trust me, will you?" But Sig's voice cracked, and she sobbed quietly, wretchedly, into her pillow, as if no one could hear.

Riley sat up, could see her sister's silhouette under the old quilts. She remembered the countless nights they'd slept up here, laughing and talking and arguing, nothing more serious at stake than whether the purple sea stars they'd found in a tide pool would go out with high tide.

"I saw Matt this afternoon." Riley kept her voice steady, matter-of-fact. "He was waiting for me outside my apartment. He's okay, Sig. Sam's death hasn't been easy on him, but he hasn't gone off the deep end. He's as stirred up as any of us about what's going on." She waited, but her sister didn't respond. "He wouldn't do anything deliberately to hurt you."

"Too late," came Sig's muffled voice.

Riley didn't know what to say. They weren't criers, she and her sister. Their parents and especially Emile had taught them to buck up and carry on, do what had to be done, no matter the pain, the hurt, the loss.

"Sig...I wish I knew what to say."

"There's nothing you can say." She sniffled, adjusted her pillow. "I'm not running anymore, Riley. I'm not hiding, and I'm not pretending everything's okay when it's not. I miss Bennett, I hate what's happened to Emile, I fear for him, I worry about Mom and Dad—and you. I'm having two babies. I can't afford not to look reality square in the eye."

Riley listened patiently, but she'd made up her mind. She was shoving Sig in the car and driving her back to Camden in the morning. Being at Emile's wasn't good for her. It wasn't helping anything.

Sig cleared her throat, got herself under control. "Matt wants to prove Emile was responsible for the *Encounter* and thus for Bennett's death. He says he wants justice, that in the end, it will be best for all of us—including Emile—if the truth is known."

"Look, we were just speculating about Sam and any proof. We were talking through our hats. There's no way to find out what really happened unless we raise the *Encounter*'s engine and have it analyzed. We all might have to learn to live with uncertainty. We'll probably never know the truth."

Sig didn't respond.

The wind gusted against the closed window. Riley imagined Straker alone on his island, felt a stab of pain as she interpreted her sister's silence, what she was thinking but not saying.

Suddenly hot and restless, she threw off a quilt. It was so damned dark, so quiet. Her sister's silence almost took on a life of its own.

"My God." Riley's voice croaked. She cleared her throat, licked dry lips. Suddenly Sig's behavior in recent months, Matt's behavior, her sister's decision to come up here to Emile's made sense. The pieces came together. "Sig, do you think Matt and Sam were working together to bring up the *Encounter*'s engine?"

"I don't know. It's at least a possibility."

"*Sig.*"

"I can't..." Her words were slurred, exhausted. "I can't think about this anymore tonight."

Riley was wide-awake now. She wanted to drag her sister downstairs, put on a pot of coffee and work out the dozen different scenarios running loose in her brain. Sort through them one by one. Come up with a plan of action.

But she forced herself to say, "It's okay. Get some sleep. We'll figure this out in the morning."

"I can feel the babies moving," Sig murmured.

Riley smiled, but she had to struggle to hold back her own tears. If Sam and Matt had been working together, then Matt's involvement was even deeper and more serious than she'd anticipated. He wasn't just latching on to Emile's disappearance, Straker, herself—he'd been involved *before* Sam Cassain's body turned up on Labreque Island.

She wondered if Special Agent Straker suspected anything. *No reading that particular mind.* Instead she concentrated on the wind, the ocean and the sound of her sister's breathing as she finally slept.

In the morning, it was as if their conversation had never taken place. Sig refused to discuss the possibility of Matt financing or otherwise working with Sam Cassain. "I was hormonal," she said. "I have no idea what Matt's up to."

She likewise refused to return to Camden, and Riley gave up, agreeing to Sig's suggestion they begin their search for their grandfather, or his trail, on the nature preserve. It was a stunning day. The acres of blueberry fields, bog, forest, sand, rock and coastline helped restore their spirits and energy. They set off along the shoreline, following trails, guiltily enjoying the peace and beauty of this beautiful stretch of New England coast.

But they didn't find Emile or any sign of him, so they drove into the pretty village of Winter Harbor for chowder. After lunch, they stopped in to see Lou Dorrman, who told them to go home.

"This isn't getting us anywhere," Sig said.

Riley sighed. "It feels like busywork, doesn't it?"

"That's why your sweetie Straker left us to it."

"He's a snake in the grass."

"No, he's just better at this sort of thing than you are, which I know you hate to admit. You rescue dolphins and whales. He catches bad guys."

"We have nothing in common," Riley said.

Sig gave a wicked grin. "That's part of the fun."

They dragged out Emile's old two-seater kayak and, Riley in front, Sig in back, paddled around the quiet, sparkling bay, visiting all their old haunts—except Labreque Island. That Riley deliberately avoided. But the nostalgia was too much for Sig, the peninsula packed with too many memories, too many triggers, and she started crying again.

Riley bit her tongue and said nothing, simply kept paddling. She couldn't swoop in to Sig's rescue. This was her hell, and it was ultimately why, Riley realized, her sister had come up here. Sig had to confront her demons and crawl, fight, scream, do whatever she had to do to free herself of their grip. Riley understood. It was one of the reasons she'd extended her weekend to come here herself. It was why she'd kayaked alone to Labreque Island.

"This is ridiculous," Sig moaned. "I'm *pathetic.*"

She swore, a long, colorful string of curse words that had her sounding more like her old self. Devil-may-care, say-anything, do-anything Sig St. Joe, who'd never cared about Matt Granger's money or Harvard education or family traditions, who'd just married him because she loved him. Never mind that she was almost five months pregnant with twins, that however much she'd loved Matt and still did, it might not be enough, she would endure, survive, *thrive.*

When she finished, Riley smiled. "Gee, Sig, that's two dollars for your mason jar."

"Two and a quarter," she said.

"Feel better?"

"Much. I *am* going to quit swearing, though. I won't be a foulmouthed mother."

"You're going to be a wonderful mother. May I make a suggestion? I say we have fishermen's platters for supper and a powwow tonight by the fire." Riley dipped her paddle into the shallow water, close to shore. Out ahead, the pink granite of Cadillac Mountain, the jewel of Mount Desert Island and Acadia National Park, stood out against a clear blue sky. "We need a Plan *B*."

"I agree," Sig said. "Just don't think you're sharing my platter. You can order your own."

Ten

Straker tied his boat up at Emile's dock. It was early evening, the sun low in the sky, the air cool and breezy. He had made up his mind to have a sensible conversation with the St. Joe sisters, but when he walked up to Emile's cottage, their car was gone.

He was not relieved. He knew they hadn't gone back to Camden. They were determined to find their grandfather.

He'd spotted them kayaking on the bay earlier in the afternoon, probably seeing if they could pick up Emile's trail. He doubted they'd accomplished any more than he had, which had its own set of dangers. Sitting idle, he imagined, was not something either sister did well.

Nor did he. Yet his own idleness had served its purpose. He'd spent the morning on the rocks where Riley had found Sam Cassain's body. He'd sat on a boulder and listened to the wind and the tide, and he'd relaxed his mind, stopped fighting the questions and frustrations and temptations.

Had he missed something?

That was the question that washed over him again and again. Somehow, some way, Sam Cassain's body had ended up on Labreque Island while he, an experienced FBI agent, was there. Had he missed a noise, a light, a movement he didn't remember—something from the moment the body was delivered onto the island?

Emile was right. The currents, happenstance, hadn't washed Cassain ashore. Someone had brought him there. His murderer; someone who'd found him dead and panicked; someone who'd made a cold, calculated decision to take his body to the island to embarrass Emile or throw suspicion on him.

Cassain drowned.

Yes. He'd drowned. *After* taking a hit on the head. The hit wasn't an accident. He could have fallen in the water; someone could have pushed him; someone could have found him there, already dead, and chosen not to be the one to explain his death to the authorities.

No specific scenario had come to Straker as he'd sat out on the rocks. He had no answers, no solutions, no deep insights to offer, simply a clear sense of resolve. Sam Cassain's death, the placement of his body on Labreque Island, had been a violation of Straker's six months there, maybe of the island itself. It was time to put things right.

That afternoon, he'd found his father and a few other lobstermen at one of the lobster pounds. They had no illusions he'd come out just to chat. They teased him about giving up the FBI to catch lobster, asked—unsuccessfully—to see the scars from his bullet wounds, reminded him of various close encounters he'd had with the law before becoming a "lawman" himself. Like he was Wyatt Earp. Without much subtlety, he'd steered their talk to the days prior to Sam Cassain's body turning up on the island. Cassain was another seaman, and they took his death personally, knew all about the burning and sinking of the *Encounter*, the deaths of the crew and philanthropist Bennett Granger. Several of them, including Straker's father, had known Bennett from his decades of summers on Mount Desert Island to the south and his long collaboration with Emile.

And what emerged from their talk had Straker here now, standing in Emile's dirt driveway. One of the lobstermen, an old man, older even than Emile, had seen the Granger yacht on the bay early in the week. "It was the small one," he'd said, "not the big one. I think it's the son's boat."

Matthew Granger.

Straker heard a car out on the main road. In another minute, Lou Dorrman pulled into the driveway and rolled down his window. "Riley and her sister are in town having supper. I saw your car down by the harbor. You want a lift?"

Straker hadn't expected to need his car. When he'd headed to Boston, he'd left his boat in his father's care. Last night, before barging in on Riley and Sig, he'd fetched his boat, leaving his car with his parents.

"Thanks," he said, and climbed in. He and Dorrman had their differences, but a ride was a ride. And he needed to see Sig, if not her little sister.

"I thought at first this body'd lead back to you," Dorrman said, his eyes on the road. "Figured you'd brought terrorists or some damned thing out here. Turns out it leads back to Emile."

It was as close to an apology as Straker was going to get, and more than he'd expected. "You've got your hands full."

"Yeah." The downeast accent was natural to Dorrman; he'd never left home, probably had grown up wanting to be sheriff. "Having those two women staying at Emile's isn't helping. Riley's a loose cannon. Always has been. The two together—well, they make me nervous."

Straker understood, but he kept his mouth shut.

"If you can talk them into going home, you'd be doing me a favor."

"Same here."

Dorrman dropped him off at a popular village restaurant that served heaping plates of fried fish, with a salad bar, baked potatoes, fries, onion rings, ten kinds of pies for dessert. The wind was picking up, the sun going down fast. Straker debated going in for a bowl of haddock chowder, but Riley and Sig emerged, laughing.

"I swear," Riley said, "I'm never touching another piece of fried food as long as I live."

Sig patted her rounded stomach. She wore an oversize hockey shirt and stretchy pants, but still managed to walk with a natural elegance. "I don't think I've ever eaten that much. A *whole* fishermen's platter. I deserve heartburn!''

Straker hung back while they got into Riley's car, with its Boston Center for Oceanographic Studies sticker and stuffed whale in the rear window. She had on slim pants and an anorak, her fit body and quick movements packed with energy and intensity. He remembered their kiss, the feel of her hand on him. They'd been on dangerous ground right from the beginning, he and Riley St. Joe. She wasn't one to crumple or go all meek with him. She was no china doll. She was a woman of strength, conviction, passion, great loyalty. She didn't make life easy on the people who loved her.

Finally he walked over and tapped on her window, which was half-open. She jumped, then groaned when she saw him. ''I thought you were still off doing your Robinson Crusoe bit.''

''You should pay more attention to your surroundings. What if it hadn't been me tapping on your window?''

''Like it's any big relief it *is* you. For heaven's sake, I just had a fish dinner in a quiet little village on the Maine coast. I'm not worried about thugs lurking in the bushes.''

He leaned in closer. ''You weren't worried about finding a dead man on your picnic, either.''

She went just a little pale. ''You're disgusting.''

''Shoot the messenger,'' he said.

Sig smiled at him from the passenger seat. ''Don't tempt her, Straker. She's probably got a .38 in the glove compartment. Now, if you two don't mind, I made a pig of myself, and I'd like to get back and walk off my dinner.''

"Fine with me." He pulled open the rear door and climbed in. "You can give me a ride."

Riley glanced over her shoulder at him, said calmly, "You've your nerve, you know that?"

He grinned. "I've done a few scarier things than get in the car. Not many, but a few."

She wasn't embarrassed or intimidated, and she wasn't about to back down. But she wasn't mad, either. Her eyes sparked, and she licked her lips. He knew she was imagining what they could be doing together in the back seat. She'd never admit it, but for once they were on the same wavelength.

"Oh, shit," Sig mumbled, sinking low in her seat.

"Sig? Riley?" Matt Granger was crossing the street to the small parking lot. He swore to himself. "Son of a bitch."

Sig glanced into the back seat. She was very pale. "Straker—quick, toss me that blanket."

He grabbed a fleece throw off the floor and shoved it over the top of the seat. She took it gratefully, unfurled it and buried herself under it as best she could.

"What do you want me to do?" Riley asked her.

"Get us out of here."

He could hear Riley fumbling for her keys. These two were as different as night and day, Straker thought, but they'd go to the ends of the earth for each other. If Sig didn't want her husband to know she was pregnant, Riley would back her up.

It was a damned conspiracy, but Matt Granger was helpless in the face of it. He stormed around to Sig's window, which was partway down. Taking no pains to be subtle, she reached up and locked her door. In Granger's position, Straker didn't know what he'd do. Push the car into a ditch, for starters. Keep these two put for ten minutes, anyway.

If Granger had ever possessed the same manners and cool bearing as his older sister, they were long gone. He looked ready to rip the window out and smash it onto the parking lot. "Goddamn you two— what the hell do you think you're doing?"

That had been Straker's line last night. Hadn't done him much good.

Sig smiled, snottily cool, in control. "Well, seeing how you asked so nicely, and so clearly have our best interests at heart, I'll tell you. We're just coming from dinner. We both had the fishermen's platter. I had apple pie for dessert, Riley abstained." She paused a beat. "Anything else?"

Every muscle and nerve ending in Granger's body went nuts. Straker could see it happen. He understood. These women would drive any man over the edge. A day by himself on an island hadn't exorcised Riley from his mind, not to mention his body.

"Go back to Camden," Granger said through clenched teeth. "Paint."

Sig yawned. "I don't take orders very well. That's one reason I'm a painter." She snuggled down into her fleece throw. "*You* go home, Matt. You have no reason at all to be here. My grandfather's family goes back generations in this area. I spent summers here as a child.''

Granger hissed through his teeth. "Sig, goddamn it—''

"Riley came up for the weekend,'' she continued, not giving him one millimeter. "We decided to spend some time together.''

This was bullshit, of course, and Granger knew it. He leaned as far into the car as he could manage without tearing off the door. "You two are trying to find Emile. You're in over your heads. He's dangerous and possibly insane. If anything happens to you, it's not going to be on my conscience.''

"Riley, start the car.'' Sig breathed in deeply, taking charge. "If my husband doesn't move back, run over his feet.''

Granger pounded the roof of the car. "Goddamn it, Sig, you won't listen!''

"I'd listen if you talked.'' She was furious now, biting out her words. "But you don't. You just want everything your way. You're so damned eaten up with your self-righteous anger...'' She flopped back against her seat. "Riley, let's go.''

Riley turned the ignition.

She wasn't fast enough for her sister. *"Now.''*

"I'm going, I'm going....''

Granger kicked the door. He was speechless with rage, fear, a tangle of emotions. Straker felt a pang of sympathy for him.

"Riley!'' Sig urged. An angle of streetlight caught her face, the high cheekbones, the long, straight nose.

Straker understood her urgency. He had seen the same green look on her little sister just a few days ago. Sig had her teeth clenched, her fingers tight on the throw. "Step on the damned gas."

Straker leaned forward, one hand on the seat behind Riley's head. "Go," he told her. "Granger'll move back."

"Straker? What the fuck—" Matt started to say.

But Riley said, "Stand back, Matt," and hit the gas.

Sig lasted a mile. When Riley hit a bump in the road, Straker told her to pull over. Her sister almost fell out of the car. He jumped out after her and held on to her while she emptied her stomach on the side of the road, sobbing, swearing, screaming in frustration and agony.

Riley paced behind them with a water bottle and the fleece throw. When Sig finished, mumbling apologies, crying, he and Riley dabbed her face with water, wrapped her in the blanket and helped her lie down in the back seat. Her teeth chattered. She clung to the blanket, sobbing for her husband.

"Maybe I should go find Matt and tell him everything," Riley said. "I don't know how much more of this she can stand. He loves her. I'm sure of it."

Straker remembered the word from the lobster boats. Matt Granger was in deep, probably over his head, too. On some level, Sig knew, feared it, and that was why she was here. "Maybe you just shouldn't meddle."

Riley didn't take offense. She sighed, the strain

catching up with her. "You're right. For a minute back there, I thought she'd hit the gas pedal or grab the wheel and run him over. Straker, they were so happy. Until last year—"

"Come on." He touched her shoulder. "We need to get her back to Emile's."

"Should she see a doctor?"

Sig groaned in the dark. "I'm okay, goddamn it. It was the scallops. I never should have eaten the frigging scallops."

It was another three minutes back to Emile's. The air was cool and crisp, the water dark. A stiff breeze gusted, making the spruce trees creak and sway. Sig tried to walk, but she was shivering, wobbly, and finally Straker just scooped her up. Of course she swore. She was an ungrateful St. Joe. But she clung to him, too, and when he laid her in one of the twin beds upstairs, she squeezed his hand.

"Are you sure you're all right?" he asked. "We can get you to a doctor."

"I'm fine." She managed a weak smile. "I threw up like that a lot in the first few weeks."

Pregnant and alone. If Granger knew, what would he do? That was what Sig couldn't face. Straker knew she was afraid if Matt found out she was pregnant, he still wouldn't end his vendetta against her grandfather. She couldn't count on him. His father's death had shattered the trust between them.

Riley covered her sister with old quilts, tucked them carefully around her. "Can I get you anything? A cup of tea...water..." But Sig was almost asleep, and Riley straightened, her hair sticking out, dark circles under her eyes. "I guess we should let her sleep."

Straker built a fire in Emile's woodstove while Riley paced. He could see that sharp mind of hers working. She had her arms crossed on her breasts and looked worried, frustrated, boiling over with unchanneled energy.

Finally, she stopped. Her cheeks were pale, her eyes almost black. She took a breath. "Thank you."

Straker stood in front of the woodstove, the fire crackling, hot against his back. She was softening, but he wasn't. He couldn't. This was his opening, and he had to seize it. "I don't want your thanks. I want you and Sig to pack up in the morning and get the hell out of here. Go back to your mother's, go back to Boston. You two must have friends who'd take you in for a few days."

To his surprise, she nodded. "I was just thinking the same thing. Sig..." She blinked rapidly, holding back tears. "What does Matt think he's doing? Doesn't he know she's—can't he *tell?*"

"He knows something's wrong, but he thinks it's him. The man's caught up in his own hell right now. He can't see your sister is, too."

"That's no excuse."

"From your point of view, no, it's not."

She sighed, looking exhausted. "I'm in no mood to be reasonable."

He smiled. "That's a mood I know well."

With another sigh, she ran a hand through her hair,

muttered about needing air and suddenly shot outside. Straker could hear her race down the steps, and by the time he'd put another log on the fire and followed her out, she was charging toward the water.

The wind had picked up, howling in steady gusts. He walked at a deliberate pace, debating whether it would be best to climb into his boat and head on back to the island. Riley stormed off to the end of the dock, her arms crossed against the cold, her jaw set.

"You want to be alone?" he asked, coming up behind her.

She turned slightly. "I want…" She stopped, swallowed, caught her breath. "I want this all to go away. I want to toast marshmallows on the fire, I want Sig's babies to have a chance at a happy life, I want Emile…" She couldn't go on. She shifted back toward the water, dark and churning in the wind.

Straker said nothing. He knew what it was to have the world close in on him. His answer had been Labreque Island, six months of solitude, of a simple, if hard, life. If he didn't do it, it didn't get done. If he was socked in with fog for days on end, there was no running down to the store for milk and videos. There had been days—weeks—when he'd thought he wouldn't come out of his exile sane or whole, able ever again to connect with another human being.

Riley suddenly leaned against him, her arms still tightly crossed on her chest, her gaze still on the bay. Her body was warm, and her hair smelled of ocean and a citrusy shampoo. The months of isolation welled up in him, seized him with an urgency so ferocious it took his breath away. He wanted her. He ached with it, burned with it.

She turned into him, draped her hands around his neck, and he knew she couldn't possibly know what he was feeling, thinking, fighting back. She whispered, "Straker, I swear I don't know what I'm doing," even as she let her mouth find his, tentatively, as if she were testing her own resolve, or sanity.

The taste of her seared through him, but he knew he was dangerous, knew he had to exert his considerable willpower over the rest of him. One slender hand drifted over his shoulder. It might as well have been on fire. His pulse raced; need surged through him. He wanted to make love to her there, then, on the old wooden dock. His head, his soul, ached with the taste of her, the possibilities.

But he controlled the urge to push and push hard, sensed that what she wanted from him was tenderness, softness, a kiss that restored and gave, when all he wanted was to take and demand, end this pounding need.

She opened her mouth to his, took herself onto very dangerous ground. Restraint was impossible. Her fingers intertwined with his, and she placed his hand on her breast, a soft swell covered in layers of fabric he imagined tearing away. In another two seconds, he would. The sand had run out of the hourglass.

Instinctively, she must have known. She pulled back. She was breathing hard, her dark eyes shining. He was thinking about the fire in Emile's woodstove, the long, comfortable couch, the blankets and cushions, the braided rug on the floor. Plenty of places to make love. They could go on all night, into the morning, until whenever Sig staggered down from the loft.

Riley smiled, touched a finger to the scar she'd given him above his eye. "I was a pretty good shot, wasn't I?"

"I let you hit me."

Finally a spark of humor lit her eyes. But it faded quickly, and she kissed him lightly, softly. "I'll take care of Sig. You find Emile, find my brother-in-law." Her eyes were black now, deadly serious. "Stop them."

She turned abruptly and ran off the dock, up the dark road. She didn't glance back, didn't hesitate. Straker kicked a loose board in the dock. He could have ripped out every board and nail and post, flung the whole damned mess into the ocean.

Honor and restraint, he thought bitterly, had got him exactly nothing. A perfectly good fire, a perfectly good woman, and here he was, standing alone in the cold and the dark.

Sig awoke in a panic. Her heart was racing, and she couldn't breathe. Nightmares. She'd dreamed of Matt. Dangerous dreams, frightening dreams. She needed air, a drink of water. Her head ached. Dehydration. She'd thrown up everything in her stomach.

Straker...he'd been damned decent. Riley was such an ass about him. Obviously he was smitten with her, even if she drove him crazy.

Air...she needed to breathe.

"Sig."

"Huh?"

"Sig."

Riley's voice. Determined, fighting panic. She was shaking her. "Stop," Sig said, feeling cranky. "That hurts."

"Sig, we need to get out of here. The place is on fire."

"Fire?" She sat up, her head spinning, pounding, her stomach reeling. Her sister stood close, her fear palpable. "Riley, you must be having a nightmare. There's no—"

"We don't have time! Get up. I can't carry you. You're too tall."

"Carry me—why would—" She stopped, could smell the smoke, could see it curling up the stairs. She saw Riley's desperate look in the dark. Heard the crackle and spark of flames downstairs. She was wide-awake now. This was no nightmare. "Oh my God."

Riley yanked the quilts off her. "We can make it through the window."

"I don't know…I…*Riley, I can't breathe!*"

"Come on, Sig. You can do it."

Sig dropped her feet to the floor. She had on socks. Straker and Riley had put her to bed in her clothes. She could feel the pull of skin over her bulging stomach. The babies were quiet. "I don't want to faint," she mumbled, and rose carefully. Riley had one hand on her elbow, steadying her.

"I've got to push the screen out."

Sig gave her a shove. "Go."

She followed her sister, crouching down, feeling the fire sucking the oxygen out of the small cottage. It was like a being, oozing, terrorizing. She heard the screen crash onto the woodshed roof below the loft window. The cold, clean air drew the smoke.

Riley coughed, grabbed Sig. "You first."

"No!"

"Don't argue with me."

Sig choked for air. "My babies...I'm so big...."

"You're not that big. You have to do this, Sig. Your babies won't have a chance if you don't. Jump onto the woodshed. Then slide off. Like when we were kids." Riley squeezed her. *"Go."*

If she didn't, they'd both die up here. Staving off her panic, Sig pulled herself up onto the sill window-washer style, then dragged one leg over, until she was three-quarters out, the woodshed six or seven feet under her. She had to get the other leg out. Any further along in her pregnancy, any taller, and she wouldn't have fit. Riley was there, helping her.

"Stand back," Sig said. "I don't want to kick you in the head and knock you out."

Riley took a step back. Sig could hardly make her out with the dark, the smoke.

"You're next. You understand me, Riley?"

"No, I'm going to stay up here and fry."

In a single, unartful movement, Sig forced her stray leg over the sill, and before she could get tangled up, sprawled forward, landing hard on her feet on the cold, scratchy shingles of the woodshed roof. Pain shot up from her ankle, and her knees buckled, but she rolled out of the way, waiting for Riley to drop beside her.

Sig heard glass exploding, saw the glow of flames, smoke pouring from the loft window. She coughed, tasting the acrid smoke. Where the hell was her sister?

"Riley!"

"I'm coming. One, two, three..."

And she landed like a panther, her dark eyes gleaming and wild. She was totally focused, just as Sig remembered on the few times she'd joined her at a whale stranding.

"You have to jump to the ground now, Sig."

Her head spun, sparks of light flashed, followed by passing waves of darkness. Everything seemed far away. *You have to jump off this woodshed.* It was a voice. She didn't know where it was coming from. Riley? Where was Riley?

"Matt."

Suddenly her sister's face was in hers. She was screaming at her. "You are going to jump off this fucking roof." Riley almost never swore. "Do you hear me? If you don't, I'm going to push you."

"Something's wrong," Sig mumbled.

"I know. Emile's cottage is on fire."

"With me. Something's wrong with me."

"It'll be okay, Sig." Riley had her by the shoulders, was scooting her down to the edge of the roof. "Listen, I can hear the fire engines. Music to our ears, isn't it? Someone must have spotted the flames."

"I can't jump. I can't think...."

"Sig, listen to me. I'm not going to count. I'm going to say 'jump!' and you're going to jump." She gave her half a beat. *"Jump."*

Sig could feel the roof disappearing under her. She didn't know if she'd jumped, if Riley had pushed her, if she'd simply fallen.

They landed almost simultaneously. Sig felt another sharp pain shoot up from her ankle and she sank to the ground. The grass was cold, damp, smelled of earth and ocean.

Riley, little sister Riley, tried to lift her from the hips, was crying, cajoling, "Sig, goddamn it, we have to get away from the cottage, it's on fire," until a voice—a man's voice, not Matt's—told her to move aside.

Sig couldn't stay on her feet.

Strong, firm hands took hold of her. She could smell smoke, her own acrid sweat, could hear the fire, thought she could even hear the smoke. She tried to claw her way to full awareness, kept losing her grip, falling back.

"My babies," she whispered, sinking again.

Eleven

They took Riley's car to the hospital in Ellsworth. Straker drove. Riley sat rigidly beside him, unable to make herself look back at Emile's burning cottage, cry, even speak. She'd managed to pull on hiking pants before clearing out of the loft with Sig, but there'd been no time for car keys, pocketbooks, anything. Luckily, she had an extra key taped inside her glove compartment.

Sig was already on her way to the hospital by ambulance. Lou Dorrman was meeting them there. He had questions, he'd said when he arrived at Emile's with the volunteer firefighters. A lot of questions. Sig had collapsed, semiconscious, incoherent, when Straker had carried her off. The woodshed had caught fire seconds later.

"If you hadn't shown up..."

Riley's words sounded unintelligible to her, but Straker, his eyes pinned on the long, dark, straight road, said, "I did show up."

The EMTs had taken over, put Sig on oxygen and

an IV as Riley hung over them, warned them her sister was almost five months pregnant with twins, aching to do something to help.

Her hands were blackened from smoke and soot, felt cold and stiff as she clasped them together on her lap. She stank of smoke. Her heart was racing, but she was very still, every muscle tensed against shaking, against a rush of emotion she knew she would never control if she let it slip through her defenses. She couldn't fall apart. Not now. Her sister needed her.

"How did you know to come?" she asked.

"I saw the glow of the flames in the sky. It had to be a fire."

"You called it in?"

He nodded. "I used the radio in my boat."

"Thanks."

He'd arrived on the scene just as she and Sig leaped off the woodshed roof. His training had kicked into gear, the tight control, the crisp professionalism. He'd dealt with the firefighters, the police, the EMTs, informed Sheriff Dorrman they were following Sig to the hospital. For once, Riley thought, she and Straker weren't at cross-purposes—but she didn't want to get ahead of herself. Right now, her interests dovetailed with his. When they didn't, so much for being allies.

"Thank God you didn't stay tonight." Her voice was distant, almost as if it were coming from the back seat. "You'd have been downstairs where the fire started."

"We might have caught it in time."

She shut her eyes. *We.* As if she'd have stayed downstairs with him. But whatever Straker was to her, at least he was there. Sig was so damned alone. Married, pregnant with twins, but alone.

Not, Riley amended, that she and Straker were a pair in the making. After months of isolation and recuperation, of course he'd have at her when he got the chance. It wasn't a ringing endorsement of her attractions, but a practical, objective look at the facts that dictated that conclusion. This was John Straker. He'd never liked her. She wasn't his type. The sexual electricity he generated just proved what all that time alone could do to a man.

As for herself, she had no explanation. The stress of finding Sam Cassain's body, Emile's disappearance? She didn't know.

And yet earlier on the dock, she'd sensed the possibility of more between them than sex. That, she knew, was dangerous thinking. There was no question he wanted sex. He was physical, earthy, unleashed after many long months of self-denial. It was a tough combination to resist, and she found herself increasingly unable—unwilling—to bother trying. But expecting anything else from him beyond hot, torrid sex was insanity on her part. She wasn't one for self-delusion.

She felt a twinge of guilt at her train of thought. It was so much easier to think about going to bed with Straker than about fires and sirens and her and Sig's narrow escape.

Riley twisted her hands together and blurted, "Sig

thinks Matt might have financed Sam Cassain to find
the *Encounter* and bring up its engine. That's where
the fire on the ship started.''

Straker nodded without surprise. "Makes sense."

"He and Sam couldn't have done it alone. They
must have left a trail."

He downshifted, turned into the hospital driveway.
"If they did, Emile knows. That's why he took off."

Riley fell back against the seat. "He's crazy."

Straker pulled up to the emergency room. "Can
you walk?"

"Of course I can walk."

But when she hit the sidewalk, her legs went out
from under her without warning, and for a mortifying
second she thought she might pass out. Some idiot
saw her and called for a stretcher.

Straker came around the car and shook his head.
"Forget the stretcher. You'd have to staple-gun her
to it."

But once inside, he turned her over to a very intense young doctor and told him to check her out.
Straker had that FBI air of authority about him, and
Riley looked like hell. Not a good combination. He
slipped off to see about Sig while the doctor checked
her blood pressure, eyes, nose, mouth, lungs. Any
bruises or sprains or pain from jumping? Her right
forearm was scraped and bloody. She hadn't noticed.
He had a nurse clean and bandage it.

"My sister," Riley said. "How is she?"

"The doctors are with her."

"What does that mean?"

It meant she'd have to wait. She staggered back to the waiting room, and after a few minutes, Straker joined her. He shoved a bottle of water at her. "Drink up. They won't let anyone see Sig yet. I called your mother. Your father's there, too. They're on their way."

"They must be out of their minds with worry."

"The hospital's calling Caroline Granger on Mount Desert."

Riley nodded dully. "She's up for the weekend. Abigail and Henry are there, too."

"Then that saves you from having to tell Matt."

She bristled. "I'm not telling that son of a bitch anything. The hospital shouldn't, either."

Straker's eyes went dark. "Sig's his wife. If they're not divorced, the medical staff won't really have any choice."

"For all I know he's the one who set Emile's place on fire!"

Straker took her by the shoulders and pushed her, not that gently, onto a chair. "You don't believe that."

"Do *not* tell me what I believe and don't believe."

"Okay. *I* don't believe it."

She started to shake. She was exhausted, irritable, smelled like a chimney. Here she was, so glad to have Straker with her, and she was barking at him. But her sister was hurting, and the only real home Riley had known as a child had just been torched. When she'd smelled the smoke, she'd assumed she'd messed up the dampers on the woodstove. She'd pulled on hiking pants and slipped on her sneakers before realizing it wasn't that simple.

"I felt the fire," she said. "I was bending down to tie my shoes, and I *knew*. I can't explain it."

"You don't have to. It happens all the time. Somehow you put together the danger signs on an instinctive level, before they register in your conscious mind."

"I was afraid Sig wouldn't make it through the window. She's tall, and her stomach—"

"She did make it."

"I had to yell at her. She was still so done in from throwing up."

Riley couldn't hold it in anymore. She couldn't keep up the fight. She sank her head into her hands and cried, sobbed, coughed, choked. She smeared black gunk over her face.

When she'd finished crying, Straker took her water bottle and dampened a couple of tissues for her. She wiped her face and hands, blew her nose. "I'm a mess."

"That's the least of your problems."

He wasn't going to pull any punches. And he was right. She flopped back against her chair. "I want to see Sig."

Lou Dorrman arrived, and Straker stood back while the sheriff had Riley tell him about her night, start to finish. She didn't volunteer anything about her brother-in-law showing up after dinner, and Dorrman didn't ask. When she finished, he turned to Straker, who calmly explained how he'd come upon the fire just as the St. Joe sisters were leaping off the woodshed roof.

"Looks like we have a firebug on our hands," the sheriff said. "Sam Cassain's place burned down the other night. Now Emile's."

"Any evidence they're related?" Straker asked.

"We got the fire out before Emile's woodshed burned completely, found suspicious materials tucked off in the far corner. He has a nice selection of firebug favorites. Linseed oil, rags, beakers, candles, matches, string, an old-fashioned alarm clock." Dorrman shook his head. "It doesn't look good."

Riley shot to her feet. "That's insane. Someone's setting him up."

The sheriff was unmoved. "Your grandpa needs to come in and explain himself."

"You can't possibly believe Emile would set his own place on fire!" She paused, tried to calm herself. Shouting wasn't going to help the situation. "Sheriff, you've known my grandfather for years. He wouldn't do something like that."

"The state police are involved. It's not like what I think or don't think's going to make a difference. They have to go by the evidence." His cop gaze settled on Riley. "We all do."

"But you have to look at the evidence with some degree of common sense."

"You talk to your FBI friend here," Dorrman said. "He'll tell you all about evidence. Now, I know you're looking for Emile. I'm going to tell you this once and only once. You listening?"

She sighed, nodded. Even her skin tingled with the frustration boiling through her.

"If you find him and don't tell us, you're going to be in a whole heap of trouble." He paused, let his words sink in. "That's clear enough, isn't it?"

"You *know* Emile's not your man." She crossed her arms over her chest as if to keep herself from flying apart. "He didn't kill Sam, and he didn't set those fires. It's just not possible."

"Then let him talk to the investigators, straighten everything out." Dorrman's tone said he was finished arguing with her and she'd better figure that out before he lost patience. The trauma of jumping out of a burning building with her pregnant sister would only excuse so much. He yielded slightly. "How's your sister?"

"I'm still trying to find out."

He nodded. "I'll talk to her later. Hope she's okay."

He left, and Riley dropped back onto a chair next to Straker. "You trying to make yourself disappear?"

"Emergency rooms aren't my favorite place. How're you doing?"

"Okay, I guess." She gulped in air, trying not to shake. "I need to see about Sig."

"Go ahead."

But as she got to her feet, Caroline arrived, with Abigail and Henry right behind her. "Oh, Riley—my God! Are you all right? We couldn't just sit out there and wait." Caroline took in Riley's soot and scrapes, her tear-streaked face. "We had to come. Is there anything we can do?"

Riley shook her head. "Thanks for being here."

"No thanks are necessary." She dipped into her expensive handbag and pulled out a handful of individually wrapped, lemon-scented wipes, which she tucked into Riley's palm. She gave a comforting smile. "You look as if you've stepped out of the pages of a Dickens novel."

Abigail was fighting off tears. She asked about Sig, and Henry promised to find out what was going on. Straker, on his feet, started to pace. Riley knew the inaction was getting to him, just being in a hospital again after his ordeal six months ago.

"I'm sorry, Henry," she said. "I know you wanted me to get far away from trouble, and here I've just jumped from a burning building."

"We'll worry about that later," he said. "The important thing is that you and your sister are all right."

Facing Henry Armistead, however, was nothing compared to facing Mara Labreque St. Joe. She burst into the waiting room with the air of a woman who'd flown up the coast on a broomstick. She was disheveled, frantic, refused to wait for anyone to tell her where to find her daughter. She grabbed Riley and took off into the treatment rooms, muttering, "Damn Emile, *damn him.*"

"Mom, I should warn you. Sig's pregnant."

"Damn it, I know she's pregnant! I have eyes in my head!"

"She's having twins," Riley added.

Her mother faltered. Her dark eyes shone. Her lower lip trembled, but she rallied. She turned on Riley as if she were Emile's clone. "And you let her come up here with you? The least you could have done was stay in a motel. You didn't have to stay at the cottage. Damn it, Riley, what were you thinking?"

"Mara." Richard St. Joe eased in behind them. "Riley's been through a rough time tonight, too."

"I know, I know, I'm sorry...." She put a hand on Riley's cheek, tried to smile through her tears. "You're okay?"

"I'm fine, Mom."

"I spoke to a doctor," her father said. "She said Sig's doing well. She sprained an ankle and had some smoke inhalation, and she's dehydrated."

"Can we see her?" Mara asked.

"Yes, but she's asleep right now. They want to get her into a regular room and keep her at least until morning."

"I want to see her," Mara insisted.

Richard nodded. "I know. Me, too."

A nurse escorted the three of them to Sig's treatment room. She was asleep on her side under a thin blanket, her pregnancy obvious even to someone who wasn't looking for it. She was still hooked up to an IV but had been taken off oxygen. Riley stood back while her parents came to terms with the reality of how close they'd come to losing not one daughter this time, but two.

"Come on," Richard said, putting an arm around

his wife, "I'll buy you a cup of coffee. I'm not going anywhere until she wakes up and I hear her voice. Riley?" He attempted a smile. "You look like you could use a whole pot of coffee."

"I'll be along."

"You're sure?"

She nodded. "Tell the rest of the crowd Sig's okay, will you? Then send them home. Henry's ready to fire me as it is." She breathed in. "Forget Straker. It won't matter what you tell him. He's going to do what he's going to do."

"He's always been that way," her mother said.

After they left, Riley moved next to her sister and tried to let the relief she knew she should be feeling register. Her *mind* was all set: Sig was okay. She hadn't died. She hadn't lost her babies. Intellectually, Riley could grasp those basic facts.

But the rest of her was still in battle mode. She was tense and shaken, her guard up. This was her sister, and she'd nearly lost her tonight. She remembered Sig after the *Encounter*, the mix of horror and relief as she'd faced her father-in-law's death and the accusations over Emile's culpability.

Her mother was right, Riley thought. She was guilty as charged. She never should have come up here with Sig, despite the fact that her sister had a mind of her own and preferred to make her own decisions.

"*Jesus.*"

She spun around. Matt was frozen in the doorway, white-faced. He stared at his wife. Riley shot over to him, put a palm on his chest. "Don't you dare go berserk on her. Do you understand? If you do, I swear I'll get the sheriff in here and have him haul you off."

His very blue eyes settled on Riley in confusion. The fury of earlier in the evening was gone. "Riley— my God, what happened? I saw Abigail. She said Sig's okay, you two were in Emile's cottage when it caught fire."

"We had to bail out the loft window. It was rougher on Sig than me."

He tried to take another step toward her bed, but Riley still had her palm on his chest and moved with him. He looked at her. "What? For God's sake, I'm not a maniac. Sig and I have our problems, but she's my wife."

"And she's my sister. If you do anything to upset her, Granger, you'll have me to answer to. I don't care if I'm a foot shorter and a gazillion dollars poorer. I will strike you down. No matter what. Understood?"

"Riley, what the hell are you talking about? I know you've had a shock, but—"

He stopped. He went still, his gaze riveted on his wife. Riley held her breath, waiting. If possible, he turned even paler. The fine lines at the corners of his eyes stood out, his mouth was drawn, and she saw touches of gray in the stubble of beard on his patrician jaw.

She let her hand drop away. He moved forward, slowly, and as much as Riley knew this wasn't any of her business, she couldn't leave. Her brother-in-law had behaved miserably, even bizarrely, for the better part of a year. A man was dead, two fires unexplained. She couldn't rely on Matt's good sense, his love of her sister. She had to make sure he didn't do anything stupid.

"Sig." He spoke in a croaking whisper, placed a hand gently on her swollen abdomen. "Jesus, Sig."

Riley shrank back to the door. She felt like a voyeur. "You really didn't know?"

He shook his head, not taking his eyes off his wife.

"She hasn't told anyone. She didn't even tell me, but I figured it out. She went to great lengths to keep you from finding out."

"Why?"

He really didn't get it. Riley decided this wasn't the time to point out what a jackass he'd been for months on end. "Would it have changed anything?"

"I love Sig. I'd die for her."

"Yeah, well, tonight she almost died for you."

It was a damned, stupid, inconsiderate thing to say, but it had been a hell of a night and Riley instantly forgave herself. Matt, however, wasn't in a similar frame of mind. He shot her a black look. "What's that supposed to mean?"

"It means," Straker said behind her, "that sucking in a couple of lungfulls of smoke didn't do anything for her big mouth. Come on, Granger. You and I need to talk."

"I want to stay with my wife."

Riley gritted her teeth. As if Matt had any damned *right*. And who was Straker to barge in and take over?

She could feel her knees starting to shake again. She wanted to slap them both. She was indignant, *furious*. Yet some part of her warned her she was done in, getting more unreasonable by the minute, that stress and fear and all the damned smoke she'd sucked in were making her irrational.

"They've got a room for her," Straker said. "Let them get her settled."

Reluctantly, Matt nodded. He leaned over and kissed Sig gently, touched her hair, her stomach once more. And he went quietly, without a parting glance at Riley.

Straker hung back a moment and thrust a finger at her. "You. Sit down before you collapse. I'll be back."

He left. She pulled up a chair to her sister's bed and plopped down, and not because Straker had told her to. Another minute on her feet and she'd collapse and end up on an IV herself.

Sig opened an eye. "He's gone?"

"Sig!"

She propped herself up on one elbow, no color in her elegant, angular face. "Bastard. I hope he feels as rotten as he sounded."

"Sig, you scared him half to death."

"Then it was almost worth having to jump out that damned window. God, my ankle's killing me. Did you push me off the roof?"

"Not really."

She fell back against her pillow, managed a feeble smile. "He hasn't touched me in months. When I felt his hand on my stomach…I was ready to forgive him everything.'' Her eyes closed; she was deathly pale. ''Go tell him I hate him, will you?''

''Sure, Sig. Before or after I tell him you love him?''

''Turncoat.''

''Well, at least you don't have the burden of keeping your pregnancy a secret anymore. Now everyone knows.''

''Lucky me.''

A nurse ran Riley out, but not before Sig warned her to watch herself. ''We cut it close tonight. Too close.''

Riley nodded. ''I know.''

Straker thrust a cardboard cup of coffee at Matt Granger. ''You look like hell.''

''I imagine so.''

He sipped the coffee, Straker suspected, more because he knew he needed the caffeine than out of any real taste for it. They were outside the emergency room. Richard St. Joe had already managed to get Granger's sister and stepmother and Henry Armistead to go home. Mara had gone up to see Sig. God only knew where Riley was. She might stay put and wait for him. She might not. He couldn't predict.

''It's not easy to love a St. Joe,'' Granger said. Even stretched to the limits, he had a patrician air to him, a private-school bearing. He wasn't a regular guy, but he wasn't a jerk, either. ''Thanks for your help. I thought Riley'd eat me alive. Sig…*Jesus.*''

"Hell of a way to learn you're going to be a father."

Granger blew on his coffee. "I never wanted the two of them involved in this business. That's why I got some distance. I should have known better, especially when Sam—" He broke off, fatigue and worry, probably even embarrassment, obviously clawing at him. "It *would* be Riley who found him."

"Look, Granger, they're not the only ones out of their element. So are you." Straker gave it to him straight. "You need to back off and leave this mess to the pros."

The clear blue eyes turned cold. "What makes you think I've done anything?"

He seemed genuinely mystified. Straker said, "Sam Cassain came to you for help. Money. He wanted to bring up the *Encounter,* at least the engine. You financed him."

"If I did, it's not against the law."

"If you did, it got Cassain killed, and now Emile's missing."

Granger held his head up, almost haughtily. "Are you suggesting I had anything to do with Sam's death? That I killed him?"

"No. He probably used you for his own ends. I think you've got your finger in the dike, and you're hoping you and your world don't drown before you have a chance to figure things out." Straker paused, gave him a chance to digest what he was saying. "Tonight you almost lost everything."

"And you suggest I do what? Leave it to you to

bring Emile in? Leave it to Sheriff Dorrman? Emile's a madman. He's past caring about anyone except himself. Who the hell do you think set that fire tonight? *Me?* No." He threw his coffee into a bush. He was deadly calm, rational, certain. "It was Emile."

"Did Cassain come to see you last week?" Straker asked. "Did he bring up the *Encounter*'s engine? Did he get his proof against Emile?"

Granger had turned him off. He started down the walk toward the parking lot. He was a proud man, rich as sin, fighting shadows and demons and determined to slay them all before they could reach those he loved. But they already had, only he still couldn't stop. Straker understood.

"When you lose yourself in the battle," he said, "you're no damned good to anyone."

Granger glanced back. "Take care of my wife."

"How can you leave her?"

The man's eyes flashed with a pain so deep and penetrating Straker felt a certain sympathy for the poor bastard. "I have no choice. I wouldn't be any kind of husband if I didn't." He hesitated, added in a strangled voice, "Any kind of father."

Hell, Straker thought, and he let the man go.

He met up with Riley back in the waiting room. Sig was down for the rest of the night, her parents still with her.

"Matt?" Riley asked.

"Gone."

She nodded, almost as if she understood.

"You don't look so good, St. Joe. Come on. You

can zonk out in the car. When we get to Schoodic, it'll be time for breakfast.''

"When we get to Schoodic, it'll be four in the morning.''

He grinned. "Like I said, time for breakfast.''

He drove back up the coast and pulled up to a one-room shack of a restaurant on the water. Riley stirred. She'd fought sleep for a few minutes, but the warm car, fatigue and adrenaline had overcome her resistance. She glanced at him now and tried to smile. Her face was still smudged with soot, her eyes heavy from sleep and the aftereffects of her ordeal. "I smell like an old fireplace.''

"This crowd won't even notice.''

The half-dozen tables and small counter of the tiny, rustic restaurant were occupied by lobstermen chatting over plates of eggs, bacon, sausage, toast, with steaming mugs of coffee. It was Sunday morning, not as crowded as a weekday. Straker's father kicked two other guys from his table and motioned for his son and Riley to sit down. Straker started to apologize to the guys—he'd gone to high school with one of them—but they assured him they were just leaving.

"Pop—"

His father held up a hand. John Straker, Sr., was a burly, gray-haired, iron-willed man with simple aspirations, all met. He called to the waitress, "Two coffees and two plates of eggs with the works over here, when you get to it.'' He looked at Riley. "I get that right?''

She smiled. "Perfect.''

He turned to his son. "You both look like you could use some good food. How close did you cut it last night?"

"It wasn't close for me," Straker said. "But Riley and her sister…"

"I heard if they'd waited another ten minutes before jumping out the window, they'd have been charcoal briquettes."

Straker turned to Riley. "I'm afraid bluntness runs in my family."

"What?" His father was mystified. "Jesus, John, if anyone knows how close she came, it's Riley. How're you doing, kid? Eggs'll be here in a minute. A good breakfast'll fix you right up."

Their coffees arrived, followed quickly by their breakfasts. Riley picked at her food at first, but after a few sips of coffee, she showed more interest. She was awake and alert, a bit less pale. She was listening, Straker knew, to his father, who had his own opinions on Emile, Sam Cassain and the fire. Despite Emile's fame and his work in waters far beyond theirs, the local lobstermen still considered him one of them. In their minds, Emile Labreque had never forgotten his roots. They thought he'd got a raw deal last year, not because he couldn't have screwed up—they weren't there; they didn't know—but because Sam Cassain should have kept his mouth shut without substantial and convincing proof of Emile's negligence.

"It's just not how things're done," John Straker, Sr., said.

How Cassain had turned up dead on Labreque Island had been a subject of much speculation all week. Emile's whereabouts, however, didn't seem to stir up as much interest. Straker thought this was curious. "We need to find Emile," he told his father. "I'm guessing he's on the coast somewhere."

"You want me to keep an eye out, pass the word?"

"Just don't do anything crazy."

"That's your department," his father said without rancor. He shifted his gaze to Riley. "It's rough, getting the call your son's been shot and might not live. I don't want to see you and your sister doing that to your mother and father."

Riley set her mug down on the small wooden table. Outside, the tide was coming in, the water almost black against the slowly brightening sky. Straker could feel his father itching to get to his traps.

"You and Sig—you two need to leave this thing to the police," the lobsterman added. "Let them do their jobs." He sat back in his chair, said grudgingly, "At least when John got shot, he was doing his job."

"Emile's my grandfather," Riley said.

"So?"

"So I *am* minding my own business."

His father leaned forward, his bushy eyebrows drawn together. "You were almost killed a few hours ago. Go back to Boston. Take your sister with you. Your grandfather never asked for your help, did he?"

She breathed in, paling just a little. "Thanks for the advice, Mr. Straker."

He snorted. "You won't take it. You're half Labreque."

He insisted on paying for his son's and Riley's breakfasts. When they were back in her car, Riley looked grimly at Straker. "He knows where Emile is, doesn't he?"

"I'd say he has a fair idea."

"Then let's follow him."

Straker started the car. "You and I think we know these waters, but we don't. My father and his friends have been working this coast for decades. Day in and day out, year after year." He backed up the vehicle, choked down his own frustration with his father before it could take hold. "We wouldn't stand a chance."

Twelve

Riley felt her stomach roll over when Straker pulled into Emile's driveway and she saw the smoking remains of the cottage. She ached with fatigue, sorrow, fear. Memories swam over her, of the countless times she'd watched the sun come up from the front porch, of the cookouts and the foggy days reading by the fire. It was here Emile could be simply a grandfather, not the famous, driven oceanographer, the researcher, the seaman. The cottage had provided continuity in the rootless childhood of his granddaughters, and now it was gone.

Straker pulled on the emergency brake, his expression serious, focused. "You've got your FBI face on," Riley told him, but her attempt at humor fell flat.

"Emile still has the land," he said, as if reading her mind. "He can rebuild."

"It won't be the same."

He looked at her. "Nothing's ever the same."

Her father had driven up from Ellsworth and was

speaking to investigators in front of the cottage. He spotted Riley, gave her a quick wave as she and Straker got out of her car. The air smelled charred. Her throat was tight, and she pushed down a wave of nausea, tensed in an effort to keep from shaking.

"I refuse to believe Emile did this." She wasn't sure she was addressing Straker or talking to herself, reinforcing what she knew, in her gut, to be true. "It just doesn't make sense. A fire this time of year, when it's so dry—he wouldn't risk having it spread to the nature preserve. Straker, if you hadn't come along, this whole point could have gone up in flames."

He nodded. "What did happen is bad enough. The might-have-beens can drive you over the edge. Stay focused on the facts and let the investigators do their job."

"What if their job is to arrest Emile and he's an innocent man?"

"They'll figure that out."

"And meanwhile the real bad guy gets away. Someone's setting him up, Straker. You know it as well as I do."

"A successful frame isn't as easy to accomplish as it sounds."

She swallowed past her constricted throat. "It is if the person you've framed ends up dead."

Straker gave her a sideways glance, but said nothing as her father extricated himself from the investigators. He looked exhausted, the eccentric scientist out of his element. "They want to talk to you," he told Riley. "They already have a theory about how the fire started. Basically, you soak a rag in linseed oil, put it over a lightbulb and drape something—a curtain, a sheet, whatever—over the lamp. Linseed oil is very flammable, spontaneously combusts easily.''

''Wouldn't Sig or I have seen the light?''

''The fire started in Emile's bedroom. They're positive about that much. If the door was closed, the light draped with the rag and a sheet...'' He shook his head. ''It's not surprising you wouldn't have noticed. The investigators tell me it's a crude but effective method of setting a time-delayed fire.''

''Gives you a chance to leave the scene,'' Straker said.

Richard glanced back at the destroyed cottage, then said to Riley, ''I find it almost impossible to believe whoever set the fire didn't realize you and Sig were staying there. I'm not saying whoever it was deliberately tried to kill you.'' If possible, his face paled even more; his beard seemed grayer, lifeless. ''I just don't think it mattered to him.''

Riley's eyes burned; she thought of Sig in the hospital, of how close they'd come to not making it out of the loft. ''I wish I'd thought to check for bombs and booby traps.''

''Emile needs to come in.'' Her father directed his unswerving gaze at her as he summoned what were clearly his last shreds of strength and energy. ''If you have any idea where he is, tell the authorities.''

''Dad, I don't—''

He ignored her. ''You won't be violating your loyalty to him. You'll be doing him a favor, especially if you're right and he's innocent. Think about it, Riley. If Emile didn't set this fire, someone else did. Do you want a seventy-six-year-old man to take that on alone?''

"I don't know where he is."

"You two work this out," Straker said. "I'll be down on the dock. Riley, let me know what you decide to do."

As he walked away, her father shook his head in amazement. "John Straker as an FBI agent. That's a tough one to get my head around. Did finding a body on the island where he was staying stir up his professional instincts?'' He glanced at Riley with a ghost of a smile. "Or is it personal?''

"Don't ask me to explain why Straker does anything. I know he considers Emile a friend."

"He seems to be looking after you, too."

She watched Straker's retreating figure, the thick, strong body, the ease with which he moved. It would be a mistake on her part, she thought, to let him or anyone else look after her. That was her responsibility. She needed to be clear about her own interests, her own motivations, what was at stake for herself and those she cared about. She was tired, drained and scared, and letting Straker take charge, with his experience and natural irascibility, could be so easy, almost irresistible. It would get her off the hook and make her feel less exposed, less vulnerable to her own fears about where this would end.

"Don't let Straker fool you," she said. "He's as unpredictable and hard to get along with as ever."

Despite his exhaustion, her father managed a grin. "Sounds like you're two peas in a pod."

"Ha! I'm nothing like Straker."

"Honey, you're kind and you're passionate about everything you do—but you're not what anyone would call easy. You need a strong personality to rub up against, keep you interested. Someone who won't back off the first time he realizes you're not the type to wilt."

"Maybe, but it's not Straker. I admit he's been a rock. He was great with Sig last night. But he's an FBI agent. He likes all this danger and intrigue." She shook her head, crossing her arms over her chest to help her keep from shaking. "Not me. I can't wait to get back to recovery and rehab."

"Your mother and I had everything in common, and it almost didn't work. You can't predict what keeps two people together. It's not a science." He smiled gently. "But you're being too intense, which proves my point. Just enjoy the man's company and be glad he's on your side."

But she wasn't sure Straker was on her side in the way her father meant. He was on his own side, operating by his own code. Being on Emile's side, she remembered, didn't mean Straker considered him innocent—it meant he'd visit him in jail if he was proved guilty.

"Sig's getting out of the hospital this afternoon," her father said. "Thank God she's all right. She needs to rest and recuperate."

"I never should have brought her up here—"

"Well, I don't know if you've noticed, but your sister has a mind of her own, too. You're not responsible for her choices. Your mother's taking her back to Camden with her. Caroline's let me use a car—I'll stay up here a bit." He paused, eyed Riley in that way he did when he had something to say she didn't want to hear. "I think you should go with them. You're running out of your nine lives, kid."

She sighed. "I understand your concerns—"

"I don't want you running around up here alone."

"That's not likely," she said with a small smile.

"You and Straker." He shook his head. "Sam's death, Emile's inexplicable behavior, some maniac setting fires. That's enough, Riley. No more."

Two investigators were making their way toward her. "I'll be careful," she promised her father. She gave him a quick hug. "Please don't worry about me."

"Aren't you even a little bit afraid?"

"Not of Emile."

Her father's eyes narrowed. "Matthew?" he asked quietly, almost against his will.

The investigators joined them, giving her an excuse not to respond. Her father left, reluctantly, urging her a final time to head for Camden when she finished here. She answered the investigators' questions, many of which Sheriff Dorrman had already asked her, and tried to stay clinical, matter-of-fact as she related how she and Sig had come to Emile's cottage, what they'd done, how they'd realized it was on fire. But as she spoke and they took notes, her heart raced and she couldn't seem to draw a decent breath.

When they finished, she walked down to the dock. She relished the crunch of the gravel under her feet, the smell of the clean morning air, the coolness of the breeze off the water. The terror and the choking smoke of last night seemed a little less close.

Straker stood on the end of the dock, his boat bobbing in the surf. She walked out to him. "Still here?"

"Yep. I was waiting to see if you'd head to Camden or go back to Boston with your father." His gaze fixed on hers, impossible to read. "I prefer to know where you are. I've decided it's in my best interests."

"I can take care of myself." She said it more to reassure herself than to argue with him.

He tilted his head back slightly, and if possible looked even more the kind of man who'd go after a gunman with hostages. "Emile can take care of himself, too. It doesn't mean either of you won't come to no good."

She smiled. "Is that a vote of confidence?"

"St. Joe, you haven't changed all that much since you were six." He motioned to his boat. "Get in."

"Don't think you've changed one whit, either, Straker. Where are we going?"

He took her by the elbow. "To my deserted island."

Straker sat out on his porch, feet up on the rail, mind on nothing more productive than Riley St. Joe skinny-dipping in the chilly ocean water off a stretch of rocks down by the dock. She was determined, she said, to rid herself of her sooty smell. She'd borrowed a towel. And a shirt. "The longest one you have. And one that buttons."

For what purpose he could only imagine, which he did in vivid detail. If she got hypothermia in Maine's chilly waters, he'd have to warm her up. He might even have to pluck her out of the water.

He jumped to his feet, cursed. He'd gone from the isolation of six months on Labreque Island to a dead body, a missing old man, arson, the goings-on among a bunch of oceanographers, a pregnant woman estranged from her rich husband and the insanity of wanting Riley St. Joe.

He did want her. There was no denying, pretending or imagining otherwise. Wishing, yes. But wishing had never got him very far.

"Hell." He grabbed the porch rail and stared out at the water, every muscle in his body rigid. Too many months of celibacy. He'd thought they'd do him good. Instead they'd led him to wanting to make love to a woman he'd never particularly liked. A snot-nosed egghead. A stubborn know-it-all.

But he'd seen the fear in her eyes after the fire, the love and concern and fight in her as she'd stood over her sister's hospital bed. He admired her loyalty to her grandfather, her willingness—to a fault—to stand up for those she loved. She'd always had a lot of heart.

Wanting her…that was another matter. If he hadn't spent the last six months holed up on an island, would he have noticed the shape of her mouth and breasts, the dark depths of her eyes, the curve of her hips?

A lobster boat rounded the point, heading for the island's old dock. Straker instantly recognized his father's colors; every lobsterman had his own colors, to easily distinguish the buoys that marked his traps. "Thank God," he muttered, grateful for the distraction. Riley was on her own. Presumably she'd have the sense to scoot her naked little self out of view.

He headed down to meet the boat. He was hoping his father had checked with his buddies and decided to come clean about what he had on Emile's whereabouts, however much, however little. While he'd waited for Riley to finish with her father and the investigators, Straker had briefly considered sharing his suspicions with Lou Dorrman. Lou would understand how to handle closemouthed lobstermen. But this was his father, his father's friends—and Straker knew he was only going on instincts that hadn't been well-tested in recent months. If he was wrong, his father would chop him up for lobster bait.

Hell, if he was right, he was lobster bait.

He hadn't gone to Dorrman. Instead he'd brought Riley back to his island and given her a shirt so she could take a cold dip in the island waters.

The boat puttered close to shore. It was an old boat, immaculate, in perfect running order. Straker could remember countless dark, frigid mornings when his father had rousted him out of a warm bed to pull traps. The smells, the gulls, the unrelenting work of checking one trap after another for lobsters that

weren't too small, too big, or carrying eggs, then bait-
ing and dropping the pots again, moving on to the
next buoy.

There was comfort in the monotony, camaraderie
among fellow lobstermen, satisfaction in a day's hard
work. But at an early age, Straker had known it
wasn't for him. He was too restless, given to wondering about life beyond the peninsula. He'd never
regretted his choice, but he'd realized in ways he
couldn't articulate that giving up this life was his loss.

It was that, more than anything else, that Emile had
always seemed to understand—the push-pull of the
coast where Labreque and Straker roots ran deep.
Emile was hardheaded and driven, but he'd shown an
impatient boy how he could move away without giving up who he was.

Straker stopped, swore under his breath.

It wasn't his father who tied up at the rickety dock
and jumped out.

"Emile," Straker muttered, picking up his pace as
he ran out to the end of the dock.

The old man was spry, at ease anywhere on or near
salt water. "I'll only be a second." He made it sound
like a warning, as if Straker shouldn't even consider
trying to impede him. "I saw my place. The investigators are still there."

"They want to talk to you."

He gave a curt nod. "Of course."

"Does that mean you'll go in?"

"It means I understand the position they're in."
He glanced out at the water; he wore a windbreaker

over his black henley, against the cold wind. "I can't stay long in case they have the island staked out. Your father's boat will give me only so much cover."

"He lent it to you or you stole it?" Straker didn't bother to wait for a straight answer; he knew he wouldn't get one. "Emile, you need to get things squared away with the police. Right now they're inclined to think you torched your own cottage. Then there's Cassain's place down in Boston. At this point you're their best bet for killing Cassain." Straker paused. "That's how I'd be thinking in their place."

"I don't give a good goddamn what they think."

"Riley's here," Straker said without preamble. "She's your most tenacious defender. I wouldn't be surprised if the police are wondering if she's conspiring with you."

"She's why I'm here." Emile's dark eyes gleamed with the kind of intensity that had sustained him over the years. The warm sun hit the deep lines in his face, made him look old but robust, capable of chasing demons, real or imagined, up and down the coast. "I know she and Sig were in the cottage last night. Sig's with her mother. But Riley—she won't stop."

Straker nodded. "I know."

"I saw her in the water. Once she's revived, she'll be back up and running again, trying to mind my own business for me."

"How is Sam Cassain's death your business?"

"He was my ship's master for seven years," Emile said simply.

Straker noticed Emile wasn't getting too far from

the lobster boat. For the past six months, Straker had watched the old man settle into life on the peninsula. In some ways, it was as if he'd never left. In other ways, it was as if he wasn't really there—he was still aboard the *Encounter,* trying to save his friend and his crew, waiting, perhaps, for the truth about what had happened to his ship to finally come out.

"Let the police solve his death," Straker said. "Tell them what you know."

The dark eyes fastened on him. "I want you to watch out for Riley. As a favor to me. I nearly got her killed last year. It was only by a stroke of luck we made it into the submersible." His jaw was set, his natural stubbornness asserting itself. "I can't count on that kind of luck saving her again."

"I've been watching out for Riley. She wouldn't agree, but that's the way it's worked out." Straker stepped over a missing plank, wondered if Riley was up on some rock buttoning buttons as fast as she could so she could streak out to confront her grandfather. "What about Matthew Granger? Did he fund Cassain's bid to bring up the *Encounter*'s engine? Is he a danger to himself or anyone else?"

Emile frowned thoughtfully. He had a keen intelligence, the weather-beaten look of a man who'd spent many years at sea. But Straker knew he would be wrong to think Emile Labreque was like his own father and the other lobstermen he'd seen at breakfast. Emile was a world-famous oceanographer. He'd founded a prestigious research center, and he'd spent a lifetime on the world's oceans, not just the coast of downeast Maine. He wasn't going after Sam's killer for himself and his own reputation—he was going after it for the five people lost aboard the *Encounter* a year ago.

Straker squinted at the old man. "Emile, I can't let you go. You have to know that. I respect what you're trying to do, but you're going about it the wrong way." He smiled. "That's what you told me when I was eighteen, remember? I listened."

"You'd stop me from doing what I have to do, what only I can do?"

More drama. "I would."

"Then I have no choice." Without hesitation, Emile reached into his jacket and withdrew a Smith & Wesson .38 that looked suspiciously like the one Straker's father kept in his toolbox. "Don't make me shoot you."

"If you shoot me, it's your choice. Not mine."

The dark, intense eyes stayed on him. Straker swore. The bastard *would* shoot him. Wing him in the leg or arm—enough to make good his exit.

"Hands up," the old man said.

"For chrissake—"

"Do it."

Straker put his hands up. "This feels like an episode of *Bonanza*."

"Emile!"

Riley. She was thrashing her way up from the rocks, barefoot, shirttails flapping, moving fast.

"Go on," Straker told him. "Get out of here before you end up shooting her, too."

"You'll watch out for her?"

"She won't like it."

"Emile, wait!" Riley was jumping from one rock to another, getting closer. "I need to talk to you!"

"But you'll do it," Emile said.

Straker nodded, and the old man lowered his gun. It would be a simple enough matter for Straker to overtake him and his damned gun, but not, he thought, the wisest course of action. Then he'd have two irate Labreques on his hands.

Emile hopped back into his borrowed lobster boat with the agility of a man a third his age.

Riley burst onto the dock, pushed past Straker and probably would have tried making the leap into the boat if he hadn't scooped an arm around her middle and stopped her.

"You're nice and dry," he said, "and I don't have that many shirts."

Emile gunned the engine and sped out into the bay.

Riley strained against Straker's arm. "Emile—damn it, talk to me!"

"Keep yelling. If any investigators are around, they'll hear you and snatch him. It might be the best thing. Maybe I'll start yelling—"

She angled her chin up at him. "You're obnoxious."

"I just had a seventy-six-year-old man pull a gun on me. I'm entitled."

"He wouldn't have shot you."

The shirt he'd given her was flannel. A blue plaid. It reached to the middle of her thighs. Her hair was wet, her lips blue. She was shivering again, this time from the cold.

"You'd have made better time if you'd put your shoes on," he said.

"You could have disarmed him. I mean, you know how to do that sort of thing."

"Yeah, and last time I ended up with two bullets in me."

"Is that why you didn't stop him? Maybe you need to spend a few more months out here—"

Straker shrugged. "I hate arguing with old men with guns."

"That's twice now you've let him go. I thought he was the reason you left the island."

"Would that my life were so simple. No, Emile was the trigger. I consider him a friend, and I didn't like the idea of his dead captain washing up on my shore. But you're the reason." He noticed she'd buttoned up his shirt crooked, and it almost did him in. "It took having Emile point a gun at my head for me to figure that one out."

Her teeth were chattering. Too much time in the damned sixty-degree bay. "He wasn't pointing at your head."

"Close enough."

"I can't..." She pushed a hand through her wet hair. "I can't think."

He settled his arm on the small of her back and said, "Maybe I should at least get you to room temperature before I ask if I can make love to you. I wouldn't want you to suggest I took advantage of you.''

She shook her head. "No. Skip room temperature. And don't ask.''

"What?''

"Just do it, because if you ask—'' she smiled in spite of her shivering "—I'll have to examine the pros and cons, the risks and rewards, and pretty much give you a dissertation—''

"I don't want a dissertation.''

"If you can carry Sig,'' she said, leaning against his arm, letting him take her weight, "you can carry me.''

Straker scooped her up. She was cold, wore nothing under his flannel shirt. He took long strides up to the cottage, then pounded up the porch steps. This time there was no emergency, no collapsing pregnant woman in his arms. This time it was Riley.

"I'm so cold,'' she whispered.

"How long were you in the water?''

"Too long. After a few minutes I couldn't even feel the cold. I sat on a rock in the water and let the waves wash over me. It felt so good.'' She smiled. "I don't smell like a chimney anymore.''

He laid her on his bed, kissed her throat, her mouth. "No, you don't.''

He slipped the shirt over her head. Her slim body was cold under his hands. He tried to hold back and go slow, ran his palms up her legs and over her stomach and breasts, lingering there, feeling her temperature rise.

"Body heat is a quick cure for hypothermia," she said.

He smiled. "Ever the scientist."

But he was past holding back. He'd been holding back for days, from the moment he'd confronted her on the rocks in the fog. He'd dismissed his jolts of desire as being driven purely by his self-imposed isolation and celibacy. Wanting Riley St. Joe for her own sake was mad. Yet here he was, consumed by the taste of her, the feel of her, the unending longing for her.

She tore at his shirt. She was breathing hard, her eyes dusky, her body warm. "You don't have the excuse of six months on a deserted island," he said.

"No, I have the excuse of seventy-hour work weeks. Don't make me wait." She slipped her hands under his shirt, spread her palms on his bare skin. "I can't wait."

"For once we're in complete agreement."

He had his clothes off, with her eager help, in an instant, and he fell onto her with a ferocity that took him aback. He couldn't get enough of her. He couldn't make himself slow down, go easy, not that she showed any sign of wanting him to do anything but what he was doing.

And what she was doing to him, the feel of her mouth and hands, the thrust of her hips, the eager movement of her legs, urged him on. The old bed creaked and moaned as they came together, her body hot now, with no sign of blue lips and chattering teeth. They rolled onto the floor in a tangle of sheets, the mattress half off the bed.

Straker didn't stop. Couldn't. He peaked once, then again as her body quaked under him, her arms clasped around him as she pulled him even more deeply into her. It was as if the last six months of isolation, meditation, running, working had prepared him for this moment. He wasn't sure he'd have survived otherwise. She filled up his mind and body, his soul, in the way no other woman ever had.

He kissed the damp ends of her hair, breathed in the smell of ocean and lovemaking. Outside the wind had picked up. The tide was coming in. A few boats were out.

"We could stay here," he said, "and make love for the next six months."

She smiled. "Tempting, isn't it?"

"Place isn't winterized. Pipes'd freeze."

"Oh, who cares," she whispered, snuggling against him; she was warm and almost liquid, nothing shivering or trembling or tensed.

She slept. They were still on the floor, arms and legs intertwined. He pulled an old blanket up over her shoulders. Her clothes were probably still out on the rocks. He'd fetch them later. Right now, he'd let her sleep against him and imagine the rest of the world falling away until it was just the two of them on their tiny windswept island.

Sig staggered into her studio. She was shaky and queasy and burning with fatigue. She couldn't imagine painting. The urge was gone. She tried to remember what it felt like to want to paint. Dipping her mop brush into water, squirting out dots of vibrant colors, pastels, earth tones. Spattering, washing, blending, playing. Being absorbed in what she was doing. Loving it.

She dropped onto her high work stool and stared at her large, empty board. For a second she pretended she was signing her name in the corner of one of her paintings. *Sig St. Joe.* Who was that? Wife of Matthew Granger. Expectant mother. Riley's sister. Mara's daughter. Richard's daughter. She wasn't sure she knew anymore.

Her mother was making her tea and toast. Her cure-alls. Whether it was the body, mind or spirit in pain, Mara would make tea and toast. Sig smiled, glad for her mother's company, her constancy.

"Matt," she whispered, choking back tears. "You *asshole.*"

But she'd felt his agony when he'd come to her in the hospital, heard it in his voice, sensed it in his touch as he'd placed his palm on her swollen abdomen. He was consumed by demons. In that moment in the hospital, with her pit fighter of a sister protecting her, Sig had known he was convinced they were his demons alone to confront. Not hers. This wasn't something they could do together.

Perhaps that was what he'd tried to explain to her months ago, however inadequately and superficially. She didn't want to understand. Couldn't. He was her husband, her soul mate, her partner in life, her lover.

She wanted to be at his side no matter the dragons that needed slaying.

Her eyes burned with exhaustion. She could still taste the smoke. The doctors had urged her to rest and drink lots and lots of water. She needed to rebuild her strength and slowly ease the shock of the fire out of her system. The doctors had assured her that if she took care of herself, her pregnancy should proceed without incident. She was healthy. Her babies were healthy.

Mara came out onto the porch with a tray. "I made green tea, and I found a lovely oatmeal muffin in the freezer. I heated it up and put a little pumpkin butter on your plate."

"Thanks."

"Oh, this was easy. Seeing you and Riley last night—that was hard." She set the tray on the gateleg table; she looked tired herself, and guilty, as if she'd done something wrong. She manufactured a cheerful smile. "I can feel fall in the air, can't you?"

Sig smiled back. "I love fall."

"I'll leave the tray—"

"No, Mom. Sit down with me. You've had a hell of a scare, too. It's not—you know it's not your fault Riley and I were up at Emile's. You couldn't have predicted..."

"Yes. I could have predicted. Riley went to sea with Emile and was almost killed. On Tuesday, she goes kayaking at Emile's and finds a dead body." Mara gave Sig a hard look. "I should have stopped you both."

"We're adults—"

"You'd have listened if I'd told you to stay put."

"I might have," Sig said with a small smile. "I'm not so sure about Riley."

Her mother inhaled, said nothing.

"Do you want to fetch a cup? We can share the tea and muffin."

Mara shook her head. "I'm fine, thanks."

But she sat on Sig's studio bed, staying on the edge, too tight and nervous to lean back and relax. "It's been a rough week for all of us. I didn't want to acknowledge how it's affected me. Seeing Sam again, then having Riley of all people find him dead—" She broke off quickly, gave herself a shake. "The *last* thing you need is to have me whining and moaning to you. We'll all be fine. You, Riley, me. We're strong women."

"That's one positive result of Emile's hardheadedness. It must be a dominant gene."

Mara nodded, biting back tears. "God, it would be so much easier if I could hate him."

"I know what you mean," Sig said quietly, thinking not of Emile but her husband.

She poured the tea. She wasn't that fond of green tea. The muffin looked and smelled wonderful, but she had no appetite. She sipped the tea, aware of Mara's eyes on her.

Her mother sighed. Her dark eyes shone with unshed tears. "You're going back to Boston, aren't you?"

"I have to." Now that her mother had articulated

it, the thought was taking concrete shape. "How did you know?"

"Because I know you, Sig, just as I know your sister. She won't stop until she finds her grandfather and proves his innocence." Mara made a visible effort to control her feelings about her two daughters, her lack of control over their decisions. "You'll need tonight to rest up. If you're not feeling up to the drive in the morning—"

"I won't leave unless I feel strong enough. Mom—"

"I know," her mother said, smiling bravely. "You need to go home."

Thirteen

──◦◦◦◦◦──

Riley slipped out of the cottage at dawn to watch the sunrise from a rock ledge. Cormorants dove for fish, gulls called in the distance, lobster buoys in a variety of bright colors bobbed in the outgoing tide. The horizon had turned lavender and purple, the sun a glowing sliver of gold where water met sky.

She had to go back to Boston. She needed clothes. Her one outfit, even after it had been washed in Straker's sink and hung to dry on his porch, still stank of smoke. Her other clothes were totaled in the fire.

But more than that, she needed space. She needed time alone to think, to process the past few days and figure out where she went from here.

"Yep." She wrapped his chamois shirt more tightly around her. "A few hours alone in your car will fix you right up."

At least, she thought, it would be a start.

She heard the cottage door creak open. A few minutes later, Straker climbed up onto her huge granite boulder and stood beside her. He wore his charcoal sweater, which fit snugly across his big shoulders. His gray eyes blended into the environment, made him seem almost a part of the island.

She quickly explained her rationale about going back to Boston. He nodded without hesitation. "Good idea. I'll drop you off at Emile's as soon as you're ready to roll."

His instantaneous reaction put her on alert. She couldn't help it. Even on a good day, he wasn't cooperative or accommodating—unless he had ulterior motives. That's why he could do the work he did. "I thought Emile wanted you to keep an eye on me."

He shrugged. "So you want me to go back to Boston with you?"

"That's a slippery answer, Straker. I think you're up to something."

"Like what?"

"Like something you want to do without my help."

His mouth twitched. "St. Joe, there are about a million things I'd like to do without your help. Where do you want to start?"

"Let's start with what you're planning to do after you drop me off at my car."

"I think jumping out of a burning building has made you paranoid."

She held her ground. "It's a fair question."

"I'm not asking you what you're going to do when you get to Boston."

"That's just a tactical decision on your part to avoid telling *me* what *you're* up to." On the horizon, the sun was a half circle of fiery orange. He was as maddening now, after years in the FBI, after six months recuperating from bullet wounds, after dealing with terrorists and fugitives, as he'd been at sixteen, frustrated with his life. "And I'm not paranoid."

He was silent for a beat. "Okay. You're not paranoid. You didn't get enough sleep. You're cranky."

"Straker."

He smiled. "I'll go put on coffee. Or would you rather I toss you into the ocean? That would wake you up, maybe bring you to your senses."

"Coffee will do. And I'm in full possession of my senses." She thumped his chest with one finger. "*You* are up to something."

"I'm not going to argue with you. Watch your sunrise. Maybe sunlight and caffeine will fire up your synapses and get you thinking straight."

But she *was* thinking straight, and he damned well knew it. She watched him retreat, acknowledged the parts of her that were still warm from the last time they'd made love, only a few hours ago. She'd half expected him to kick her out yesterday after they'd first made love. Okay, months of celibacy finished, out you go. There'd been an urgency, a potency, to that first encounter that left her reeling even now. When it was over, he didn't suddenly wince and say, "Oh, God, Riley St. Joe. I must be out of my mind."

Instead they'd walked around on the island. She didn't remember what all they'd talked about. Some about the past week, but not much. It was comfortable talk, about his work, her work, families, friends,

Maine, nothing overly intimate or soul searing. If anyone had told her a month ago she'd be chatting with John Straker about ways to reduce the fat in a good beef stew, she would have laughed herself silly.

She wondered if she'd have laughed herself silly at the idea of her and Straker making love. Probably. That or gagged. Now, with the morning sun spilling out over the eastern sky, it had seemed inevitable. Destined.

Late in the evening, after dinner, when the cottage was dark and the bay quiet, empty of boats, they'd made love again. Slowly, tenderly, but with no less urgency. Straker had always been a supremely physical man. The feel of his scars, long healed but still recent, reminded her he was physical on more levels than those she'd personally experienced.

When he'd touched her in the pitch blackness before dawn, when it was so dark she couldn't even make out his silhouette, she'd felt a connection to him that went beyond physical, went beyond two people who'd known each other forever and now had found themselves in bed.

Falling in love with him, she warned herself, was not smart. It wasn't good for her. It was, in fact, insane.

Yet she could stay on the island and make love to him all day, have her fill of that thick, strong, amazing body. Pure sex with him was tough enough for her to digest. *Liking* him was tough enough. But this overwhelming emotional connection—it had to be smoke inhalation.

She turned away from the sunrise, watched him trot up the steps into the cottage. He was holding back on her. No question about it. She charged down off her boulder and pounded up the porch steps. He was used to doing things his own way, flashing that FBI badge, not answering to anyone. His own mother had given up trying to tell him what to do when he was eleven and nearly flunked out of sixth grade.

Riley let the door slam shut behind her. "You think Sam brought Emile the *Encounter*'s engine, don't you? You think he's stashed it somewhere."

Straker shoved a log into the woodstove without answering.

"If Emile has the engine," Riley continued, "it's to protect it as evidence. It's not to protect himself. If he did wrong, he'd own up to it."

"Not easy, stashing an engine as big as the *Encounter*'s."

"Maybe Sam only needed to bring up parts of the engine to prove what happened—maybe he didn't bring up anything, just took incriminating pictures."

"You're speculating."

"I'm brainstorming," she said. "There's a difference."

He straightened, looking strong, powerful. She'd need a weapon if she was going to stop him from following through with whatever sneaky plan he was implementing. "Don't even think about it," he told her.

"Quit reading my mind."

"Then quit thinking about taking a poker to me.

You want that ride to Emile's or shall I leave you out here on an uninhabited island without a boat? I've laid in enough supplies for a week or so."

It was his way or no way. "Forget it. I'll draw my own conclusions about what you're up to." The man was infuriating. She started back to the bedroom. "And never mind coffee. I'll get some on the way home. I want to leave now."

Straker rocked back on his heels. He was about three yards away and irritatingly calm. Let him contemplate his options, she thought. He could come clean and accept her as a full partner...or not.

Finally, he said, "I agree. I think Emile got hold of whatever it is Cassain found when he searched the wreckage of the *Encounter*. The engine, presumably. Other evidence."

"That's why he went to Sam's house the night of the fire."

"It explains why Matt Granger was there, too."

Riley nodded. "It also explains why Sam's house was torched—someone didn't want the police, or anyone else, finding any evidence of what happened aboard the *Encounter* last year."

Straker yawned, as if he'd figured all this out days ago and now it bored him. "Satisfied?"

"Emile's seventy-six. He's not up to this."

"He was up to pulling a gun on me."

"That's because you're obnoxious. *I'd* pull a gun on you. You drive people over the brink, Straker."

He grinned, eyes half-closed as they raked her from head to toe. "Yep. No argument there."

She groaned. "I rest my case. You're an outrage. I don't know how I ever ended up in bed with you."

"I do. You going to drive back to Boston in my shirt?"

Utterly outrageous. "You're just trying to distract me. Do you know where Emile is?"

"No."

"But you have a pretty good idea. Damn it, I know you do—"

"I'll be on the boat. If you're there in three minutes, I'll take you to your car. If not, enjoy your little island vacation."

"You know, Straker, you're awfully cold-blooded when you want your way. Did you consider the list of places I said Emile could be? Did one of them resonate with you? Or are you thinking about your father and the other lobstermen and what they know?"

"I don't want my way." He tore open the front door and glanced back at her. "I want you out of it."

"It's the lobstermen," she said.

"The clock is ticking."

"Just remember, you drive me every bit as crazy as I drive you. Probably crazier. It's *my* grandfather we're talking about. It was *my* sister who was almost killed."

He gripped the door. She could see the muscles in his forearms tense. He banged the door shut, marched over to her, grabbed her by the shoulders and kissed her. It was a hard, possessive, spine-melting, Rhett Butler kiss. Straker lifted her off her feet with it.

When he released her, she had to call on all her various forms of physical conditioning to keep from collapsing.

She cleared her throat, caught her breath. "What was that about?"

"I'll reset the clock at two minutes."

He stormed outside without another word. Riley knew he'd seize any excuse to leave her there. She'd find a way off the island. She'd flag down a passing boat, see if he had a kayak, build a raft if she had to....

She managed to throw her things together and leap into his boat as he was untying it.

It was chilly out on the bay. His shirt was big on her and made her think of the three times they'd made love, the incredible feel of him inside her. But when he pulled up to Emile's dock, he didn't even turn off the engine, just unceremoniously motioned her out.

"Go straight to your apartment," he said. "Stay there. I'll be in touch."

"I hate dictatorial men."

"St. Joe, how many burning buildings do you need to jump out of before you realize this is serious?"

"Okay, okay. I'll go straight to my apartment. I'll stay there. I'll wait for you." She hesitated. "Do you have a gun?"

"No, I don't have a gun. Who the hell would I shoot?" He narrowed his eyes on her. "*You* don't have a gun, do you?"

"I'm just thinking—"

"Don't think. Just go before I change my mind and take you with me."

"Take me with you where?"

"St. Joe. Get off my boat."

Definitely a man with a mission, and one he wanted to take on alone. He didn't want her as a distraction, a target, a hindrance. She jumped onto the dock and watched him speed off toward the mouth of the bay. Something must have jiggled loose and he had at least a pretty good idea where Emile was holed up. And he didn't care if she knew it.

One of her sleeves unrolled, dangling several inches past the tips of her fingers. Emile was her grandfather. She didn't believe he'd gone off the deep end. She believed he was trying to put things right and make sure no one else ended up dead on the rocks. He wanted justice for the five people who'd died aboard the *Encounter.*

She thought of Bennett Granger, his dignity, his kindness and generosity. He wasn't a marine scientist, but he'd loved the ocean every bit as much as Emile did, had wanted a marine life that was healthy and vital for future generations. *For his grandchildren. Sig's babies.*

If someone had sabotaged the *Encounter,* Emile would go to the ends of the earth to find out who. Let them set him up. Let them frame him for fires and murders—let the world think whatever it wanted to think. He wouldn't care.

Riley kicked a loose stone into the bay. She had responsibilities, a lot at stake. Straker had *nothing* at stake, which was probably why he'd gone off on his own.

Such was her state of mind when she drove into the village and parked in front of his parents' house. Mrs. Straker was in the garage with an unlit cigarette in her mouth and an upholstery hammer in one hand. "Riley St. Joe," she said, beaming. Her alert gaze took in her oversize shirt, and she shook her head. "I guess that rumor's true."

"What rumor?"

"You and my son on Labreque Island." She removed her cigarette, sighed almost as if she were exhaling smoke. "I wondered if you two'd ever get together after you bloodied him that time."

"Mrs. Straker, we're not—I mean—" Knowing she was doomed, Riley rolled up her errant sleeve. "How did that particular rumor get started?"

"Honey, nothing happens on this coast the lobstermen don't know about."

Riley nodded. "I understand. In fact, that's what I'm counting on. Can we talk?"

Straker didn't know how long he had before Riley tracked him down. It was a foregone conclusion she'd try. He'd kicked her out of his boat to buy himself a little time. In her place, he had to admit, he wouldn't sit quietly on the sidelines, either. And he'd never been much on anyone telling him what to do.

He docked in the village harbor. It was a small, picturesque harbor, relatively quiet at this time of morning with its moored boats, its glistening water and surrounding landscape of modest houses, Victorian bed and breakfasts, shops. The only eyesore was the old sardine cannery.

This was his home turf. Riley could pretend it was hers, too, but she'd never spent a long, cold, damp winter here. She'd never warred with herself over staying and leaving, over wanting something more yet wanting this to be enough, knowing it could be if only he'd let it.

He didn't see his father's boat. A few other lobster boats were in. Straker was aware of eyes on him as he walked out onto the ancient wooden pier. He stopped, waited to see what would happen. Nothing did. These were men he'd known all his life, and they were treating him like a rich yachtsman.

Maybe he was wrong. Maybe they didn't know anything. Last night over dinner he and Riley had rattled off a long list of places Emile could be, had winnowed it down to a dozen realistic possibilities. She and Sig had already checked out a few of them Saturday before the fire. That left several summer houses owned by Emile's friends, boats he might have appropriated or been loaned, lobster pounds, uninhabited islands—places he could slip in and out of with ease.

They didn't have the kind of time required to search them all one by one. *He* didn't have the time. He'd just spent the better part of a day and a night making love to Riley St. Joe. That alone dictated a certain measure of urgency on his part. He was out of control. After they'd made love their third time, he'd stared into the darkness, exhausted but unable to sleep, knowing he needed answers. *They* needed answers. They needed to know why Sam Cassain's body had turned up on Labreque Island. Then they could figure out what was going on between them.

"Hey, no dead bodies and women keeping you busy today?"

Straker smiled at A. J. Dorrman, one of the sheriff's lobsterman nephews. "The day's still young. How are you, A.J.?"

"Upright and taking nourishment. You?"

"I need to find out where you all have Emile stashed," Straker said bluntly.

A.J. twisted his mouth from one side to the other. He was in his early thirties, beefy, used to a life of hard physical work and answering to himself. He rubbed his chin. "Shit, Straker."

"Lou will have your head if he finds out you've been hiding a man wanted for questioning in a suspicious death."

"Emile didn't kill anybody. You know that. He's just a crazy old fart."

"His house was just torched. He's being set up to take the fall."

"I know, I know."

Straker waited. Silence was often his most effective tool. Also, he'd known A.J. all his life. Pelting him with questions, pressuring him, would only convince the man to dig in his heels and keep his mouth shut.

A.J. scratched one side of his jaw. "You think he's in any danger?"

"Yes."

"So what happens if the wrong person comes down here hunting for him? I get shot and go recuperate on an island by myself?"

Straker shrugged. "If you're lucky."

"Yeah, Lou'd finish me off before I got my sorry ass to any island." He started past Straker, said, "But if I snitched to you, I'd get stuffed into a sardine can and left to rot."

He kept walking toward the parking lot, and in case Straker didn't take the hint, A.J. wiggled a finger in the direction of the old sardine cannery. It was a dilapidated, rambling wooden structure, long abandoned. With the touted health benefits of Omega-3 oils and the depletion of the populations of so many commercially popular species of fish, sardines were making a comeback. This building, however, had seen its day. Emile's own grandfather had worked there years ago. The village had wrangled over its removal for years.

With the lay of the land, the inflow and outflow of pleasure boats and working boats, it was the perfect, if surprising, choice for a base. It had access and cover. No one would notice a network of lobster boats helping a discredited, brilliant, world-famous old man who was, when all was done and said, one of their own. Just as Straker was, no matter how many cases he solved for the FBI, how long he stayed away.

He walked around back. The building came right up to the edge of the water. Windows were broken and missing, boarded up. He spotted a ground-level door hanging half off its hinges in a corner formed by a six-foot concrete retaining wall and hill that sloped down to the water.

He picked his way over shards of glass and through overgrown brush, but when he got to the door, it opened before he had a chance to kick it in. Emile poked his head out and snorted in disgust. "I should have shot you yesterday when I had the chance."

"I see where Riley gets her charm."

"Where is she? I thought I asked you—"

"I know what you asked, and the best way for me to watch out for her—and you—is to get to the bottom of this thing. She's supposed to be on her way back to Boston."

Emile scoffed. "She's probably right behind you."

Straker ignored the obvious point. "You have the *Encounter* engine in there?"

"Pictures. I still don't know what Sam did with the engine."

"Christ, Emile. I should haul your butt over to the sheriff's myself."

The old man gave a curt, dismissive wave and ducked back inside. Straker cursed silently and went in after him. If Emile shot him, so be it—but he didn't seriously believe that would happen.

The door opened into a small entry, with dusty, sagging stairs leading up into the main part of the old building. Emile had set up housekeeping in a dark corner. He was using a turned-over wooden crate as a table. He had crackers, peanut butter, a six-pack of tomato juice, another six-pack of orange juice, a box of raisins.

He was perched on a stool, close to the door. "You listen, Straker. Then you leave me alone and let me do what I have to do."

Straker glanced at the old man. He had on his khakis and black henley, no obvious place for his .38. "You're turning the lobstermen around here into accessories."

"Sam brought up the *Encounter*'s engine two weeks ago," Emile said, ignoring his last comment. "Matthew Granger funded him. In secret."

"Your granddaughters figured as much. Have you talked to Granger?"

"No. I don't know if Sam even told him he had the engine. Sam had his own agenda. If it tied in with Granger's, fine. If not—" Emile shrugged his stringy shoulders. "Tough."

Straker thought a moment. The air was damp, smelled of bad food and dirty socks. Blankets and a pillow were tangled up on a small air mattress in the opposite corner.

"All right," he said, "what happened to the *Encounter?*"

"Sabotage."

Straker was silent.

"It was a quick, easy job, if you know diesel engines. When Sam pulled up the engine, it was obvious what happened—it's there in the pictures." He nodded to a nine-by-twelve manila envelope amid his provisions. "Someone opened up the lube oil drain.

The valve's padlocked. The padlock's cut, proving it wasn't an accident."

"Cassain found it?"

"So he says. I don't know if the pictures are fakes or what. That's why I want to find the engine itself. You cut the padlock, then just turn the valve. Easy as pie. Engine can't run without oil. You get a main bearing failure on the crankshaft, which destroys the engine. On an old ship like the *Encounter*, that'd be the end of her."

"But the engine's safety features should kick in," Straker pointed out.

"Normally, yes. There's an automatic shutdown panel. Alarm goes off when there's a problem, the engine shuts down. It's like the engine's brain." Emile spoke clinically, as he did in his documentaries. This unusual mix of intensity and unemotional stating of the facts, keeping his natural drama in check, had served him well over the decades. He was credible, believable, principled. "Disable the safety features, and the engine doesn't know it has a problem. It doesn't automatically shut down. It just keeps running."

"Did Cassain find evidence the shutdown panel was defeated?"

"Jumper wire. A piece of wire with two alligator clips. It'd do the job."

"It wasn't destroyed in the fire?"

Emile shook his head. "I think our saboteur got more than he counted on. The crankcase explosion by itself probably wouldn't sink the ship. When you open the lube oil drain and defeat the alarm panel, you also defeat the controls to the number-two fuel tank. It overflows into the bilge, and now you've set off a fatal chain reaction.''

"Number-two fuel's more flammable than lube oil.''

"Yep. Lube oil draining into the bilge is a mess. Number-two fuel's a catastrophe. Meanwhile, the engine runs dry without lubrication, it explodes and ruptures a disk on the side—''

"How do you know that?''

"Sam brought up the ruptured disk. It's in the pictures. With the disk ruptured, flames can pour out of the engine and light the mix of fuel and oil in the bilge.''

"Jesus,'' Straker whispered.

Emile was very still, his expression grim. "It was a huge, tremendously hot fire. Not much burns hotter than number-two fuel. It warped the bulkheads, fed on the fuel in the main tanks. The *Encounter* took on water.'' He sighed, looking tired and old, except for his eyes, which were alert, gleaming with determination. "With that kind of fire and flooding, she didn't stand a chance.''

"It couldn't have been an accident,'' Straker said quietly.

"No.''

"Once the shutdown panel was disabled and the lube oil drain valve opened, an explosion was virtually guaranteed. It's just a question of whether the saboteur realized how catastrophic the explosion would be—the chain reaction he'd cause." Straker imagined Riley amid this chaos, the *Encounter* burning, flooding, her friends dying. "What about timing? If the engine had exploded closer to land, you might have had a better chance of getting the fire out, getting the crew out. On the open sea—"

"On the open sea, we were doomed. Timing with this kind of sabotage would be hard to predict. An explosion was certain, but when..." He shrugged. "I don't think that mattered."

"What did matter? What did the saboteur want to accomplish?" Straker narrowed his gaze on his old friend. "You have ideas, Emile. If the explosion was unpredictable, it's unlikely a particular individual was the target—murder wasn't the point. Our saboteur didn't use this as a way, for example, to kill Bennett Granger."

"No," Emile allowed.

"You don't believe the saboteur intended for the *Encounter* to burn and sink, killing five people."

"No, I don't."

"Cassain?"

"I need to find the engine." Emile sprang up from the stool. "That's why Sam's place was burned down. Someone wanted to make sure the police didn't find any evidence of what he'd been up to these past few months. Then they came up here and set my place on fire to throw suspicion on me."

Straker moved toward the old man. "If I found you, someone else can. Trust me, Emile. Let me get you the protection you need. You're not safe here."

Emile nodded. "I know."

"Tell me about Sam. When did he bring you the pictures?"

"Saturday afternoon, right in broad daylight. Riley got here Monday morning, found his body on Tuesday."

"I take it he didn't come up here to apologize," Straker said.

"He had no reason to apologize. It wasn't my idea to bring up the *Encounter*'s engine," Emile said with a trace of disgust. "She was lost. I did nothing to find out what the truth was."

"You believed it was your fault."

"If I'd had a watchman on duty—"

"Then you'd have six crew dead instead of five." But Straker wasn't here to make Emile feel better about what he'd done, or failed to do. "Was Cassain interested in the truth?"

The old man slipped back outside into the sunlight. Straker followed. Emile was staring out at the glistening harbor. "He'd suffered this past year. He wanted his pound of flesh. If it was in the form of cash, the more the better. He showed me the pictures for my reaction."

"And?"

"We both had the same idea about what happened—that whoever sabotaged the *Encounter* didn't count on the day tank overfilling." The old man continued to stare out at the lobster boats, sailboats, the odd yacht. His expression was unreadable. "I don't know who sabotaged my ship or why. It could have been a crew member with a bone to pick with another crew member. Sam could have faked the evidence, the pictures. I have to find the engine.''

"That doesn't explain his murder, the fire at his house, the fire at the cottage. Go ahead, Emile. Speculate. Based on what you know, what's your best guess about what happened to the *Encounter,* what's going on now?"

He inhaled, shifted his gaze to Straker. "Look at what's happened in the past year. Look at what the loss of the *Encounter* accomplished—"

"It killed the center's chief benefactor and drove out its founder."

"No one could have predicted Ben's death," Emile said, "or that I would tuck my tail between my legs and flee home."

"From what Riley tells me, this past year has been a public relations disaster for the center."

"Initially. Henry Armistead, Abigail Granger, my son-in-law, Riley—the entire center staff has worked tirelessly to turn it around. I asked myself, and Sam asked himself, what would have happened if the *Encounter* hadn't gone down in flames, if there hadn't been any loss of life."

"If it was a near thing instead of a catastrophe, you lose the *Encounter* because of a crankcase explosion, but no one gets hurt."

Emile eased back against the retaining wall. "People loved that ship—it was part of the romance and adventure of our work. A new ship was in the works, but it was underfunded. We weren't sure when, or if, we'd be able to finish it. And our supporters, even some of our own staff, didn't want to give up the *Encounter*."

"As long as it could put out to sea, people wouldn't get excited about its successor."

"You can't underestimate their sentimental attachment to it."

"A narrow escape for the great Emile Labreque and his crew would elicit sympathy and galvanize support for a badly needed new research ship. The old ship dies in battle, so to speak. Let's honor her memory by building a new one."

"The *Encounter II* is back on schedule. Support's up. The catastrophe of the *Encounter* was a setback at first—"

"But now things are working out." Straker frowned, shaking his head. "I don't know, Emile. It's a hell of a stretch. Wouldn't our saboteur *want* the *Encounter* and any evidence of his handiwork at the bottom of the ocean?"

"Immaterial. People would have been outraged at the idea of sabotage. Support would have poured in."

"And the police would have investigated."

"You're an FBI agent," Emile said. "You tell me how many criminals you've apprehended thought they'd get caught."

Straker didn't argue. Emile's theory was sound enough, if far-fetched. And he'd asked the old man to make his best guess. If this was it, this was it. "What about Cassain? Did you encourage him to go to the authorities with his evidence?"

"Of course. He refused to listen."

"Blackmail?"

"That's my guess. He was getting his ducks in a row before bringing his proof to the saboteur and exacting his pound of flesh. He came to me to help solidify his theory."

"But he didn't give you a name, any hint of who he thought was responsible?"

Emile's dark eyes shone with intensity. "*I* was responsible for the *Encounter*. It was my ship, my crew."

Straker let that one go. This was no time to try to out-argue a Labreque. "You know what I mean."

"Sam played his cards close to the chest. He knew I'd go straight to the authorities. I'm convinced he was still flailing around, figuring out his next moves."

"And he flailed in the wrong direction and got himself killed." Straker could see it. He gave the old man a hard look. "We're taking your pictures to the police."

Emile shook his head. "I need to finish what I started."

"No, you don't. You need to let the police do their job. Sam was murdered, Emile."

Emile drew himself off the retaining wall, pointed down the slope. "You have bigger problems than stopping me."

Straker turned, and there she was, marching up from the water with her jaw set hard and her hands clenched into fists at her sides. She'd spotted them, but she had the sense not to yell out.

"Nowhere to run," Emile said lightly, "nowhere to hide."

"You should have shot holes in her kayak," Straker muttered.

Riley stopped between them. "Emile, Straker— what are you *doing?*" She was out of breath and talking through clenched teeth. "Emile, for God's sake, you can't keep sneaking around. You're going to get yourself killed or tossed into prison for a million years."

"I'm leaving," he said calmly.

"You can't leave. Your cottage—you must know what happened. They found all this firebug stuff in your woodshed. Someone's setting you up."

He ignored her. Straker stayed out of it. Emile was as maddening as she was, and they'd been doing this dance over a variety of subjects ever since Riley started to talk. Her grandfather pointed a finger at her. "You never mind me and listen to Straker. Follow his advice. You know about cetaceans. He knows about arson and murder."

She inhaled. "I am *not* letting you go."

"You have no choice."

That didn't sit well. She was prepared to argue her case, but Straker said, "We have a lot to talk about."

She glared at him. "You're not letting him go!"

"Someone sabotaged his ship and caused the deaths of his best friend and four of his crew. You nearly died. He nearly died." Straker sighed, knowing he must have been infected by the Labreque sense of drama, their way of looking at things. "What would you have me do?"

"Sabotage?"

She was pale, could barely get the word out. Emile seized the moment to slip off. Straker didn't stop him.

Riley spun around, made a move to go after her grandfather. Straker touched her arm. "Don't. You'll just draw attention to him. He has a lot of friends up here. They'll look after him. He left Cassain's pictures of the engine and the evidence it was sabotaged. We need to get them to the police. Then they need to find the engine to make sure it really is the *Encounter* and not something Cassain faked."

"Do you think he faked it?"

"No."

"I hate this," she said.

"I know." Straker rocked back on his heels, eyed her and considered the various possibilities of how she'd found him. One stood out. "My mother ratted out my father?"

Riley gave an absent nod, a small smile. "She doesn't miss anything."

"There'll be a battle royal over that one. Well, let's go."

"You go on." She fixed her dark eyes on Straker, and he could see her fighting to be reasonable, smart, not simply to inflict her will on everyone else. "I'll head to Boston. You can pretend I never saw any of this."

Straker grinned. Her motives, he thought, were obvious.

"Quit acting like you know what I'm thinking," she said.

"I do know what you're thinking."

"I'm just trying to be sensible and reasonable."

"No, you're not. You're looking after your own skin. You're afraid if you go to see Lou Dorrman with me, he's going to put you in protective custody or otherwise restrict your movements. I think he would. He's pretty much had it with you Labreques."

"I'm going."

Straker fought the urge to stop her, to bring her to Lou Dorrman for safekeeping. "Don't make me regret not tying you up in my boat."

She smiled faintly. "You'll be in touch?"

"Count on it."

Fifteen minutes later, Straker was telling Emile's story to Lou Dorrman, who if he didn't understand oceanography, did understand boats. "That's a hell of a damned thing to do to a ship setting out to sea."

"So is Emile off the hook?" Straker asked.

But he knew the answer. It'd be his answer, too, if this were his case. The sheriff scowled. "No. And neither are you. Sit down."

Straker sat, and after he told his story to Lou one more time, he had to wait for the state detectives and tell it to them. They weren't pleased with him for letting Emile go. Straker wouldn't have been pleased, either. A seventy-six-year-old man and a trained FBI agent—he could have brought him in.

"Next time," Teddy Palladino said, "you'd better."

"Next time, I will. Meanwhile," Straker said, "I think we're giving Riley St. Joe way too much time to get herself back into hot water."

Palladino agreed, and Straker was on his way.

Fourteen

———⋘∙⋙———

Sig plopped down on a squishy, comfortable sofa in the front room of her house on Chestnut Street, not far from Matt's childhood home on Louisburg Square. They'd picked this house together. Although she hadn't contributed a dime, she'd never felt it was any less hers than his—and he'd never indicated otherwise. That wasn't how they operated. They were partners, equal, even if his bank account had more zeroes than hers.

Her babies jumped, startling her. It was their strongest movement yet. She placed a palm on her lower abdomen and sank deeper into the cushions. She'd fought melancholy during the long drive from Camden, could feel it again threatening to overwhelm her. She wanted to be plucky and resilient, but just couldn't summon the energy.

Her gaze drifted to a framed picture of her father-in-law and Caroline at their wedding. Matt so missed his father. He was self-contained, not one for open displays of emotion. He'd insist his actions in recent months had nothing to do with his grief, but with facts, logic, truth and justice. He and Bennett weren't demonstrative or openly affectionate, but they'd enjoyed each other's company.

Her father-in-law had been delighted when she and Matt had announced they wanted to marry. Bennett and Emile had been friends and partners for fifty years. "I don't care if you know a whale from a dolphin," Bennett had told her. "I'm thrilled to have a Labreque in the family."

His tragic death had changed everything, shattering Matt's world, and thus, Sig thought, her own.

She imagined her husband standing in their elegant living room in tattered jeans that hung low on his slim hips, his hair tousled, his eyes that memorable, piercing blue. He didn't hide his intelligence, his education, his money, nor did he flaunt them.

"Hell's bells," Sig breathed. "You're getting maudlin."

She popped up off the couch and headed straight for the front door before her thoughts could get away from her, take on a life of their own. She might not be a fighter like Riley, but damned if she'd turn into a brooder.

It was warm outside, warmer than Camden would be at this time of the afternoon. She walked down to Charles Street, saying hello to a neighbor she recognized, enjoying the feel of the brick sidewalk underfoot, the sense that she was home and trying, at least, to take charge of her life.

The markets and coffee shops, the flower shop, the

antique shops, were all crowded with people coming home from work. She stopped at a small market for milk, juice, bread, coffee. Could she live here without Matt? She didn't think so. It was difficult enough making a place for herself on Beacon Hill with him in her life. Without him, she'd probably always be known as Matthew Granger's ex-wife.

The thought made her gasp, unable to get a good breath. She'd felt the same way in Emile's loft with the smoke oozing up the stairs. *Matthew Granger's ex-wife.* But that was where they were headed.

She carried her grocery bag up to Louisburg Square. Abigail would be back from Maine by now. Sig hadn't talked to her in weeks and didn't want to put her sister-in-law on the spot—but Matt was in trouble, at least on the edge. If Abigail had any insight into her brother's state of mind in light of the fires, Sam's death, the pending birth of his children, Sig wanted to hear it.

Her sister-in-law answered her front door in slim pants, her blond hair pulled back. She looked sleek and poised, while Sig felt bloated as she huffed and puffed over carrying a bag of groceries up Mount Vernon Street. Her hair hung down her back in a thick braid, and she wore one of her voluminous dresses. She felt frumpy, a little sick to her stomach.

"Sig! What an incredible surprise. Come in, won't you?" Abigail drew her into the entry, unchanged since her father's death, probably since her grandfather's death, too. "How are you feeling? Have you recovered from—my God, I can't even say it. We came too close to losing you.''

Sig managed a smile. "No argument from me."

"And you're pregnant." She smiled. "With twins?"

"Lively twins."

"I can't wait to tell my kids they're finally going to have cousins. Where are you staying?"

"At the house."

Abigail frowned. "Alone?"

"It seems that way. I got back this afternoon."

"I meant to visit you in Camden," Abigail said. "Oh, Sig—are you sure you're up to staying by yourself? You're welcome to stay here with me."

"I'll be fine."

Abigail seemed dubious. She was so different from her brother—more formal, more mannerly. "Let's have a drink and catch up, shall we? Coffee, tea, whatever you'd like. Have you had dinner yet?"

"No, but the thought of food…" Sig shuddered. "A drink would be great, though."

"Then come downstairs. You can leave your groceries right here in the hall. Is there anything we need to stick in the freezer?"

"No, it'll be fine."

She set her grocery bag on the floor, ambivalent about having stopped in. There were so many questions about the fire, Matt's behavior, Riley, Emile— even John Straker and his role. Sig didn't want to get into any of them. She just wanted Matt to come to his senses.

Abigail started down the hall. "Henry and I were just making coffee."

"Henry's here? Don't let me interrupt—"

Abigail blushed, tried to cover for it. "You're not interrupting anything. He'll be delighted to see you."

With that, she led Sig down a flight of stairs to the kitchen, a cozy mix of modern and nineteenth century with its brick fireplace, copper pots, granite countertops and cherry cabinets. Henry got up from the table, greeting Sig warmly. "Thank God you're all right. You and Riley gave us all quite a scare."

She smiled. "We gave ourselves quite a scare."

"I imagine so. Have the police—well, let's not talk about that right now. There's fresh coffee. Can I pour you a cup?"

"I can put water on for tea if you prefer," Abigail said. "I didn't drink coffee during either of my pregnancies, but I doubt one cup'll hurt someone who survived a burning building."

Sig laughed, relaxing. "Put that way, I'll say yes to coffee. I'll just add a lot of milk."

Henry poured the coffee, moving about Abigail's kitchen as if he were comfortable there, familiar. He filled a small pitcher with milk, set it and the heavy mug on the table. "I'll let you add your own milk. I'm sure you and Abigail have a lot to talk about. I'll scoot upstairs for a bit."

"That's not necessary," Sig said.

He held up a hand, smiled. "It's fine, Sig. You two catch up."

When he was gone, Abigail put her hands on her

hips and scrutinized her sister-in-law. "Are you *positive* you're well enough to stay alone? You still look pale to me. I think you should have stayed with your mother a few days at least to recuperate."

"I'm just tired. It was a long drive." Sig poured milk into her coffee, sipped it. It was hot, not too strong. She avoided Abigail's eyes. "I'll be fine."

"Mara must have hated seeing you go off on your own under these circumstances. Wait until you have those babies, Sig. Then you'll understand. There's no off button when you're a mother."

"You were divorced when your children were young. Do you think—"

She cut Sig off with a firm shake of her head. "You and Matt are *not* going to divorce. Don't even think about it. This is just a bump in the road. You'll see."

"Don't pay any attention to me, Abigail. I'm not thinking straight. I..." She sighed. "I'm just worried about him. I wish I understood what he's trying to accomplish."

"Matt has a good head on his shoulders, Sig," Abigail said gently, sitting across the table from her. "He's not stupid. He sometimes asks a lot of the people who love him, but you have to have faith."

"For how long?"

"For me, it's forever. But I'm his sister."

Sig bit her lip, refusing to cry. She'd cried too much already.

"By the way," Abigail continued, "you must be wondering if there's anything between Henry and me. There is. Sort of. We're trying to be low-key because of our roles at the center, and now with Sam's death—well, I'm sure you can understand our reluctance to become a subject of gossip and speculation.''

Sig suddenly felt enervated, as if she wouldn't even make it back out to Louisburg Square. She drank more of her coffee, nodded. "You're both entitled to your privacy."

"We've only been seeing each other a few weeks. Henry was very nervous at first, especially since we were beginning to see signs that some of the rawness of the *Encounter* ordeal was easing. Then it just…" She smiled, her eyes not quite meeting Sig's. "It just seemed so natural."

"I won't say anything if you don't want me to," Sig said.

"We should probably wait until Sam's death, the fires…" Abigail groaned, as if it were all too much to articulate. "Until this whole mess is sorted out."

"I understand. Abigail, everyone only wants happiness for you. You've done so much for the center, and your family, too. Matt likes Henry, and I'm sure Caroline's fond of him. Of course, that shouldn't matter. You just need to follow your own heart."

"Ah, Sig. You make everything sound so wonderfully simple. I've missed you." Her expression clouded, and she leaned forward. "Sig, what do you think's going on with Emile?"

"I wish I knew. That's why Riley and I were at his cottage. We wanted to find him, get him to talk to the police."

Abigail sighed, got up to pour herself a cup of coffee. "He's always had a very fine opinion of his own abilities. I wouldn't be surprised if he thinks he can sort out Sam's death better than the police. Either that or he's gone completely nuts."

"To be honest, I've never been very good at figuring out how Emile thinks. Riley's much better. Me—I can't even figure out what my own husband's thinking."

"Don't be too hard on yourself."

Abigail returned to the table with her coffee. Sig noticed her slender fingers and manicured nails, looked down at her own unpolished, blunt-cut nails. She needed to take better care of herself. Ultimately, she realized, that was why she'd come home. Not to do her nails—to focus on her, on Matt, on their marriage, on the family they were in the process of creating.

"Henry's waiting for you," Sig said, struggling to her feet. "I'll head on back. I just wanted to stop in and say hello."

"I'm glad you did. Are you sure you won't join us for dinner? We're just ordering out. Nothing fancy."

But Sig was sure, and when she walked back out to Mount Vernon, she found herself feeling a little foolish. Even in her confusion over whatever was going on with her brother, Abigail was confident, poised, well-mannered and in her element. Sig constantly felt as if she were spinning out of control. She had no plan of action, no clear course she was following. She simply responded to events as they happened.

She'd call Riley when she got back. Find out what her wild little sister was up to and whether the sparks were still flying between her and Straker. Find out if she was safe. If she'd learned anything more about Emile and the fire.

"There," she told herself as she unlocked her front door. "You're taking action."

She pushed open the door, saw the shadow of a man in the front room and screamed, her bag of groceries crashing to the floor. The milk carton split open, soaking the bag.

"Sig..." Matt stepped out of the shadows. "I didn't know it was you."

She was shaking, far more terrified than she would have been if she hadn't just escaped death in Emile's loft. Her knees went out from under her and she sank to the floor. She couldn't stop herself. Her head spun. Her stomach lurched, and she thought she'd pass out.

Matt caught her by the elbows and lifted her into his arms. She ached to lean into him, let him take her weight, but she stopped herself, stiffening against her own attraction to him, her own need.

"Are you all right?" He sounded panicked, tortured. "Sig, what can I do?"

She had to look at him. At those blue eyes, that square jaw, that lean body. He still held her. "I'm not going to pass out. I'm okay."

"You're sure?"

She nodded, and he took her face in his hands and kissed her cheeks, and she realized he was crying. So was she. She'd started to say something, she didn't know what, when his mouth found hers.

"Oh, Sig," he whispered. "I love you."

She wanted this, had dreamed of it for months. Her mouth opened to his kiss. He slid his palms over her shoulders, and she quaked when he touched her breasts, swollen from pregnancy. It had been so long. "I've missed you," she said. "I've missed you so much."

He smoothed a hand over her lower abdomen. "Twins. My God." His voice cracked. "I want to be a good father, Sig. I'll do my best. I promise."

She covered his hand with hers. "I can feel them moving. Most of the time it's this little flutter."

"You're okay? After the fire—"

"Yes."

He kissed her again. "I remember when we made these babies. I don't know how I've done without you for so long." He curved his hand slowly back up to her breast, found her nipple, circled it with one finger as he deepened their kiss. "Just let me sleep beside you tonight."

"And then what?"

His eyes flashed. "What do you mean?"

"I mean what happens in the morning?" She fought past her longing for him, called upon all her convictions, her determination that she had to stand her ground. For her sake, for his, for their babies' sake. "I'm expecting twins, Matt. There's too much at stake for me. For us. I need to believe in you—I need you to believe in me. *Talk* to me. Tell me what's going on with you, Emile, Sam. Let me in.''

"Sig…''

"No half measures, Matt. I won't be a sometimes wife. I *can't* be. Either you let me in, let me help you through this, or you walk out of here.'' She gave him as hard a look as she could. "Or I do.''

"I love you. I'd die for you. I'd die for our babies. Isn't that enough?''

He was so persuasive. So handsome. Her body burned with wanting him. She hated being alone. She liked having him in bed with her, liked waking up to the rub of his beard on her, liked hearing him thrash around in the kitchen. She desperately wanted their life back. But how much could she give?

"I know you asked me to give you space and let you work this out for yourself, and I was willing— for a time. I've been more than patient. And I never expected…'' She blinked back more tears, squashing a rush of conflicting emotions. "Sam Cassain was *murdered*. Riley and I were nearly killed. Matt, this isn't about you and your grief anymore.''

"It never was. That's why you have to let me do this on my own.''

"What if you're next? What if Riley finds your body washed up on the rocks? I know you gave Sam the money so he could probe the *Encounter*. You must have left a trail. The police are bound to find out—''

"They already know. I called and told them this afternoon. It wasn't a crime, Sig.'' He stood back, and she could see the impact she'd had on him. "If not me, Sam would have found someone else. He'd have stolen the money."

"I'm glad you've finally told the police." She held up her head, refused to give him one damned inch. "But I don't see why you couldn't see your way through to telling me."

He didn't answer.

"Because of Emile? Or because you knew I'd try to stop you?"

"Because it's not your fight."

As much as his words hurt, she didn't wither. "Your fights are my fights."

"Not this one." His voice hardened, more against his own conflicting emotions, she thought, than against her. "I thought you understood."

"Understanding doesn't mean I'm patient, and it doesn't mean I'm going to sit back and passively let you do whatever you want to do, get yourself killed, end up in jail. I *won't*. We're partners."

"No, Sig. Not on this we're not partners. We can't be. It's too dangerous."

She stood her ground. "If it's too dangerous for me, it's too dangerous for you."

He hissed through his teeth. "Damn it, what kind of man would I be if I didn't see this thing through? If it's my fault Sam's dead—" He broke off, raked a hand through his hair. His eyes were a searing blue, radiating all his frustration, anger, grief, fears, everything he tried so hard to keep banked down. "This is my doing, Sig. My problem. The fire at Emile's, your pregnancy—how much more reason do you need to stand back?''

''How much reason do *you* need?''

Suddenly he looked exhausted, defeated. She ached for him. But she couldn't back down.

And neither could he. ''It's more reason for me to redouble my efforts.''

She clenched her fists, refused to cry. ''Damn you, Matt.''

''Don't ask for what I can't give.'' He sighed, his expression softening slightly. ''Let's not fight. You look tired. Can I get you anything?''

''A good lawyer.''

He swore under his breath and stalked across the room, slamming the front door on his way out. Sig didn't have the energy to go after him. She collapsed onto the couch, her body still hot with the feel of his touch, his kisses. She sobbed, cried, swore and finally threw the needlepoint pillows across the room one by one.

She should have let him stay the night. At least then she'd know where he was. So much, she thought miserably, for taking action. All she could do was sit in her empty house, wait and worry.

Riley picked up a few things at her favorite market in Porter Square and almost deluded herself into thinking her life was normal. Which it wasn't and maybe never would be again. Murder, fires, sabotage, a crazy grandfather and a shot-up FBI agent coming off a self-imposed exile.

"Phew," she said, walking up the shaded street with her bag of groceries.

When she turned the corner onto her street, she saw Straker sitting on her front steps. He didn't get up. It was a warm evening, and he wore jeans and a dark navy pullover that made his eyes seem darker, duskier.

"You beat me here," she said.

"I thought that might be a wise move."

"It wasn't wisdom," she told him, "it was luck."

"You have a lousy track record, St. Joe. I don't trust you to mind your own damned business for a change."

She climbed the steps with her groceries. He still hadn't gotten up. He seemed at ease, thick legs stretched out, his back against the steps.

"I haven't been sneaky. I just haven't been particularly lucky," she said.

"Did you stop in Camden on your way back?"

She nodded. "Sig left for Boston this morning. She's back at her house on Beacon Hill. I don't know if that's smart—Mom didn't, either. But there's not much either of us can do about it. I'll call her, make sure she's okay." She glanced down at Straker. "How'd it go with Lou?"

"Our good and true sheriff is still hoping he'll get me into his jail before this is all over. He's on the case. I don't know how long he and CID can sit on the pictures before word gets out."

"The sabotage of the *Encounter* is big news."

"The suspected sabotage. It hasn't been proven."

He got to his feet, and she felt a warm shudder, knew that yesterday and last night had settled nothing between them.

"You're looking a little spooked, St. Joe. Does that mean I get the futon tonight?"

"Don't flatter yourself, Straker. I'm not spooked by you." Unraveled, maybe, but not spooked. She balanced her grocery bag in one arm and whipped out her keys. "And you can stay at the Holiday Inn."

"Not a chance. Emile asked me to look out for you. I'm a man with a mission." He stood next to her as she unlocked the door; even in the night light, she could see the scar above his eye, his wry smile. Shot up, six months on a deserted island, and he was as confident as ever, as sure of who he was. "You wouldn't want to come between me and my mission."

She pushed open the door, let him walk in ahead of her. "Are you going to check my place for bombs and booby traps?"

"For starters."

So much for normality.

Her apartment almost seemed to belong to another person, as if she'd taken a quantum leap in her life since she'd left for Maine. She eyed the clutter, the work that meant so much to her, the little things that soothed her soul and just made her smile. She didn't know how she could go back to being the person she'd been before she'd found herself trapped in the fog and had stumbled on Sam Cassain's body, before she'd made love to John Straker.

"I'll put the groceries away," she said. "You make sure nobody's been fooling around with my lightbulbs."

She was just kidding—she told herself she was just kidding—but when Straker started poking around in the corners of her apartment, she couldn't deny a sense of relief. Nobody'd blow up her apartment tonight, anyway.

She set her bag on a cleared stretch of counter and unloaded the milk and juice. Her phone rang, and she shut the fridge, debating whether to let her machine take the call.

She picked up the receiver, and Sig said, "Riley? Just checking in."

Riley frowned. "You sound terrible."

"Physically terrible or emotionally terrible?"

"Both."

"Well, not to worry. I've got my feet up and a talk show on the tube. I'll be fine."

"But you're not fine right now," Riley said.

"Matt was here a little while ago. We—" She seemed to choke back a sob. "I've never felt so helpless in my life."

"What are you going to do?"

"Take the night off. When I'm painting and run into a brick wall, I find it best just to stand back, abandon the project for a while, then come back to it fresh." She inhaled, sniffled. "I know you'd find a way to go through the brick wall if you had to, but I have to—"

"Sig, do you want me to come over?"

"No, no. I'm fine. Are you alone?"

Straker appeared in the kitchen doorway and gave her a thumbs-up. No linseed oil rags draped over her lightbulbs. Riley sighed. "No."

"John Straker's there? *Riley.*"

"It's not what you think." Well, it was, but she wasn't getting into it with her sister. "There's something you need to know. Be discreet, okay? It's not public yet."

She told Sig about the *Encounter*'s engine, Sam's pictures, Emile's theory of sabotage. Straker didn't look too happy about it, but he didn't jerk the phone out of her hand or rip it out of the wall. Riley left out nothing, not even the parts about her brother-in-law's role in bringing up the *Encounter*'s engine.

When she finished, she said, "Are you still sure you don't want me to come over?"

"No." To her surprise, Sig sounded firm, more in control. "I need to mull this over while I watch the talking heads."

She hung up, and Riley let out a long, cathartic breath. She was restless, her mind racing in a thousand different directions at once. She turned to Straker. "How about dinner out? There's a quiet little Thai restaurant a few blocks from here. We can walk over and pretend we're normal people."

"I didn't know any normal people lived in Cambridge."

"Straker, you are so damned obnoxious. I don't know how anyone stands you."

He grinned. "You stand me pretty well, as I recall."

"That was post-traumatic stress. It took jumping out of a burning building to get me into bed with you."

"Ah."

"No sane woman would go to bed with a shot-up, burned-out FBI agent who never could get along with anyone."

"But you've regained your sanity?"

She eyed him, felt the traitorous reaction, low and deep. She licked her lips. "I'm trying."

"Try away, St. Joe. Come on, we'll do dinner out. It'll remove temptation for an hour or so."

Unfortunately, she thought, temptation would be right across the table from her.

But maybe he, too, needed some semblance of normalcy, some balance between the life he'd led for the past six months and the highly charged atmosphere, the danger and questions and fears, of the past week—which, she presumed, was more like his "normal" life.

They sat in the back of the tiny restaurant and ordered too much food, and by unspoken agreement, they talked about things other than fires, murder and sabotage. He wasn't a regular guy. She'd known that when she was six. But he was even less of a regular guy at thirty-four. Regular guys didn't rescue hostages from terrorists. They didn't, she thought, have friends like Emile Labreque, and they didn't touch her the way John Straker had.

"Do you like being an FBI agent?" she asked.

"I'm good at it."

"That's not the same."

He smiled. "It suits me. It's good work, rewarding work. For a while back in April, May, I thought I'd quit, buy a lobster boat."

"But you've changed your mind," Riley said.

"I figure dead bodies would keep turning up until I got the point."

When they walked back to her apartment, she found her hand in his, found herself leaning against his strong shoulder, whispering, "You don't have to sleep on the futon."

"What about the Holiday Inn?"

"A cheap Mainer like you paying for a room when a free one's available?" She smiled. "I don't think so."

"A free room and a willing woman. Life could be worse."

She punched his arm.

"St. Joe, you've been waiting for years for me to walk back into your life. You need a man who doesn't tiptoe around that big mouth of yours."

"You didn't walk back in, Straker. You barreled in."

He squeezed her hand. "Sexier that way."

When they reached her apartment, he made no pretenses, just scooped her up and carried her back to her bedroom caveman style, smothered her laughter with a breathtaking, spine-melting kiss. He was indeed, she thought, an intensely physical man, with an enthusiasm for sex that was staggering, that made her feel as if he would never get enough of her.

They had a cycle going. The more he wanted her, the more she wanted him; the more she wanted him, the more he wanted her. On and on it went, until the cycle fell in on itself and they couldn't stop, couldn't breathe, couldn't imagine release.

And when it happened, when release came, it wasn't gentle, or slow, or easy, but soul penetrating, washing over them in great, searing waves, as if it had a logic and a will of its own, one that bypassed all careful reasoning, all knowledge, all common sense.

"I can't fall in love with you," she whispered, drawing the blankets up over them as she settled against his shoulder.

He slid his hand over the curve of her hip, moved lower, eased his fingers between her legs. "Of course you can't. Falling's not your style."

And his mouth found hers, his tongue probing with the same erotic rhythm as his fingers, beginning the cycle again. "What's your style?" she asked as he kissed her throat, took a nipple between his lips.

"I'm better at action than words."

He raised up off her and eased his fingers away, then entered with a deep, hard thrust that made her cry out with its intensity. He didn't follow with another, but stayed in her, caught up her hand in his and locked eyes with her. A man of action. A man of great physical needs. He was asking her not to fall, but to take control, to choose.

"Again," she breathed. "Don't stop."

"As if I could," he said, thrusting harder, deeper.

Much later, she slipped out of bed, pulled on a bathrobe and went into the living room. She turned on a light and sat on the futon with a clipboard and a pencil, drew a line down the middle of a yellow pad. On the left, she jotted everything she knew to be a fact. On the right, she jotted everything else.

When she finished, her hands were shaking and she was fighting tears. There was more under the "everything else" column. None of it looked good for Emile.

Straker came and sat beside her. He'd put on jeans, nothing else. He took her clipboard, examined it. "Not bad. You'd make it through Quantico."

"I'm afraid for Emile," she said. "He's always believed in destiny, fate. That's how he could take on so much for so many years, without fear. He's never been able to look over his shoulder and see his enemies coming. And Matt—" She gulped for air. "I'm afraid for him, too. He's in over his head, isn't he?"

Straker was expressionless. "He should tell the police what he knows. Bow out and let them do their job."

"Sig couldn't stand to lose him. Straker, she's pregnant, she can't—"

"She knows all the risks." He laid Riley's clipboard on top of a stack of magazines. "Sig might be a free spirit instead of a scientist, but she's no one's fool."

Riley stared at her columns of facts, rumors, musings, suppositions. "Bennett Granger came aboard the *Encounter* at the last minute. I wrote that down under facts. I don't know if it makes any difference—I just jotted down stuff as it came to mind."

"Why the last minute?"

"Spur of the moment, he said. He did that sort of thing from time to time. This wasn't one of Emile's big research expeditions—we were just going out for a few days to test an experimental submersible. My own reasons for being aboard were tangential." She swallowed, barely able to continue. "Do you suppose whoever sabotaged the *Encounter* would have done it if they'd realized Bennett was aboard?"

"It's something to consider." Straker's tone was professional, unemotional.

She shivered, suddenly cold. "I don't know how you do this kind of work for a living."

"Because it's necessary."

She nodded. "If this was your case—"

"It's not my case. I haven't been treating it as my case. I'm Emile's friend. I'm your friend. I told you right from the beginning I'm not acting in a professional capacity." He managed a quick smile. "Which is a good thing. Otherwise I wouldn't be able to sleep with you, and that wouldn't be any fun."

She smiled, feeling less cold. "Thank you."

"It's easy to be reassuring in the middle of the night. In the cold light of day..." He got to his feet, touched her hair. "We'll take another look at your list in the morning."

Fifteen

~~~∽◦⟋⟋⟍◦∽~~~

Straker listened to Riley explain her plan of action—or, more accurately, *inaction*—as he drove her into Boston in the morning. With her leather tote on her lap and wearing a crisp white shirt and black pants, she was ready to spend the day as director of recovery and rehabilitation for the Boston Center for Oceanographic Research. Henry Armistead, she said, would just have to put up with her.

"I'm going to try to sit tight," she said. "I think it's important to give the authorities a chance to pick apart Sam's movements in the past few weeks and get on with finding out how he died, who's framing Emile and setting fires."

Straker had his doubts about Riley St. Joe ever sitting tight, but he kept silent.

"I suppose answers would be easier to come by if my damned grandfather and brother-in-law quit their cloak-and-dagger games and talked to investigators." She inhaled, her frustration with them palpable. "But I understand. I was aboard the *Encounter,* Straker. If

I were in Matt's or Emile's place, I'd probably do what they're doing."

"You haven't been much better," he pointed out. "It's going to be a close call whether they end up with charges against them."

Her arms tensed, and her eyes darkened a fraction. A week ago he might not have noticed. Now he noticed everything she did. Which, he knew, would be of no comfort to her whatsoever. She said, "Emile won't care. Matt..." She inhaled. "He's probably never even had a parking ticket. But he can afford a good lawyer."

Straker shook his head. "Yep. You're going to sit tight." His tone was laced with sarcasm and amusement at how unself-aware she could be. "You'll start to twitch the minute someone hands you a report on the skin problems of a moray eel and you realize this is it, no bad guys to root out."

"I *like* my work."

"So?"

She shot him a stubborn look. "So what?"

"So I give you thirty minutes before you start climbing the walls."

"You're not going to give me anything. You're going to leave me alone. Got it, Straker? I mean it. Henry still has you down as a stalker, you know."

He smiled. "Is that a threat?"

"It's bad enough I'm showing up today. If you show up, too, he'll have a fit. And I don't blame him. Caroline's round of parties on Mount Desert was supposed to signal a new beginning for the center—the end of our year of mourning the *Encounter* and the five lost.''

"Then Sam turns up dead.''

She winced, staring out the open window. It was a cool, beautiful morning. "I didn't mean to sound hard-hearted. Sam had his downside, but he didn't deserve—'' She stopped, and Straker knew she was seeing the body on the rocks. "He didn't deserve to be murdered.''

Straker negotiated the maze of Big Dig detours and the city traffic, and was struck by the normalcy of something as simple as dropping Riley St. Joe off at work.

"I need to let everything simmer,'' she went on, almost absently. "Sig does that. She's convinced that abandoning a problem for a while is the best way to solve it.''

"I thought you were giving the authorities a chance.''

"I *am*. But if I come up with any answers, what's wrong with that?''

"Nothing if you call them first and don't go off half-cocked.''

She scowled. "Typical FBI agent. You don't trust anyone.''

"I don't trust *you*. You get a lead on Emile, you'll be out of there.''

"Well, fine. What are your plans for the day?''

"I thought I'd pay your sister a visit.''

Riley nodded, obviously concurring with the idea.

"I plan to call her after I get in. She's so unhappy. Are you shifting your focus from Emile to Matt?"

"Nah, I'm taking you to work."

She groaned. "Were you this bad before you were shot? Never mind. I know you were. That's why I threw that rock at you."

"You threw more than one rock at me. Lucky for you only one hit."

"Lucky for *me?*"

"Definitely."

He pulled up to the plaza in front of the center, and a wild-haired man in his late twenties jumped out in front of Riley's car. He thumped the hood in excitement. "Riley St. Joe. A word?"

"I'm not talking to reporters, Straker. Can you—"

Straker shook his head. "I'm not running him over. He has a right to do his job."

"If he jumps in front of a moving car, he should expect to get run over." But she sighed. "This is all Henry needs to see. You at the wheel of my car, a reporter pelting questions at me."

The reporter held on to the driver-side mirror as if to keep the car from pulling away. He stuck his head in Straker's window. "John Straker," he said. "You're the FBI agent who was wounded in the hostage situation up on the Canadian border earlier this year. You were on Labreque Island when Riley here found Captain Cassain's body."

"That's me."

"So there you were recuperating from your injuries on a quiet coastal island and a dead body turns up.

How did that feel? Did it bring everything back? Did
you have a flashback to your own near death?''

Straker kept both hands on the wheel. This wasn't
a professional journalist, this was an idiot. He was
feeling fewer qualms about running him over. "I'm
not answering questions this morning." There. That
was reasonable.

"You and Emile Labreque are from the same small
town in Maine. Are you two friends?" When Straker
didn't answer, the reporter squinted at him, undeter-
red. "You know where he is? Don't you think it's
virtually impossible for a widely recognized man like
Emile Labreque to elude authorities for this long
without help?"

Riley placed her hand on her door handle as if to
make a run for it.

"Okay," Straker said to the reporter. "Riley needs
to get to work, and I haven't had my second cup of
coffee." He put one hand on the gearshift. "You
might want to back away from the car."

The reporter—or whatever he was—hung on to the
mirror and leaned farther in the window. Straker
could easily give his scrawny neck a twist. "Riley,
what about you? Are you hiding your grandfather?
Do you think he killed Sam Cassain?"

She clenched her tote, glared at him. "That's a hell
of a question—"

"I've heard rumors Cassain could prove your
grandfather sabotaged the *Encounter*."

One of the many lessons Riley had yet to learn,

Straker thought, was turning the other cheek. Her eyes darkened; her jaw set hard. "He did no such thing."

"Rumor has it that's what got Cassain killed. Emile popped him on the head, let him drown, dumped his body where he thought no one would find it. Didn't he try to discourage you from kayaking to Labreque Island?"

She grabbed Straker's arm, ready to jump over him and go for the guy's throat. "That's outrageous. Who's spreading these rumors?"

"Well, then, maybe you helped your grandfather dump Sam's body, then pretended to find it to divert suspicion—"

She was going for the window. She shoved her tote on the floor with one hand and tightened her grip on Straker's arm, ready to crawl over his lap and jump through the window. He could smell her hair, her light perfume, felt a jolt as he remembered last night. Now, however, she wanted blood.

Straker held her off and turned to the reporter. "Okay, ace, time to back off. We're done here."

The reporter stood his ground smugly. "I'm not."

Straker ignored him and hit the gas, pulling forward, giving the guy about half a second to let go of the mirror. He did, but he smacked the trunk as a final *gotcha*. Straker plopped Riley back in her seat, gunned the engine and whipped around to the parking garage, where, presumably, she'd have a better chance of avoiding other reporters.

"You're an FBI agent," she muttered. "Can't you arrest him?"

He glanced at her. "An ounce of prevention is worth a pound of cure."

"What's that supposed to mean?"

"It means I'd rather keep a violent act from happening than clean up after one."

She snorted. "You think that weasel would have tried to hurt me?"

"Other way around, sweetheart." He smiled as he pulled to a stop just inside the garage. "I can see why the center doesn't have you do PR. The pitbull approach."

"He was horrible. Unprofessional. He deserved—"

"He deserved worse than he got. That's not the point. You let him get under your skin, which is exactly what he set out to do."

She picked up her tote bag, her cheeks flushed. She was still poised for battle. "This is why I'm an ocean-ographer."

Straker smiled. "Go take care of your fish."

"When you see Sig, if there's any sign she's not doing well—"

"I'll slap her into the hospital."

Riley nodded and pushed open her door. "I'll check in with you later and let you know how long I plan to stay. If you learn anything, call me."

He waited until she'd made her way to the center's side entrance, then dove back into Boston morning rush hour traffic and headed up to Beacon Hill. Lots of cars, lots of aggravation. He located Chestnut Street, located the attractive Federal Period town house that, according to Riley, belonged to her sister and brother-in-law. It had black shutters and a cream-colored, brass-trimmed front door.

He parked in a spot designated for Beacon Hill residents and rang the doorbell. If Sig wasn't home, he had no Plan *B*.

She was home. "Straker," she said in surprise, as she opened the door. "What are you doing here?"

"I thought I'd stop by and see how you're doing. Mind if I come in?"

"Of course not."

She stood back, and he walked in past her. She shut the door quietly behind him. It wasn't, he thought, that she looked like hell. Sig almost never looked like hell. But she was pale, drained, eyes puffy, the few lines in her face more prominent. She had on one of her oversize dresses, this one way too big, and her hair hung in tangles down her back. She wasn't her usual vibrant self.

She smiled weakly at him. "I look that bad?"

"Nah. You look like a pregnant lady who jumped out of a burning building a few nights ago."

"I'm feeling fine," she said. "Just a little tired. I already went for a walk this morning.

"Good for you."

"Can I get you a cup of coffee?"

He could drink about a gallon of coffee, but he shook his head. Like her little sister, Sig didn't have the kind of internal barometer that told her when she'd had enough. She'd keep going until she dropped. Straker followed her into a pretty front parlor that was surprisingly livable, had her sit. She took the couch. He took a wing chair across from her.

She cleared her throat, stared at her hands as she twisted them together on her lap. "The police were here when I got back from my walk."

Straker wasn't surprised. "They want to talk to your husband," he speculated.

She nodded. "They said he's a potential...a material witness, I think it was."

"Bottom line, Sig, he needs to come in. He needs to grab the first uniform he sees and start talking. It's squeeze-play time. He's got too many competing things going against him." He paused, debating the wisdom of his next statement. "He's in over his head. Way over."

"I know, I know. He's a Harvard MBA, not an FBI agent. I don't know what the hell he thinks he's doing!" She collapsed back against the couch. "I told the police he was here last night. Everything. God."

"It was the right thing to do."

She nodded, fighting tears. "I still feel like a fink."

He couldn't resist a smile at her choice of words. The St. Joe sisters were a dramatic, colorful pair. They got that from their grandfather. Their mother, too. "Did your husband give you any idea—"

"No. Not about anything." Her dark eyes dried; her expression hardened. "I'd tell you if he did. I'd love for you to track him down and knock some sense into him."

"Unfortunately, I'm not that good at knocking sense into people."

She waved a hand. "Oh, you've just been spending too much time with Riley. *No one* can get through to her when she's got the bit in her teeth. You have to wear her down." She gave a sudden wry smile, her melancholy lifting. "And I'm sure you have your ways of doing just that."

He judiciously said nothing.

Sig sat up straight, almost gleeful. "Straker! You and Riley *are*—"

"Stop right there, before you say something that'll get us both in hot water." He wished he could keep her spirits up, but he knew he couldn't. "Sig, various lobstermen, including my father, have given your grandfather a hand. I don't think they've stepped over the line yet, but they've come damned close."

"I know. Riley told me. Are they in any danger?"

"Nothing they can't handle, I expect. They'd love a chance to nail anyone who'd sabotage a ship." He leaned forward, eyed her intently. "What your sister didn't tell you, because I haven't told her, is that some of the lobstermen saw your husband's boat in the bay shortly before she discovered Sam Cassain's body on Labreque Island."

Sig frowned. She'd sunk back against the couch again, her dress draped over her bulging stomach. His words didn't seem to register. "Matt's boat?"

"Yes."

"Well, he was on Mount Desert that weekend. Everyone was. Caroline, Abigail, most of the center's staff. My father, Riley. My mother didn't go up—she doesn't have anything to do with the center anymore.

It wouldn't surprise me if Matt ditched Caroline and his sister to sail up to Schoodic.'' She added softly, ''We both have a lot of memories up that way.''

''The police have probably talked to the lobstermen. They'll have told them they saw him. Sig, I'm not suggesting he had any direct involvement with Sam's death or how he ended up on the island.''

''But that's how it looks,'' she finished for him. She shut her eyes, breathing out in a mix of frustration and resignation. ''The police didn't say anything about lobstermen, Matt's boat—''

''They wouldn't, necessarily.''

Her eyes brimmed with tears. ''I don't know what to do.''

''Trust your instincts and call the police the next time you see your husband.''

She leveled her artist's gaze on him. ''He's not a killer.''

Straker didn't respond. What response was there?

''He's *not*.''

If Emile was right, someone had sabotaged the *Encounter*. Someone who knew boats. Someone who, according to Riley, probably hadn't realized Bennett Granger would be aboard. That opened up the possibilities.

''Sam's death could have been an accident,'' Sig said. ''Matt's never been that interested in the center. He indulged his father and Abigail, but he had no scores to settle, no grand plan for preserving the world's oceans. He just wants to know why his father died.''

Straker could see she was getting upset; her face was red, her hands twisted into knots. Time to change the subject.

"My God," she said, going even paler, "it's not as if *he* sabotaged the *Encounter*."

"Sig, I'm not jumping to any conclusions. Neither should you."

"Why would he fund Sam to find out what really happened if he knew? If he'd done it himself? Why would he—" She gulped for air. "I suppose if he's guilt ridden and the explosion, the fire, the flooding were all worse than he expected, he might want to know what happened. He could—"

"Sig. Stop."

She placed a hand on her brow, tried to control her rapid breathing.

"Tell me about Abigail," Straker said quietly.

Sig licked her lips, calming slightly. "She's wonderful. Riley and I have known her since we were little kids, but she's older than we are. She was always good to us. I think she might have liked to become a marine scientist, but she never did."

"Your sister did."

"Oh, there was never any question of that. You remember. She and Emile were joined at the hip from the minute she could dip a hand into a tide pool."

"Did you feel left out?"

Sig smiled, looking better now. "Are you kidding? With Riley tramping around after Emile and Mom and Dad, I was free to draw, paint, do my own thing.

My mother and I have grown closer since she moved to Camden and took up nature writing.''

"What about your father?''

"He's a great guy, and he and my mother are happy together now, even if they have unconventional living arrangements. I'm not sure I could stand it myself. I *know* Riley couldn't.''

Straker made no comment.

Sig went on. "My father can't wait for the *Encounter II* to get finished. He doesn't have Emile's charisma, but he's just as committed to the center's work.'' Her expression hardened suddenly, and she glared at Straker. "He didn't blow up the *Encounter.*''

Straker sighed. "You and Riley have to quit trying to read my mind. You're no good at it.''

Unlike her sister, Sig had the grace to blush. "I'm sorry. I'm defensive. There's one more thing about Abigail I probably should tell you—she and Henry Armistead are having an affair. I'm not surprised, really. Abigail's divorced, Henry's charming and handsome, and they both live and breathe for the center. They've had a traumatic year, trying to make up for the loss of both Emile and Bennett.''

"They're keeping their relationship secret?''

"For now. I suspect they want to have a better idea of where it's going before they open themselves up to that kind of publicity and scrutiny.''

"She and Armistead have to fill pretty big shoes.''

"Yes, they do.''

An awkward silence followed. Straker had never

been much on small talk. He got to his feet and motioned for Sig to stay put, but she didn't. Her color had improved, and she seemed to have more energy, even a little fight, now that she'd had a chance to talk.

She touched his arm. "My sister isn't as invulnerable as she likes to pretend. You'll be gentle with her?"

He smiled. "If I don't throttle her first."

Riley lasted in her office just over ninety minutes, thinking about the fall whale migration south, before Henry stormed in. He inhaled sharply and dropped into her extra chair, frowning at her. "The Maine State Police were at Abigail's this morning."

Matt. They would want to talk to him about his role in bringing up the *Encounter*'s engine. Riley nodded. "I hope they'll get to the bottom of this mess soon."

"They'd get to it a lot sooner if your grandfather—" He stopped himself, waved a hand in frustration. "Well, you know my position on Emile. I'd hoped we were over the hump when Caroline had us to Mount Desert last week. It'd been a year since the *Encounter*, and—" He sighed, throwing up his hands. "Obviously I was wrong."

"You weren't wrong, Henry. We had a great time at Caroline's. None of us could have predicted Sam's death."

"I hope not."

Riley felt her stomach turn over. "You're not saying—"

He raised his eyes to hers. "Let me be plain, Riley. I hope for your sake Emile's exonerated."

"He will be," she said. "If he's not, I'll resign. You won't have to fire me. What about my father?"

"He doesn't have your visibility. He's pure research, and he's been more willing to allow the possibility that Emile has gone over the edge."

"I understand," she said quietly. "But I'm not worried. I know my grandfather, Henry. He didn't kill Sam or set those fires."

He sighed, as if he couldn't expect her to say anything else. "Abigail's terrified for her brother. Nearly losing Sig just about did her in, and now the police are looking for Matt."

"It's a mess. I know that. With any luck the police will find Matt before he does anything really stupid."

His chin shot up, his eyes sparking. "Are you implying—"

She gave him a quick smile. "I'm not implying anything."

Henry rose, stiff, formal, carefully controlled. "Riley, if something else is going to blow up in my face, I need to know it."

"Hey, I'd like to know it, too."

Her halfhearted attempt at humor didn't go over well. "I'm asking you to keep me in the loop."

She groaned. "There is no loop, Henry. I wish there were." She jumped up from her desk, suddenly restless; she couldn't imagine focusing on her work.

"We're all in difficult positions. We're all under a great deal of stress. Believe me, I'm not trying to make things worse for you."

"I know, I know." He exhaled, looking less angry and frustrated, more tired. "Forgive me. It wasn't my intention to downplay the ordeal you've been through in recent days. Abigail said the police left her with the impression they have information they aren't willing to share with her. I was hoping you had some idea what might be—"

She did have some idea. She had plenty of ideas. But Straker would have her head if she sat Henry down and told him everything. Instead she mumbled, "I'm just doing the best I can."

His eyes narrowed, again suspiciously. The look of fatigue instantly vanished. "Riley?"

She'd never been a good liar. "Look, I'm not going to get anything done around here. I thought—well, it doesn't matter what I thought. You don't mind if I head out, do you?"

"Of course not."

His tone was clipped, wary. She didn't know what had tipped him off that she was in fact holding back on him—probably recent history. But how could she explain that her grandfather had been hiding out in an abandoned Maine sardine cannery with his pictures of a sabotaged *Encounter* engine?

"What about your FBI agent? John Straker. Where's he?"

"He doesn't exactly keep me informed of his movements." She tried to seem casual. She swooped up her leather tote. "I'll stop by Sig's. If she's seen Matt, I'll let Abigail know. Okay?"

Henry remained cool. "Be sure you do. She's worried about her brother, as you can imagine. None of us wants him to be the next victim."

"Henry—"

He held up a hand. "I'm not suggesting anything. I imagine the police have interviewed your sister as well. She would cooperate, I'm sure."

"I'm sure," Riley echoed, annoyed.

After Henry left, she finished packing up for the day. Tension and fatigue had eroded her ability to concentrate. Usually the opposite occurred, and the more stressed out she was, the more she buried herself in her work. It was, she thought, her own form of self-imposed exile. Straker had gone to an island after his ordeal. She had dived into the world of marine recovery and rehabilitation. There was nothing more exhilarating than returning a healthy dolphin, a healthy whale, to the wild.

Instead of going directly to Beacon Hill, she slipped out to the small, rusting, outdated research ship moored at the back of the center. It wasn't the *Encounter,* and it wasn't even a shadow of the *Encounter II*. Her father was down below, trying to work in cramped temporary quarters.

Riley managed a smile. "This old tug doesn't quite compare to the *Encounter II,* does it?"

He leaned back in his ancient chair, visibly shook off his total immersion in his work and focused on her. "It's going to be a fabulous ship."

"Bennett's dream come true," she added.

Her father nodded sadly. "He always had tremendous vision. Emile, too. They were remarkable men."

"Emile still is. He's not dead."

"I didn't mean it that way."

He raked a hand through his scruffy hair. His research into the endangered right whale—a large, slow, acrobatic, oil-rich species long favored by whalers—consumed him. The northern right whale, *Eubalaena glacialis,* was near extinction, although the southern right whale was showing signs of recovery. Their slow breeding hindered their recovery and thus was a focus of much of Richard St. Joe's research and restoration efforts.

"You're okay?" he asked.

She nodded, realizing with a pang of regret that she couldn't tell him about Emile and the *Encounter* sabotage, either. She'd simply wanted to see him. "Sig's back in town."

"Mara told me. We're in constant touch since the fire at Emile's. I heard you came to work today—I was going to stop in later. I think it's a good idea to try to maintain your routines as much as possible until this all gets sorted out."

"In theory, anyway. I'm heading out right now. I thought I'd go up and see what Sig's up to."

"I don't like her staying in that house alone."

"I wondered about that, too. Maybe I'll stay with her or make her camp out at my apartment."

He nodded approvingly. "What about John Straker?"

Riley deliberately misinterpreted his words. "What, do you think I need to keep an eye on him?"

Her father smiled. "No, but I suspect he's keeping an eye on you. That thought helps me sleep nights." He gave himself a shake, sighed. "I can't believe I said that. Amazing. Trusting John Straker with one of my daughters. But he's here in Boston, isn't he?"

"He most certainly is."

"If you need me—"

"I know, Dad." She gave him a quick hug. "You and Mom are both rocks. Thanks."

The sun was bright, the air perfect for an afternoon of playing hooky—if only she could, Riley thought. She'd love to walk through Fanueil Hall Marketplace, sit on a bench and look out at the harbor, or just go to the Department of Motor Vehicles and replace her driver's license after it burned up in the fire at Emile's.

Instead she spotted Straker at the marine mammal fountain. His thick body, the ease with which he stood at a Boston fountain or on a rickety Maine dock, were unmistakable. He turned to her, his gray eyes sweeping over her. "No whales to drag back to sea?"

"Thankfully, no. Did you see Sig? How is she?"

"Hanging by threads."

"She can't stay alone. I'm going to insist we stay together."

He nodded and gestured behind her. "Company."

Caroline Granger joined them at the fountain. She looked composed, perfectly groomed and coordinated in her stylish pantsuit and gold jewelry. "Riley,

you're just the person I'm looking for.'' She smiled
at Straker, narrowed her ladylike gaze on him. ''You
must be John Straker, the FBI agent.''

He smiled back, a gleam of wry humor in his very
gray eyes. This was a man, Riley realized, who didn't
take himself too seriously. ''And you must be Caroline Granger.''

''The widow,'' she added with a light note of self-
deprecation. ''I heard all sorts of stories about you
this summer in Maine. You were a topic of much
speculation. Were you a hero or a wounded lion raging on his own private island? No one quite knew
whether to lock up their daughters.''

Riley tried not to squirm. Straker laughed. ''Nothing like a little drama to perk up a summer afternoon.''

''Well, you've become quite the legend. Don't
deny it. I came to invite Riley here to lunch. Won't
you join us, Special Agent Straker?''

If Caroline Granger could charm Straker, she could
charm anyone. Riley, who had no such ability,
watched in fascination. ''I was just on my way to see
Sig—''

''I won't keep you long. We can have lunch right
here at the hotel.'' One of Boston's finer hotels was
a short walk from the plaza. ''To be honest, Riley, I
need to talk to you.''

''Then lunch it is. Thank you.''

Whether because he was charmed or simply determined to keep watch on her, Straker joined them. Caroline had a table waiting at the waterfront luxury ho-

tel, its menu nothing like the one at the shack of a restaurant where his father and fellow lobstermen ate.

"You must try the clam chowder," Caroline told him when they were seated. "It won't compare to sitting down to a bowl of steaming haddock chowder in a good Maine fog, but it's really a wonderful recipe."

Straker agreed to try it. Riley could see he was taken with Caroline. Who wouldn't be? Caroline asked about Sig, shared Riley's concern about her sister staying on Beacon Hill alone. As their table filled up with warm bread, salads, chowders and drinks, she said, "I'm going to tell you both something. A secret."

Riley glanced at Straker, but his expression was unreadable.

Caroline continued, "I don't eat, sleep and breathe oceanography."

"Horrors," Riley said with a laugh.

But Caroline was serious. "I took an interest in the center because it meant so much to Ben. It was like having a third partner in our marriage. I knew that going in, of course. I accepted it. I loved his passion for oceanographic research, his love of the ocean. That kind of intense commitment, I find, is rare." She turned to Straker. "Did you ever meet my husband?"

"A few times during the summer when I was growing up in Maine. He'd take his yacht up to see Emile when he wasn't off on some grand research expedition."

Her eyes moistened, but no tears spilled out. "Oh,

he loved Emile. He truly did. This past year has been devastating. Losing Ben, losing Emile. I thought I'd never recover.''

Riley picked up her tall glass of cold sparkling cider. She hadn't followed Caroline's lead and had wine; neither had Straker, who stuck to water. In contrast to the sudden somber tone of the lunch, the restaurant's atmosphere was cheerful and elegant. "It seemed like having everyone to Maine last week helped—it felt like a kind of transition to me," Riley said. "I mean, before Sam..."

Caroline lifted her slender shoulders, let them drop. "I loved being around all of you, all that dedication and intelligence, all your wonderful energy and enthusiasm. You've helped me stay connected to Ben. I wanted that. I *needed* it."

"I think I understand," Riley said. "You've helped us stay connected to Bennett, too. We all miss him."

She nodded. "I know. He's hard not to miss. But now..." She paused, sipped her wine. She seemed to be talking to herself as much as to her lunch partners. "All that's happened this past week has made me realize, or acknowledge, what I already knew—that I need to move on with my life. Perhaps if Ben and I had had children it would be different. But we didn't, and now I have to make a decision."

"Caroline—"

She shook off Riley's interruption. "Ben has two children. Abigail will carry on her father's work. Matthew will carry on his father's commitment to his family's businesses."

If he didn't get himself arrested or killed, Riley thought. But she could detect no such concerns, nor any bitterness, in Caroline Granger. "Caroline, you've been amazing this past year. We would all miss you. I hope you know that. Do you have any plans yet?"

"I have a condominium in Florida. I think I'll go there for the winter. Then I'll reexamine my options in the spring." She smiled at Riley, every hair and careful smudge of makeup perfect, in place. "I'm grateful for the seven years I had with Ben and his family and friends."

"As they—we—all are for you."

Caroline seemed relieved simply to have stated her intentions out loud. She turned to Straker, gave him a clear-eyed, businesslike look. "I should tell you, and Riley, that Emile came to see me last night at my apartment here on the waterfront. He's back in Boston. I haven't mentioned his visit to the police."

Straker had no visible reaction. "What did he want?"

She stared at her wineglass as if transfixed. "He asked me if I was the one who encouraged Ben to go aboard the *Encounter* on its last voyage. You know he went aboard at the last minute."

"And?"

She didn't lift her gaze from her wineglass.

"I was."

Riley didn't move. Straker's eyes met hers briefly, shifted back to Caroline. "Why?"

"Oh, he was champing at the bit to go. It was so

obvious. I wanted us to do a few things together, spend some time on Mount Desert, go sailing with friends, just take a long drive in the country." She sighed, wistful. "But I knew he wanted to go. So I told him I'd prefer to wait until fall, when the leaves had changed and the crowds had eased. I said I'd go to a spa while he was away, visit old friends. I said— I said, 'That's where your heart is, Ben. Go.'"

"And you told this to Emile?" Straker asked.

She nodded. "He thought it was Matt who'd urged Ben to go. It would explain why he's had such a difficult time accepting what happened. But it wasn't Matt. It was me. I've lived with that guilt...."

Riley reached over and touched Caroline's hand. "Unless you blew up the *Encounter* yourself, it's not your fault."

"Reason and guilt often don't go hand in hand. But thank you."

"What about Emile?" Straker asked.

"He simply nodded and left. I urged him to go to the police before anything else terrible happens, but he ignored me completely. He's always had that way about him when he's on a mission—you can't divert him." She sipped more wine; she'd hardly touched her food. "I haven't told the police about his visit. I suppose I should."

Riley was ready to tell her not to bother, just to spare her the trauma, but Straker went all-FBI and said, "Yes. You should."

"I'll do so at once," Caroline said, and smiled.

"Thank you both. I hope—I know this will all work out. It has to. None of us can take any more tragedy."

She stayed to pay the bill, shooed Riley and Straker out. When they reached the brick plaza in front of the hotel, the sun was breaking through clouds that had floated in off the water.

Straker said, "I wonder what Emile's up to."

"From what Caroline said, I'd say he has the bit in his teeth about something. Well, that's nothing new. But if he sticks his face into the wrong hornet's nest and gets himself killed—"

"Don't jump ahead, Riley. We just had lunch. Where to now?"

She thought a moment, knew what she had to do. "I want to see my sister."

Sixteen

$\backsim\!\!\!\!\curvearrowright\!\!\!\curvearrowleft\!\!\!\!\sim$

Riley was struck by how happy, even relieved, she was to see her sister when Sig opened the door to her Chestnut Street house. "Where's Straker?" Sig asked, peering out at the street.

"What makes you think he's with me?"

"Because he is."

Riley scoffed. "I'm lucky I can breathe without him."

"The question is, would you want to?"

"Sig..."

She smiled, motioning Riley inside. "So is he here or isn't he?"

"He's parking the car."

Sig led her into the living room, where Riley flopped onto a chair and tried to ease the tension in her neck and shoulder muscles. Sig's house was tidy and spotless, not that she was tidy and spotless by nature—she and Matt had help. Her sister's artistic touch was everywhere, in the placement of furniture, the choice of fabrics and artwork. Riley had no such

knack. She just piled up stuff where she had room
and bought what caught her fancy, and what she could
afford.

Her sister smiled knowingly. "I think you've finally met a man who knows your bark is bigger than
your bite."

"Now, don't be jumping to conclusions. And never
mind *my* bark. His bark's just as big as his bite.
He—" Riley frowned, sat forward as she listened.
"Did you hear that?"

Sig frowned. "What?"

"Shh."

They listened, silent, as a distinct rattling sounded
from down the hall, toward the kitchen and the back
door. A garden courtyard connected with a narrow,
secret alley that led back to Mount Vernon Street, one
of Beacon Hill's many nooks and crannies.

"Quick," Sig whispered, moving toward the hall,
"grab a vase or something."

Riley picked up a heavy, handblown glass vase
from a gleaming side table. She moved in behind her
sister, kept her voice low. "How would someone get
in? You keep your doors locked, don't you?"

"Of course."

"Maybe they broke in while you were taking a
nap."

"I haven't slept."

"Have you been out?"

"I took a short walk this morning, but other than
that, I've been here." Sig placed a hand on the cream-
colored woodwork and leaned forward, peering down

the hall. "If someone knows the alley and had a key—unless they broke in—"

"Matt?"

Sig didn't answer. She eased into the hall, Riley on her heels with the vase. "Let me go first," Riley whispered. "I can move faster than you can."

"Do you think we should call the police?"

"If it's Matt..."

She nodded, and Riley edged in front of her. The vase was heavy and awkward, a bit slippery, but it would do damage if she had to hit someone over the head with it.

"I hope Straker finds a parking space and gets in here," Sig said quietly.

"It's okay. We can handle—"

"That's the spirit."

It was Emile's voice behind them. Riley was so startled that the vase slipped out of her grasp and shattered on the hardwood floor. Sig clasped her bulging stomach with one hand. They both whirled around.

Their grandfather smiled at them. "I'm glad I taught my two granddaughters how to stand up for themselves. I was trying not to startle you."

"Well, you blew that," Riley said, picking her way through the shards of glass.

"We thought you were down the hall in the kitchen," Sig said.

"I was. I came through the drawing room."

Riley had never seen him look this tired, this worn-out. Even after the *Encounter* had gone down and the air was running out in their submersible, he had been numb, fatalistic. Now, she could see every second of the past year's trauma etched in the lines in his face, in its grayish color, in the stooped way he walked. Only his dark eyes reflected any of the old fight, intensity and spirit.

"How long have you been here?" Sig glared at him, obviously unsure of her own reaction to Emile sneaking around in her house. "Why didn't you use the front door and knock?"

"I had a key. I didn't realize you were here. I thought I might catch Matthew by surprise."

"Obviously he's not here. Emile..." Sig threw up her hands in frustration. Clearly at a loss. "Damn it!"

Riley squatted down to pick up the thick pieces of the broken vase. "Straker's on his way. He'll make you go to the police this time, Emile. He's ready to go FBI on us. I think he's about had it with cutting you any slack. Me, too."

"Listen to me," Emile said. His voice was ragged, exhausted. "Both of you. The police searched the Granger house on Mount Desert. They found the *Encounter*'s engine stashed in an outbuilding. Not the whole thing—the alarm panel, a ruptured disk, the lube oil drain valve. The evidence that proves it was sabotaged."

Riley nearly cut herself on a piece of glass. "Emile, good God, how do you know?"

"That doesn't matter."

"Caroline told you," Riley said. "She knew.

Straker and I just had lunch with her. Why didn't she tell us?''

"Because of me," Sig said, white-faced. "She thinks Matt—she thinks he and Sam had a falling out and...*oh, God*."

Probably true, Riley thought. Caroline knew she and Straker were on their way to see Sig, wouldn't want to upset her further with more incriminating evidence against her husband.

Emile's expression softened. "We can't jump to conclusions. Sam could have brought his evidence there for safekeeping with or without Matt's knowledge, or Matt could have brought it there himself."

"Holy shit," Sig breathed, sinking into a chair. "The stupid bastard *has* to come in."

"Does this take any heat off you?" Riley asked her grandfather.

He shook his head. "No. The police are still very eager to talk to me."

Count on Emile for a straight answer. Riley got to her feet, thick pieces of glass in her palm. "Then let's call them. Right now."

The front doorbell rang. It had to be Straker, Riley thought with mixed feelings. He'd back her up and Emile would finally be in safe hands, but she also expected she and Sig had seen the last of maneuvering around Boston on their own.

Sig, either sharing her expectation or too tired to move, motioned for her sister to get the door. Riley looked for a place to put the shards of glass. "Never mind the damned vase,'' Sig said. ''I don't think I'd even feel it if I stepped on a piece of glass.''

Riley let the glass fall back onto the floor and pointed a warning finger at her grandfather. ''Emile, you stay right here. Do *not* try to sneak out. I mean it. I'll sic Straker on you.''

She didn't give Emile a chance to answer. Not trusting him for one minute, she quickly slipped into the hall and tore open the front door.

Matt Granger fell in on her, his tall, rangy body slumping into her arms. ''Oh, God,'' she said, catching him as best she could.

Riley saw the smears of blood on the door, on his hand as he tried to steady himself. He was too big, and all she could do was cushion their fall as they both sank to the floor.

She screamed. ''Sig! Get out here—Matt's hurt!''

Her brother-in-law was barely conscious, virtually a deadweight on top of her. He was a lean slab of meat, crushing her as he moaned and struggled against his own incapacity. She could feel his sweat, his blood.

''Don't try to move,'' she said softly, holding him by the shoulders.

He had a bloody scrape on the left side of his face; his left eye was puffy, bloodshot and bruised, his fair hair caked with blood. He moaned, and she saw that his left arm was also scraped and bruised.

Sig dropped onto her knees beside her husband, took in his bloodied appearance. ''Matt—oh, *Jesus.*''

Emile was right behind her, swearing under his breath.

"Riley, call an ambulance," Sig ordered, taking charge. "Emile—Emile, there's a first aid kit in the kitchen. Get it for me. Hurry."

Matt's good eye focused. He put more effort into sitting up. "Emile's here?" His voice was rasping, pain racked. "Goddamn it, who do you think did this to me?"

He pushed Sig's hand away and, with sheer force of will, pushed himself to his feet. Riley slipped out from under him. Except for the blood and bruises, he had no color in his face. He fell against the hall wall, just managing to stay upright. "Where are you, you fucking bastard?"

Riley shot up, touched his arm. "Matt, come on. Let's get you to a doctor."

He elbowed her back, not gently, and staggered down the hall. She doubled over, the wind knocked out of her. Sig grabbed her by the shoulders, her dark eyes focused, intense, in control. "Riley, listen to me. You need to get the first aid kit. It's in the cupboard above the refrigerator."

"What about Emile?"

"We can't count on him if Matt wants to kill him."

After a few steps, Matt slumped against the wall. He was raging, almost incoherent. "*Emile!* I know you did this to me. Damn you! You killed Sam, you killed my father."

"Straker would be out parking the damned car,"

Riley muttered, pushing past her brother-in-law as she made for the kitchen.

Her grandfather was there, had the first aid kit out on the table. "You take these," he said, shoving gauze bandages, a tube of antibiotic ointment, into her hands. "I will end this, Riley. I promise you. Take care of Matt and Sig."

"I know you didn't do this to him—"

He gave her a quick, fierce hug, ruffled her hair as if she were six again. "I'm counting on you."

"Emile, damn it, you can't slither out of here now. We need you!"

"I'm one old man. You can go on without me." He sounded fatalistic, even pessimistic.

"Straker's on his way."

"Good."

But that didn't stop him. He slipped out the back door into the courtyard just as Matthew kicked open the swinging door and staggered into the spotless kitchen. Blood streamed down his face. He cradled his left arm, unable to stand up straight. He glared at Riley. "You let him go?"

"No, I didn't let him go, damn it, he just went. It was follow him or get some bandages for your stupid head! My God, Matt, Emile's not a murderer. You *have* to know that."

Sig slammed into the kitchen behind him. It was a warm, cozy, modern kitchen with dark wood cabinets and a collection of a half-dozen different kinds of Depression glass, which she'd said reminded her of watercolors. "Matthew, you can't go after him.

You're seriously hurt. Let me take you to the emergency room."

He stumbled to the back door. "I don't need a doctor."

But his eyes rolled back in his head, and he fought to stay on his feet even as he reeled, knocking a chair over, cursing. Sig slipped her arms around him from behind. Riley dove in to help her, and they got him down to the floor.

"Asshole," Sig said, crying. "Good for Emile if he did this to him. It's the first thing he's done in months that makes any sense."

Straker materialized in the hall doorway, hissed something under his breath as he quickly assessed the situation. Riley was unreasoningly relieved to see him. And annoyed. "Why the hell are you always *late?*"

He ignored her and dropped down beside Matt. "Is he conscious?"

"Unfortunately," Sig said bitterly.

Riley wet a dishcloth in the sink, handed it to Straker and tried not to notice her own trembling hand. "We have a first aid kit."

"He needs to get to an emergency room." Straker took the cloth and dabbed at Matt's bloody face; Riley supposed they'd taught him basic first aid procedures at Quantico. "Did you fall?" he asked Matt.

"Hit from behind," Matt mumbled. "Pushed me down the stairs."

"Where?"

"Abigail's."

"Is she okay?"

He winced. "She wasn't there. I used my key to get in."

"Why?"

"She's my sister. That's the home I grew up in."

"Oh, horse shit," Sig said. "You and Emile are the two biggest goddamned liars. Like you're Sherlock Holmes. What the hell were you doing sneaking around Abigail's house?"

Straker held up a hand, silencing her. For no reason she could fathom, Riley thought of all the quarters her sister would owe her mason jar. Straker examined Matt's injured arm. "Looks as if your forearm's broken. Did you see who hit you?"

"No." He grimaced, his hands shaking. "But it had to be Emile. I followed him to Abigail's. He shoved me down the stairs to the kitchen. I was half-unconscious, and he came down and kicked me in the head and chest a few times. I probably have a cracked rib or two."

"But you didn't actually see him?"

He closed his eyes, shook his head slightly, painfully.

"That's it." Sig stood up, raked a hand through her hair. "My car's right outside. If I can have some help, I'll take him to Mass. General myself."

Massachusetts General Hospital was only a few blocks away. Straker set the bloody towel on the floor. "Come on, Granger." He pulled Matt's good arm over his shoulder and took his weight. Matt was taller, Straker more thickly built. "You need to let a doctor take a look at you."

Sig grabbed her keys and handbag, pushed into the hall with a force of will Riley hadn't seen in her in days. She herself hung back. She debated saying anything, just melting into the woodwork, then finally mumbled, for honor's sake if no other, "I'm going after Emile."

Straker thrust a finger at her. "You wait."

"I will not wait. Emile's going to get himself killed."

"And you with him."

"You can catch up with me." She gave him a faint smile. "I'll leave a bread crumb trail."

"Riley—"

"I've always wanted to see you in action."

As if she hadn't, she thought with a jolt, remembering last night.

Straker gritted his teeth, with Matt slumped against him. "Trust me, St. Joe. You don't want me to catch up with you."

But she'd made up her mind and charged out the back door, into the pretty courtyard garden and streaming sunshine.

Straker was rusty. It was his only excuse. An old man, a pregnant woman, a sexy spit of an egghead and a thrashed blueblood—and he was out parking the car. He stuffed Matt Granger into Sig's sleek car. "Do you want me to drive to the hospital with you?"

She shook her head. "Go after that stupid sister of mine."

"With pleasure."

"She and Emile…" She brushed at tears with the back of her hand, but Straker had no illusions. She'd be fine. She was fully engaged, determined. "They're devoted to each other. You know it, you've seen it yourself. And they're just alike. They act first, think later. They're so smart they usually can get away with it."

"Not this time. This time, they need to goddamn back off."

"They won't. Neither one."

He nodded. "When you get to the hospital, call the police. Tell them everything."

"I will. I promise."

He believed her. In her own way she was as strong as the rest of her family. It would be a mistake, Straker thought, to underestimate Sig St. Joe Granger's strength.

Matt was regaining consciousness, and Sig shut the door on him before he could fall out or try to go after Emile himself. She hurried around to the driver's side and climbed in, started the engine, gunned it and was off.

Straker headed back into her house. It was quiet, its elegance marred by the smears of blood on the walls, floor and woodwork. He went down to the kitchen and out to the pretty courtyard garden, which had obviously been neglected in recent months.

No trail of bread crumbs. He reined in his frustration, knew there was no point in following Riley on foot. He wasn't worried about her few minutes' head start, but she knew Beacon Hill better than he did. He'd be lucky to find his way back out to the street from the damned courtyard.

He went back to his car. He'd missed Granger's entrance; he'd missed Emile. He shook his head, disgusted with himself.

The snaking network of hilly one-way streets, originally designed for horses, tangled him up and slowed him down. He stopped in the middle of Louisburg Square, realizing Riley could have followed Emile all the way to Logan Airport and onto a plane to Greece or South America by now.

He double-parked and checked Abigail Granger's house. Locked up tight. He rang the doorbell, knocked. No answer. He stood on the front stoop, imagined himself on Labreque Island. It was a clear, warm, perfect September day. He'd take his kayak out, sit on the rocks, maybe dip his feet in the bay. But that life seemed remote now, as if the past six months had collapsed into a matter of seconds.

So what was Matt Granger doing here that got him pushed down the stairs and thrashed?

Straker drove down the hill to Mass. General Hospital. No Sig in the ER waiting room. No police arriving to take her and her husband's statements. Straker swore under his breath and pushed his way to Matt Granger's treatment room. The doctors had gotten right to work. His broken forearm was already set, and he had his ribs wrapped and the cuts and bruises on his face treated. He looked like hell, physically and emotionally spent.

He glanced at Straker. Even beaten to shit, the man had a patrician look about him. "Where's Sig?" But Straker's hesitation told him, and he jumped off the treatment table and grabbed his shirt, shrugged it on as he addressed the doctor who'd been shining a light in his eyes. "I have to go."

"Mr. Granger, I don't recommend—"

"My wife is in danger. You have any Tylenol or something you can give me?"

"You need something stronger."

Granger shook his head. "Anything stronger'll knock me out."

The doctor sighed, handed him samples of Extra-Strength Tylenol and Tylenol with codeine. "I want you back here. You're leaving against my advice."

"I know, Doc." Matt gave a rakish, Robert Redford grin, despite his swollen, bloody face. "I won't sue you."

The doctor wasn't amused. He kept arguing as Granger headed for the door. Adrenaline and pain had him focused and alert. Straker didn't try to stop him. If Sig St. Joe was his own wife, he'd drag his ass off an ER treatment table and go after her.

"I'll look after him," he told the doctor, "and get him back here as soon as I can."

The doctor didn't like that, either, but there was nothing he could do.

"Sig would blithely walk into the mouth of a dragon," Granger told him as they headed outside.

"She's oblivious. Here she's nearly been killed, I've nearly been killed and she goes off—" He grimaced, as if he'd thought too far ahead already and couldn't stand what he saw. "What the hell is she thinking?"

"Riley took off after Emile."

"Damn it. They're both impossible."

"You said it yourself. Loving a St. Joe isn't easy."

Matt half fell into Straker's front seat. "If I brought this on Sig—"

"That kind of thing won't get you anywhere," Straker warned, and shut the door.

He took Cambridge Street to Government Center, snaked through the jammed traffic and endless waterfront construction and tried to push back his own rampant thoughts. "If you're right and Emile killed Cassain, he wouldn't deliberately hurt his own granddaughters. He had that chance back on Chestnut Street. Instead he got out bandages for you."

Granger cradled his broken arm, swallowed the Extra-Strength Tylenol without water. He had to be in immense pain. "You don't think it's Emile."

Straker reluctantly slowed for a stoplight, clenched the wheel. "No, I don't."

"I just don't know anymore. My family..." Granger shut his eyes briefly, every fiber exuding misery on a large scale. He swallowed. "Christ."

"Maine CID talked to your stepmother this morning. They found the engine parts Cassain brought up from the *Encounter* in an outbuilding at your family house on Mount Desert. Do you know how they got there?"

Granger sat in tight-lipped silence. Straker didn't push it. He pulled up in front of the Boston Center for Oceanographic Research. No reporters jumped in front of his car, which was at least something. "You stay put. Security's suspicious of me as it is. They don't need to see me walk in with a bloodied Granger. Keep the car running." He gave Granger a hard look. "Ten minutes. That's all I need. You steal my car and pass out and kill a pedestrian—"

"Ten minutes. Go."

On his way Straker called Richard St. Joe on his cell phone. "I've lost both your daughters. You want to let me in?"

"I'll meet you at the main entrance."

"Henry Armistead has me down as a stalker."

"Screw Henry."

Despite his rumpled, distracted appearance, Richard St. Joe commanded a certain respect among the center's staff. The security guards let Straker pass.

Straker didn't mince words. "Your son-in-law just had the shit kicked out of him at Abigail Granger's house. Is she here?"

"I don't know. I think so. John, what the hell's going on?"

"Someone sabotaged the *Encounter* last year. It should have been a nice little explosion that made everyone feel bad. Instead it was a great big explosion that sank the ship and killed five people."

"Jesus Christ," St. Joe said.

"That's the short version."

"Emile?"

Straker gave a tight shake of the head. "No." For

the first time, he was convinced his instincts were right. It wasn't Emile. "Sam Cassain came out and blamed Emile, and that suited the saboteur just fine. With the *Encounter* at the bottom of the ocean, there was no proof of what really happened. Then your son-in-law secretly funded Cassain's bid to bring up the ship's engine. He succeeded."

"And the engine showed evidence of sabotage. Do you think that's what Sam expected?"

"Initially, I think he was just looking for something that proved conclusively that Emile was responsible."

"But he found evidence of sabotage," Richard St. Joe said, "and it got him killed. Knowing Sam, he tried to blackmail whoever was responsible for the *Encounter*."

Straker nodded. "That's my guess." He provided a quick rundown of the day's festivities. He tried to be clinical, professional, objective, tried to ignore the twist of pain in his gut that told him he was long past playing this one as an outsider.

"Will Matt be all right if he doesn't get back to the hospital?" Richard asked, white-faced.

"He won't be comfortable, but he won't die."

"Emile couldn't have done that to him."

"No."

"I want my daughters safe. Just tell me what to do."

Richard looked as if he'd be sick. Straker had seen both his daughters get sick, and they'd had that same aura about them. But Richard held on, and they reached Abigail's office. It was her father's old office, tucked in a corner down from the main administrative

offices. She had no regular hours, no full-time secretary.

She wasn't in, and the door was locked. Straker
held on to the doorknob, glanced at Richard St. Joe.
"You up to a little breaking and entering? If not, look
the other way. Is there an alarm?"

"No. Security's not that tight once you're inside
the building. If you need an extra shoulder—"

But the door came with one good, hard shove.

Richard St. Joe followed him inside. "What do you
expect to find in here?"

"I don't know. Matt was attacked at Abigail's, and
she and Henry have worked hard this past year after
the *Encounter* tragedy."

"She's devoted to the center, as much as her father
ever was. She fought long and hard to get him and
Emile both to pay more attention to membership. She
wants more programs, more community outreach."

"You?"

"That's not my area of expertise."

Straker sat at her desk. The furnishings were surprisingly utilitarian, the view spectacular. He tried to
get into her computer, but it was password protected.
He spun around in her chair, St. Joe pacing nervously.

Definitely rusty, Straker thought. He could sense
the connections spinning around him, but he couldn't
put them together, make any sense out of them.

He stood up, examined Abigail's wall of framed
pictures. "Are these her pictures?"

"No, they're still from Bennett. She's hardly
changed a thing in here since his death." Richard

smiled wistfully as he fingered a vase of flowers. "A new computer and flowers."

"Who's this?"

Straker pointed to a small framed picture of a man in fire fighting attire. Richard peered over his shoulder. He was fidgety, a little less green. "That's Henry Armistead—and that's Bennett next to him." He pointed to a tall, white-haired man; Straker realized he wouldn't have recognized Bennett Granger. St. Joe went on, "Bennett had flown out to California during wildfires that threatened delicate stretches of the coast. He wanted to see for himself if there was anything the center could do."

"When was this?"

"About four years ago. Henry was the executive director of a small, private California marine research institute. He trained as a volunteer firefighter for those wildfires that get out of control there. Bennett liked him, and when the job opened up here, he brought Henry in."

Straker continued to stare at the picture. An administrator-oceanographer who would know ships. A firefighter who would know fires. And a man in love with a wealthy woman whose father wasn't killed in an accidental explosion, after all.

The puzzle pieces stopped spinning. They settled, connected together. "Here's what you can do." Straker started for the door, feeling a sense of certainty he hadn't in days. And a sense of urgency. He glanced back at Richard St. Joe. "Call the police. Tell them to pick up Henry Armistead. Tell them I said so. Throw in that I'm a damned FBI agent if you need to get their attention.''

St. Joe paled. "John? What the hell—''

"Just do it. I don't have time to explain. I have to find your damned father-in-law.'' And his daughter. Riley. She'd be right with Emile, barreling in because she was an optimist, because she believed in her grandfather.

"Go,'' Richard croaked. "I'll call the police.''

When Straker reached his car, Matt Granger was struggling not to let his pain get away from him. Straker understood. He'd fought pain on every level for months. For a while he'd let it get away.

But he couldn't let empathy affect his need to act. "You've been hanging on to the last shreds of hope that this thing could still be laid at Emile's feet. Better your wife's crazy grandfather than your sister. But you know better, don't you?''

Granger sank against the seat, nodded. His skin had a gray cast; his one good eye was bloodshot, almost vibrating with pain.

Straker shoved the car into gear, released the emergency brake. "You should have told me you suspected your sister. That's why you snuck into her house, isn't it?''

"I hope I'm wrong.''

"You are wrong. She wanted a dramatic gesture to galvanize support for the center and the *Encounter II*.'' Straker pulled out in front of a car, ignored the angry blare of its horn. "But it's Henry Armistead who gave it to her.''

Seventeen

❧⤛❧⤜❧

Sig raced up Pinckney Street and turned onto Louisburg Square, her head spinning, throbbing with tension. She'd hated to leave Matt in the ER, but she'd had no other choice. She couldn't stand by while her family destroyed itself.

She'd pelted him with questions. How had the *Encounter* engine ended up at his family house in Maine? Why would Emile be at Abigail's to push him down the stairs? Where was his sister?

He hadn't responded. Had refused to answer. His injuries weren't stopping him. He was closemouthed, stubborn, maddening. Overprotective. She was Sig, the free spirit, not Sig, the fighter.

Not this time. She knew her husband, knew how to read his silences, his fears. She trusted her intuition, relied on it in her work as a painter—she didn't need to be a damned scientist to know that Matt was terrified his sister somehow had gotten herself involved in Sam Cassain's death, the fires, perhaps even the attack on him.

Sig was as positive, as certain, as she'd ever been about anything. And it was ridiculous. Absurd. Matt had lost all perspective or he'd know. Of *course* Abigail wasn't involved. Of course she hadn't sabotaged the *Encounter* or murdered Sam Cassain. The idea was insane.

Sig felt the strain in her lower back, knew she needed to slow down and stay calm. She simply wanted to allay Matt's fears, *then* tackle the police and all their questions.

Louisburg Square was quiet, bathed in sunshine, as if to remind her of the life she used to lead. She slowed her pace, tried to consider her actions. Was she being like her sister, like Emile? Acting first, thinking later?

No. She'd thought this through, if rapidly.

"Sig!" Riley jumped out from the private park and landed at her sister's side. "What are you doing here?"

Sig put her hand on her heart. "Scare me to death, why don't you?"

"Sorry. I was lying in wait for Emile, hoping he'd walk by and I could nail him. How's Matt?"

"I left him in the ER."

"What? Why? Did you sneak out or did he let you go? Forget it, you snuck out. He'd never voluntarily let you come up here."

Sig inhaled through her nose. "I make my own decisions."

"Just as well he's in no condition to come after you," Riley said.

"You're exasperating. Did Emile give you the slip?"

"I never picked up his trail. He must be ex-CIA or something, I swear."

"What about Straker?" Sig asked. "He went after you—he looked ready to throttle you."

But John Straker, Sig could see, had her sister in knots. "He drove past me once. I thought about flagging him down." Riley glanced sideways at Sig. "I didn't trust him not to run me over and call it a day."

"Anyone in his place would."

"Look who just abandoned her beaten and battered husband in the ER. You're worried about the same things I am." Riley frowned, a bundle of pent-up energy and frustration. She pointed at an expensive car parked in the square. "Look, there's Abigail's car. I rang her doorbell a little while ago, but she didn't answer."

"Maybe she's indisposed."

But Riley clearly didn't believe it. "And maybe she was there when Matt got helped down the stairs."

Sig licked her lips, which were dry and parched, and her babies gave a fluttering little kick; the skin on her lower abdomen felt tight, stretched. She cleared her throat and focused on the mission at hand. "I have a key."

"Good. Let's let ourselves in and hope we're just catching her in the tub."

"Do you suspect Abigail?" Sig asked bluntly.

Her sister seemed surprised. "No, of course not. She wouldn't know how to sabotage a ship engine or dip a rag in linseed oil and set Emile's cottage on fire, never mind want to do something like that.''

"Then why are you here?''

"Emile." Riley marched up to Abigail's front door. "Matt followed him here, says Emile pushed him down the stairs and beat him up. So what was Emile doing here? What did he see that he didn't mention to us? And if he didn't attack Matt—which he didn't—then who did?''

"Abigail?''

Riley groaned in exasperation. "*Sig*. I just said she's not on my list any more than Emile is. If you apply the process of elimination and a little common sense, you come up with—''

A stab of pain nearly brought Sig to her knees. She almost couldn't speak. Her head pounded. "Henry. He was here yesterday. He and Abigail are having an affair…damn.''

"The only problem is he doesn't strike me as someone who'd know how to commit arson and blow up ships, either. He's an administrator. He studied oceanography, but he hasn't really been in the field in years and—'' She stopped, stared at her sister. "What is it?''

"But he would. Riley, remember?'' They stopped at Abigail's brass-trimmed front door, and Sig swallowed, her throat tight and dry. "Henry was one of those volunteer wildfire fighters out west. That's how he and Bennett met.''

"No, I didn't know. I didn't pay much attention

when he was hired. We were revamping the recovery and rehab program.''

Sig smiled feebly. "You and your one-track mind.''

"But fighting wildfires isn't the same as committing arson.''

"Who knows what all those firefighters sat around talking about during breaks? The fires at Sam's house and Emile's cottage were both caused by crude time-delayed devices. Henry could have chosen his timing.''

"And he was desperate," Riley said.

"Yes. If he sabotaged the *Encounter*, he's responsible for the deaths of five people. He'd lose everything, including Abigail.''

"I hate this. Explosions, fires, assaults and murder—they aren't exactly my area of expertise.''

"Maybe we should find Straker," Sig said.

"I don't see Henry's car. He's probably still at the center. Maybe he and Abigail rode together and no one's here.'' She gave Sig an encouraging smile. "This could be our best chance to look around her house and settle our minds. Maybe we're way off the deep end here.''

"Do you think so?''

Riley shook her head. "No.''

Sig wasn't sure. All the threads and pieces seemed to float past her, and she couldn't put anything together. She fumbled with her keys, too nervous to single out her copy of the key to the Granger house.

Riley, ever impatient, grabbed them from her. "Which one?"

Sig pointed, her hand shaking. "That one."

Riley grasped the key, stuck it in the door, pushed it open. "It's not really breaking and entering," she whispered as they slipped into the cool, elegant home. "We're just taking a look around."

Sig called out, "Abigail? You home? It's me, Sig."

Total silence. Given her mood, it seemed eerie. On another day, it would be refreshing, soothing to encounter such a place of peace and elegance in the heart of the city.

"I'll check the kitchen," Sig said. "You look around here and upstairs."

Riley nodded.

Sig stifled a surge of guilt. Her sister-in-law had never faltered in the past year. She'd been strong, capable, determined. Without her energy and focus, the center might never have survived Emile's downfall and Bennett's death.

Thinking of her husband's battered body, Sig started down the kitchen stairs. She looked behind her after every step, not wanting someone to shove her from behind, then give her a few kicks while she was down. She shuddered, pushed the images out of her mind. Matt was in good hands now. He'd be okay.

She peered down the stairs, balanced herself with one hand on the wall. She could see something at the foot of the stairs. She leaned forward to get a better look.

Abigail.

She was sprawled on the floor at the foot of the stairs. Sig jumped back, shrieked. Her breath went out of her. She lost her footing and grabbed the railing, caught herself before she could tumble down the stairs.

"Sig!" It was Emile, down in the kitchen. "Run! Get out!"

She turned, tripping on her long skirt, and, almost on her knees, scrambled up several steps.

Something tugged at the hem of her skirt. She kicked backward, and a hand grasped her lower leg, twisting. If she didn't go with it, she'd break her leg. She turned over, sat on the step.

Henry snatched her hand and jerked her to her feet. "Abigail's alive."

Sig gasped for air. "What the hell's going on here? Henry, for God's sake—"

"Shh, shh." He put a finger to his lips. He was dressed casually in a cotton sweater and trousers, handsome, totally calm. "It's okay. Shh. I don't want to hurt you."

Riley. Her sister must have heard the commotion in the kitchen. She would call the police. She would get Straker. She would run out into the street and get someone in here. Sig couldn't give her away. She had to be brave. She kept her eyes pinned on Henry, refusing to glance back up the stairs and alert him that Riley had come in with her.

"What did you do to Abigail?" Her voice was hoarse, breathless. "Did you push her down the stairs and beat her up the way you did my husband?"

"I could have killed your husband. I didn't. Be grateful."

"You *monster*."

"If your husband had minded his own goddamned business, we wouldn't be here right now."

"His father's death *is* his business."

Henry's eyes darkened, and he jerked her down the stairs, not caring if she stumbled, if he had to drag her. She managed to stay on her feet. Adrenaline shot painfully through her. Her knees weakened. She should have found a gun, grabbed a poker from the fireplace.

He tightened his grip on her arm and elbowed her in the chest to break her momentum and keep her from toppling into him. She tried to pull herself free. "Ouch—Henry, you're hurting me!"

"Armistead," Emile yelled from deeper in the kitchen. She'd never heard him sound so certain, so furious. "If you hurt her, I'll kill you myself."

Henry smirked, cocky, nasty. He didn't even look in Emile's direction. "Your grandfather doesn't seem to understand he's tied up and can't do anything. It's his life that hangs in the balance. Not mine."

"I'll haunt you from the grave," Emile said. "You won't have a second's peace."

"Henry," Sig croaked, gasping for air, "for God's sake, you can't believe this is going to work."

"The police already suspect Emile. I just need to help them reach the correct and logical conclusion, provide proof that what they believe he's done, he did, in fact, do."

"What about Abigail?"

He ignored her and pulled Sig over Abigail's prone body. Sig was sickened, terrified for herself, for her sister-in-law, for Emile.

Henry touched her hair. "Sig, you of all people should understand."

"What? I don't understand any of this."

"Loving a Granger. Wanting to be one of them. You don't understand?"

Bravado, anger, kept her on her feet. "You don't love Abigail. You don't know what love is. And I never cared about being a Granger. I cared about my husband."

"I never meant..." He broke off, his eyes misting, not with regret, Sig thought, but self-pity. "No one was supposed to die."

"Five people *did* die. And now with Sam's death, six."

Henry's gaze hardened, his grip on her tightening painfully, to the point she thought her arm would break. "Trust me, no one misses our good Captain Cassain."

He shoved her backward, sent her sprawling against the table. She stumbled, held on to the back of a chair. A knife. Where did Abigail keep the knives?

She saw her grandfather in the corner by the stove, his hands and feet tied to a chair. He was white-faced, old, trembling not with fear or pain, she thought, but unbridled anger. "Emile," she breathed. "Oh my God."

His dark eyes leveled on Henry. "Kill me. Leave Sig."

"That won't work, Emile. I'm not stupid. I've examined every option. You're the one who backed me into a corner. If you'd just left me alone—"

"You sabotaged my ship. You killed members of my crew. You murdered my captain."

"Your captain discredited you. He tried to blackmail me. Why would you risk your life for him?"

"That's my duty," Emile said simply.

"If no one had died," Henry sneered, "you would have thanked me for getting rid of the *Encounter*."

Emile's expression was stony. "Abigail saw you before you hit her."

"No, she didn't." Henry was confident, arrogant. "She'll blame you. You hurt her brother, now you've hurt her."

"She suspects you, Henry. You know she does."

"Shut up."

Sig felt bile rise up in her throat, and she put her free hand on her abdomen as if to soothe her babies. She needed a weapon. Some way of stopping this from happening. How could it be Henry? How could he have killed Bennett, four other crew members, Sam Cassain?

And where was Riley? Sig felt sick to her stomach.

Henry turned to her, as if reading her mind. "Where's your little sister? She's a pill, that one."

"I left her with John Straker. They'll have the police here any second. You should stop now while you still can." She raised her chin, breathed in. "Damn you, Henry."

"Oh, yes. I'm damned. But not today. Today, finally, I'm free."

"What do you want from me?"

"You, Sig?" He smiled, an unsettling mixture of sadness and relief. "I want you to prove to the authorities just what a madman your grandfather has become."

Riley searched madly for a telephone. She needed to call the police; she needed help. She raced silently through the parlor. "Even the damned Grangers have to have phones!" she muttered under her breath, forcing back panic. Henry had Sig. Something had happened to Abigail. And Emile—he was down there, too, in danger.

She stopped in the middle of the thick Persian rug, tried to remember the layout of the huge, old house. There would be a phone in the kitchen, but Henry was in the kitchen. Wasn't there an office upstairs? And bedrooms—surely there would be a phone in the master bedroom.

If Henry heard her, she was sunk.

She eased out into the hall and stood at the top of the stairs, listening to the low, intense voices coming from the kitchen. If only she knew how much time she had!

There.

A phone. She spotted it on a table at the end of the hall. She'd have to be careful and speak quietly to keep Henry from hearing her. She moved quietly, quickly, down the hall, lifted the receiver and grimaced as she tapped out 911. She didn't waste any time with explanations, told the dispatcher there was a hostage situation on Beacon Hill and gave the address.

The dispatcher wanted her to stay on the line, but she heard her sister scream. The police wouldn't get there in time.

"Hurry," she told the dispatcher, and hung up.

She ran into the parlor, grabbed an expensive, heavy brass poker from the marble fireplace. This was madness, she knew, but she couldn't hide up here while her sister and grandfather were in imminent danger. Even if she raced outside, it was a quiet weekday afternoon. She couldn't count on running into anyone who could help.

Straker...

He wasn't here. She was.

She slipped silently down the stairs, concentrated on maintaining her footing, on the feel of the poker as she refused to let her fears overcome her. She didn't think back, didn't think ahead.

She managed not to gasp and give herself away when she saw Abigail at the bottom of the stairs. Farther into the kitchen, Henry stood with his back to her, Emile's gun pointed at Sig. She was at Emile's side. Their grandfather was white-faced, furious, determined.

And he saw Riley. She knew he did. His expression didn't change, he didn't move, but she knew.

Abigail moaned incoherently, but Henry didn't turn around.

"If you kill me," Sig said coldly, "you kill my babies."

Henry scoffed. "I'm not killing you." His voice was high-pitched and jittery. "Your grandfather is killing you."

"My husband will hunt you down."

Riley could feel her body moving almost of its own accord, instincts taking over. Her world slowed down, enough for her to see, maneuver, act. Emile kicked forward, distracting Henry, and she swung her poker, hitting him in the arm.

The .38 flew from his grip, and she whacked him again. He cried out in pain and surprise, spun around and snatched the poker, raging as he backhanded her. She fell against the table, tripped backward over Abigail.

Sig dove for the gun, kicking it aside. Henry grabbed her from behind, held the poker over her pregnant stomach. She went still, her face drained of color. "No. Henry...my babies."

"No more, Henry," Emile said. "For God's sake, no more."

Armistead pulled Sig backward toward the counter, tightened his grip around her middle. In one swift movement, he dropped the poker and whipped a knife off a magnetic rack, put it to her throat.

Riley went still. Her grandfather didn't even seem to breathe. The police would be here any minute, she thought. They had to be. Neither she nor Emile said a word as Henry pushed Sig toward the stairs. Abigail, still moaning, rolled onto her side, coughed. Henry went around her, started up the stairs with the knife still at Sig's throat.

When they were almost to the top of the stairs, Riley staggered over to her grandfather. "The police are on their way. They'll get him. He won't hurt Sig. Oh, God, he *can't*." She grabbed a knife, cut the duct tape and rope around her grandfather's wrists. "He must be out of his mind—the police are on their way."

"He's past thinking." Emile pushed off the dangling ropes, nodded to her as he tore at his bound feet. "Go. See what you can do."

"I'm so scared. I've mucked things up as it is—"

"You bought us time. Sig would be dead if you hadn't acted. This is Henry's last chance. He knows it. Riley, you'll know what to do. Trust your instincts."

Abigail collapsed again, vomiting. Riley reclaimed her poker, and Emile waved her upstairs, even as he struggled with the last of his ropes and duct tape.

"Go," Abigail echoed, her voice rasping, hoarse. "Stop him."

Riley took the stairs quickly, silently, praying the police would arrive before Henry had a chance to harm her sister. She didn't know what to do in a hostage situation. She just knew she couldn't let the bastard hurt Sig.

She slowed her pace as she came to the top of the stairs. She held her poker high and took a breath, but before she could assess what was happening in the hall, a hand shot out and whipped the poker from her grip. It clattered to the hall floor. She opened her mouth to scream, but Straker was there, scooping an arm around her.

"I didn't want you to ram me through with that thing," he said.

She started sobbing, gripped his shoulders, "Sig— he's got Sig. Henry. He has a knife."

"Not anymore."

"I'm okay." Sig's voice, weak and shaky and angry, came from down the hall. "The son of a bitch ran into Matt and Straker. He didn't stand a chance."

Riley focused, and she took in her battered and bloodied brother-in-law holding Henry's knife at the bastard's throat. Henry had his face in his hands. Henry wasn't crying, he wasn't raging. He was simply sitting there quietly.

Straker rubbed a hand over Riley's hip. "You hurt?"

"Bruised."

"Good." His gray eyes were unamused. "You St. Joes. Don't you believe in calling the police?"

"I did call. They're on their way. I just couldn't wait for them to get here. Henry would have shot Sig."

He nodded. "Then you did what you had to do."

"Emile's down in the kitchen. I think he's okay, but Abigail—Henry did a job on her. We need an ambulance."

"I think we need a couple of ambulances."

"I'm fine." But even as she spoke, Riley felt her legs going out from under her. Straker steadied her, and she grumbled, "I can't believe you get paid for doing this. How did you know to come here?"

He winked, tightened his arm around her. "I'm the FBI."

"Well, I'm glad you showed up." She squared her shoulders, sniffled and managed a quick smile. "I didn't feel like catching Henry all by myself."

Eighteen

~⊷⊶⊷~

Riley breathed in the clean Maine air, shoved her hands in her jacket pockets as a breeze blew in off the bay. It was a shining autumn afternoon, as beautiful as any she remembered. Evergreens and hardwoods with leaves of red, orange and yellow were outlined against a deep, endlessly blue sky. The bay was choppy, the tide coming in hard. Lobster boats were out, their multicolored buoys bobbing in the swells. Cormorants dove for fish. In all the important ways, she thought, life here hadn't changed.

Emile and his lobstermen buddies had hauled off most of the rubble that had once been his cottage. They were still arguing over drawings for a new one. They all had their own ideas about propane heat versus fuel oil, natural light, windows, keeping it simple or "yuppifying" it. Emile was tireless. Henry Armistead hadn't succeeded in destroying him.

The police had conducted a thorough analysis of the engine parts Sam Cassain had brought up from the remains of the *Encounter*. They had uncompromising proof of sabotage. Sam Cassain had been wrong about Emile.

But instead of exonerating the oceanographer immediately and publicly, and turning the investigation over to the authorities, Sam had slipped behind the scenes and tried to make a profit.

He'd fingered Henry Armistead early on. It was Sam who'd let Henry aboard the *Encounter* shortly before it set out to sea that final day. Abigail Granger had known. She hadn't realized its significance, she'd explained from her hospital bed, until it was too late. When she'd finally confronted Henry, he'd tried to kill her. He loved her, wanted the status she could give him, but he'd been desperate, knew the walls were closing in on him.

Emile joined Riley down on the water. She smiled at him. He was sweating, in his element as he worked on his new cottage. "I think it needs more windows," she told him.

"You going to pay for them?"

"Only if I can visit whenever I want."

His dark eyes gleamed. "You'll do that anyway."

"I'll miss the old place," she said.

"I won't. It had mice and snakes."

"Not that many." She squinted out at the water, felt the chilly breeze on her face. "You won't change your mind and come back to the center?"

He shook his head. "No. This is my life now. It's a good one. I have friends here."

"Lobstermen. They're lucky Lou Dorrman didn't lock them all up."

"Lou's a good man," he said.

"How did you know, Emile?" She turned to him, felt that pang she always did these days when she realized how close she'd come to really losing him. "That it was Henry, that he was as desperate as he was?"

"I didn't know he was that desperate or I wouldn't have ended up trussed up like a Christmas turkey. That it was Henry... I talked to your mother. Her last visit with Sam—he always wanted to put his best foot forward with her, even if he knew they could never be together again. He told her he was trying to put the *Encounter* right. She didn't think it meant much of anything at the time."

"It meant he knew what he'd found aboard the *Encounter* would exonerate you."

"If he hadn't tried to blackmail Henry, if he'd just gone to the police, to me, even to Matt... Sam underestimated Henry, and it cost him his life." Emile shook his head sadly. "Sam's was a life of missed opportunities."

"Do you think Henry meant to kill him?"

"He let him die. That much we know from the police examination of the boat Abigail let Henry use while he was staying with her and Caroline on Mount Desert Island. That's where Sam confronted him. I don't think it was an accident. I think Henry hit Sam over the head, pushed him into the water and let him drown."

"Then he thought better of letting the police find him off Mount Desert Island and pulled him out."

"And dumped him on Labreque Island," Emile said grimly. "He probably cut his engines, slipped in under the cover of dark. Henry was bold in many ways, cowardly in others."

"If Straker had caught him—"

"It does no good to go back and imagine what might have happened. It's enough to deal with what did happen."

"Henry chose Labreque Island because he'd already formulated a plan to blame the *Encounter* on you."

Emile nodded, accepting this information philosophically. "His one problem—he couldn't find Sam's proof. He checked his house in Arlington, burned that down. Checked my house, burned it down—which also suited his plans to frame me."

Riley sighed, continued to stare out at the water. "But Sam had tucked the engine on Mount Desert. Even Matt didn't know where it was. That's what brought him out here the weekend Sam died—he was looking for Sam's evidence." She could feel her grandfather's sudden melancholy. She turned to him and smiled. "Thank God it's over."

Emile's dark, intense gaze zeroed in on her, didn't let up. "Riley, if you want a kayak, I can find you one. Yours burned up in the fire. You can paddle out to the island—"

She shook her head. "I'm not rattling that particular cage."

Straker was there, had been for ten days. He'd settled affairs with the Boston police, the Massachusetts

State Police, the Maine State Police and Sheriff Dorrman, and, after making love to Riley a final, bonemelting time, had retreated to his deserted island. He didn't say why. He didn't ask her to wait or to understand. He just said he'd be in touch, and went.

"He can't stay out there through the winter," Emile said.

"I wouldn't put anything past him."

A car drove all the way up to the dock, and Riley, surprised, recognized her sister's BMW. Sig popped out, looking even more pregnant. But the pale, serious look was gone, her free-spiritedness back. She waved, smiling. Matt climbed out from behind the wheel. He had a small cast on his forearm, his bruises had faded somewhat, but he'd lost weight.

"They're both wounded," Emile said. "They need some time away together."

"They can afford to go anywhere they want."

"'Anywhere' isn't here."

They got packs from the trunk. Riley gave Emile a questioning frown, but he was off to greet his older granddaughter and her husband. She gave up and joined them.

Sig beamed at her. "A week on the island is just what we need."

"What island?"

"Labreque Island, idiot. It's peak fall foliage, the weather's not too cold." She blushed, smiled at her husband. "Not that it matters."

Matt slipped an arm around her. "John's laid in provisions. He's even appropriated a canoe for us."

Riley stared at them. "A canoe?"

"We'll be the last two people to stay at the cottage," Sig said, as if Riley knew what she was talking about. "Then the island becomes part of the nature preserve."

Emile nodded, pleased. Riley scowled at him. "You knew?"

He blinked at her. "Knew what?"

"Oh, phooey, you know what I'm talking about. Has Straker been to see you? How do you know—"

"You ask too many questions," her grandfather told her. "Come on, Matt. I'll help you with your packs."

Matt grinned at Riley. "You and your sister talk. I'm with you, Riley. I think you've been plotted against."

"You just be quiet," Sig said, giving him a shove.

He and Emile took the packs down to the dock. Riley saw Straker's boat, out across the bay, beelining in their direction. Her sister dropped her sunglasses over her eyes. "Don't kid yourself, Riley. You're in love with him." She laughed. "Thank God I'm not the only idiot in the family."

"Matt really loves you."

"I know." Her laughter faltered. "When Henry had that knife on me, that's what kept me going. Just knowing that single-minded dope loves me, that he'll love our babies."

"Sig…"

"We're going to be okay. A week out here…" She breathed in the cool air. "It's perfect."

"Straker's idea?"

"He called a few days ago. We accepted immediately. I can't explain it—it's as if he knew this is what we need to put this whole thing behind us. Maybe it's because it helped him put his own ordeal behind him."

"I hope your week doesn't bleed into six months."

Sig shook her head. "It can't. I'm not having twins out on a damned island. And I plan to be back on Beacon Hill before the snow flies." She turned to her sister. "Thank you, Riley. For all you did."

"I didn't—"

"You and Straker saved Matthew, and you saved me."

Riley swallowed. "Straker..." She sighed, never one to articulate her feelings easily. "We have nothing in common."

Sig grinned. "I beg to differ."

And when Straker pulled up to the dock, Sig waved and ran down to greet him. He jumped out of his boat, kissed her on the cheek. The sight of him took Riley's breath away. She walked slowly down to the dock, hyperaware of those gray eyes on her as she helped Matt and Emile load up the boat.

"I stocked up," Straker said, "but if you want any gourmet food, I hope you brought it."

Sig laughed. "Nope. We're going to rough it. Beef stew, hash and eggs, lots of lobster. I think we'll manage."

"If you need anything—"

"We'll call Emile. Don't think Matt's going out to

a deserted island with a pregnant woman and no phone.''

They finished loading the boat in a flash. Emile promised to look after their car, and Matt tossed him the keys. For weeks he'd operated in Sam Cassain's and Henry Armistead's shadows, sometimes one step behind, at other times two steps ahead, always trying to keep from pulling his family into what he believed he'd created when he'd funded Sam's efforts to bring up the *Encounter*'s engine. Yet without him, Henry's act of sabotage would have gone undiscovered.

''Oh,'' Sig said, turning to Emile, ''Mom said to tell you she and Dad are coming up tomorrow to help with the new cottage. We stopped in Camden on our way up. She says you'd forget to put in a bathroom without her.''

He smiled. ''She doesn't know how I survive without her.''

''And did Riley tell you? Dad wants you to be on the maiden voyage of the *Encounter II*.''

His old eyes misted, and he nodded solemnly. Riley had forgotten about her father's message. She wasn't surprised. She hadn't been thinking clearly.

The boat pulled away, and Emile said, ''So, John, I hear you're going back to the FBI.''

''Yep. I've been assigned to the Boston office.''

''Heading up a new domestic terrorism unit's what I hear.''

Straker smiled. ''My father exaggerates.''

''Well, don't plan on Riley here pressing your FBI suits. She doesn't iron.''

"Hell, she doesn't clean. She's a scientist. Me, I cook, clean, capture bad guys." He grinned. "The perfect man."

Riley was at a loss. "Straker—"

Emile climbed into the BMW. "Fun having a rich granddaughter," he said. "I'll see you two later."

He backed the car up to his skeleton of a cottage, and Straker eased closer to Riley. "You look as if you've just been caught in a whirlwind."

"I have been," she said. "You want to tell me what's going on?"

He held up a paper bag. "I have marshmallows and a fire ready to be lit on a narrow stretch of beach not far from here."

"You've been thorough."

"Always."

"Straker, if you want to stay up here in Maine, I can—"

He shook his head, cutting her off. "Toasted marshmallows, fire. Then we'll talk."

The narrow stretch of beach was a short walk from the dock, where she'd put in her kayak what seemed like a million years ago. True to his word, he had a fire built. He lit the kindling and stuck marshmallows on green sticks. She could smell the smoke, feel the heat of the fire on her face. It was romantic, healing.

He held a marshmallow in the flames, watched as it caught fire. "Rumor has it you like your marshmallows charred on the outside and gooey on the inside." He blew out the flames. "Your men, too."

"Sig. That rat fink. Is that what she told you? Well, I haven't had that many men in my life."

"Too busy rescuing whales?"

She shook her head. "Too busy being busy."

He handed her the blackened marshmallow. It was perfect, just the way she liked it. He touched her lips, kissed her lightly. "I love you, St. Joe. I think I always have."

"Even when I hit you with that rock?"

"You've always been willing to take me on. You don't back down, you don't let me intimidate you, even if you are a little spit of a thing." He smiled, kissed her again before she could protest about being called little. He said close to her mouth, "Back in the spring after I got shot, I came to the island because my world was closing in on me. You've opened it up again."

"I don't think anyone's said anything more wonderful to me. Straker, the past ten days while you've been out here plotting and God knows what else—" Her breath caught. "I tried to imagine going on without you…" She looked into those gray eyes, past the scars and the hardness to the kind, strong man she had fallen deeply, forever in love with. "But I couldn't. I didn't want to."

He put another log on the fire, the bright, hot flames glowing on his face. He sat back, moved in close to her, so that she could smell the sea and the sawdust, see the scar she'd given him when she was twelve, and he said, "Whatever demons we face from here on out, we face together."

*From one of America's best-loved authors...a story
about what life, joy and Christmas are all about!*

DEBBIE
MACOMBER

Shirley, Goodness and Mercy

Greg Bennett knows he's made mistakes, hurt people,
failed in all the ways that matter. Now he has no one
to spend Christmas with, no one who cares.

Greg finds himself in a church—and whispers a simple
heartfelt prayer. A prayer that wends its way to the
Archangel Gabriel, who assigns his favorite angels—
Shirley, Goodness and Mercy—to Greg Bennett's case.
Because Gabriel knows full well that Greg's going to
need the assistance of all three!

Shirley, Goodness and Mercy shall follow
him...because it's Christmas.

*On sale **October 22, 1999**, wherever hardcovers are sold!*

MIRA